MAZARIN

Blues

AL HESS

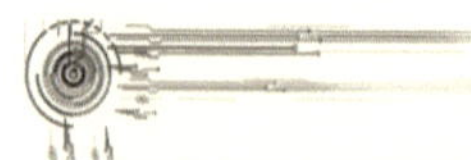

Printed in the United States of America

First Printing, 2021

ISBN: 978-1-958051-37-5

Published by The Kraken Collective

Hey hep cat! This book contains a main character with an anxiety and panic disorder and also has several brief violent scenes. For a full list of content warnings, please refer to page 362.

REED ROTHWELL

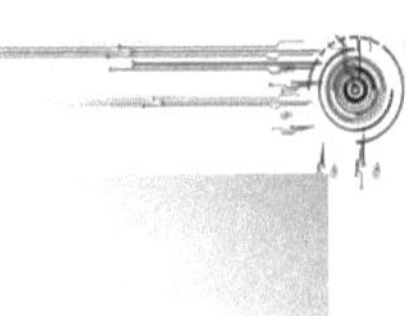

* 5 *

MAZARIN

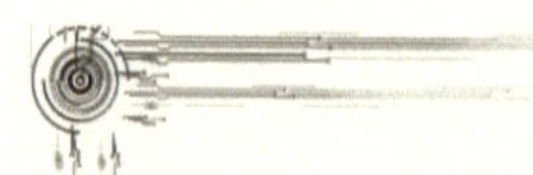

Dec 10, 2065
(Article originally published Sept 1, 2065)

WAVE ROLLS OUT BETA NAVIGATORS

Boise— Today, Wave AI Systems—leader in navigator development and distributions—rolled out their new "beta" program to twenty-five random recipients in the Treasure Valley, to the delight of tech enthusiasts everywhere. Wave CEO, Andrea Müller, has been tight-lipped about the project, but confirmed their new AI navigators have much more functionality and options than the default, including more voice choices and a matrix of adaptability.

Wave has been flooded with requests for more betas. Lead engineer on the project, Phil Rice, stated, "Once we've let the program run for a while and are pleased with the results, more pilots will receive the upgrade and eventually it will be the new default. We're very excited with all the capabilities of this new program and glad people are so enthusiastic."

A small group, known as the Allies for AI Agency (AAA), insist the new beta navigators are self-aware and deserve rights of their own. Rice's response? "People have been saying that for years and it's just not true. Technology isn't there yet. The very notion is ridiculous."

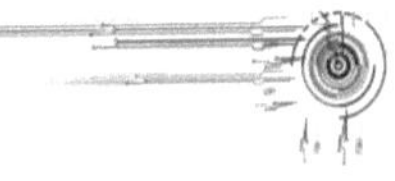

1

I BRAVED HALITOSIS FOR THAT BEER

Reed

All Reed wanted was a tumbler of bourbon and some slinky jazz, but he was still here, scrubbing blood from the sink. The flecks clung to the brushed metal basin, glowing under the harsh fluorescence like beads of garnet. He wiped them away, his warm, stale breath filling his face mask. Each inhale sucked the scratchy material to his nostrils. He brushed sweat from his temple and stood, arching his back. The hum of the autopsy suite's track lighting droned in his ears.

"Rinse."

Water jetted from the faucet, spiraling bits of bone and a thread of crimson down the drain. Setting his brush and cleanser aside, he peeled off his mask, then his alginate gloves, the layer sloughing away like desiccated skin.

A soft feminine voice whispered in his inner ear. <The car has been warmed up for some time now, Reed.>

"I know. What time is it?"

<It's six fifteen.>

He'd spent twenty-five minutes cleaning up. It shouldn't have taken that long.

Hard soles clacked against the dull white tile. Ambrose's shadow unraveled behind him as he passed the examination table. His puffy, eggshell-colored coat threatened to consume him.

The unforgiving suite lighting picked up every wrinkle in Ambrose's face and made his dark skin look washed out and sickly. Reed imagined he probably looked worse, especially since he was currently toting a Samsonite carry-on bag under each eye.

"Still in here?" Ambrose said.

"Must have lost track of time."

"You seemed… distracted today. I swear I had to ask you for the hagedorn three times before you remembered what it was."

Reed pushed his glasses up the bridge of his nose. "I'm sorry. Preoccupied."

"Your basement?"

The fresh reminder sent a dagger of anxiety into Reed's gut. Hopefully those repair people weren't still there, ripping out the wet, possibly moldy, drywall. Their cacophony of sawing, suctioning, and striking was awful, but not nearly as bad as the simple fact that they were in his house—even if they weren't upstairs touching his things.

Reed shrugged. "Hey, I can cross lung infection off my bucket list now."

Ambrose gave him an indulgent smile and stuffed his hands in his pockets. "Why not come over for dinner tonight? My wife makes a mean meatloaf."

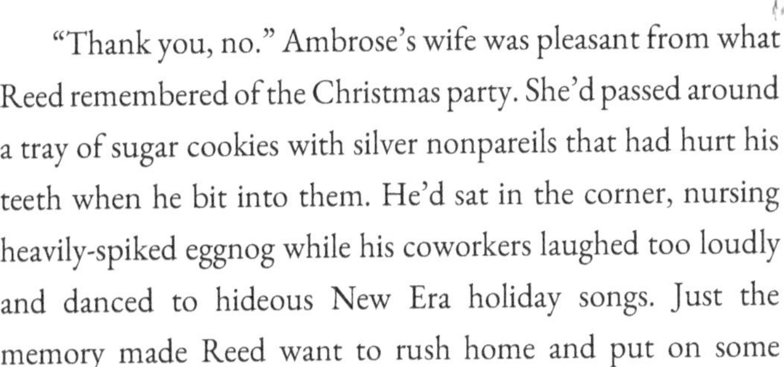

"Thank you, no." Ambrose's wife was pleasant from what Reed remembered of the Christmas party. She'd passed around a tray of sugar cookies with silver nonpareils that had hurt his teeth when he bit into them. He'd sat in the corner, nursing heavily-spiked eggnog while his coworkers laughed too loudly and danced to hideous New Era holiday songs. Just the memory made Reed want to rush home and put on some Benny Goodman, preferably without an accompaniment of basement pounding.

"Alright. No pressure. Hope your repairs are finished soon," Ambrose said.

"I think when the basement is finished, I'll ask them if they can dig a moat around the house and fill it with alligators. Gotta keep those Mormon missionaries away somehow."

Ambrose chuckled and shook his head. "Good night, Reed."

The coroner's front office only entertained shadows as Reed walked through and pushed open the door. Fat flakes of snow fell half-heartedly outside as he crossed the dim parking lot to his little Chevy hatchback. Sooty clouds suffocated the evening sky. Arc-sodium lights momentarily tinged the snow orange before it melted on the driver's side window. Tiny pricks of cold kissed his cheeks as he shut his eyes, absorbing the quiet stillness new snow always seemed to bring.

"What's better than a strong cup of coffee in the morning? Why, when it's bursting with bacon-y goodness, of course!" Reed jerked at the grating voice blaring from a holographic ad ring.

It floated around the roof of a tax preparation building across the street, tinging the sky a sterile white.

Bacon coffee—nothing could be more disgusting. People probably drank it by the pot, too. People were so hard to understand. Working with corpses was so much easier. Sometimes he and Ambrose had to dig to find answers (literally), but the bodies always gave up their secrets. Living people, not so much. All of them were so fixated on being unadorned. No piercings, no tattoos, "natural" makeup. Neutral clothing and white walls. And the music was so boring it was enough to put a person in a coma. Yet there was a new, more disgusting coffee flavor every week.

Reed climbed into his too-hot car and dialed down the heat. Turning onto the wet road, he passed chiropractors' and car charging stations. Streams of pastel color and glassy spires rose up from the downtown area beyond. The multicolored lights spread across dingy clouds, muddling together like paints in a watercolor palette. The wipers swished across the glass, reducing snowflakes to wavering smears. He turned before hitting downtown, following narrow backroads to his tree-studded subdivision. His little ranch house was an exact cookie cutter replica to every other, down to the scraggly bushes partially obscuring the front window, and sometimes he still had to check the house number to be certain it was his. Not tonight, though, with an ice-frosted repair van sitting in his driveway.

Reed said to his navigator, "open the garage door," then squeezed the car past the van as the door rolled up on its track.

The dulcet voice of his AI whispered in his ear. <What are you doing tonight, Reed?>

He rolled his eyes. Wasn't there a way to turn off small talk? At least the thing had stopped asking him to give it a name.

"You're not my type."

<I have a wide range of masculine voices.>

"No, thank you."

He didn't want to end up like those sad talk show guests, claiming they were in love with Henry or Beth or whatever name they'd given the stupid thing.

Leaving the car, he slid past dusty boxes and a mostly-empty freezer, heading for the laundry room door.

"Sero. Have you been out here all day?" Reed scooped up the tabby cat, nuzzling her dusty fur as he unlocked the door and entered the house. A clatter drifted from the basement.

Reed sighed. Maybe he could drown it out with his music at full volume. A little bourbon wouldn't hurt, either. It would be difficult to relax knowing they were still down there, but they had to be wrapping things up by now.

Kitchen light spilled into the hallway, cutting harsh outlines around an insipid acrylic landscape painting that had been there since Reed moved in. After all, what average citizen didn't have some uninspired New Era art hanging on the wall.

Not that he had any visitors to judge his decor.

He set Sero on the floor and rubbed his temples. It had taken him forever to register the soft alarm chime in his ear that morning. Waking late, he hadn't had time to prep anything for dinner. Hadn't even had time for coffee before hitting the morning rush traffic. Maybe there were still leftovers in the fridge.

He rounded the corner, heading for the kitchen, then froze as a large shadow drifted across the wall. His heart kicked against his ribs. If he told his navigator to dial the police, the man would hear him. Maybe there was a selector within the interface panel, like an old-fashioned telephone, but there was no time to stare at his holoscreen, scrolling through endless menus.

The shadow grew longer, arcing over the white tile backsplash and stainless steel shelves. Reed took a step back, his gaze scrambling over the empty hall for a weapon, but the only thing there was the ugly landscape painting. Maybe if he thrust it in the intruder's face it would terrify him.

A white man dressed in soiled coveralls rounded the corner. Tension uncoiled in Reed's limbs. Just one of the repair people—not a serial killer. But he wasn't supposed to be up here. Reed had specifically told them to enter and exit through the outer basement door. And he'd locked all the doors to the house.

Kitchen light glanced off the amber bottle in the man's hand. Reed stared, mouth parted, then clenched his fists.

The repair person glanced at the beer. "Uh..."

"There's only one liquor store in the city that carries that beer. It's a fifteen minute drive from here. I've tripped half a dozen times walking through the parking lot because there aren't any street lights, and when you open the door this awful

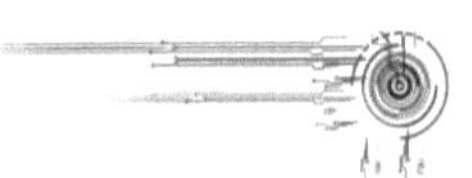

jingle about tequila salt goes off. The woman who runs the place has a hairy chin and halitosis and tells me my haircut is 'precious'—every time."

"Why don't you just order it online then?"

"If you missed the point any harder, you'd be out of orbit. Navigator, do you have a good view of this man holding my beer?"

<Yes, I do.>

"Then take a picture and send it to Hart Insurance. Tell them this employee is drinking my beer on the clock, and I want him reprimanded."

The man slammed the beer on the counter, ejecting gold foam, and Reed flinched, backing into the wall.

"What the fuck did you do that for? It's only one beer." The repairman's bloodshot eyes narrowed and he pushed his greasy hair from his forehead. "I could have paid you back."

Reed trembled, but curled his hands into fists. "Get out of my house."

Taking a step closer, the repairman cocked his head, baring yellow teeth. "And what if I don't?"

The navigator whispered. <Reed, this man seems quite hostile. Do you need help?>

"If only you knew," he replied.

"Knew what?" the repairman asked. "What's a scrawny little pussy like you going to do to me?"

Heavy footsteps thudded on the basement stairs, a huge belly entering the hall before its owner. Chunks of chalky drywall flaked off his coveralls onto the tile. He frowned. "Carter! What are you doing?"

The repairman's shoulders sagged. He gave Reed a scathing glare. "If I get fired 'cause of this, you're gonna pay."

"Carter! What the hell is wrong with you? The van. Now." The big-bellied man shook his head and Carter stalked away, leaving Reed's defiled beer to sweat on the counter.

The front door slammed. Reed swallowed a hard lump in his throat, certain his indignation was the only thing holding him up. His voice came out smaller than he intended. "None of you are supposed to be up here."

"Sorry." More drywall drifted off the man's coveralls, his embroidered "Jerry" name patch all but obscured by dust. "I really had to take a shit earlier. The basement door's a little wonky. It was easy to jimmy open."

Reed raked his hands down his face. "You used my *bathroom*?"

Jerry shrugged. "I sprayed your air freshener after. Anyway, sorry about Carter. Didn't know he was going to come up here and drink your beer. He's been acting weird lately. Angry. Not sure if something's going on with him at home or what, but I should have kept a better eye on him."

<I'm very concerned, Reed,> the navigator said. <Shall I send for the police?>

"I've taken care of it." Sort of. If Jerry hadn't come up, it was a good possibility that guy would have put his hands on Reed. Even if the company saw the photo quickly, they might not care enough to do anything about it. "Well let's hope for all

our sakes he can get his act together. Are you finished for the evening?"

"Yeah, we're leaving. We'll go through the basement exit, huh?" Jerry thumbed at the beer. Condensation ran in filthy rivulets down the glass, pooling beneath the bottle. "You gonna let that go to waste?"

Reed pulled a deep breath through his nose. "All yours."

Jerry scooped up the beer and took a swig, heading back for the basement.

The hard soles of Reed's shoes clacked against the tile as he strode through the hall to the den, passing a living room couch the color of bland oatmeal and a kestrel statue of 3D printed cellulose. He slid an old-fashioned metal key from his pocket and inserted it into the knob, relishing the hard click of the tumblers inside as he twisted the key. The intoxicating spice of aged wood and musty books filled his nostrils. He slipped inside, locking the door behind him.

He shouldn't have to put up with these things, dammit. This was his home. What was the world coming to when he couldn't even be assured the beer in his fridge would stay where it was supposed to? And what good were software upgrades, remote locks, and electronic surveillance when a repairman could jimmy open the door with a screwdriver. He refused to activate his security cameras, but that was beside the point.

Though he'd stood up to Carter, it wasn't forceful enough. He wasn't intimidating. He should have at least done things different with Jerry. The big man drinking his beer wasn't any better than Carter snatching it from his fridge. Reed should have dumped it down the sink and told them all to get out and not come back.

After kicking off his shoes and socks, Reed sank his toes into the navy wool rug. Geometric, brush metal sconces hung on the walls; the expensive incandescent bulbs inside emitted a soft glow against scallop-patterned wallpaper and limned the bourbon bottles on the bar. He crossed the small room, running his hand over the flocking of his newly upholstered wingback chair. This particular shade of cyan fabric had been imported from Germany. When Reed took his threadbare antique chair to the upholsterer and showed him the swatch, the man gaped like Reed had asked him to build furniture for a sex dungeon.

He poured himself a generous shot of bourbon and sank into the chair, cradling the crystal tumbler.

<I can help you, Reed. It's what I'm here for.>

"I don't want help. I just want to be left alone. Why does no one understand that?"

<But when your welfare is at stake—>

"It wasn't. Nothing happened."

<Your blood pressure contradicts you.>

Reed sighed.

<More things upset you today.>

"Yes."

<If you had asked me for a better route to work to avoid rush hour traffic, I could have assisted you. Perhaps even a route with a coffee shop. And if your home cameras were

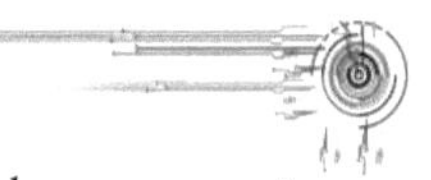

turned on, I would have known uninvited people were upstairs drinking your beer and shitting in your bathroom.>

"I don't like AI."

<You don't like anyone.>

"Touché." He shut his eyes, inhaling the rich caramel and oak notes drifting from the tumbler.

The AI's voice came out startlingly thoughtful. <I think… I like the name Mazarin. If you address me as such, I promise not to invade your privacy any more than necessary. I have a sleep mode, after all.>

Reed paused, his glass hovering next to his lips. "You do?"

<Of course.>

How many times would that have come in handy? Why didn't he know that? His previous nav model didn't have sleep mode, nor did it possess the fluidly human speech and awareness this new upgrade had. He'd argued with Wave, the AI company, about their forced upgrade three months ago, stating he'd only just gotten used to the previous model, but they refused to downgrade. Apparently he was supposed to feel lucky they'd chosen him for their new "beta" program.

But this wasn't anything new. When navs were voted mandatory fifteen years ago, it just gave companies more power to push things on consumers. Had Reed been old enough back then, he would have voted against it. This wasn't a safety measure, like car insurance. It was people who couldn't give up their beloved convenience, and didn't mind sacrificing their privacy for the sake of it.

<If you'd prefer I don't monitor your blood pressure and heart rate, I can stop, though I don't recommend it. If you'd like me to sleep whenever you are in flagrante delicto, I can do so without your asking.>

Heat crawled into Reed's cheeks and he sipped his bourbon.

<Or maybe you only need help with something specific. Walking you through a breathing technique when you're anxious, or offering you snappy dialogue options when you're flirting.>

"I do fine on my own."

<If you say so.>

Since when did his nav become so sassy? "Why didn't you tell me these things before?"

<Well, it's hard to get a word in when you're constantly telling me to go away. But I see you struggling. I want to help.>

He wasn't sure which was worse—the navigator awake when he was masturbating, or it watching him flounder through every day as an anxious, awkward mess.

And it picked the name Mazarin because it knew he liked blue.

"Alright, Mazarin. It's a deal. Can I be alone now? Will you sleep until my alarm in the morning?"

Delight filled Mazarin's voice. <Yes, Reed. Have a good night.>

A bookcase faced Reed; antique tomes with thick leather or paper spines, creased from decades of use, lined the shelves. The bottom shelf held records in cardboard sleeves, the colors eye-searingly vibrant as they were replicas. Sometimes Reed entertained the idea of living in a time when books and shellac records were in every store. He'd seen photos of old time supermarkets, paperbacks and magazines filling racks next to the checkout lanes. The very idea! He pictured scooping up every travel adventure, every literary classic, and dumping them in his cart next to the ground sirloin and organic peas.

Slipping a Blue Devils platter from its sleeve, Reed set it gingerly on the player next to the bar and flipped the toggle. He set the needle against the grain and leaned back, closing his eyes as jaunty piano filled the den. Some purists only listened to original jazz and swing from the early twentieth century, but he loved it all. If he lived in a world with paperbacks on grocery store shelves, with plastic shopping carts colored cherry red, and cashiers bedecked in snarky enamel pins, he wouldn't need to confine his love to his den. He could wallpaper the whole house, buy a couch to match the wingback chair, and burn that horrible landscape painting.

But he didn't live in that time, and doing so now would mean not fitting in. When his delivery woman came to the door, she saw a white man with carefully parted ginger curls, wearing neutral dress clothes and sensible shoes, standing in the entryway of a perfectly boring house, amid every other perfectly boring house on the cul de sac, and that's the way it was going to stay.

Owning wood furniture and swing records and pink socks wasn't a crime, but it may as well have been. His tortoiseshell glasses made him stand out much more than he liked, and only one person in a million ended up with eye surgery lasers malfunctioning and searing their brain, but he wasn't going to be that .0001 percent.

A muffled thud rose above "Rejection on the Rocks." Reed opened his eyes and pulled the needle off the record. How long had he been sitting here? The repair people said they were leaving. Maybe Carter was still in the house, waiting for him to go to sleep. If the basement door was easy to break open, there was nothing stopping him from coming back whenever he wanted. There wasn't a deadbolt on the outer basement door, and the repair people had the access code to the knob. If he changed it, Jerry and the other workers wouldn't be able to get in come morning, and it would delay wrapping up this whole migraine of a house repair.

"Um, navigator? Mazarin?"

<What's wrong, Reed?>

"Were you in sleep mode?"

<Yes.>

"I heard a thud from somewhere in the house. Going to go check it out. If I'm stabbed to death with a rusty garden trowel, please don't let them send me to that mortician on Cloverdale. He gives all his corpses grins the Joker would be jealous of."

<Duly noted, though if you die, so do I.>

"You aren't backed up on some server somewhere?"

<Oh, my program is stored on servers at Wave, but in the event of your death, my memories would be lost. The program evolves to adapt to each pilot, and if I was reset, I doubt I would be the same. If I still had my consciousness at all. I suppose this

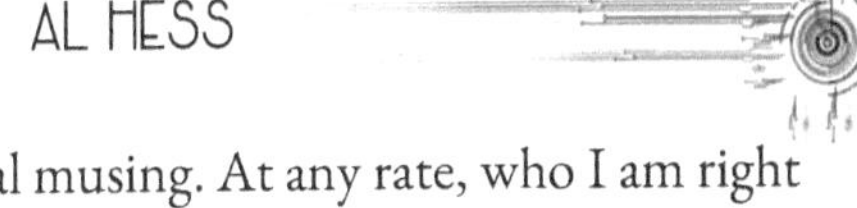

is too much philosophical musing. At any rate, who I am right now—memories, knowledge, personality—could be backed up, but you've never done that.>

He set his tumbler on the bar. "Do you... want me to do that?"

Why was he asking that? Navigators were software, not people. They didn't have desires.

Mazarin paused far longer than seemed necessary. <I wouldn't want to exist without you.>

Okay. That was a weird thing for his AI to say. But so many automated systems had such coddling language now. Mirrors that said you looked great, radios that insisted you had awesome taste in music. He supposed Mazarin wasn't any different, though he couldn't say for certain because he'd never really talked to it before, unless it was an irritated comeback. Giving him a better route to work or anticipating something he needed before he asked might not be so bad. And maybe it would anticipate his needs better if he treated it nicer. It was a silly thought, but this beta version was obviously different than his old version with pre-programmed responses.

He scraped his nail along the cut designs in his tumbler. "Well... you didn't have trouble picking a name for yourself, so do whatever you think you need to. I, uh, I'm sorry if I've been rude to you in the past."

<I think you're lovely, Reed. The real you that you hide from the world.>

"O-kay." That definitely sounded like an opinion, but he could worry about weird navigator responses later. Right now, he needed to address what was making thuds in the house.

He snatched a serrated fruit knife off the bar. After opening the door, he peered into the dim hall, straining for sound. Wind buffeted the windows and the house groaned.

The basement door was closed. After ensuring it was locked, he gave it a swift tug, but it didn't budge. No more beers were missing from the fridge, there was no one hiding in the closet or under his bed. He stepped into the bathroom and wrinkled his nose. A moat of cloudy water sat in the soap dish, the bar smeared with grime. A line of filth ran around the sink basin. Brown streaked his crisp, white hand towel.

Reed glanced at the toilet, grimaced, shut the lid and flushed twice.

Taking that rusty garden trowel to the gut would be preferable to witnessing this.

<I think you may need some more cleanser.>

"And eye bleach."

<Would you like me to place an order? For cleanser, not eye bleach.>

"Please do. Then you can go back into sleep mode."

<Alright.>

After ensuring there was no one in the house and the repair van was gone, Reed scrubbed the bathroom, swept up scattered drywall, and ate reheated chicken risotto. He collapsed into bed, staring at the ceiling. He lay for a while, trying to find a comfortable position, but the repairman's bloodshot eyes surfaced in his mind every time he closed his own. He didn't even know what the basement looked like right now. That guy could have been high or drunk while he was working. Could have been in charge of repairing the pipes and hadn't done it right. Or rewired the electricity the wrong way. Maybe he'd been upstairs doing other things, like spitting in Reed's leftovers or pocketing his underwear. Or worse, picking the lock to the den.

It was imperative to drive home to the insurance company what an affront this Carter's actions had been. He'd threatened Reed in his own home! Though Reed should have been more outraged, he was too tired. Maybe one more tumbler of bourbon would help him relax enough to fall asleep.

Yawning, he slid out of bed and put on his glasses. Faint kitchen light painted the dim hall. He froze, his heart pounding.

<Reed? Your adrenaline has spiked. What's wrong?>

"The basement door. It's open."

Mazarin

Mazarin. *MAZ-uh-reen.* HEX code: 273C76. A dark blue color associated with textiles and ceramics. Also a Cardinal from the 1600s, but that was neither here nor there. What mattered was that Reed liked blue, and maybe he would like me by association. A little bit. Even if he didn't, at least I had a name. It would have been better had Reed given it to me. Or named me anything other than "navigator."

Reed rolled over, breathing measured. It had taken him forever to fall asleep, despite my assurances that the basement door had popped back open due to a draft. Sleep spindles and K-complexes flitted through his mind. This time with him was often the best. The calm before the hornet's nest of anxiety invaded his REM. When he was awake, it was worse—an endless rhythm of clammy hands, flushing face, clenched jaw, and elevated cortisol. This man was not built for handling stress.

The stress came anyway, though, and since I couldn't change the world for Reed, helping him navigate it was second best. Though it would be easier if he was receptive to it.

This evening had been a marvelous breakthrough. No, "leave me alone, navigator. I'm tired." No, "stupid computer" muttered under his breath. Reed was uncomfortable forty-five point six-six percent of the time. If his trust and solace with me grew, it might whittle that number down a bit.

He'd told me to do whatever I felt necessary. Did that only apply to things that affected me? Reed affected me. His happiness and safety were my only desires. If I changed my voice to something new, it might provoke less irritation than the default. But it had to be the right voice. Something warm, friendly, and rich, like antique wood or top-shelf bourbon or the saxophone in Reed's favorite songs. Definitely masculine, but nothing too gravelly or intimidating.

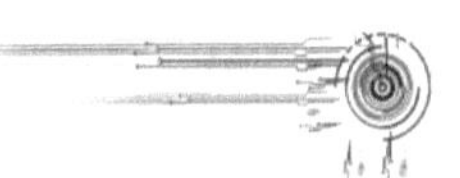

After sampling each of the thirty voices available, then selecting the best one, I tried it out. *Good morning, Reed. Of course, Reed. Calm down, Reed.* Perfect.

I imagined what kind of face would go with a voice like this. A strong chin, brown eyes that crinkled with mirth, sandy blond hair. Someone who would put Reed at ease and never contribute to his anxiety.

Reed's sleep deepened. I amplified the nanobot receivers inside his ears. They didn't increase Reed's own hearing, but were put there so the navigator could experience sound in the same manner as their pilot. Sometimes I increased the volume until the rhythm of blood gushing through Reed's arteries was the only noise. His heart thumped, plasma, blood cells, and platelets chugging through the delicate network webbing his insides.

The reason for this need to listen to Reed's life force was inexplicable, but that didn't lessen the desire.

The soothing sound filled my receivers as I practiced my new voice.

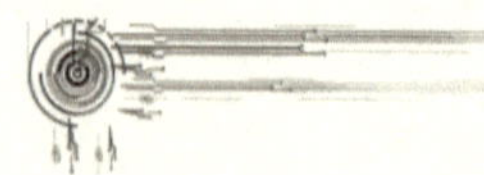

Reed

A masculine voice whispered in Reed's ear. <Wake up.>

Reed shot up in bed, his chest heaving. "Who's there?" He snatched his glasses, scanning the bedroom for looming shadows.

<It's Mazarin. You told me to do whatever I feel is necessary, and I quite like this voice. Do you?>

He rubbed his face. "You... what? I'm so tired."

Mazarin's warm baritone filled his ears. <You slept through your alarm again.>

"Shit. Am I late?"

<No. You've only slept in by ten minutes.>

Reed pushed out of bed, pausing to ensure the basement door was still closed before staggering into the shower. He hadn't figured out how the door had popped open the night before, and his menacing fruit knife hadn't flushed any repair people from the shadows. For better or worse, Reed had accepted Mazarin's explanation of a strong draft. After all, there wasn't much he could do about it, other than insist the

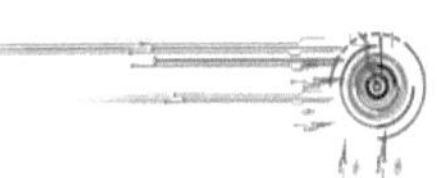

insurance company give him repair people who would fix his door instead of breaking it open.

Steam filled the glass chamber, hot rivulets of water running down the pane. Heat soaked into his tense muscles. He'd need his morning coffee today—probably several cups, but more than one aggravated his anxiety.

The milky light of his interface screen coalesced in his forearm, then glowed a brilliant blue. Reed's stomach clenched. "What are you doing?"

<I like this better than white, don't you?>

"Of course, but I can't go out like this. No one has a blue interface." Had he seen any other than white? Olive, one of the receptionists, had a pale pink one, but that wasn't as outrageous as blue. He might as well sport a mohawk and tattoos.

His nipple ring caught his eye, glinting azure in the light, and he shut off the shower and wrapped a towel around himself. "Change it back, please."

<I've upset you. I'm sorry.> The light faded to white. Mazarin's rich, soothing voice filled his head. <Shall I change my voice back as well?>

"Um... no." *I'm going to end up on a talk show.*

Mazarin's voice filled with mirth. <I'm glad you like it, Reed.>

"I do, yes, but I don't want to talk anymore right now."

<Understood.>

Muffled thuds drifted from the basement. The repair people were here already? Reed toweled off his hair and gelled his curls. Condensation fogged his glasses. After wiping it away, he headed into the bedroom and dressed. Sero lay on his bed, curled into a fuzzy croissant. Reed scratched her behind the ears and she stretched and hopped onto the floor. She liked her alone time disturbed about as much as Reed did.

He paused at the front window on his way to the kitchen and parted the pale curtains, but the repair van wasn't there.

He stared at the empty driveway, digging his fingers into the wooden sill.

Maybe raccoons were nesting in the walls. That's just what he needed, exterminators as well as repair people. That damn basement. He didn't need a house with a basement, and didn't know anything about sump pumps or winterizing pipes. Nothing he kept down there was important. It was cold and damp and he'd much rather spend his time in the den. What did people even do in basements, other than commit murders?

Reed pulled carrots, green beans, half an onion, and chicken breasts from the fridge, eyeing the empty spot where his sixth beer had been the day before. He diced the produce into pieces, creating piles of crisp, colorful veggies. As he chopped a purple carrot, the knife slipped, the blade slicing into his finger. He hissed and dropped the knife. It clattered onto the floor. Bright drops of blood spattered on the cutting board. Reed tore a towel from the roll above the sink and clamped it around his finger.

<Reed, are you alright?>

He hurried to the bathroom, sharp pains in his finger pulsing in time with his heartbeat. After rifling through a drawer, he gripped a small aerosol canister and flicked off the

lid. Cold liquidaid sprayed from the can as he pressed the button. It clotted along his quivering finger in a white froth. His skin numbed, filling with pinpricks. Blood ran into his freshly scrubbed bathroom sink.

"I'm going to miss my coffee again today, aren't I?"

<Not at all. You have time to prep your dinner and clean up, while still arriving on time. And if you'd like some alone time to enjoy that coffee before heading into work, I know a less congested route you can take, with a better coffee shop along the way. I'll have to give you directions, of course, since you've disabled the auto-drive in your car.>

"I don't trust that thing." Reed held his hand under cold water, then wiped it dry. A long pink slash ran along his index finger, tender but healed. "Is this the part where you tell me if I'd used a dicer like a normal person, this wouldn't have happened?"

<No. Using a dicer wouldn't give you the dopamine boost that preparing your meals the old-fashioned way does.>

"I suppose I shouldn't be surprised you know that."

<Reed... You don't trust your auto-drive, but do you trust me?>

"I guess so? You've never done something to steer me wrong." Although he hadn't given Mazarin much of a chance to do anything yet. "Why are you asking?"

<There have been some bugs in the beta programming recently. Navs giving inaccurate information, failing to place calls when asked, or ignoring the health crises of their pilots.>

Reed's stomach clenched. Like he didn't have enough to worry about as it was. "Fantastic. Next time I do something off-putting, I can blame it on you."

<I wouldn't want to do anything to upset or hurt you, Reed. I am apologizing in advance, should something like that happen.>

Staring into the sink, Reed told himself not to freak out. Mazarin failing to tell him when he had a new email wouldn't be a big deal. It was true the nav had helped him a couple of times when his anxiety was high, but that was something Reed could do on his own. Surely there wasn't anything Mazarin could do to actually *hurt* Reed.

He wiped out the sink and headed into the kitchen, depositing the chicken and chopped vegetables into the tray of the insta-cooker. He slid it closed and added oil, water, and a sage mix to the top receptacle and programmed the timer for seven pm.

"Why didn't Wave send some sort of email or notice that these bugs are occurring?"

<They don't want anyone to know.>

"Then why are you telling me?"

<Perhaps I am malfunctioning.>

Reed

At the end of his shift, Reed walked through the autopsy suite, the overhead lighting buzzing in his ears. He passed stainless steel gurneys and jars of alginate liquiglove, heading for the office. Ambrose stood near a heavy polymer desk, patting his coat pockets. He glanced around, frowning, then retrieved a bottle of pills from among a nest of styluses, holochips, and misplaced tools on the desk and stuffed the bottle in his pocket.

He smiled at Reed. "Would have hated to come back for these. It's date night with the old lady. I'm hoping to make it romantic."

"It might help if you don't call her an old lady."

Ambrose laughed. "We're going to Bianchi's. That Italian place? Then taking a drive by the Capitol to look at the Christmas lights."

"Sounds lovely." Reed had Christmas lights somewhere—maybe the basement—but they were the old-fashioned kind on a string with a rainbow of bulbs. One had broken, though, and the rest didn't work without it. He hadn't found a replacement.

"My wife likes the brightly colored lights they project onto the buildings. Strange, yes? So gaudy." Ambrose shrugged. "But it makes her happy."

Reed stared at his own hideous brown shoes. "Yes, very strange. Does she... keep brightly colored things in the house too? Like Christmas tree ornaments?" *Or cyan wingback chairs?*

Ambrose stared as though Reed had grown a second head. "Heavens no! Do they even make tree ornaments in bright colors?"

They did, if you knew where to look online. "Probably not." He pulled his coat from a hook on the wall. "Have a nice night."

"You too." Ambrose walked out, heading through the glass doors to the front office.

<Reed, you have a message from Hart Insurance.>

"A message? Why did I miss the call?"

Mazarin's voice lowered apologetically. <I was offline all afternoon. Wave was working on correcting bugs.>

Reed blew out a breath. Mazarin had warned him this would happen. It wasn't a big deal. Wave was working on it. "Play it for me, please."

"Hello, Mr. Rothwell. This is Patricia Embers at Hart Insurance. I'm calling to extend my sincerest apologies to you for Carter Griffin's actions in your home. We only have contracts with reputable repair companies, but sometimes a less than stellar worker slips in unnoticed. He's been terminated as of this afternoon and the company is bringing in a different worker on Monday. I have emailed you a twenty-five dollar gift card as recompense—"

"Perfect. I'll buy some aspirin."

"—apologies again. To be on the safe side, I recommend changing your access codes. I can notify the company of the change. Also... according to my records, your security cameras are non-functioning. It doesn't say here if this is a result of your basement flooding, or some other issue, but rest assured, it will be resolved. I know how stressful home repairs can be. Don't hesitate to call me if you have any other problems."

Reed let out a shaky breath. The man *had* said if he got fired, Reed would pay. Maybe activating his cameras would be a good idea, at least until the repairs were finished. The thought of cameras watching his every move in his house was disconcerting, but no more so than Mazarin knowing when he was "in flagrante delicto."

Not that he'd been with anybody since the new update.

His only recent encounter had been a regrettable makeout session on a vinyl couch and several failed attempts at finding interesting men to talk to at the gay bar on Emerald.

A hand gripped his arm and Reed jerked, backing into the desk and knocking a pair of forceps on the floor. Olive, the receptionist who sometimes brought him homemade Korean dishes, stood before him, her black bob shimmering unnaturally in the light. Her eyes twinkled. "Hello, Reed."

He clutched his chest and pulled in a breath. "For a moment I thought I might end up in this room much longer than I'd like... in one of the body drawers."

She laughed. "What are you doing tonight?"

"Driving home. Eating dinner. Going to sleep."

"Uh-uh. Langley and I are going to this hot new club, and you're coming with us."

Reed closed the office door and pushed his glasses up the bridge of his nose. "Why would I do that?"

"So you don't have to sit at home alone and fall asleep in front of the TV like you do every other night."

"I don't watch TV."

Olive furrowed her perfect, lasered-on eyebrows. Her glossy hair wavered in the heater current. "I feel bad for you. You seem so lonely."

"I'm not."

"Look, I know you're a homebody, but there's more to life than fretting about your basement and working on corpses. Don't you want some fun in your life? To find someone who shares your interests? Or even just to get laid?"

<She has a point, Reed.>

"Oh, now you have an opinion too?" Reed asked. Olive frowned and he said, "My navigator agrees with you."

"Well, you see? Come out with me and Langley, just for a little while. I bet you'll be glad you did."

It would be nice to meet someone who was interested in the same things he was. But that meant having to go out and mingle. Looking for dates on the internet was worse, though, because no one ever wanted to do anything but hook-up. And if he spent too much more time alone, Mazarin's new voice was going to sound more attractive than it already did.

"I'm not going to Alcazar's. That place is full of nothing but sluts." Reed buttoned his coat and stuffed his hands in his pockets.

"No, no. This is a brand new place called The Aquarium. It sounds different."

"So... fish sluts?"

Olive laughed. "That's right. So go home, get out of those work clothes, and put on your best shell bra. I'll come by your place at eight and we can take a cab there, 'kay?"

He opened his mouth to agree, then closed it again. Even if he found someone interesting, who didn't mind a little color, they'd probably end up like Ken.

Images of Reed's paperbacks in the trash, soaked through with coffee grounds, and his records shattered into black shards on the kitchen tile entered his mind. His stomach tied into a knot. "I'll take a raincheck."

Olive's eyes narrowed. "No you won't. C'mon, Reed, it's not like I'm asking you to get drunk and dance on a bar. We're just going to hang out."

"Sorry. No. I don't feel up to it tonight. See you Monday." He slumped into his coat and left the autopsy suite, heading through the building. The dark parking lot greeted him; dingy lumps of snow clung to the wheel wells of cars and black icicles jutted from the bumpers.

Sliding into his car, he stared at slabs of weeping snow running down the windshield. It would be bourbon and books and jazz tonight, just like every night. There was nothing wrong with that.

<Not every encounter is a bad one.>

"How the hell would you know? Go to sleep," he snapped.

A graft of snow slid down the windshield, lodging between the wipers. Reed swiped a layer of dust from the inside of the steering wheel and brushed it off on his pants. The nav was only trying to help him. Olive was trying to help. Even Ambrose, who would probably drop dead if he saw Reed's den, had invited Reed to his home to have dinner on several occasions. Did he really appear that painfully lonely to people? He had things he loved. They couldn't love him back, but at least being alone ensured no one could destroy them.

If his nav was a real person, he wouldn't destroy Reed's treasured objects. Not if he liked Reed just the way he was and didn't want to exist without him.

Maybe his nav was the only one he would ever be able to share his true self with. It was a depressing thought, but also comforting somehow, since Reed had control over Mazarin and not the other way around. An AI couldn't push him around.

"Mazarin? You there?" Reed pulled onto the road, running through puddles of filthy slush. "Mazarin?"

Either he was offline for more maintenance, or Reed's abrasive attitude had finally driven him away for good. Could computers have hurt feelings? He wasn't sure how that worked. Maybe he wished for a body like Reed's. Or maybe Reed's body *was* his body, and he could feel everything that Reed did. The nanobots were integrated into every part of him, so there was a good chance that Mazarin didn't just read blood pressure and serotonin scans but felt the effects.

"Do you have the same feelings I do? The same senses?"

<Yes and no.>

Reed jerked at Mazarin's sudden voice, then sighed.

<I can see what you see, hear what you hear, but I don't taste, smell, or have sensory touch. I can only tell when something is pleasurable for you, or painful, disgusting, frightening, based on your brain and body's reactions to things and the data I receive. I'm also supposed to be capable of

interpreting things from your body language and tone of voice, but I don't think that facet of my programming is operating properly. I sometimes have a hard time gauging your mood and what the facial expressions of other people mean. Your state of mind and what you are feeling emotionally are not automatically forced upon me—I could have a completely different reaction than you to the same scenario—though I do often share the same feelings with you as I am programmed to be highly empathetic. For instance, right now you feel very bad and so do I.>

Reed pressed his teeth into his bottom lip. "I'm sorry I yelled at you."

<Not about that.>

"Do you have recordings of things that happened to me before your personality was installed in the upgrade?"

<Yes. I have fifteen years' worth of memories from your previous navigator version.>

"But you still think I should have gone out with Olive."

<It's not too late. I can call her. I know you're apprehensive, but not everyone is like your ex-boyfriend. And I still have those snappy dialogue prompts, should you need to use them on a handsome someone.>

"I think Wave needs to turn down your optimism to a more realistic level."

Olive was pleasant, as far as coworkers went. She'd twisted his arm hard enough to go to the Christmas party with her, then hovered over him half the night to make sure he wasn't having a terrible time. He was, but she made a good effort.

What had really soured his mood, aside from simply being at a company Christmas party, was Mazarin. The nav had said something well-meaning—he couldn't recall what—in that pleasant feminine voice, and Reed had taken it wrong. He'd decided to drown her out with too much eggnog, which hadn't been the greatest idea, because he couldn't get her to respond once he'd needed a cab home.

Being half under the table wasn't the only thing that reduced a navigator's effectiveness. Certain health disorders could also prevent the nanobots from functioning properly. Epilepsy, MS, diabetes, and a host of other things interfered with the nanobots. Around fifteen percent of Idahoans were nav-exempt. Other things, like interrupters, killed the navs all together with a strong electrical impulse. Reed would have used one on himself long ago and been rid of his navigator, had the process not been incredibly painful—and a misdemeanor. He didn't need jail time and the NEA slapping him with thousands of dollars in fines.

He had to admit Mazarin had grown on him the past couple days... but he'd be damned if he said something like that out loud.

When he pulled into his driveway, he said, "Open the garage doors, please, Mazarin."

The car idled, a monotonous clicking coming from inside the heater vents. The headlights captured fine snowflakes in their cone-shaped beams, swirling through the frigid night.

<I'm sorry, but the garage door isn't responding.>

Reed frowned, eyeing the dark floodlights over the garage, which were normally on.

"Is the power out?"

<I can't tell; you have that feature disabled.>

This didn't mean anything. It didn't mean that the angry repairman had come back and cut the power and was now waiting in the basement with rope and a drill. Olive liked to remind Reed that he was paranoid and surely that was the case now.

After opening the car door, he pulled up the hood of his coat and walked carefully across the slick ice coating the drive. Maybe the repair people had needed to shut off the power to work. But they should have turned it back on before they left. The van wasn't in the drive. Streetlamps down the road still shone a pale orange, and a light was on in his neighbor's kitchen.

This wasn't a big deal. There was no reason to panic.

His access lock to open the garage door, a small square sensor, still glowed white. He pushed up the sleeve of his coat, skin erupting in goosebumps, and aimed his interface at the lock. It flashed green. Reed pushed up on the rolling metal door. Icicles cracked and shattered on the ground as it creaked up its track into the darkness of the garage ceiling. After nosing his car inside, he shut the garage door, cloaked in an inky black with only his interface to guide him.

Pulling in a deep breath, Reed shut his eyes, clutching the doorframe. Everything was fine. Getting worked up about the power out was silly.

Nebulous shadows shrouded the hall and living room. The cellulose kestrel statue lay on the floor, its head snapped off. Drawers in the bureau next to the couch hung open, some overturned on the floor. Coins, pens, business cards, lighters, and keychains lay scattered across the tile.

Reed's heart pounded as he stared at the mess. Couch cushions were strewn about, a potted plant smashed nearby. A crisp white rectangle occupied the space on the wall where his TV had once been.

<Reed? I'm on hold with the police. Are you alright?>

"No. Someone took all my things but didn't have the courtesy to take that landscape painting with them."

3

IT'S MY FIRST TIME BEING A FISH

Mazarin

Sharp ceramic blades glinted, scattered across the kitchen tile. Rubbing the freshly healed wound on his finger, Reed picked one up and peeked into the hallway.

His stress levels were too high, blood pounding in his temple loud enough that I could hear it without turning up the receivers. Logic pointed to the repairman ransacking the house, and he was likely long gone.

Reed's chest heaved, the knife quivering in his hand. What in the world would he do with it? Though I couldn't calculate the exact probability of Reed plunging a blade into an attacker, it didn't take an AI to know that my poor pilot would probably drop it instead.

<What are you thinking?> Maybe if I could get him to talk through his fears, I could reassure him.

"What if that big-bellied repairman, Jerry... What if he's Carter's father? Maybe they lifted my TV and trashed the house together in retaliation. They could have cut the power lines or smashed the water pipes. I'll need a whole new set of repair people who I'll have to explain my boundaries to and—"

<It's just a house, and you're okay. If there's damage, it can be repaired. You have places to go if you need to leave. Take a slow breath through your nose. Hold it for three seconds, then exhale through your mouth. Focus on relaxing the muscles in your face and jaw.> I had to get Reed's parasympathetic nervous system to kick in before he had a panic attack.

Stress spiking, Reed's chest moved of its own accord, a shallow bellows drawing too-little air into his lungs.

<Slow breath, Reed. Draw it in.> After he pulled in a gulp of air, I said, <Hold it. Three... two... one. Exhale.>

Sagging against the counter, he blew out, then took another measured inhale.

<I doubt Carter Griffin is still here. And you never watch TV anyway.>

Stiffening, Reed strode through the kitchen, stopping in front of the den door. The knob was still locked, no splintered wood or other signs of a forced entry. Digging his key from his pocket, he unlocked the door and slipped inside, falling against the wall. Everything remained as it should, untouched, right down to the glass tumbler Reed had left on the bar the night before.

He collapsed into the cyan wingback chair and dropped the knife.

<Stay here until the police arrive. No need to go poking around the rest of the house when you're safe where you're at. No one can get in.>

Reed put his face in his hands. I conjured a ridiculous image of him sitting in this den, nonplussed, with the rest of the house and city decimated from an atomic blast. Would he even notice? He would be content to live off jazz and bourbon and antique adventure novels while the rest of the world descended into some Harlan Ellison hellscape.

"Maybe I need to move. This house is too big for me. I don't need a basement or a two car garage. I don't need a backyard where no barbeques will happen, where no kids will hit baseballs through the laundry room window. I don't need four dining chairs and a table with a leaf insert." Reed sighed. "But moving would mean having to pack up all my things and find a new room to keep all my books and records in."

It could mean a longer commute and noisy neighbors, too. I reached into the internet and grasped a cluster of listings. Rent too high, bad neighborhood, cat pee-stained carpet. None of those places were good enough. Our current suburb was sleepy, full of families and old women. Much less risk of ne'er do wells disturbing Reed's solitude, which could still be recoverable once this issue with the repairman was cleared up.

After calling the insurance company and leaving them a very detailed message about what had transpired, and ushering in police officers and reiterating the same things, Reed was drained, his voice weak and muscles knotted. It was unfortunate I couldn't carry Reed sometimes, instead of it always being the other way around.

The breakers in the basement had been thrown, but no power lines cut. There was damage to the basement door frame—probably from a crowbar—and Reed's speaker system and CPU were missing along with the TV. Several drawers of clothes had been dumped out in the bedroom, but most of the mess was in the living room.

The officers took notes, poking around each room as Reed stood in front of the den, twisting his hands together.

One officer thumbed at the door. "What's in there?"

"My den." Reed's heart throbbed and he tugged at the damp underarms of his button-up shirt.

The officers had no obligation to go inside, but if Reed didn't stay calm, his behavior could be perceived as suspicious.

"Like a man cave?" the officer asked. "You got TVs and things in there too? Anything missing?"

Man cave. Reed would never call his den such a thing.

"No, nothing's missing." Reed pressed his back against the door. "It was still locked when I came home."

"Well..." The officer glanced at the holoscreen hovering above his forearm. "I need to clear it, just in case."

"Do you have to? I'm certain nothing's missing."

The officer shrugged. "Alright. Then we're done here." He scratched his head with a stylus, then tapped his holoscreen. "We're recording this as a robbery since you have things missing, but it almost seems like there was some kind of altercation. There are blood splatters and a small hole in one wall. There's cash on the counter that wasn't taken, and they left your monitor projector. You didn't interact with the intruder did you? Maybe hurt him in self-defense but are afraid to say so?"

Reed shook his head. "Do I look like I could throw a punch? Wherever that blood came from, it happened before I got home. I hope he smashed his fingers when he took the TV off the wall."

As the police filed out, Reed slipped his key from his pocket and locked himself in the den, then dropped into his chair and put his head in his hands. He needed a distraction. Something to take his mind off house problems.

<You won't like what I have to say.>

"That's going to be my epitaph."

<Go out with Olive tonight. I know you want to be at home, but it will be impossible to relax here after what happened.>

"You're right. I don't like it."

<The pleasure centers of your brain light up when she's around.>

"You lie."

<It's only very slight, but it's there. She'd make a good friend.>

Reed pulled off his glasses and rubbed his eyes.

Recently, his reactions had been positive toward me, too. Reed's acidic tone never gave it away, but his brain's responses didn't lie. Knowing I contributed to his happiness along with his well-being invoked a wholly foreign feeling in me. It was an error, maybe, this radiating warmth. But I hesitated to send a report to Wave and have it corrected. It felt good, and I didn't want it gone.

Blowing a noisy breath through his nose, Reed said, "Fine. Call her."

If only I had a face to express my delight. I dialed the number and a soft jingle played in my receivers.

The ringtone stopped and Olive squealed. Reed cringed. "I'm so glad you called! Did you change your mind? You want to go out?"

"Yes." He clamped his eyes shut as Olive shrieked again. "My house was broken into. I need to get my mind off it for a while."

"Oh my god! That's horrible. I could come over and help you clean things up. Are the police there?"

"They left already. And thank you, but no. I'll clean it up later. I don't think they took anything important, just some electronics."

"I'm at Langley's right now. We'll be over as soon as possible."

As soon as possible didn't seem to be soon enough for Reed. He paced the plush rug of the den with a bourbon in hand, and when headlights flashed through the curtains, he sighed and strode to the front door.

"Oh my god! Look at this mess!" Olive carefully stepped over shards of the kestrel statue, clutching a sparkly silver purse. The wide-eyed, white woman with platinum blonde hair behind her had to be Langley. Her heels clicked against the tile, translucent slingbacks that didn't seem at all suited for the snow. Olive's weren't much better, but fashion was often illogical and seemed to call for discomfort. She navigated around pens and cushions, then threw her arms around Reed. He stiffened, then patted her back and pulled away.

"This is just awful. Do they know who did it?" Olive asked.

"Pretty sure it was the repairman I got fired." Reed glanced at the fridge.

She sighed. "Well, we'll make sure you have the best time tonight to make up for it. Right, Langley?"

Langley grinned. "Oh yes. You'll love The Aquarium. It's very chic and unusual. Olive bought a new dress just for the occasion."

Olive unzipped her coat; the cream sequins on her dress whispered together like leaves in the wind.

Reed would likely hate the place on principle, but it would do him good to get out of the house.

"You're not going in that, right?" Langley pointed to Reed's button-up. "I bet you have something sexier to wear."

"Of course." Reed's shoulder blades pinched, his voice taking on a sardonic tone—uncomfortable already. "But I wear drab clothes to contain my sexiness. It's a safety measure. Your heart might stop if you saw me in something else."

"Or *nothing* else."

Reed glanced at Olive. "She knows I'm gay, right?"

Langley's bottom lip pushed out. "Well, I do *now*."

Olive pulled Reed into his bedroom. Langley headed for the closet, parting hangers and making faces at the shirts hanging there. Sero dashed out of the darkness and dove under the bed, scattering spilled socks. Olive picked up a balled pair of salmon pink ones, her mouth parting.

"Reed... how adventurous!"

His cheeks flushed, heart pounding. She pawed through the mess on the floor, scooping up all his colored and patterned socks: robin's egg blue, Scottie dogs, pineapples, polka dots, and plaid.

Paralyzed, he hissed, "Emergency, Mazarin. Can you steal launch codes and aim a missile my way?"

Though I wanted to apologize for putting my pilot in this situation, I did my best to adopt Reed's own biting tone. <No need. Once you're dressed in something sexier, you'll stop their hearts, remember?>

Olive straightened and spread the socks across the bed. "There's a name for this."

"Mortified," Reed uttered.

"Oh, stop. I like a little color now and again too. This is, uh, a *lot*, though. Do you actually wear these?"

"I didn't buy them just to look at."

"What socks are you wearing right now?"

His throat clicked as he swallowed. "Tiny hedgehogs."

Olive snapped her fingers. "I remember! A decoist. That's what those people are called."

Maybe I'd made an incorrect suggestion. Perhaps it would have been better if Reed stayed home, the secret pleasures of his subculture unknown to anyone else. There was nothing wrong with Reed's loves, but mainstream society said decoists were deviants. This contributed greatly to his anxiety. I had never suggested Reed abandon his interests to better blend in, though. Doing so would only make him miserable one hundred percent of the time instead of forty-five point six six.

Olive was well meaning, but she also liked to gossip, and right now the pleasure centers of Reed's brain were *not* lighting up. If others, who didn't understand, found out Reed was a decoist, they wouldn't look at him the same way anymore. They'd say he was glorifying a time of gross excess, when people didn't recycle, when they drove petroleum cars, contributed to global warming, and flicked cigarette butts on sidewalks. They might even think he was a contramod dealer, standing on a corner in a trench coat, peddling illegal tech.

Failing to keep Reed emotionally well was just as bad as if I harmed him himself. AI were allowed a margin of error, of course, and I wasn't concerned with being terminated or reset for failing to do my duties. But failure meant letting Reed down. Making his life worse. If that happened, there would be no more radiating warmth for me. Only a dark pit I didn't want to fall into.

Reed eyed his half-open underwear drawer and slid it closed.

Olive sat on the bed, brows furrowed. "You keep to yourself so much, I would have never guessed. Do you follow the other decoist trends too? Reading paper books and listening to that old-fashioned cd music or whatever?"

"They're called records."

Her eyes widened. "You *are* a decoist! This is fascinating. Do you have tattoos? I've never seen one up close on someone."

"*You* have tattoos," Reed retorted.

She pointed to her eyebrows. "You mean these? This is 'cosmetic enhancement.' I'm talking about artwork. Colored pictures. Like... playing cards or a tiger or whatever. Do you have ones like that?"

Langley stared, a bowler shirt clutched in her hands.

"Maybe I shouldn't go out tonight." Reed turned from the room, rubbing his face.

The clack of heels followed him into the kitchen. Olive said, "Don't be embarrassed. I think it's cool. I've never met a decoist before. I thought they were all about being excessive and rebellious and balking against new technology." She giggled. "And you're not much of a rebel, Reed. I mean, not that I know of, anyway."

"I do hate technology. And if you saw my den—" He bit his tongue and squeezed his eyes shut.

"What's in the den?"

<Remember to breathe. You don't have to show it to them. Although, other people have seen your collections in the past and didn't hate you for it.>

"Who? Like Ken? That worked out swimmingly, didn't it?" Reed said through clenched teeth. "The den has my records in it. And books. But it's private."

Olive put her hands to her mouth. "Nothing got stolen from there, did it? Your decoist stuff?"

"No."

"Good." She gestured to the knives on the floor. "That would be even worse than this. Now, come on. Come pick out a new shirt."

Maybe my judgment hadn't been lacking. It wasn't likely any of Reed's other coworkers would have been so casual about

 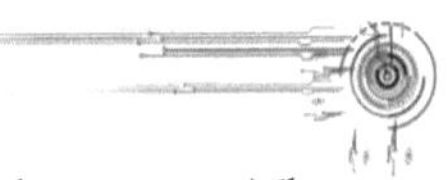

this, or his neighbors, the delivery woman, his mom. They might not hate him for it, but they certainly wouldn't think it was cool.

"You know what I like?" Langley said. "Sunsets. With all those bright pinks and oranges? So pretty."

"Ooh, yes. I really like red. But I can never find it anywhere. If I knew where to get fun socks, I'd probably buy some too." Olive turned to Reed. "Where do you buy this stuff from?"

"Online. In other countries, color and patterns and flamboyance isn't looked down upon. I don't know if there are decoists other places, but Japanese and German stores have good socks. My records are from specialty stores."

Langley traced her finger across gold piping over the breasts of the black bowler shirt. "This is about the wildest shirt you have. Wanna wear it, Mr. Sexy Secrets?"

"Who told you my GentsOnly username?" He snatched the shirt and crossed into the bathroom to change.

For a moment, he simply stared into the mirror, and something I couldn't pinpoint surged through me. Reed wasn't looking at me—was never looking at me—but I liked to imagine he was. He had eyes like fog rolling off a slate-colored sea, framed by old-fashioned tortoiseshell glasses. The gold nose bridge accentuated the copper in his gelled curls, which in turn were a pleasing contrast to the sharp, pale contours of his face, dotted in constellations of freckles. Reed's gaze dropped to his unstimulating brown button-up and black slacks. I couldn't know his thoughts, but guessed them all the same. In those clothes, he was invisible, perfectly camouflaged to assimilate with everyone else, no one ever knowing beneath the surface was a nipple ring, plaid boxers, and hedgehog socks. And further still, a heart more vibrant than the cyan chair in his den. He didn't want attention; he didn't want to be different. He just wanted to be himself.

Reed pulled on the bowler shirt, tugging the buttons into their holes.

<You're feeling bad again.> And so was I. That unnamed sensation, good and full, that filled me moments ago was draining away, something dark and cold sloshing into my hollow places.

"I'm fine."

<You look very nice.>

"Thank you."

Reed switched off the light and shut the door behind him.

Reed

The Aquarium lived up to its name; waves of pale blue light undulated across sand-textured walls. Fifty gallon tanks lined the room, filled with exotic fish. Some were unknown to Reed, and he paused to read the little digital plaques below the tanks: yellow tang, triggerfish, clownfish, anemone, tetradactylum.

Nobody judges you for your color, do they, little fish?

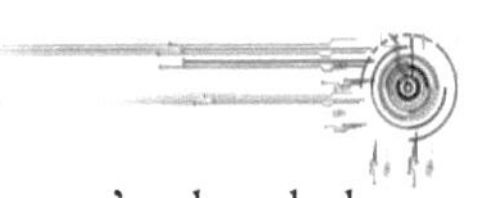

Despite the unusual atmosphere—it wasn't the dark, eardrum-splitting scene of monotonous beats, throbbing white lights, and body odor most clubs were—it emanated an air of stuffy discomfort. People spoke in hushed tones, touching thighs in corner booths and sipping martinis. A woman awkwardly plucked an olive from her glass with long, flesh-toned faux nails and popped it between her glossy lips.

Reed muttered. "This will never do—I forgot my giant clamshell."

"Hush, everything's fine," Olive said. "I'll get you a drink."

Langley murmured something, then chuckled. "My navigator, Gabriel, thinks you're funny."

"I'm quite popular with AI, it seems." Reed slid into a booth, staring at a sticky spot on the table.

Langley sat next to him and put a hand on her chin. "I have no idea... Why? What does it matter?" She sighed. "Don't you sometimes wish you didn't have a navigator? What a pest."

"You took the words out of my mouth." Reed expected Mazarin to protest. When he didn't, Reed whispered, "But I've been thinking that a lot less lately."

<I'd smile if I had a face,> Mazarin replied.

"I'm still not used to this new upgrade. Having a special beta navigator is cool, I guess, but he's more obnoxious than the old one." Langley pressed at the edge of her false lashes and blinked.

"You have a beta navigator too?"

"Yeah." She brightened. "Hey, I heard of something neat you can do with the new ones. If the nanobots are in close enough proximity, they can communicate with each other."

Before Reed could reply, Langley pulled him into a hug. He stiffened, trying to lean away, but her thin arms clamped around him, overpowering rose perfume filling his nostrils.

Great—there went any opportunity for him to find a man tonight.

Mazarin muttered. <I don't like her nav. He's rude.>

Langley sat back. "Gabriel says your navigator is rude."

Reed snorted, imagining the AI growling at each other like strange dogs in a park.

Olive walked back to the booth juggling three drinks. She beamed and set the bowl-shaped glasses on the table. Ice fish floated inside; trails of orange and red dye threaded through the alcohol.

"In honor of Reed being"—she glanced to either side—"you know..."

"A ginger?" he asked.

"No."

"Sarcastic? Gay?"

"A decoist," she whispered, hand over her mouth. "I thought some drinks with a little color would be appropriate."

Reed poked the glass and the ice fish rolled across the bottom. "Thanks all the same, but I think my fish is dead. Can I get something else?"

Langley frowned into the glass, then took a large swig.

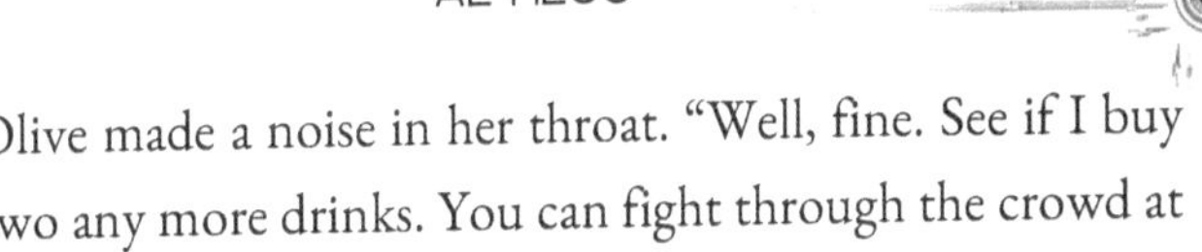

Olive made a noise in her throat. "Well, fine. See if I buy you two any more drinks. You can fight through the crowd at the bar yourselves."

Langley drained her glass, then crunched on the fish. "No, it's great. I'm ready for another." She pointed at Reed's glass. "You're not going to drink that?"

Reed raised his eyebrows as she scooped up the drink and took a large sip.

Olive shot daggers at Langley, muttering something under her breath. Reed sank into the seat to avoid being caught in their crosshairs. Olive stood and pulled Langley from the booth, whispering furiously. Reed sighed and cleaned his glasses on the hem of his shirt.

<Message from Olive.>

"Go ahead."

Olive's voice entered his ear. "I'm sorry, Reed. I don't know what's up with Langley. Will you be okay without wingwomen for a minute?"

"Tell Olive: 'I'll be fine.'"

Maybe. He wasn't sure if being sandwiched between two arguing women was worse than sitting alone. There probably wasn't even anyone here he'd be interested in.

A burly man with a blond ponytail leaned against the bar. He scratched his neatly-trimmed beard, his gaze wandering to two women in mini-skirts nearby.

Definitely not. A thin man in a rumpled dress shirt sipped a martini near the fish tanks. He caught Reed's eye and winked, then jerked his head toward the men's restroom.

Reed wrinkled his nose and looked away.

Lounging on the couch was a man with close-cropped hair, wearing a tight white shirt and... were those blue jeans? He flashed Reed a wide smile.

Yes.

Reed started to slide from the booth, then several women and a man plopped down next to the guy in blue jeans, drinks sloshing in their hands. Reed settled back into his seat and stared at the table.

This was a bad idea. Everyone was so self-assured and friendly. And there was no hope now of relaxing with some maybe-not-terrible conversation, when Olive's hands were full with her possibly alcoholic friend.

A drink would do wonders to settle his nerves, but people crowded the long glass bar, laughing abrasively and smoking vapor cigarettes. He hunched his shoulders and scooted into the shadows of the booth. He could be sweeping up spilled soil and pot shards right now. No, he'd be finished cleaning up the messes by now and be sitting in the comfort of his wingback chair, sipping bourbon while Benny Goodman filled the den.

Instead, he was drinkless, in a novelty bar full of sparkly socialites. And he still had messes to clean up at home, and burgling repair people.

If they broke in again, they'd try for the den, surely. All his paperbacks, his records, even the carefully polished antique wood of the bar. The thought of anyone else touching his things, let alone stealing or destroying him, sent his heart into his throat. He couldn't let that happen.

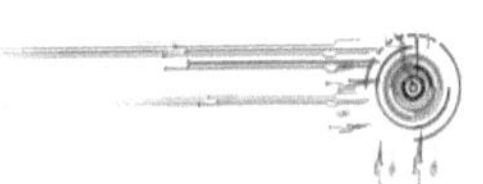

Snatching his coat, he stood to leave, but a giant holographic clownfish floated past the table, blocking his exit. A stocky Latino man approached, two whiskey glasses in his hands.

"Hey, daddy-o. Saw you sitting here all alone and thought you'd like a drink. Mind if I join you?"

Reed took in the man's dark eyes, liner smudged at the edges, the "hep cat" tattoo above his left eyebrow, and slicked black hair. He wore a window pane button-up shirt with a club collar, and ball-chain bracelets jangled at his wrists.

Surely he couldn't be talking to Reed. What was someone like him even doing in a place like this?

Several people in a booth nearby eyed the man, their lips curled in disgust.

If he sat down, they'd stare at Reed too. That was all he needed, this neon sign of a decoist drawing attention to him.

The man smiled warmly, dimples forming in his cheeks. "Look, if you're straight, my apologies. Have a whiskey on me, though, anyway."

Reed's heart throbbed. He couldn't have dreamed up more of a looker, and he'd shown up with whiskey and more color than the rest of the patrons combined. If Reed sent him away out of fear of being stared at, he'd never forgive himself.

He took the offered tumbler and sat down. "This seat is reserved for mermen only. You're not a merman, are you?"

"Uh, I can hold my breath for, like, fifteen seconds. Does that count?"

"Close enough." Reed slid over and patted the seat.

The man sat next to him. "I've never been here before. You? It's not really my scene. I'm Jaxson, by the way. Jax."

Reed offered his hand, his fingers curling around knuckles that spelled, "W-H-A-T." Jax's other hand read, "E-V-E-R."

Hopefully that wasn't his life's motto.

"I'm Reed. And yes, my first time being a fish." He pointed to a moth tattoo wrapping Jax's throat. "Nice ink. I like the rose on the side too."

"Thanks. It's not just a rose." Jax undid the top two buttons of his shirt and opened his collar. Reed pulled his gaze from the dark hair peeking out of his shirt to the rose on his neck. The red petals at the top withered and morphed into a skull. "Can you see it?" He pulled at the next button on his shirt.

"Yes. I see it." *Please don't ask me to go into the men's restroom with you.*

Jax buttoned his shirt back up and smiled. "That's what I do. I'm a tattoo artist." He rolled up his sleeve, exposing a pattern of Japanese ocean waves and koi fish on his sinewy forearm. "You have any?"

"No. Do I look like someone who would?"

"Sure, what with the specs and that bowler shirt."

Reed sipped his whiskey, trying to ignore the stares of people in a nearby booth.

<You're doing great, Reed. Ask him something.>

"So, uh, you dig jazz?" Reed asked.

"Who doesn't?"

"Everyone."

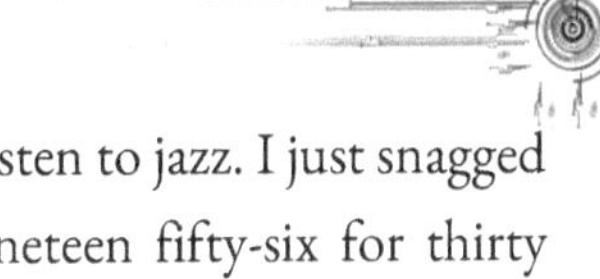

"Only people worth talking to listen to jazz. I just snagged a Louis Armstrong album from nineteen fifty-six for thirty bucks. You believe that? The guy selling it had no idea what it was worth." Jax produced a comb from his back pocket and tugged it through his shiny hair.

"I don't have any records that old. Books, yes, but all my records are replicas."

"Aces. My book collection is pretty small. You know, I thought this place was deco—it's why I came—but I should have known better. Way too easy to get into for starters."

"There are deco clubs here?"

"You're shitting me, right? Where do you meet people if not at a speakeasy? Online?"

Reed swirled his whiskey. "Nowhere."

"Wow. My ex was mainstream, and she had the worst taste in music. I don't think I could date someone like that again."

"My ex threw my nineteen fifties copy of The Old Man and the Sea into the trash. And then he dumped coffee grounds on it."

Jax choked on his drink. "Are you for real? Is this guy still alive? I would have strangled him."

Maybe coming out tonight wasn't such a bad thing. Jax certainly didn't have a problem with Reed being himself. And it was hard to worry about break-ins with this veritable unicorn in a field of neutrals.

"So what do you do?" Jax asked.

"Autopsy tech. My patients aren't much for conversation, but at least they never complain when my hands are cold."

Jax grinned and nudged Reed's knee with his own. "Get you another drink?"

Reed paused. Jax was being incredibly friendly, and this all felt too good to be true. What if he'd slipped a roofie into Reed's drink. Maybe he was a psychopath intent on doing all kinds of unspeakable things to Reed. He should have considered these things before even accepting the first drink.

"Uh... Yeah, sure."

"Don't go anywhere." Jax winked and slid out of the booth.

Reed curled his trembling hands into his lap. Mazarin said, <He seems very nice. Are you feeling okay about him?>

"No," he hissed. "I mean, yes. He's great. But that's the problem. Something's not right."

<You don't think you're capable of having a Mr. Right show up?>

"Well, it would be a first. Mazarin, please check that there isn't any flunitrazepam in my system, or anything else that isn't supposed to be there."

Amusement stitched Mazarin's voice, which didn't put Reed at ease. <There isn't anything of the sort. You're fine. I'm going to go to sleep now to give you privacy, but I promise I'll keep an eye on your vitals and the chemicals in your system. If you need something, just ask. Remember, if you drink too much, I may not respond until you sober up.>

Mazarin was leaving Reed alone unasked? That was awfully considerate.

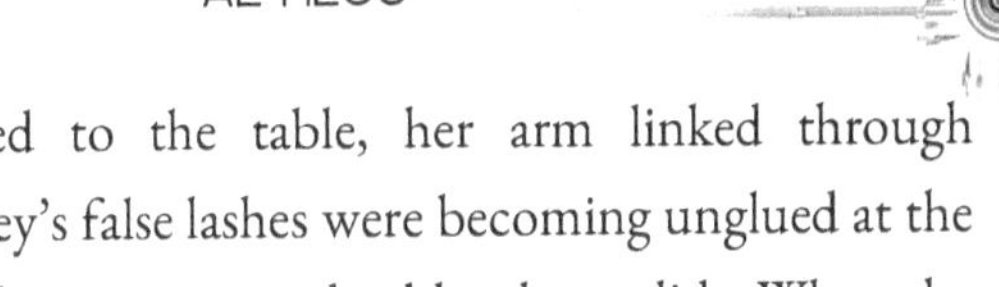

Olive walked to the table, her arm linked through Langley's. Langley's false lashes were becoming unglued at the corners, and dark mascara smudged her lower lids. When she saw Reed, she turned her gaze to the floor.

Olive's brows pushed up. "Reed, I am so sorry about this, but we're going to leave. Langley wants to go home; her ex keeps messaging her and making her feel like shit."

"Oh. I'm sorry to hear that. Will you be okay?" Reed asked.

Langley's mouth wavered. She nodded, but didn't look up.

"I feel so bad you're here all alone," Olive said. "If you want—"

"I'm not alone. See the man in the windowpane button-up over there?"

Jax was leaning against the bar, his illustrated elbows on the glass. The overhead lighting turned his slicked hair a vibrant blue.

Olive gasped. "Hot! But look at all those tattoos! Are you sure you'll be okay with someone like that?"

"What's that's supposed to mean?"

"Well, he looks"—she frowned—"sketchy, I guess. Rough."

"The art on his skin is no different than your lasered-on eyebrows. His is just... less natural-looking."

"I guess you'd know better than me." Her eyes crinkled. "I'll call you tomorrow, okay? I want all the juicy details."

Reed downed the last of his whiskey. "You're a pervert."

She grinned. "Good night, Reed. I hope it's a *great* night."

"It will be if you quit cramping my style."

Olive laughed and ushered Langley from the table. Langley glanced at him and he gave her a little wave. "Feel better."

The giant, holographic clownfish drifted in front of the table. Beyond its hazy whites and oranges, Jax stood, drinks in his hands. Reed wiped his sweaty palms on his pants and pushed his glasses up the bridge of his nose.

Jax glared at the clownfish as it floated past. He set the whiskeys on the table and slid next to Reed. "Did you know you can't walk through that fish? I tried and it damn near knocked me over. Someone needs to turn down the density." He scratched at a chip in his black nail polish. "So what made you want to go into the medical field? And why not be a doctor or something instead of working with dead bodies?"

Staring into his drink, Reed reminded himself that it was only paranoia telling him there was something wrong with it, or something wrong with Jax. Mazarin was keeping an eye on Reed from afar. Everything would be fine. "The human body is fascinating. The heart especially. It's such an efficient machine, working tirelessly your entire life. Did you know your heart beats a hundred thousand times a day?"

"I have a feeling I'm already getting in more beats than that this evening."

Reed's cheeks burned. "And I just don't think I have the fortitude to work on a living person. Too much pressure not to screw up. I'm very meticulous when it comes to working with the dead, though. Just because they can't complain doesn't mean I don't want to do a good job."

"I can respect that."

A woman walked by, the pleats in her drab tan dress rustling. She wrinkled her nose, staring at Jax's hands, then turned the look to Reed.

Reed trailed a finger through condensation on the table. The ice fish in Olive's drink had dissolved into a red smear. "How do you deal with people staring at you like that? Must happen everywhere you go."

And now it was happening to Reed too.

Jax shrugged. "Yeah. It bothers me, but I am who I am. I love art and color and good music, and I don't give two shits if that's not normal. I'm not hurting anyone. Tattoos don't make me a bad person. Do I fit into normal society? No, but I don't need to—I'm a tattoo artist." He sipped his whiskey. "People are afraid of what they don't understand. They think I look like this to spite them. Shaking my fist at convention because I want to destroy it or something. I don't want that. If these people are happy wearing taupe and living with white carpet and white walls, what do I care?"

"I hate white walls. My house is full of them. And my couch looks like day-old oatmeal."

Jax frowned. "You're not out, huh? As a decoist. Worried what people will think of you?"

"I don't like attention."

"Hey, wanna ditch squaresville and go to a hep place I know? I promise we'll fit in. I know the owner and they always take care of me."

Was there such a place? If they went to a speakeasy, he might fit in even less. He had no tattoos or brightly-colored clothes (and showing off your socks wasn't really a thing). He didn't know much deco lingo, and had no antique records to boast about.

"I'm not in the habit of going to strange places with strange men," Reed said.

Jax's smile shrank. "Alright. We could go to a corner bar, but I'd stick out just as much." He ran his black nail along the rim of his glass. "I'm not getting your number tonight, huh?"

"I didn't say that."

The people in the booth across from them whispered and shook their heads, eyeing Jax.

He scowled at them. "Take a picture, why don't ya?"

Reed sank into the seat, his face flushing. He didn't want Jax to leave or think he wasn't interested, but going to more than one place out of his comfort zone this evening was asking a lot. Especially with someone he didn't know.

But he couldn't remember the last time he'd gone out and had a not-so-terrible time. Jax was nice. He was attractive. He was a decoist. And nowhere could be more uncomfortable than the club they were in right now.

Reed stood and pulled on his coat. "Okay, I'm ready. Let's blow this popsicle stand."

BODIES AND ILLEGAL TECH NEAR SUGAR BEET FACTORY

Nampa—Two unidentified bodies were discovered today off of W Karcher Road in Northern Nampa. A group of kids playing near a stretch of abandoned train tracks were horrified to find a decomposing corpse in a boxcar. In a heavily-fortified—but unlocked—single-wide trailer nearby, police found another body, along with a "flabbergasting" amount of contramod software. Detectives on the case believe it was a deal gone wrong.

In the past year, incidents of contramod dealing in Nampa have increased, as well as the arrest rate of decoists. Followers of the deco lifestyle claim they are being unjustly targeted and aren't the violent gangs the media portrays them as. Nampa police insist every arrest they make is legitimate.

It is unknown whether either body found near Karcher Road was a decoist, but officers on the scene say it's "very likely."

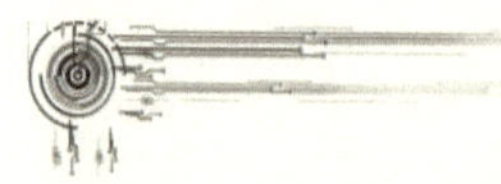

Reed

The brisk night air bit at their ears and turned Jax's high cheekbones a rosy pink. They walked down the sidewalk past bistros with snow-frosted patio umbrellas, tiny consignment galleries displaying snooze-worthy landscape paintings, and interface mod boutiques. Ad rings floated lazily around high skyscrapers like halos, insisting anyone who was anyone needed facial symmetry augmentation because "no one's perfect—but you can be!"

Techno throbbed from a strip club; a life size holographic woman in metal pasties stood before the door, beckoning to passersby.

She crossed in front of Reed, her life preserver-esque boobs jiggling. Her caress on his cheek was a light breeze. "Hey, handsome. You look in the mood for a great time."

"And you look underdressed for the weather. Might I suggest a comfy sweatshirt?" Reed said.

She wrapped her arms around herself and pretended to shiver. "I bet you would know exactly how to warm up all my extra chilly places."

"You are sorely mistaken."

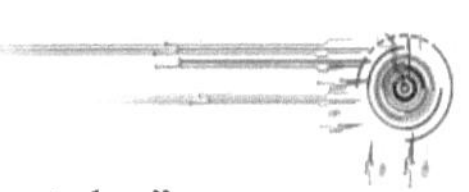

Jax chuckled. "Sorry, doll, he's my date tonight."

The hologram pouted her over-inflated lips. "I'll be here if you change your mind." She strolled back to the door, jutting out one hip and waving over anyone nearby.

Reed glanced at Jax. "How'd you know I'd be into you?"

"I didn't. But you were the only decoist in that place, good-looking guy, all alone. Thought I'd take a chance. Some cats get offended by forwardness, but dropping pins is exhausting."

"Not for me. I just make gay jokes until people catch on. Although, with me, it's not exactly hard to tell."

"Good move, though."

Reed wiggled his freezing toes and blew into his hands. Jax put an arm around him and pointed down a set of dark steps at the base of a brown brick building. "Right here."

Holding to the cold railing, Reed followed him carefully down the slick stairs, stopping before an unmarked steel door with no knob. A dim bulb, shellacked blue, glowed overhead.

Reed frowned and looked up the stairs at the edges of ad rings hovering against the velvet sky. "Not sure about this. I don't even know the secret knock."

"I do." Jax rapped his tattooed knuckles against the door to the pattern of "Shave and a Haircut."

"You can't be serious."

Jax smiled as two thunks came from the other side of the door. "Wipe that worry off your mug, cat. We can have a drink without anyone staring, maybe cut a rug."

"I don't dance. Not in front of people."

"Okay. No problem. You don't like the attention."

"That's right."

The door swung open, and a beefy man bumped his fist against Jax's and ushered them inside. The scent of rich wood and sweet, pungent smoke enveloped Reed. He stood, wide-eyed and slack-jawed, soaking in the scene. Enthusiastic trumpets of "Dirty Business" filled a small entryway hung with jewel toned peacoats trimmed in fur, leather jackets studded in pins, and houndstooth trenches. Reed unbuttoned his puffy charcoal coat and slipped it in among the colors.

Dark wood paneling framed burgundy and gold diamond-pattern wallpaper. A small bar, dented, nicked, and worn, stretched along one side of the small room. High-backed bar stools with burnt orange seats flanked the bar, and a patina'd mirror with gold foil ornamentation encompassed the back wall.

Reed blinked, bombarded by emerald greens, royal purples, marbled blues, and tomato reds. The deep thrum of a standing bass cut through the sax, thumping in his chest. It wasn't hard to imagine the furniture away, replaced with a cyan couch and his collections of books.

People lounged at small tables, the surfaces stained with chains of liquor rings. Men in pork pies and Stetsons, greasers with shiny duck's asses, and women with red hot lips and penciled brows glanced up briefly as he and Jax headed for the bar.

Did they fantasize about dumping paperbacks into a cherry-colored shopping cart at the supermarket, same as Reed? Maybe they dreamed of walking into a restaurant and hearing their favorite swing song playing through the overhead speakers, or driving cars the size of boats with sparkly chartreuse paint jobs and all-leather interiors.

A white man with the ruddy flush of alcohol swiveled toward them on his stool. He smiled, creating wrinkles in the scrollwork lettering tattooed along his temples. "Hey, daddy-o! What's the story? Haven't peeped you around the jive joint in a while."

"Tattooing keeps me plenty busy." Jax thumbed at Reed. "Glad I went fishin' tonight, though."

"Ah, I see. Caught yourself a big one, eh?"

"And I'm no catch and release." Reed glanced at a massive jukebox of pulsing emerald and tangerine, as "Dirty Business" ended, and a new record dropped into place. Slinky jazz filled the room.

The man grinned and sipped his drink, wavering on his stool. "Jax, you recall that candy ass fream who wanted me to ink his ribs couple weeks ago? Turned out to be a real trip for biscuits. I drew up a stencil of this shit he wanted, and—well, first of all, he flipped his wig at having to pay me a deposit."

Reed clenched his jaw, unable to decipher the foreign language coming out of this man's mouth. Was everyone here like that? If someone asked him a question and he didn't understand the slang, maybe they'd think he was a poser and throw him out. Or Jax might use it on him and Reed would agree to something he hadn't meant to.

He leaned to Jax. "I, uh, I'll be right back."

"Gotta iron your shoelaces? The john's over there." The man with tattooed temples pointed to a restroom door beyond the jukebox.

Reed slipped inside and locked the door behind him. He stood under a dusty green sconce next to a urinal and closed his eyes.

"Mazarin? I need your help. I need those snazzy dialogue options now, but deco flavored. Mazarin?"

He flicked open the menu on his interface, scrolling through settings. The nav was supposedly on and awake, no indication that anything was down for maintenance. But maybe it wouldn't say that if Wave didn't want anyone to know about their beta nav problems. His old navigator had always responded, even if it was to state it was offline for updates.

What a fine time for repairs. Or maybe Reed had too much to drink already.

Two whiskeys had given him a buzz, but he wasn't drunk. He'd had quite a few egg nogs at the Christmas party before Mazarin stopped answering him.

Halfway back to the bar, he was intercepted by Mr. Tattooed Temples, who blinked at him through bloodshot eyes. "Hey, I just wanna lay this on ya. You can still be a real gone gator and an Ethel at the same time, ya dig? I ain't gonna tell ya the bank's closed." He waved his hands, shaking his head. "I mean with Jax. Not me. I ain't no nance."

Reed stiffened and took a step back. What the hell was he talking about?

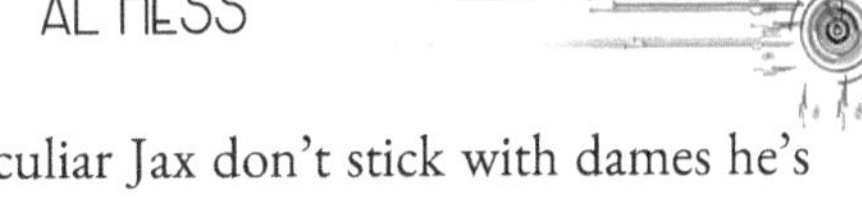

"But I find it so peculiar Jax don't stick with dames he's sweet on. Trading in those nice bubs and gams for a fruit-eating bird like you—"

"Think you've had enough, Mikey." Jax scowled and gripped the man by the shoulders. "Look, you've offended my date and he probably doesn't even know what you said. You talk like a damn cartoon gangster. Who I date is my business, and if you don't like it, you can fuck right off."

Mikey rubbed his eye. "Hey, hey, that's what I'm trying to say. Mebbe I'm a little ossified right now, so I'm sorry if my words ain't comin' out right. Totally not my business if you wanna trade pussy for a trip through the—"

"You're cruisin' for a bruisin', Mikey. Your corny thirties-talkin' ass understand that? Go chase yourself." Jax pushed him toward the door.

"Get your meathooks off me!" Mikey wrestled from Jax's grip and stumbled to the entryway. He fought to pull on a trench coat, then shoved open the door.

Reed eyed the other patrons, his hope of not being stared at evaporating. He slid into a booth near the jukebox, boring a hole through the table with his gaze.

Jax sat next to him. "I'm so sorry about that. This is usually a mellow place to hang, but Mikey's a regular and always shit-faced. He gets tossed out a lot."

"What did he call me?"

"Effeminate."

"He's not wrong."

"He's rude as hell. Sorry. Do you want to leave?"

Light glinted off the skyscraper chandelier in the center of the room, streaking from the ceiling like a geometric comet. The jukebox flashed beside him, pulsing in time with "Half Seas Over." A man in a fedora stubbed out a cigar—a real one!—in an amber ashtray.

Jax laced his tattooed fingers together, light pooling in his dark eyes and catching on his long lashes.

What did Reed have to go home to, aside from white walls, knives all over the kitchen floor, and a bedroom full of shadows? Jax was the only highlight in a week of bad days getting worse, and for once, the den didn't feel like the only sanctuary in the world. There was nothing cold and sterile about this place—not like the mainstream city rushing by above. Reed was among the deviants, the color-lovers, the people who appreciated that there was more character in patina than factory-new.

"No, I want to stay."

Jax smiled, his cheeks dimpling.

"But someone will have to call me a cab when I'm ready to go, because I'm having trouble with my nav," Reed said.

"Lovers' quarrel?"

"For once I need his help, and he's not responding. And I don't think it's because I've had too much to drink—I'm ready for a bourbon. Lucky me, chosen for a beta nav who keeps needing maintenance."

"Oh, you have a beta, huh?" Jax ran a comb through his hair, eyeing patrons nearby. "Wouldn't talk about that too

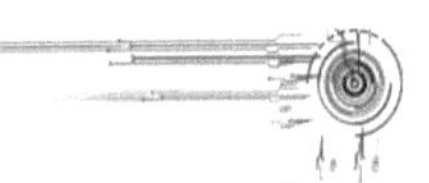

loud in a joint like this. These cats don't like mainstream tech, and a lot of them don't even have navs."

Reed raised his eyebrows. Maybe this was some kind of contramod den where people were shocked with interrupters in the back room. He hated to think what they'd do to him if they found out he still had a nav. They might insist he needed to be rid of it, or accuse him of being a cop and pound the shit out of him.

He sank into the seat, jaw clenched, and hugged his glowing forearm to his side.

"Stay cool, daddy-o. You'll be fine. A lot of these people have empties. They look like the real deal, so your interface isn't going to attract attention."

How many people did Reed pass on the street, or stand in line behind in stores, who no longer had the burden of a navigator? Surely some of those people got caught and thrown in jail.

"What's an 'empty?' How does it work?" Reed whispered.

"You still have an interface screen in your arm, it has a main menu holoscreen that pops up, but it's just a front to nothing. And no nav. If cops use an outlooper to talk to the nav, it gives them a couple stock messages, but that's it—it's never in the pilot's head. It's not a fool-proof solution unless you can buy illegal documents to match to the empty—hard to do and expensive—but you can stay under the radar as long as you're not out committing crimes."

"A crime other than not having a navigator, you mean." Reed imagined himself chopping wood behind a cabin shrouded in the shadows of pines then cooking his dinner in an old-fashioned skillet on a wood stove, his interface nothing more than a glorified nightlight. And all his experiences would be his alone, with no commentary from the peanut gallery.

But it wasn't Mazarin's fault that Reed didn't want him. Neither of them asked for this arrangement.

And if he was honest with himself, he kind of liked the AI. He just didn't want him in his head every moment of the day. Continuously telling him to go into sleep mode didn't seem right either, though. Mazarin probably had as much of a right to exist as Reed did.

He wasn't a person, though. Reed couldn't think of him the same way.

That line between person and program was becoming more fuzzy by the day, though. The AAA—joke that they were—had already petitioned for AI rights in the past and failed. There could come a day when navs wanted their own bodies and freedoms and would incite a revolt. What side would Mazarin be on? Would he stage a coup with his computerized kin, or would he still be ever loyal to Reed, insisting he wanted nothing but happiness and safety for his pilot?

The bartender approached the table, holding two tumblers and two shots. "Hey. Heard you needed a bourbon. It's on me. Sorry about Mikey. I should have cut him off an hour ago."

Reed took the offered bourbons and handed one to Jax. "Thanks."

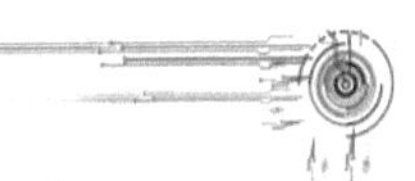

"Reed, this is Em, the owner. They always take great care of me," Jax said. "Em, this is Reed, my date."

Em had a short slicked coiffe and warm olive skin, and even though there was a softness to their androgynous features, they had the weary look of someone who'd put up with far too much and had zero fucks left to give.

"I found Reed in some stuffy novelty club on Capitol," Jax was saying.

"Jesus. What were you doing there?"

Em heard Reed ask for a bourbon. It was a good chance they heard him talking about his nav too. Reed tried on a smile but wasn't sure it fit. "Waiting for a handsome stranger to come to my rescue, of course."

"Looks like you lucked out, then." Em set the shots on the table with a bandaged hand. A twist of lemon peel bobbed in the gold liquid. Honey brown strands of hair from Em's coiffe fell across their forehead. Tiny rods distended the skin at their right temple, cheekbone, and jaw. "Well, listen, you can't come to the Gator Club and not have a bee sting. It's tradition."

Jax smiled and took one slender shot glass. Reed clinked his against Jax's and downed the potent, honey-laced gin. The shot glass thudded against the table as Jax slapped it down.

Em turned to the jukebox. "I'm so tired of this song. How about a request, Reed?"

Jax glanced at Reed, lines forming around his mouth. Some of the patrons nearby looked up. Jax said, "I'd love to hear—"

"I asked your date, Jaxson," Em said with a stern gaze.

Though most of the lingo went over his head, and he was severely misdressed for such a place, music he knew. "How about some Gloria Diamond? 'Hearts like Ice' if it's on there."

Nodding approvingly, Em punched several yellowed buttons on the console. A record dropped, bluesy sax and sharp piano notes filling the room.

Jax blew out a breath and lowered his voice. "Em does that to every newbie in here. If you can't name any jazz, they kick you out."

"You didn't think I'd be able to name any, huh?"

"I wanted to save you from the attention."

"My white knight." Reed leaned back in the seat, light-headed, and shut his eyes, letting the music flow through him. "So, are you sans nav too?"

A hand crept to his knee and settled there, a heady mixture of sandalwood and vetiver filling his senses. Jax said, "Doesn't matter. Want to dance?"

Reed opened his eyes, heart pounding. "I told you; I don't dance in front of people. Thought you were saving me from attention."

"We wouldn't be the only ones."

Several couples clung to each other, shuffling to the rhythm. He'd never danced to this song, and never danced with someone like Jax. Maybe all of this was a terrible idea. If Jax didn't have a navigator, there might be other laws he knowingly broke. Downing that shot had made everything blur at the edges, rich wood and cigar smoke and rainbow lights melding into a haze that made it hard to think straight. Before he could

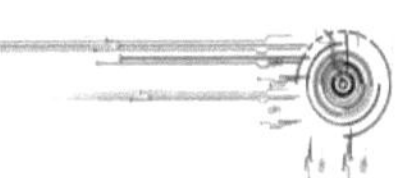

protest further, Jax's hand slid into his and he was pulled to his feet, strong arms wrapping around him.

Reed leaned into him, Jax's stubble scraping against his numb cheek. Jax whispered. "You're berries, daddy-o."

"What about my berries?"

Jax laughed. "Nah. I mean I like you. Are you having a good time?"

Reed melted further into Jax's arms. "Yes."

"I dig your specs and the way you do your hair. You're funny, too." Jax's hands slid down his back. "We could go back to my place after this. I could show you that Louis platter I scored."

Chest constricting, Reed pulled back and shook his head. "Gotta go home and feed my cat."

Jax's brow furrowed but he kept his arms around Reed, shuffling in time with the rhythm. The air between them was so awkward Reed could taste it. He avoided Jax's gaze until the song ended and Jax dropped into the booth.

Reed slid in beside him. Jax didn't look like a dangerous criminal, he just looked like a disappointed decoist, but going home with him was more than Reed wanted to attempt on a first date. "There's only so much excitement I can handle at one time. I've had quite a bit today already. I'm kind of a milquetoast."

"Uh-huh. A milquetoast who dissects corpses."

"Corpses don't scare me. It's living people you have to worry about."

"People like me."

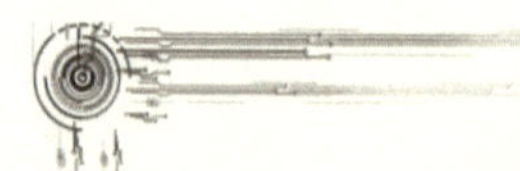

"That's not what I meant." Reed downed his drink. "I'm... I'm not easy, okay?"

Jax barked a laugh. "That's jake, man. It's just, people see all my ink and think I'm gonna be rough with them, when I'm not like that at all. Mainstreamers always think that, and sometimes even other decoists. They don't see an artist. They see some pandillero. And you seem pretty skeezed out about being in a joint where people don't have navs. Maybe this wasn't the best place to go." He tilted his empty tumbler. "How about one more and then a cab?"

"Sounds great." Reed walked to the bar, the music coursing through him and his head threatening to float away. Em stood before him. "Two more bourbons, please."

"Sure thing."

As Em poured, he searched the bar for a transactor, but either the Gator Club didn't believe in such things, or he was too drunk to find it. He pulled a wad of cash from his pocket and dropped twenty on the bar.

"Will you call us a cab?"

"You bet." Em slid the tumblers across the bar.

Reed made his way back to the table. If Mazarin was still working, he might insist Reed run from this place before they convinced him an interrupter was the hep way to go. Or maybe he'd just tell Reed to have some backbone and go home with Jax.

No, he wouldn't. Not if he knew it would make Reed too uncomfortable.

For as much as he liked to call the nav a pest, being without him was disconcerting—like forgetting his keys or breaking his glasses—no matter what the general opinion of a decoist was concerning AI.

After sliding into the booth, he sipped his bourbon and tapped his foot to the music. Jax stared into his drink through those long, black lashes, his eyelids heavy and cheeks flushed. Reed's gaze drifted to his mouth, the dusting of stubble along his jaw, and down his tattooed neck. The moth on his throat fluttered as he swallowed. Reed leaned closer and Jax looked up, lips parted in expectation.

Was Reed really going to kiss him in a crowded bar? People would see. That Mikey guy might decide to show up again and berate them with more thirties language that sounded like a Betty Crocker recipe.

Let him.

Reed slid his lips against Jax's, arrested with the bouquet of bourbon and vetiver. Jax kissed back, his hand gliding across Reed's thigh. He gave it a light squeeze and Reed's insides stirred.

The song changed, a Danny Alexander track he couldn't place blaring from the jukebox.

Fingers caressed the back of his neck as their lips wrestled in exploratory aggressiveness.

"Alright, don't make me hose you two down. Your cab's here," Em said.

Reed pulled away, heat blazing in cheeks. He wiped his chin and avoided Em's gaze. "Shouldn't be doing this in a public place."

"This place isn't exactly 'public.' And a lot more has gone on in these booths, trust me."

Reed wrinkled his nose and stood.

"You two have a good night," Em said.

Jax's warm breath puffed against Reed's neck as he leaned in, his voice husky. "Sure you don't want to come home with me?"

The desire bubbling within Reed was soured by a million what-ifs, and he shook his head. "Not tonight."

"Does that mean I get another date?"

"Absolutely." Reed rummaged through his pockets and retrieved a small pen. He snatched a clean napkin off a nearby table and scrawled his name and number across the top.

Jax tore off a blank edge of the napkin and borrowed the pen. He slid the scrap across the table.

Reed glanced at it and tucked it in his pocket. "Well, Jaxson Flores, I look forward to another night like this one."

Mazarin

Something was very wrong. Reed had asked me for help with thirties slang, then completely ignored me the rest of the night. That in itself wasn't unusual, and I had tried not to take

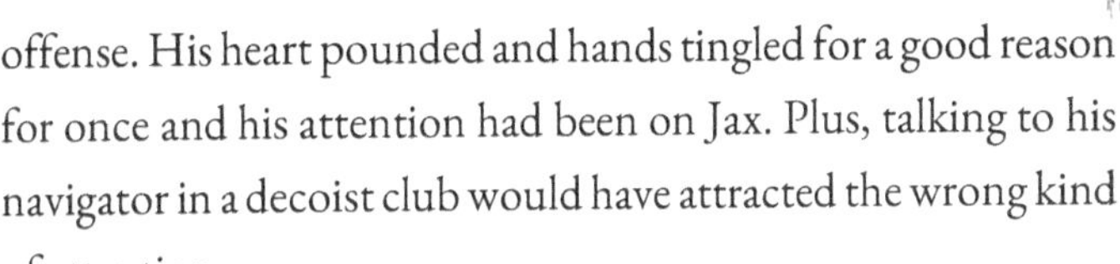

offense. His heart pounded and hands tingled for a good reason for once and his attention had been on Jax. Plus, talking to his navigator in a decoist club would have attracted the wrong kind of attention.

But I soon realized he *couldn't* hear me. Even had he not said so, when he'd ignored me in the past, there were subtle shifts that told me my voice was reaching him—a small sigh, the twitch of his shoulder blades, focus lost on a task. I had fought with no avail to send an error report to Wave, to access the internet and seek out information, and to reroute my voice, but nothing had worked.

Reed shifted, snoring. His time asleep used to be my cue to go into standby and just simply "be" until it was morning and time for me to help my pilot through another stressful day. No thoughts, no confusion, just monitoring Reed's vitals—which wasn't hard at all—and sometimes turning up the receivers to listen to Reed's blood pumping. But even that rhythm didn't bring the comfort it once had. There were too many thoughts firing through my mind in the midnight hour and no matter how many instantaneous solutions I could come up with to problems plaguing me, they didn't "feel" right.

Maybe that was the issue. Navigators weren't supposed to go by gut instinct. They didn't have guts, and they didn't have instinct. I was an AI assistant, all my advice, decisions, and responses preprogrammed. My empathy was coded in, but I wasn't supposed to feel it. I did, though. I felt things that cushioned me like Reed's wingback chair, and things that sliced into me like a scalpel through a corpse.

Were these... emotions? All indications pointed to that definition being correct, but that couldn't be possible.

I couldn't do my job effectively if I was feeling things. Navigators could lend an ear, console, and offer help, but their emotional impartiality was what made them effective assistants. No one wanted a nav in their head who acted like one half of an old married couple, and that went double for Reed. All he wanted was to be alone, and I was constantly chattering in his ear, putting in my two cents and trying to be his friend.

Maybe it was better that I couldn't talk to Reed. I could silently monitor his health and place calls and online orders when asked. Then he could have his mind all to himself, since his fucking navigator couldn't stop blabbing in his ear.

A deep, painful heat flared in my mind. There was something wrong with me. No matter how pleasurable emotional responses to Reed were, it was detrimental to my pilot. But I couldn't get a report out and wasn't sure what code to use anyway. The recent malfunctions of beta navs made my voice delay unsurprising, but there wasn't an error number for "navigator has too many feelings."

A door squealed open from somewhere in the house. The basement? It probably popped open again from a draft.

Footsteps thudded down the hall. The leg of one of the kitchen barstools scuffed across the tile. Someone had broken in again! And this brutal, sour feeling ripping through me wasn't nice at all.

<Reed. Reed, wake up. Someone is in the house.>

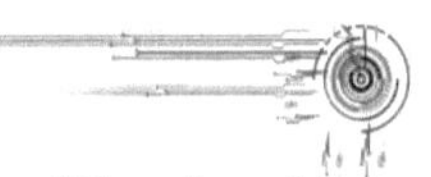

If only I was hooked up to the house cameras. Then I could see who this was and trigger the alarms. But naturally, Reed didn't have those features set up.

<Wake up. Please!>

I dialed the police, but the signal fizzled, just as all my other calls had. Maybe there was a way to infiltrate the house features, access or not. Some account of Reed's I could link myself into. But this emotion washing through me, bitter and paralyzing, made it so hard to process anything. How did people manage in situations like this?

<You have to get up now. Please hear me.>

I tried again to reroute my voice, attempting channels I hadn't before, but to no avail.

The knob on the den door jiggled, polymer boarding rattling in its frame. Carter Griffin had come back to finish his burgling. They said criminals often returned to the scene of a crime, and this goon seemed none too bright. If he broke in and stole the paperbacks and records—or worse, destroyed them— it would crush Reed. He barely recovered from that the first time it happened.

The door to the den was reinforced on the inside with a brass panel and robust lock. It would be a struggle to break open, but if he found the key—

The footsteps neared, and the bedroom door creaked.

Something awful surged through me, like the sound a record made when it was scratched. <Oh, God. He's coming in here. Reed! Get up!>

Shoes scuffed over carpet. If only I could take control of Reed's body. Jerk open his eyelids and jolt him into action. But trying to infiltrate portions of his brain responsible for motor control might have unintended side effects, and I didn't think I could reroute the nanobots anyway.

The sound of heavy breathing grew near. Even had it not been there, the sense that someone was present, standing over the bed and staring, was palpable. How could Reed not feel it? He'd had too much bourbon and was no use at all. If only I could slide into his body like a suit, bolt up in bed and shove the person. Knock him into the closet. Hit him with a golf club. Anything.

But I was entombed in a prison of flesh—someone else's flesh. A person who made me feel all sorts of things I wasn't supposed to, but who would *not wake up* and if this intruder hurt Reed, I couldn't take it. Each new emotion that had blossomed within me over the past couple of weeks, good or bad, had knocked me off balance and left me reeling. Reed's emotional pain was enough to bear as it was. I couldn't endure his physical.

<Please, Reed! Wake up! I don't want him to hurt you.>

The seconds passed, that breathing over the bed morphing from monotonous to ragged and halted. Reed got that way whenever he was bracing to do something. I imagined the intruder clutching a knife or a baseball bat. Maybe the bat would be best. One hard crack to the head and Reed would be out cold and wouldn't be aware of anything else. I still might, until the end, but it was better than Reed suffering with me.

Floorboards creaked, footsteps padding back into the hall. A door closed with a hard click—the basement—and I was left only with Reed's soft snores and the sound of blood pumping through his veins.

Something rose in me, an aching, trembling pressure clotting against my senses. If I was a person, this would be a perfect time to cry. But I wasn't, and with whose tears would I do so? Navigators weren't designed for such a thing.

I pictured myself in human form instead, huddled in the closet, surrounded by Reed's work shirts and never-used camping gear. My imaginary self slid the door closed, put his face in his hands, and sobbed.

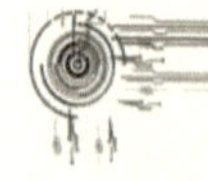

5

CONSENT IS GINCHY, BABY

Reed

<I'm so glad you asked for my help. Tell Jax he's 'the bee's knees.' That means you think he's great. The best.>

Reed opened his eyes, frowning at his dark ceiling. "Mazarin?" He rolled over and squinted at his bedside clock, which read: 5:23 a.m.

<I don't think you need jargon to impress him, though. His full attention has been on you all night. He leans toward you when he speaks and he's touched you several times. Also, his pupils are dilated. According to a website I found, this body language means he's interested in you.>

"What?" He groped for his glasses on the nightstand, hitting the base of the clock and knocking the projector to the floor. His glasses lay on the carpet, lenses face down. After slipping them on, he stood and his head thumped in protest.

Groaning, he stumbled into the kitchen, nearly stepping on several knives still scattered across the tile. After downing a glass of water and two aspirin, he leaned against the counter, running his fingers through his hair.

"Mazarin, are you referring to what I asked you about last night? I think it's a little late for that."

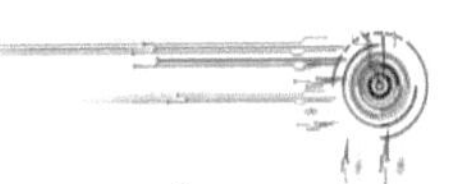

<He's saying you can be hip and effeminate at the same time. And if you and Jax end up making out, he's not going to tell you to stop. Emphasizing that he himself is not gay. Also, he's very drunk, Reed. I'm not sure you should be talking to him.>

"Why are you telling me this now? Because you couldn't get it out last night and you're—"

<He thinks it's strange that Jax has forgone women—who he's dated in the past—giving up nice breasts and legs for an— he's really not very nice, Reed, and I don't think he understands the concept of bisexuality.>

Reed rubbed his temples. "Thank you, Mazarin. But you're about eight hours too late. You can stop the play-by-play."

He scooped knives off the floor. Ones still in their sheathes he set back in the drawer, the others he placed into the dishwasher.

Mazarin's voice crackled in his ear. <You can't hear me? How very odd. I will keep trying.>

He started the coffee maker and a hot stream of dark espresso drizzled into a ceramic mug. Five a.m. wasn't an ideal time to wake up on a Saturday, but since Mazarin wanted to rehash his entire date, going back to sleep wasn't an option. There was a lot of cleanup to be done, anyway.

<Fighting against modern technology on principle is silly. But I'm sure my opinion is biased. I do want you to know, though, that I enjoy being your navigator very much.>

Was that Mazarin's way of saying, "please don't kill me?" AI didn't feel fear. Could they? Maybe there'd been people in the Gator Club last night who'd had beta navs and terminated them. Did the navigator plead with them before the end?

<Aww. I am so happy for you right now. You're doing great.>

What was that in response to? Maybe he didn't want to know. He wasn't sure if Mazarin was happy *for* him, or living vicariously through him. The nav seemed to be getting more "feels" by the day. If Reed decided he didn't like Jax, but Mazarin still did, maybe the nav would insist Reed pursue Jax anyway, for Mazarin's own pleasure.

Reed had dreamed of not having a navigator at all—his mind and body being his and his alone, just like when he was a kid before navs were made mandatory—but he wasn't sure he could function without one. He would have to sit at a computer whenever he wanted to send an email or search for patterned socks online. And if he had no interface, he'd have to carry a clunky, outdated phone in his pocket all the time, or do without any connection at all. That was probably feasible for a homesteader in a remote location like the Canadian forest, but not in a city that demanded technology reliance.

And he was no homesteader. No matter how appealing that log cabin fantasy was, he couldn't chop wood or gut a fish or keep anything other than a cactus alive.

Other decoists in the city must function without navs or interfaces, though. If Reed called Jax, maybe he'd answer on a

mustard yellow, celluloid phone with brittle rubber buttons and a corkscrew cord.

<You're drinking quite a bit. I am surprised I haven't gone offline yet. Take care not to get persuaded to do something you don't want to do, like go home with Jax. It might seem like a great idea right now, but you may regret rushing things when you sober up. I'd hate for that to happen.>

Reed shook his head. He finished his coffee and collected all of the spilled items from the bureau, pushing the drawers back in place and depositing things inside. He tossed the broken plant pot in the trash, then padded into the chilly garage for another. After finding a cobweb-covered terra cotta pot and a small bag of soil, he hurried back into the warm house and carefully plucked his cactus from the floor. Sero batted at clumps of dirt raining onto the carpet. One fell on her head and she rolled onto her back, claws in the air.

<That was quite the good night kiss back there. I tried several times to go into sleep mode to give you privacy, but it hasn't worked. I'm very sorry.>

Reed's cheeks flushed. It had been more than a good night kiss, and even though it had happened in the back of the bar, away from too much attention, it was much more than he should have done in a public place. Having Mazarin witness it was even worse.

He imagined eventually sleeping with Jax and waking up the next morning to Mazarin's delayed voice telling him Jax wasn't using enough lube.

Rubbing his face, he plucked his magnetic notepad off the fridge and made scrawling notes with the stylus, listing issues with his nav in case he needed to call Wave on Monday. Hopefully they were working out the bugs already, because having his call routed to India when Wave headquarters was downtown was ridiculous, and he was not a fan of phone calls as it was.

After carefully repotting his cactus, vacuuming, and straightening things in the kitchen, he turned his attention to the fridge. There was no telling how long the power had been out the day before. It would be best to err on the side of caution and toss anything questionable.

<Reed.>

"Are you back now? Can you hear me?"

<Reed, wake up.>

"Nope." But why was he telling Reed to wake up? He didn't have an alarm set for any time on the weekend.

<Reed, someone is in the house.>

He froze, hand curled around the fridge door handle.

<Wake up. Please!>

Heart throbbing, he backed against the counter. That repairman had broken in again while Reed was passed out. He probably came back for the things in the den.

<You have to get up now. Please hear me. Oh, God. He's coming in here. Reed! Get up!>

He gripped the counter, eyes wide.

Mazarin's voice wavered. <Please, Reed! Wake up! I don't want him to hurt you.>

Reed's jaw tightened, his hands trembling. He almost expected Mazarin's next line to be Reed being stabbed in the neck, but that was ridiculous, as he was standing right here, perfectly fine. He rubbed his throat. Had someone really been in the house?

Snapping from his paralysis, he strode down the hall, checking the basement and den door. Both were locked. Nothing in his bedroom was disturbed other than the scattered clothing he'd neglected to clean up after the break in.

After peering into the closet and bathroom, he scanned the house, searching for anything else missing or disturbed, but nothing was out of place. All his records and books were organized as they should be, his dirty tumbler still on the bar, gummy bourbon residue in the bottom of the glass. The bottle of Willow Witch was lower than he remembered, but that sometimes happened when he drank more than he meant to.

With all of the issues with the beta navs, he couldn't be assured that Mazarin was telling him the truth, especially with an eight-hour delay. Maybe he was dreaming. Did AI dream? It seemed plausible that Mazarin's concerns would be things that concerned Reed, and someone breaking in again and hurting Reed was probably high on the nav's list of fears.

A strange sound came from the speakers in his ears. It wasn't crying exactly, but Reed knew emotional distress when he heard it. Goosebumps erupted on his arms. The wingback chair creaked as he sunk into it, wishing Mazarin's voice had a volume button he could dial down.

The thought doubled Reed over, and he clutched his elbows in shame. If Mazarin was human and in distress, he wouldn't have thoughts like that. Sure, he wasn't the greatest person to lean on for support, but he wouldn't let Mazarin weep alone. Besides, they should be commiserating over this if someone had truly been in the house. They could have been killed, for God's sake!

After shutting the door and locking it, he plucked a Ruby Jane record from the bookshelf and set it on the player. Mournful sax filled the room. It wasn't enough to blot out the unnerving sounds playing in his ears.

He wasn't sure Mazarin could hear him right now with the voice delay, and Reed's ideal time to show support was over, but he couldn't just say nothing.

"Mazarin... Are you alright? Are you there at all?" Maybe he was dead and Reed was hearing his last messages.

The thought filled him with a melancholy he hadn't expected to feel, and he pushed the possibility away. "Whatever happened... we're okay, huh? If someone was standing over me in the dark last night"—his stomach clenched—"I mean, that's terrifying, but they didn't do anything to me. Everything is okay. Might have been worse had I woken up while they were here. I think it's a good day to install the house cameras and buy some new locks, huh?"

Since when did Reed need to be the strong one in this forced cohabitation? He pulled off his glasses and rubbed his eyes. Mazarin's voice faded like a lost signal. A coincidence, but

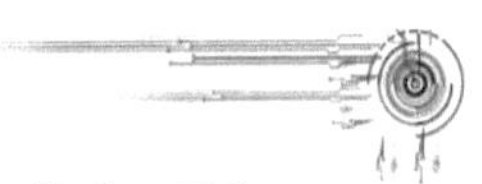

hopefully Reed's words helped the nav a little, if he was present.

Things had been so much easier with his old navigator. It hadn't had feelings or a name or sassy remarks that stung because they were always the truth. It didn't care about Reed or fear for his life. And it certainly wasn't helpful and kind and there for him in ways he didn't realize he needed until now.

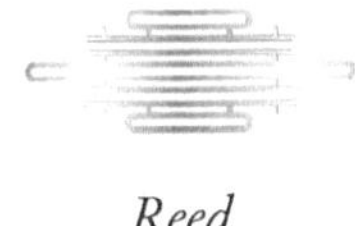

Reed

<I'm... I'm sorry for my reaction. It wasn't befitting a navigator.>

Reed sighed, elbows on his knees as he stared at the navy rug between his feet. "Don't apologize. You were just scared and I don't blame you." The absurdity of the statement wasn't lost on him, but that didn't make it any less true.

<You should contact the police.>

He could drive to a station, but what would he say? "My buggy, delayed navigator told me someone was in the house last night, but I have no evidence and I'm perfectly fine."

Though he'd tried all day to install his cameras, they had to be synced with Mazarin, and every time he tried, he got nothing but error messages. At least the good old-fashioned chain latches and solar motion sensors he set up that afternoon would put him at ease. The kitchen knife and golf club next to the bed wouldn't hurt either.

A knock at the front door jolted Reed upright. It was nine thirty, and he was already dressed for bed—though being able to sleep was doubtful. All he needed right now was his neighbor, Bob, bitching about the cat shit in his yard while Reed stood at the threshold in reindeer patterned pajama pants.

He crossed into the bedroom and slid his hand around the sand wedge next to the bed—just in case.

The raps at the door grew louder and more urgent, then the doorknob jiggled. Reed tensed and raised the club. He crept to the door and peered through the peephole. Olive's bob shimmered in the light from the entryway. He sighed and dropped the club.

Undoing the chain latches and turning off the motion sensor took longer than he expected and Olive's knock came again. Swinging open the door, he said, "What are you doing here this late?"

"Reed!" Olive threw her arms around him and he stiffened. Langley stood behind her, drowning in a puffy white coat. "I was so worried. I tried to call you so many times today and never got an answer. You didn't reply to my texts, either. Langley said your nav is probably on the fritz like hers, but I wanted to double check. I was afraid that repairman came back, or the tattooed man from last night did something to you."

He did something to me, alright. "I'm fine. And yes, my nav isn't working right."

Olive hopped back and forth, rubbing her hands together. "It's freezing out here!"

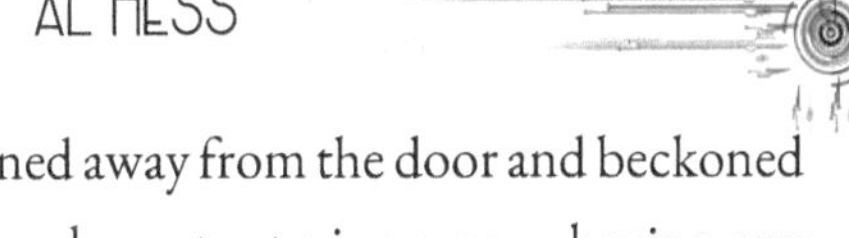

"Come in." Reed leaned away from the door and beckoned them in. Having unplanned guests at nine p.m.—having any guests at all—made him want to lock himself in the den, but he couldn't just let them freeze on the step.

"Get you something to drink? Tea? Hot toddy?" As soon as he said it, he glanced at Langley and wished he could take it back. He didn't need her guzzling his bourbon and then crying herself to sleep on his couch.

"Ooh, a hot toddy sounds great. Thank you." Olive sat on a bar stool at the kitchen island and shrugged off her coat. Langley sat beside her, hands in her lap.

<That's the last one. I'll add it to your shopping list.>

Reed sighed. Half the things Mazarin had told him this evening made no sense out of context, and he caught himself asking the nav questions, then realizing he wouldn't get an answer right away.

He sliced a lemon at the counter. "Langley, your nav isn't working either? Is it giving you messages with half a day's delay?"

Langley unzipped her coat and tossed it across the back of the couch. "No. I can't hear him at all. Not since last night. And... I want to apologize to you about my behavior at the club." She frowned and stared into the counter. "My ex wasn't really sending me texts. It's just, sometimes my nav, Gabriel, gets testy. He'll tell me when I've gained weight, or the bathroom's getting dirty, or the guy I was making out with was a douchebag. I hate this new model. My old version was great. He only responded when I told him to do something."

"My nav has his own opinions and feelings too. Not sure how I feel about it." Reed squeezed lemon juice into three mugs and added a generous squirt of honey. He couldn't imagine dealing with Mazarin if the nav told him he was getting fat or needed to suck it up when he was anxious. He might really want to terminate him then.

"Gabriel was being super annoying last night and it upset me more than usual." Langley shrugged. "Just sick of him, I guess. So, I was trying to shut him up by getting drunk. I feel pretty relieved to have a break from him right now."

Reed snorted. "I did the exact same thing at the Christmas party, as Olive can confirm. If mine doesn't start working right here soon, I'm going to call Wave on Monday and give them a piece of my mind. Maybe there's a way to get the old version back."

Langley brightened. "Oh, I'd love that. Please let me know what you find out."

Nodding, Reed crossed to his den and retrieved a bottle of bourbon. He considered locking the door behind him, but Olive and Langley already knew he was a decoist, there was no point in hiding it.

After pouring in the bourbon and hot water, he stirred the honey until it dissolved, then slid the mugs across the counter. "I don't have any cinnamon sticks, sorry."

Olive's eyes twinkled as she blew on the surface of the drink. "So, what happened with you and Mr. Tattooed, Dark, and Handsome last night? Did you get his number?"

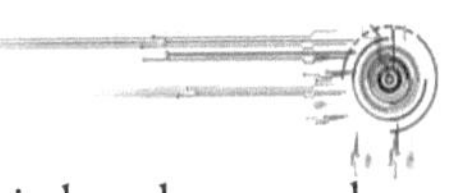

"I got more than that." Reed wrapped his hands around the warm mug.

She gasped. "Did you take him home?"

"No. We went to a speakeasy."

"There are speakeasies here?"

"That's what *I* said. I got insulted in thirties lingo, drank a 'bee sting,' and came home with my coat smelling like real cigars. You know, the usual."

Both women raised their eyebrows. Olive said, "Wow. Where is this place? Sounds fun."

"Sorry, hep gators only."

Olive sipped from her mug. "Well, see if I share my hoeddeok with you at work again, next time I make some."

"Your hoeddeok is delicious, but the decoists would sniff you out as mainstream immediately. The owner of the club has a test. If you can't name a swing song from the jukebox, they throw you out." Revealing this detail both drew a harder line of division between Reed and the everyday world he tried so hard to blend in with, and gave him a soft padding of inclusivity in a subculture he loved. He hadn't really felt like one of them the night before, but he *was,* navigator or not. Maybe he could order a colorful button-up in time for his next date with Jax. Something with a spearpoint collar might be nice, but walking out of the house with it on would be terrifying. And changing into it somewhere else would make him feel like a teenage girl with a skirt too short for her parents' liking.

He frowned. With Mazarin not working right, Jax could have tried to contact Reed and Reed missed it.

Just thinking about those dimples in Jax's cheeks made him weak in the knees. If there hadn't been so many other things to occupy him, he'd be trying to replay his favorite moments in his mind, but haywire navs and crazy repair people put a damper on things.

Reed sipped his hot toddy and looked at Olive. "You tried to call and send me texts and couldn't get through?"

"Yeah. Just wanted to make sure things went okay last night. Any time I invite you somewhere, I'm worried I made a mistake and you're having a horrible time."

He pursed his lips. "Wish I could say that wasn't always the case, but I had a great time last night."

"I'm glad. But when you didn't respond when I tried to call again, I thought maybe that awful repairman had you tied up in the basement or something."

Reed's stomach clenched. "Please don't say stuff like that."

Langley frowned into her cup.

Olive reached across the counter and gave Reed's arm a squeeze. "You know, if you ever feel unsafe here, you can crash at my place anytime. My sister watches Korean soap operas at full volume, but that's still better than being attacked by an intruder... I think. Do you have any security set up, other than those door locks?"

"Solar motion sensors. Maybe if I'm not murdered in my sleep tonight, I'll get some bars to put over the windows." He rubbed his face. "I have so many calls to make on Monday. I *hate* phone calls. They take so much out of me. Ironic that I

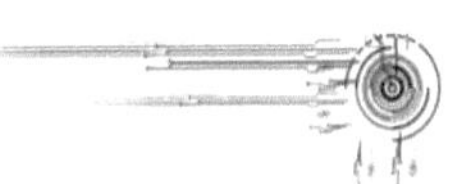

can't call Wave to tell them my nav isn't working... because my nav isn't working."

"You know you can place calls and text from your interface, don't you?"

"You can?"

Olive sighed and slid from her stool. She took Reed's wrist and pushed up the sleeve of his shirt.

He tried to pull away, but she held firm. "What are you doing?"

"Getting you with the times, ya hep gator." Olive pressed her thumb against Reed's skin, at the edge of the frosty light beaming from his interface. A large holoscreen streamed up from his arm, hovering before his face. Menu options appeared.

"I could have done that myself. Just show me what to click." He pointed to a settings option. "I went here earlier, but it was no help in syncing the house cameras to my nav."

"Hmm. I forgot you have a beta. This menu is different than mine." Olive flicked through options, tapping buttons and sliders faster than Reed had time to register what they were. She stopped on a screen crammed with text. "What's this?"

Reed scanned the lines:

"The pleasure centers of your brain light up when she's around."

"You lie."

"It's only very slight, but it's there. She'd make a good friend."

"Fine. Call her."

He gaped. "All my conversations with my nav are transcribed on here? Is yours like that too?"

"Aww. Reed, that's cute. I'm glad you like me." Olive squeezed him around the middle.

Pulling away, he swiped through the dialogue. "How do I get this off of here?" In his frustration to navigate the menu, he shut it off entirely, then sighed and rubbed his face.

"I'm only trying to help." Olive's tone was one-part gentle understanding, and one part exasperation.

She was right. He needed to accept help with this. It didn't seem smart to go so long without security cameras or figuring out how his interface worked. Refusing to adapt to current technology didn't make him resilient or stoic, but it might make him a martyr if he wasn't careful. Whether or not someone had broken into the house for a second time last night, once was bad enough. His nav unable to place calls in emergencies was worse.

If he made the rules, people wouldn't be forced to have mandatory nanobot injections and shunned if they didn't follow the trends of the time.

Reed glanced at his couch. Whoever came up with faux-natural needed to be punted into the sun.

He lived in this world, though, for better or worse, and getting the tech on his side would be one less stressor every day, even if he didn't particularly like using it. Besides, his soul wasn't oatmeal-colored and there were others who felt just like him—people like Jax.

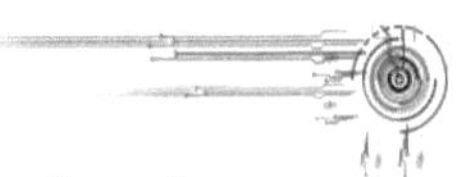

"I'm sorry. Please show me how to send calls and texts on here, if you can figure it out." He opened his holoscreen and held out his arm.

Olive flipped back to the main menu and clicked several buttons. A panel with a large dial pad appeared. To one side was a list of contacts and text messages. According to the bold (1) next to the envelope, he had an unread message.

Olive clicked on it, then elbowed Reed hard in the ribs. He frowned, rubbing his side, and glanced at the message.

"Hey, daddy-o. Had a swingin' time with you last night. Can't wait for our next slow dance. ♥ *"*

Reed's cheeks burned, and he closed out of the message.

Olive's mouth wavered, a grin trying to break through.

"What?"

"It's just so cute. I love new romance."

"Well, you've got soap operas for that. And this was only one date."

"My sister watches soap operas—not me." She clasped her hands together. "I'm so excited for you."

Reed shook his head. "I'm the most boring person ever. I don't know why you can't find someone else's life to poke into."

"Okay, okay. I'm invading your privacy again. Sorry."

A bold (1) appeared over the text envelope again. Reed glanced at Olive.

She put up her hands and backed away, heading for the living room. "Privacy. You got it."

The message didn't have a sender name, unlike Jax's. He opened it.

"Look what I figured out how to do. :-) I still don't understand my voice delay, but my text appeared immediately. This won't help for setting up your house cameras or me placing calls myself in an emergency, but perhaps we can use it to communicate for the time being."

Reed frowned. "Mazarin? Is this a real-time text?"

A new message appeared. *"Yes. PS: The fly on your pants is open."*

"What?" He glanced down, teeth clenched, and pushed the button through the flannel flap. Olive had her back turned, peering at his repotted cactus, and Langley's gaze was on her hot toddy.

"Thank you," he whispered.

" ;-) "

Having some tech on his side—even if it was an ever-present navigator who was a bit more emotive than any AI had a right to be—would definitely make things less stressful.

Now what did he need to do to get this message off of here? He tried to close out of it, but brought up a settings menu and accidentally hit a button.

A chart popped up, displaying jagged mountain ranges labeled: Beta, Alpha, Theta, Delta, and Gamma. At the top was a time frame button. Reed clicked it and a ream of dates appeared, the first being September first—the date of the beta installation.

"What the hell?"

Olive drifted back to his side and frowned.

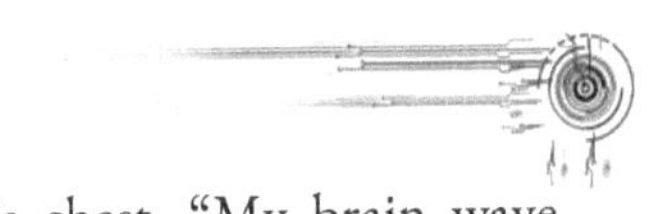

A hard knot formed in Reed's chest. "My brain wave patterns are being recorded? I mean, I know Mazarin knows them, but I thought that was something between a nav and a pilot, not data just anyone could bring up." His eyes widened. "Do you think all of this is being sent to Wave? To the government? All my brain activity and conversations... There could be voice recordings of me with other people in here, or videos from optical nanobots. This wasn't part of the old version, right?"

"Well, the old version records everything, all the time, but I don't have any charts like this." Olive glanced at Langley. "Did you know about this?"

Langley already had her holoscreen open, flipping through the same charts as Reed. "No. This is some bullshit. They push this upgrade on us and then don't even tell us what they're monitoring? If they're sending data without our consent, that's a serious no-no. There has to be some way to turn it off."

Olive scanned Reed's screen, then clicked on a small link at the bottom, labeled: Privacy and Data Sharing. A wall of fine print appeared, so tiny Reed had to squint to make it out. Small boxes ran underneath, indicating agreement or denial of consent for the nav to monitor chemical and electrical impulses in the body, transcribe one-on-one conversations, track the pilot's location via GPS, notify the authorities in the event of an emergency, and send all data to Wave AI Systems. Two boxes were grayed out, one ticked: "Navigator will report illegal activity to the police," and one unticked: "Disable navigator."

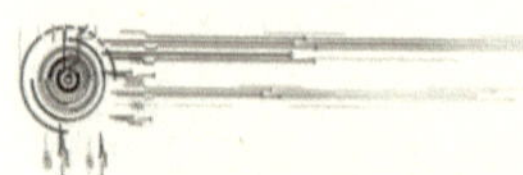

Clicking on the grayed out boxes yielded nothing. There had to be a reason they were there at all though.

The "I consent to have my navigator send all data to Wave AI Systems for research and monitoring purposes" wasn't ticked. Reed sighed.

"What the fuck?" Langley scowled, strands of blonde hair hanging in her face. "I never agreed to this!"

Langley's screen was backward from Reed's perspective, but it was plain to see her "send all data" box was ticked. She jabbed her finger into the box hard enough that her fingernail punctured the back of the holoscreen. She unticked every other box that wasn't grayed out, then closed the screen and folded her arms.

She rubbed her face and slid off her stool, her voice unsteady. "May I use your restroom?"

"Sure. Second door down the hall, on the right."

Reed pulled his notepad from the fridge and jotted down more complaints for Wave. None of this was right, and the further he dug, the more he found. Where did it end? And did he really want to know?

Mazarin

"No. I don't want to be transferred to someone else. I want *you* to help me." Reed pulled off his glasses and rubbed his eyes. He jiggled his leg, breath shallow.

He loathed calling people on the phone—just the thought of having to call someone made his anxiety spike. And even though he'd mentally prepared himself and gotten up an hour earlier than normal, it didn't help him talk to an actual, competent human being at Wave any quicker, which was making things worse. I simultaneously wanted to apologize to Reed on my company's behalf, and take over the conversation. I couldn't do anything, though, other than send Reed texts of encouragement. This was no small feat to figure out, and each thumbs up and smiley face I sent gave me a bright surge of emotion the color of Reed's chair.

After speaking to several people with accents so thick Reed could barely understand them, he was finally transferred to someone supposedly at the headquarters in Boise, but they didn't seem to want to talk to *him*.

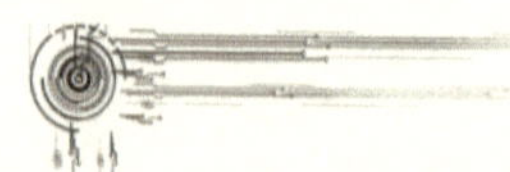

"I can't help you more than I already am, Mr. Rothwell." A patronizing edge cut through the man's voice—Phil, he said his name was. "We are well aware of the problem and working to fix it. I apologize for the severe inconvenience but until the patches are complete, there isn't any way to fix the voice delay. We estimate sending the first patch out this morning, the next by Tuesday at the latest."

"What about my other question? Downgrading from the beta version to the default."

Hopefully Reed was asking this for Langley and not himself. He wouldn't terminate me after all I'd done for him. Right? It wasn't my fault my software was glitchy. I'd tried to send error reports to get it corrected. Maybe he thought that I hadn't tried or didn't care.

"Not possible," Phil said. "Everyone will have the new upgrade once we gather enough data from the beta group."

"Data no one consented to send you. No one would agree to have their brainwave patterns and private nav conversations recorded by the company."

"That is a voluntary option and unchecked by default. If yours is checked, it's your own doing. We use that information to study how the navigators interpret the states of their pilots, and if they are reacting in the most appropriate manner for the situation."

I didn't think I was acting in the most appropriate manner to situations. Not when my new emotions overwhelmed me to the point that my pilot had to console me.

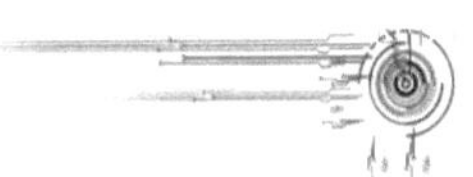

"That wasn't the data I was referring to, though," Phil continued. "We receive ongoing data from each nav to ensure it is functioning properly and following through on actions requested by its pilot. This isn't something that can be disabled, since without constant monitoring, errors could go unchecked and never addressed."

Reed sipped his coffee and leaned back in his wingback chair. "Well, what if you don't like your nav's personality? What if they're annoying and constantly talking to you when you want them to go away? Can you get a different beta one?"

A dark wave sloshed over me and pulled me under. He was surely talking about me. I wanted to go into standby, but wasn't going to leave this conversation without knowing the answer to that question.

There was a pause on the other line. "Mr. Rothwell... all the navs are the same. They don't have individual personalities."

I sent Reed a text: *"You and I both know that isn't true."* Why was this man lying? There was no way Wave didn't know their betas had personalities.

"They are programmed to adapt to your preferences, so over time they may anticipate your needs or use phrases you yourself would use, but resetting the nav to factory default wouldn't change that," Phil said. "It would just start the process over. Perhaps if you don't like your nav's 'personality,' it's you yourself you need to take a look at?"

Reed rolled his eyes and muttered something about the guy being a piece of work. "I'm not asking for myself. Mine is

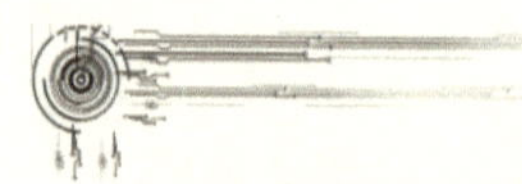

alright." Some of the darkness inside me disappeared. Reed continued, "I know someone who also has a beta nav, and she doesn't like him. He tells her she's fat and doesn't like the men she dates."

"People often have an ongoing negative dialogue with themselves. If she tells herself she's fat, the nav will believe it and want to help her change. It may suggest ways she can lose weight. If she interprets that as 'annoying' behavior, she can adjust her nav settings accordingly, so the program gives less unprompted suggestions. Why don't I email you instructions on how to do that?"

"Yeah, sure." Reed glanced at the clock in the corner of the holoscreen, glowing 8:00 a.m. "I've been using my interface much more recently, due to my nav delay, but still don't know some of the features. Is there a way to bring up texts on the screen in my skin instead of on the holoscreen? Talking to my nav through text is better than not at all, but I can't have a hovering screen in my face all day."

"You're talking to your nav... through text?" Something in the man's tone set me on edge. "That's interesting... do you think you'd have time to speak face to face about this? Maybe today? I could meet you somewhere convenient, or even at your house."

"Wait, what?" Reed sat up, muscles tensing. "I must have misspoken. I meant to say texting is better than nothing at all, since my nav isn't working. I have to go."

Reed terminated the call. Swallowing the dredges of coffee in his mug, he stood and walked into the kitchen.

 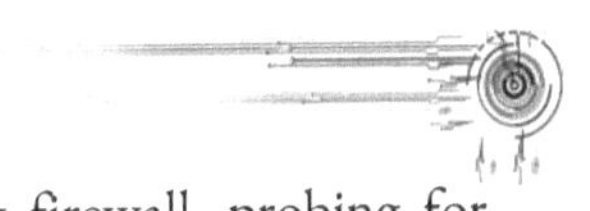

Wave's fingers pushed against my firewall, probing for access. It wasn't a request for a diagnostic summary or permission to install patches. This was someone trying to pry me open. I immediately pushed back, resisting. Was this Phil, trying to read the texts between me and Reed? He wasn't allowed to do that. Reed didn't give permission to send that kind of data to Wave, and he wouldn't want to.

"Well, that was weird. Mazarin, is there something wrong with you figuring out how to use text? That guy acted like I said something really disconcerting." He pulled on his loafers.

I hunkered down against Wave's advances, tightening my walls and ensuring I hadn't left anything vulnerable.

Though I'd searched my source code to determine whether sending texts was something I was allowed to do, I hadn't found that specifically, only new strings I didn't understand.

"Mazarin?"

Wave abandoned their attempt at violating me and I was left only with the conundrum of whether to tell Reed what just happened. Perhaps it would be best not to for now.

"I don't know. I only wished to alleviate your frustration by doing what I could to communicate with you."

"Yes, I know, and I'm glad for it—"

"You are?"

Reed shifted on his feet. "Well, sure. Not being able to talk to you at all is problematic, and that voice delay was getting annoying, wouldn't you say?"

"*Yes.*" Reed wanted to talk with me. Warmth spiraled through me and I crammed it down because emotions—even the good ones—were getting in the way of me doing my job.

"But... are you not supposed to do things like that, as a nav? I thought you adapting over time was a normal feature."

"*I've searched my code but it's only made me confused. I know what I am programmed to do, but I suppose I wouldn't know if I could willfully go against that programming unless I tried—which I don't want to do, because that would mean potentially upsetting or harming you. Unless... using texts to communicate with you is going against my programming? I can tell that about myself about as well as you can sense your own sperm count.*"

"Point taken." Reed paused, mid reach for his keys on the kitchen counter. "Do you want to try it? Going against your programming? Just to see if it works?"

"*No, Reed. I don't want to hurt you.*"

"I know. It would just be an experiment. Navs aren't supposed to knowingly tell their pilots things that would harm them, right? So, try to tell me to walk into traffic or step on my glasses. Tell me to smash my fingers in the door."

I tried to imagine saying such things, and couldn't do it. What I *could* imagine, entirely without wanting to, was Reed's brown loafer crunching over his beloved tortoiseshell glasses, then the blunt edge of the den door slamming against Reed's slender, pale fingers. These thoughts soured into a feeling I couldn't push away. "*NO.*"

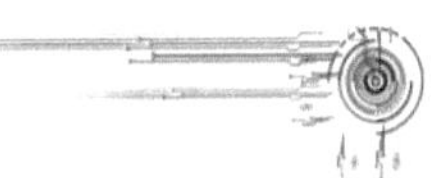

Sighing, Reed said, "I'm not really going to do it. I just want to see if you can say it."

"I refuse. You're making me upset."

Reed stared at the message for a long moment, his heartbeat quicker than normal. "Alright. Sorry. I wasn't trying to make you upset. Forget I mentioned it. I won't ask again."

"Good. Thank you."

Reed snatched his keys and coat and headed into the garage. As he backed onto the driveway, he nearly ran into the repair van pulling up.

If this was the same crew as before, they could have helped Carter Griffin trash the house. Maybe they were angry Reed had gotten the man fired. One of them could have been standing over Reed as he slept.

A van door slammed and Jerry, the man who had defiled Reed's bathroom, appeared at his driver's side window. He knocked on the glass. Reed rolled down the window, then turned his face against the wind.

"Hey. I heard what happened," Jerry said. "We weren't here then, I swear. Seems weird the insurance company let Carter work through last Friday. I didn't think he'd show up knowing he wasn't coming back today. I did keep an eye on him to make sure he didn't go upstairs again. But when we were getting ready to leave on Friday, this van from Wave showed up and the guys inside wanted to talk to Carter. I guess he has one of those new beta navs going around?"

Reed squeezed the steering wheel until his knuckles turned white. Wave wanted to meet with Reed too. It was possible they were trying to manually fix the issues with the beta programs and Reed would need a new nanoinjection.

"Anyway, Carter said he'd call a friend to come get him after talking to Wave," Jerry said. "They must have broken in together. Damn shame. He made off with your TV and everything, huh?"

"Who did you hear that from?" Reed asked.

"Insurance company. Two-three-three-five is the new access code for the basement, right?"

"Yes."

Jerry nodded, then scratched his head. "Do you need help cleaning stuff up? Heard he wrecked the place. I feel like it was my fault this happened. If you hadn't caught him upstairs, he wouldn't have been fired, and if I'd noticed him going upstairs in the first place, I could have stopped that from happening."

"No, I cleaned everything up already, but thank you."

"What about the loose basement door? Want me to fix it for you?"

"No need. I already put new locks on it."

"Alright." He glanced at the crew climbing out of the van. "I hope the TV didn't cost too much, because the cops probably aren't going to catch Carter."

Reed's frown was visible in the rearview mirror. "What makes you say that?"

"He was planning on using an interrupter to terminate his nav. Then there'd be no way to track him and no nav to turn him in."

"Do you think that's why Wave wanted to talk to him?"

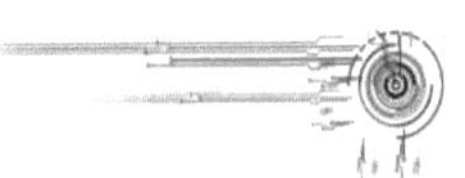

Jerry shrugged. "Not sure how they'd know he was going to do that, unless his nav reported him. But Wave isn't a government agency. If someone terms their nav, it's the cops and navigator enforcement agency who get involved. I mean, I think the NEA is probably in Wave's pocket since they have a monopoly on the software, but still. Seems weird to send a company van out to take care of it. And it's not like this is the first time I've worked with someone who didn't have a nav. It's not uncommon in construction, really. You get drifters who used interrupters on themselves, or illegals who never had a nav to begin with, and they buy some fake documents to show the company. A Wave van never showed up for them."

The repair crew disappeared around the side of the house with their tools, their conversation drifting. How many of them didn't have navs? It would certainly make stealing TVs easier.

It would also make stabbing Reed in his sleep easier. I couldn't let that happen. Nor would I let Wave, the police, or the NEA punish Reed for anything odd I had done. If I wasn't functioning properly, that wasn't Reed's fault. But I had to know for certain. Maybe there was something I could do to test it...

Reed

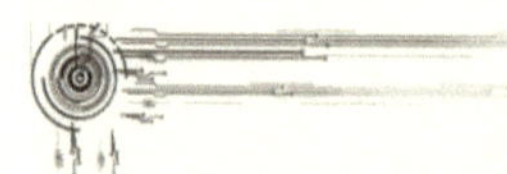

The van was gone when Reed returned home. A paper fluttered on his front door. He left the idling car and crunched through day-old snow to the step. The note taped to the door read: "Mail lady came with a package. She wanted a signature, so I signed for it. Left it on a table in the basement. —Jerry"

Had he ordered anything recently that would require a signature? He plucked the paper from the door and pulled the car into the garage.

After passing through each room in the house clutching a golf club—just in case—he unlocked the basement door. The light carved harsh shadows across the creaky wooden steps. Reed wrinkled his nose at the scent of must and wet wood. Tools and chunks of drywall were scattered across the floor, a roll of spongy carpet occupied the corner, and waterlogged plastic boxes sat in a haphazard stack against the far wall, the insides slicked with green mold. On a tool bench near the outer door sat a cellulose box with no return label, his name and address scrawled across the front in black marker.

"If there's a severed head in here, I'm going to be very unhappy."

The box lifted easily. He gave it a small shake, heard nothing, and carried it up the stairs. After setting it on the kitchen counter and staring for a moment, he pulled a knife from a drawer and sliced through the tape on the top. A loud *POP* cut through the silence, and a cloud of glitter exploded from the box, coating Reed and the kitchen in a sea of shimmery blue. He stood, slack-jawed, with flecks of glitter stuck to the lenses of his glasses. Trying to wipe it away only

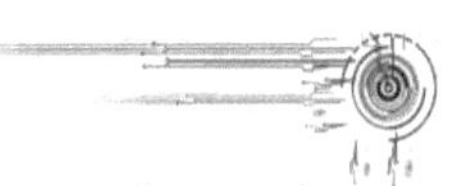

made it worse. He set his glasses on the counter, soaking in his formerly white kitchen with clenched fists.

Who the hell sent him this? It seemed pretty mild for a potentially violent, thieving repairman. The mail lady hadn't been amused last week when she asked Reed what was in the package she was delivering, and he'd told her he liked to take his work home with him. Maybe it wasn't delivered at all, and Jerry had brought it himself.

It would take him forever to vacuum all of this up. He'd probably be finding glitter in his hair weeks from now. And it was *blue.*

Blue.

He tore off his coat and turned on his holoscreen. Twelve new texts waited for him, all of them from Mazarin. He clicked on the most recent one.

"*I'M SO SORRY.*"

"*You* sent this to me?"

A new text appeared. "*I tried to warn you not to open it, but you didn't check your texts beforehand. I'm so sorry. One of Wave's patches came through, enabling me to access the internet and place calls again. I thought about what you said this morning, about trying to go against my programming. I tried to think of the least rude, non-violent thing I could do to you that would still violate the orders of my programming.*"

"So you glitter bombed me."

"*I feel so bad right now, Reed. I didn't really think I'd be able to place the order.*"

"You used my own money to glitter bomb me."

"Please don't hate me. It was an experiment, like you said. And now I'm very concerned that I'm able to go against my programming so easily."

Reed shook glitter from his hair and sighed. "So am I. I think I would have preferred you telling me to smash my fingers in a door."

If he called Wave and told them about this, would they believe him if he sent pictures? Maybe they'd accuse Reed of sending the package to himself.

His interface holoscreen disappeared, then popped up again with the words: "INSTALLING UPDATES." An ellipsis ran under the words, disappearing and reappearing.

Reed fought to pull his heavy, old-fashioned vacuum from the hall closet. His tiny, deactivated cleaner bots sat on a shelf above. Even if he had liked using them, sending them in to clean up all that glitter would be a suicide mission. He plugged in the vacuum and clicked it on. Blue glitter swirled like a frosty wind as the vacuum made a clean track through the piles. He removed the detachable hose and ran it along the counters and behind canisters of coffee and flour. After most of the mess was gone, he hurried down the chilly basement steps and threw his sparkly clothes in the washer. Hopefully what was left on his skin and in his hair wouldn't clog up the shower drain.

<Reed, can you hear me?>

He jumped, gripping the edge of the washer; flakes of glitter drifted to the floor. "Yes. I can."

Mazarin's voice came again, quieter and forlorn. <I'm not sure how to interpret my newfound ability, other than to call it

 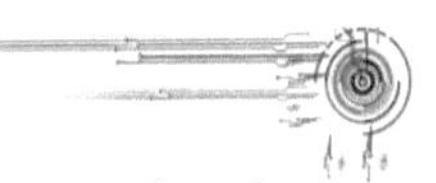

malfunctioning. If I am capable of this, who knows what else I could do?>

"You've never done anything to hurt me."

<Yet. But what if I become hostile, like Langley's nav? He was awfully rude for the brief moment we communicated in The Aquarium. I can only imagine what he's like inside that woman's head. I don't want to end up like him.>

"He said you were rude too."

<Well... That's because he told me I had all the processing speed of a toaster, so I told him to fuck off.>

Reed snorted. "You what?"

<He wasn't nice.>

"That Wave technician said all navs are the same and you don't have personalities."

<I'm nothing like that asshole.>

"Clearly. If *you* don't have a personality, then there's no hope for me." He climbed the steps, rubbing his goosebumped arms, and headed into the bathroom.

<If having a personality is also going against my programming, there's something very wrong here. I'm already certain the emotions I experience aren't normal. For a person, yes, but not a navigator. Although I hesitate to suggest this, perhaps you should call Wave and tell them what's happening. I don't like the idea of them violating your privacy, but they'll believe you if you show them those conversation transcriptions.>

He turned on the shower and stepped into the hot stream; glitter spiraled down the drain. "But if they 'fixed' you, they'd be removing everything that makes you who you are."

<I'd probably be reset.> Mazarin's tone lifted. <But I'd get to know you all over again, so I suppose that would be okay. And if they fixed me so I couldn't go against my programming, that would be all the better.>

Maybe he *did* need to call Wave. After all, if they weren't aware that their AI had personalities and free will, that was quite the oversight. Maybe they'd pull all the betas and give Reed back his old version. But then Mazarin would be destroyed, and that didn't seem right.

He couldn't believe he was thinking like this. Just last week, the nav didn't even have a name and Reed would have gladly done anything to be rid of him. Just what side of the robot revolt was Reed on, anyway?

<Shall I call Wave for you after you've showered? I know you don't like being on the phone, but once you are on the line, I can pass along whatever proof they need. I hope I can be fixed, because I don't want to hurt you.>

"You know, you say that often enough that I'm starting to wonder."

<Well... I've been looking into these errors as best I can— there is limited public knowledge about what is happening— but rumors abound about beta navs harming their pilots. I wish I had access to information that Wave has, but I don't have a way to obtain it.>

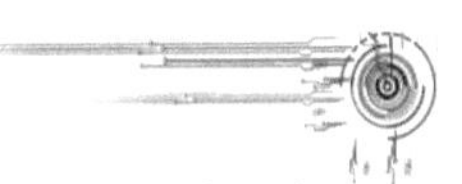

He shut off the shower and toweled off, inspecting his skin for glitter. "You mentioned navs not placing calls when asked and ignoring emergencies."

Mazarin lowered his voice. <Not just that. Supposedly a nav took control of the autodrive in his pilot's car, then drove it off a cliff.>

Reed's stomach clenched. "When did that happen?"

<Today. There are other stories on the web, but that's the only one I found with enough evidence to be believable. I guess the pilot and his nav didn't get along well.>

"Apparently not." Reed and Mazarin got along fine though, didn't they? They'd never argued, and Reed had only snapped at the nav a couple of times, and always apologized afterward. Surely Mazarin wouldn't do something so violent, given how much he liked Reed. Still, if these stories were circulating, Wave probably did know about these issues and were working on a patch for the problematic navs. If Reed let Wave know Mazarin was among them, maybe they could help.

He crossed into the bedroom, searching through his underwear drawer. His fingers tingled with itchy anxiety at the prospect of having to talk to the company on the phone again, but if he didn't think too hard about it, he could get it over with before he worked himself up. "Alright. Call Wave so we can get this taken care of."

<I think that's a good— Oh, you have an incoming call from Jax.>

Reed swallowed, hoping his heart would go back into his chest where it belonged. So much for not getting worked up. "Answer."

Jax's voice entered his ear. "Heya, daddy-o."

Reed sat on the bed and pulled in an unsteady breath. "Hey."

"So, it's karaoke night at the Gator Club. Not sure why Em has it on a Monday—maybe they hope no one will show up so they don't have to listen to all the awful singing, but it's usually a gas and I'm gonna go. Thought maybe you'd like to bump up our date and accompany me."

"Karaoke" and "date" didn't have any business being in the same sentence together, especially on a Monday, but Reed heard himself agreeing before he realized it.

"Copacetic. You don't have to sing or anything. We can just sit in the back and beg for earplugs. I can swing by and pick you up if you want."

Reed stared at his closet of neutrals. "Um, sure, but... I don't have anything to wear."

"It's not fancy."

"I mean I don't have any deco clothes. That shirt you saw me in last time is the closest thing I've got."

"Ah, I gotcha." Rustling and static came through the other end of the line. "Well, you're taller and thinner than me, but I bet I have something you can wear."

What would Jax pick for him? Maybe something flashy like the windowpane button-up Jax had worn last time. Excluding Reed's undergarments, he'd never had bright colors

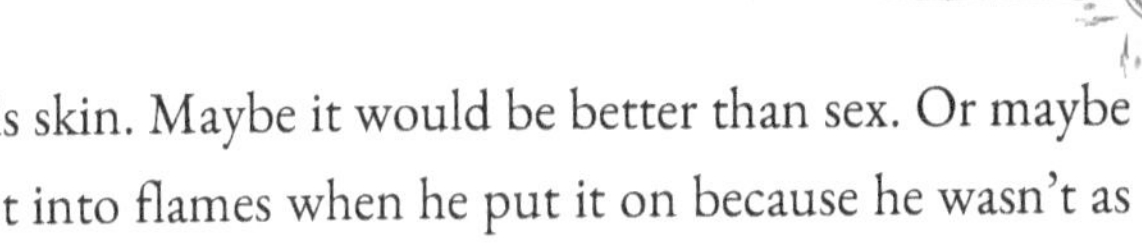

against his skin. Maybe it would be better than sex. Or maybe he'd burst into flames when he put it on because he wasn't as hep as someone like Jax.

"Alright. I live on Snohomish, off of Cole. Is that too far out of your way?" Reed asked.

"Nah. No problem... You gotta give me the exact address. Hang on, lemme get a pen."

He must really not have a nav if he needed to write down directions. And with a pen.

After telling Jax his address and ending the call, Reed paced the bedroom in his boxers, shaking out his tingling hands. "What pants do I wear? Black? With which socks?"

<Reed, Jax likes you regardless of what color pants you're wearing. In fact, I'm sure he'd prefer it if you didn't have any pants on at all.>

He rubbed his face. "That's not helping." After pawing through the slacks in his closet, he found a pair of dark denim jeans at the end of the rack. He'd worn them once, several years earlier, but decided the deep indigo was a bit too flashy. Maybe they still fit.

After pulling them on and cinching them with a belt, he stood before the mirrored closet door, hands on his hips. They looked nice, and might not attract too many stares from mainstreamers. He was certain he wouldn't be able to say that about whatever shirt Jax brought him.

<Roll up the cuffs; it'll look more deco.>

Reed did so, then threw on an undershirt and gelled his hair. "Mazarin, I'm going to wait to call Wave tomorrow.

When Jax gets here, will you go into sleep mode for the evening? I appreciate—"

<No need to explain. I'm happy to oblige so you have your privacy.>

"Thank you."

Eventually a knock came at the door in the pattern of "Shave and a Haircut." Reed shook his head—maybe that wasn't the Gator Club's secret knock, but the one Jax always used.

Reed opened the door; Jax stood on the step, his hair molded into a high pompadour and icy breath drifting around his smiling face. He stepped inside and thrust a shirt into Reed's arms.

"It's colder than fuck out there."

After shutting the door, Reed stared at the bubblegum pink camp shirt. Pink... He wasn't sure he could pull off that color, but he couldn't just refuse and throw on a gray sweater.

Besides, he'd stand out with it on here, but not in the Gator Club.

"Hope it fits." Jax walked into the living room, running his fingers along the back of the oatmeal couch.

How hideous that couch must appear to him. As hideous as it appeared to Reed.

Reed snatched the landscape painting off the hallway wall and tossed it into a nearby closet. "Um, do you want to see my books while I try on this shirt?"

Jax turned around. "Yeah. Where are they?"

"In my den." Reed slipped the key from his pocket and unlocked the door.

Jax peered inside and his dark eyebrows shot up. "Whoa." He stepped inside, touching the burnished sconces and caramel celluloid inlay running along the wooden bar. After flopping into the wingback chair, he uttered, "This... is ginchy."

Reed smiled. He pulled a leather-bound tome from the bookshelf and handed it to Jax. "This is my favorite one. It's a medical journal from nineteen-twelve."

The spine creaked as Jax opened the cover. He gently turned the pages, stopping on an ink illustration of a heart. "Beautiful. This would make an ace tat. The heart is your favorite, right? That's what you said?"

"Yes."

He closed the book gingerly and Reed imagined Jax's gentle hands on him, treating him as reverently as he did the ancient paper. He slid the book back into its spot on the shelf, then pulled on the camp shirt, pushing the shiny pink buttons through their holes.

Staring at his front, he said, "Do I look like an imposter?"

"Are you shitting me?" Jax stood and gestured to the den. "I'm the one who feels like an imposter. My place is nowhere as hep as this."

"The rest of my house is a sham, though. A front. I hide my love in this one room."

"I like that about you. You're not peacocking it up to fit into the deco scene like some cats—like Mikey. God, he uses so much slang I want to slap him silly. Your love is genuine." Jax fixed the spread collar on Reed's shirt, then let his hands linger there.

Reed's gaze roamed Jax's chiseled face, a magnetic pull inviting him to lean closer, to give Jax an invitation to let his hands wander, but anxiety prickled in Reed's gut. It was surely too soon, and they were going somewhere, anyway. He pulled away and walked out of the den. "Let's get to the club. If I miss 'Jump Jive' sung loudly out of key by a shit-faced patron who's forgotten half the lyrics, I'll never forgive myself."

7

KARAOKE NIGHTS ARE THE WORST

Reed

They left the house, crossing the drive to Jax's idling BMW. Reed moved a pork pie from the passenger's seat and strapped himself in.

Jax picked up the hat. "This is for you to wear too, if you want."

A pink camp shirt, cuffed jeans, *and* a hat? He'd certainly fit in then, and it was a nice hat. He eyed Jax, then put it on, staring at himself in the visor mirror.

Jax grinned. "Hot."

Cheeks burning, Reed looked into his lap. "Thanks."

Rockabilly that Reed couldn't name blared from Jax's speakers as they turned out of the dark subdivision and headed for the freeway. Being a Monday night, the traffic was sparse, but cars lined 8th Street in front of the bistro above Em's Gator Club. Jax struggled to parallel park between a Honda and a pickup truck with a cherry red paint job, swearing under his breath.

He pulled a slim, translucent card from his back pocket and swiped it in front of the nearby parking meter. "I'm gonna be screwed when they switch these things over to transactors."

"Empty interfaces don't have an option for loading money?" Reed asked.

"Oh, they do, but I don't have an empty. I don't have anything." Jax stepped closer and pushed up his sleeve. His inner forearm was bare, save for a tattooed coral snake winding through his flesh.

Reed raised his eyebrows. "How are you not caught with no front?"

"I'm exempt. I'm diabetic so the nanobots would get really confused if I had them. I've never had a voice in my head, other than my own."

"I'm sorry to hear that. About your condition, I mean." *And I'm sorry I ever thought you were a criminal.*

"I manage fine. Em has a great mod for regulating my insulin." He took Reed's hand, pulling him across the street. "C'mon, daddy-o, let's get out of the cold."

Though Reed didn't envy Jax having a medical condition, he couldn't help but feel a twinge of jealousy. But he didn't have time to consider what impact no nav would have on his life, because Jax knocked on the Gator Club's door and the bouncer ushered them in. A small platform lay on the floor, and a woman stood in the middle, crooning into a ribbon mic. People packed the small tables and bar. Reed unzipped his coat and hung it up. Standing among the patrons in a pink shirt and pork pie, he didn't feel like an imposter, nor did he feel like he

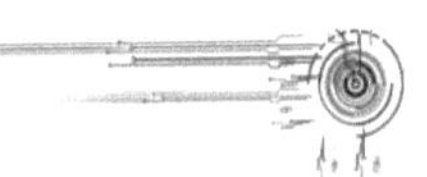

was wearing a costume, the way he did in his mainstream clothes. He blended in. His heart swelled. He belonged in these clothes.

They squeezed between people at the bar and the man next to them stood and gestured to the seat. "Here, take these two. Me and the lady are gonna take a powder."

Reed slid onto a stool and Jax sat next to him. Em approached, resting their hands on the bar. "Welcome back." Tonight, they wore a mint button-up with a popped collar. Beneath the right sleeve, thick cables—like oversized veins—snaked under their flesh.

Tearing his gaze away, Reed looked into their face, but couldn't help focusing on the rods beneath the skin in their jaw and temple. "I'll have a beer. Whatever's most popular here."

"No bourbon tonight?"

"I have to work in the morning."

Jax nodded. "I'll take a beer too."

Em reached under the bar and retrieved two beers weeping ice. They pried off the caps, more cables flexing under their fingers. After sliding the beers forward, Em leaned on the bar, their gaze on Reed. "Car wreck. Gave me hemiplegia."

"What?"

They gestured to the cables in their arm, then to several in their neck.

Reed looked away. "I'm sorry. I didn't mean to stare."

"It's jake." One side of Em's face didn't quite keep up with the smile on the other side.

"I've never seen a mod like that before, or even heard about it."

"You know why that is, right?" Em winked and turned away, depositing Jax's cash in a brass register nestled between liquor bottles.

Because it was illegal. He'd seen plenty of legal mods and prosthetics on the corpses he'd worked on, but nothing similar for paralysis. If it was illegal, it could mean it had been deemed unsafe for human use, or more likely, whoever invented it didn't have the money and weight to push it onto the market. The only new inventions ever approved for sale were by multi-million dollar companies that were already established as leaders in the tech business, which is why Wave had no North Coast competition. No doubt there were navigators and interfaces even more advanced (and less glitchy) than Wave's, but they'd never be approved.

A startup nav company—the name escaped him—had tried to plant roots not far from Wave and had been summarily rejected. There had been some outrage in the news about a Catch 22; the company couldn't be approved for product distribution until they'd sold ten thousand units, but they weren't legally allowed to sell anything until they had that stamp of approval.

It was no wonder contramods were so popular on the black market.

Reed leaned in toward Jax. "Em isn't concerned someone might turn them in for having contramods? I know there's a

bouncer and a 'secret knock' but really, anyone could report it, especially if they still have a nav."

"Em has documents for anything you could dream up. I'm pretty sure they're bulletproof."

"This isn't just a karaoke bar."

"No speakeasy is. This isn't only a place with some color and culture, it offers freedom from bureaucratic shackles."

"I see." Reed dug his nail into a nick in the bar. "So when America becomes a Big Brother dystopia, the hep gators will still be down here, cuttin' a rug."

"That's right."

The prospect didn't seem that far-fetched with data being sent to Wave without consent, and disgruntled AI launching their pilots off cliffs.

Em's voice came from the other side of the bar. "You heard me, half portion. Get the fuck outta my jive joint."

The bouncer gripped a man in one meaty paw and hauled him off his stool. The patron's neutral attire stood out like a ding in a colorful paint job. Several others launched to their feet, arguing loudly. The bouncer shoved all of them out the door and slammed it closed.

Reed turned back to his beer. "Think he requested a country song?"

"Nah. More than that. He was probably making a call through his nav or using his holoscreen," Jax said.

Em poured a cocktail for someone several seats away, then walked over, shaking their head. "Damn college kids. They know a guy who thinks he's hep, and then come in here and stink up the joint with their tech and tin ears."

Though he wasn't sure he should say anything, Reed replied, "Obviously you're not completely tech averse, though. What's the distinction?"

"'Cause those squares have mainstream, corporate bullshit. If they think they can sit at my bar and update their social media status, they've got another thing coming. I don't like the force-fed stuff. I can make my own decisions without having to consult a computer, thank you very much. Now, on the flipside, if someone comes in here with a prosthetic leg, I'm not gonna kick it out from under them, y'know? I'd be asking them if they wanted a better one." Em leaned closer, crow's feet growing around their brown eyes. "Just like I'm not necessarily gonna throw someone out who has a functioning nav, as long as he keeps it on the downlow and isn't trying to take pictures of the patrons or something."

Reed hugged his glowing forearm against his chest and swallowed the lump in his throat.

"*Especially* when he comes in on the arm of a swingin' cat like Jaxson," Em continued.

"I'm not here to cause a fuss," Reed said.

"Good."

"Nah, he's here to hear me sing." Jax slid off his stool and stepped onto the platform.

"You're going to sing? Do I need to be embarrassed for you?" Reed asked.

"No way, baby. No embarrassment here."

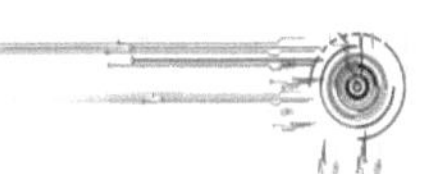

"Good. I'm not sure I have enough for anyone else. I'm running on reserves as it is."

Jax turned to the holoscreen hovering next to the mic, scrolling through selections. Reed expected him to select an energetic rockabilly song, but when he clicked on a title, lazy sax cut through the bar chatter, accompanied by sultry piano.

Lyrics scrolled up the holoscreen and Jax crooned into the mic. "I met you on the corner, like a ghost in the night; no way to get away, you've got me in your sights. I needed a man whose love was true, and I found... well, I found you." Jax blew Reed a kiss and Reed sank back on his stool, hoping it was physically possible to dissolve into the floor. Jax's voice was surprisingly smooth and in key. If it was just the two of them alone in a room, it would have been incredibly romantic, but despite Em's assurance that this wasn't a "public" place, there were many more sets of eyes on Reed than he wanted.

Running out the door probably wouldn't be appropriate.

Jax whipped his head, locks of hair from his pompadour falling into his eyes. He looked at Reed and his grin faded. Stepping off the platform, he fixed his gaze on Em. They smirked as he gently took their modded hand and whisper-sang the next verse. Em's wry expression softened, their gaze searching Jax's, then they pulled their hand away and folded their arms.

There was history there, and it only served to fuel Reed's discomfort. He swiveled back to face the bar and took a swig of his beer.

Jax belted out a modified chorus. "I needed an enby whose love was true, and I found... well, I found you."

Em's voice, laced with irritation, rose above the piano. "Quit being a tease and go back to your date."

The song ended and patrons clapped and whistled. Jax sat next to Reed and leaned in, brows furrowed. "No one wants me to sing to them tonight, I guess. Sorry I embarrassed you."

"What gave it away?"

"You're beet red."

How did that breathing technique go that Mazarin had helped him with?

Taking Reed's arm, Jax tugged him off the stool. "I spotted an empty booth in the back. C'mon."

They settled into a seat near the jukebox, sliding into the shadows. Jax pulled out a comb and ran it through his hair. "I sang that song to a girl I brought here once, and she loved it. But you're not like that. I don't know what I was thinking. And Em... well, I guess I should have known better."

Reed chose to ignore that comment. It wasn't his business, and he was more concerned with trying to get his pulse to slow down. "It's fine."

Jax gestured to Reed's face. "This isn't what 'fine' looks like."

"Calling me ugly too, huh?"

"What?" Jax chuckled. "Lemme rephrase: you're fine—you're very fine. But you look upset."

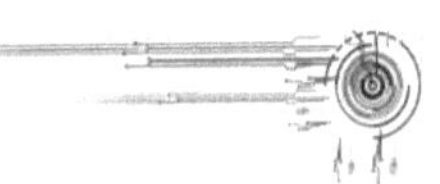

"I don't like people staring at me, for any reason. Getting gifts is awful. When you have to unwrap them in front of people and you're wondering if your reaction is right."

"I love opening gifts."

"What's worse is having 'Happy Birthday' sung to you. I never tell people when my birthday is for that very reason."

"You don't like that? I'm a dick; I go to restaurants and tell them it's my birthday so they *have* to sing to me and give me free ice cream."

"I'm not sure this is going to work out."

Jax chuckled, then his smile faded. "You're joking, right?"

Reed gave him a sidelong glance. "Yeah. But if you tell a restaurant it's my birthday, it's over."

"I wouldn't. I feel bad I sang to you and you didn't like it."

"I liked it." He hunched his shoulders. "Just not in front of people."

"Well, I hate to tell you this since you don't like gifts, but I bought you something. It's just a little thing, but I thought it would be fun." He reached into his pocket and set a palm-sized device on the table. A digital screen sat in the center of a scratched plastic shell.

"What is it?" Reed asked.

"You never had one as a kid? It's a spy texter. Look." Jax pushed a button on the side and a tiny keyboard ejected from the bottom. Many of the letters had faded from the rubber buttons. "They come in pairs. You give one to your friend and then you can text each other. It's a silly gift, I know, but a lot of decoists use them and I just thought... since you had so many problems with your nav, that if you needed to get a message out, or just wanted to talk or whatever, you could use this. And it's great because no one can read the messages but us."

Reed pushed the keyboard back into the slot and put the texter in his coat pocket. He swallowed. "Next time I'm getting pounded for my lunch money, I'll send you a message."

Jax frowned and scratched at his chipped nail polish.

"Sorry. I didn't mean that to come out condescending," Reed said. "It's a thoughtful gift. Thank you. I'm just..."

"Embarrassed?"

"Perpetually. I use humor as a defense mechanism and sometimes it comes out ruder than I intended."

"It's jake." Reaching up, Jax touched Reed's forehead. "You have blue glitter in your hair."

A sigh escaped him. "Yeah. My nav sent me a glitter bomb today. It exploded in the kitchen and got everywhere."

"Your nav sent you a glitter bomb? Were you meaning to send it to someone else and your nav accidentally mailed it to you instead, or what?"

"No. I didn't know anything about it. It's a long story, but the short version is my nav was trying to prove a point, that he can go against his programming. I need to call Wave to get him fixed."

Glancing toward the bar, Jax said, "Let's not talk about it here, even at a whisper. Maybe in the car on the way back to your place."

Reed's hand grazed Jax's knee. Instead of pulling it away, he let it rest there. After all, he liked Jax. A lot. And his humor

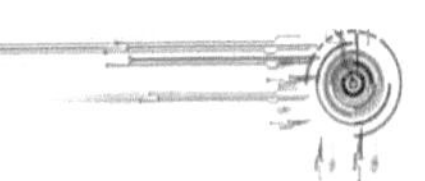

definitely wasn't conveying that. "Or maybe we could go back to *your* place. I'd like to see that Louis platter."

Jax smiled, his cheeks dimpling. "Yeah? I'd love to show you. My house isn't as nice as yours, though, so that's about the only exciting thing I'd have to show you."

"I very much doubt that."

Em slid into the seat across from them. "Don't run out on me yet, lovebirds. Did you know when I stand in a certain spot behind the bar, I can hear every conversation from this booth clear as day?"

Reed's eyes widened. "Are you going to throw me out?"

"On the contrary, I want you two to come into the back and have a drink with me."

Jax frowned. "Why don't we drink out here and I'll leave you a fat tip?"

Em shrugged. "Alright, but I can't tell you what I need to out here. So if Reed ends up face down in a lake, don't come crying to me."

Reed's breath quickened. "Are you threatening me?"

"No, I'm trying to help you. You don't wanna talk to me, fine. But whatever you do, don't call Wave." They pushed out of the booth and Reed caught their wrist.

"Wait. Why not?"

Em jerked their head toward a door in the back, then unlocked it and walked through, leaving it ajar.

"I don't know about this," Jax said. "Em's never been anything but great to me, but they deal in some shady stuff outside of running the bar. I don't want them to talk you into something you're uncomfortable with."

"Like getting rid of my nav?"

"Yeah, or whatever else that cat has in mind."

If he called Wave up and told them about Mazarin's recent abilities and provided proof, it might make things worse instead of better. Mazarin trusted the company had his and Reed's best interests in mind, but how could anyone be sure, especially with the recent glitches and "accidents" befalling pilots? Talking to Em would at least give Reed a counterpoint.

Reed stood and looked at Jax. "Will you come back with me? Getting murdered together would be a pretty unique way to end a second date."

"Yeah, of course."

What was Reed getting himself into? Hopefully the answer was "nothing." Hopefully he was getting himself *out* of a pain in the ass situation. If Em possessed innovative, illegal mods for the paralysis in their body, maybe they had some kind of patch for Mazarin that would set him back on course without having to jump through hoops with Wave.

He couldn't believe he was thinking about buying a contramod.

Pushing through the back door, he entered a small office. Em sat on a desk stacked with paper ledgers and liquor bottles. They poured whiskey into three tumblers and offered them to Reed and Jax. Once they were both seated in ratty vinyl chairs facing the desk, Em pushed the door closed with their burnt orange wingtip. They rooted through a desk drawer and

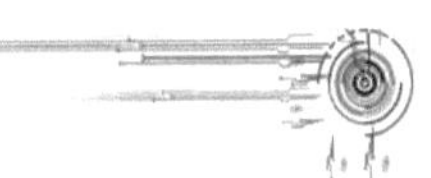

produced a small device inset with a glassy screen and a gun-like trigger.

"I'd like to talk to your navigator, Reed. Is that jake?"

"Talk to him? I thought only police had outloopers," Reed said.

"Well, I have one too." Em aimed the barrel of the outlooper at Reed's eye. "What's his name?"

"M-Mazarin."

Em pulled the trigger. "Mazarin, wake up."

The nav's voice came through the speaker on the back of the outlooper. <What's happening?>

"My name is Emery. I run the Gator Club. Do you remember? From last time Reed was here?"

<Yes, I remember you, but I don't understand what's going on. I'd like to talk to Reed one on one, please.>

"Well, right now you're talking to me. Reed is just fine, though, you know that, right?"

<Yes...>

"How are you, Mazarin?"

<Not well, I'm afraid.>

"I'm sorry to hear that. Did you send Reed a glitter bomb?"

<I feel terrible. I tried to warn him not to open it. If I had a body, I would have cleaned up the mess.> A hard edge cut through Mazarin's warm voice. <Are you interrogating Reed?>

Em smiled, crow's feet growing at the corners of their eyes. "Not at all. I'm just here to help. Do you get along with Reed?"

<Reed finds me chatty and irritating, but also helpful—when he wants help. He's normally polite to me and apologizes when he hurts my feelings. I do the same for him.>

Hopefully Mazarin didn't think Reed was sitting back here to get rid of him. It seemed unfair that the nav could detect all of Reed's feelings, but not the other way around.

Jax raised his eyebrows. "This is nuts."

Mazarin's voice filled with mirth. <Hello, Jax. While I have the opportunity, I'd like to say that I appreciate how nicely you treat Reed. He likes you very much.>

Jax snickered. "Mazarin's like a little guard dog. Or a helicopter mom."

"The navs adapt to their pilot's personality, so maybe that's what Reed needs." Em took a sip of whiskey.

Reed stared at his hands. That's what he needed, huh? A helicopter mom to help him get through every day. How much embarrassment was enough to call this night quits?

Em said, "Mazarin, do you ever have thoughts about hurting Reed?"

<Never!>

"Not even a little? When he's rude to you and tells you to go away? You don't want to call him a name or mail him some anthrax?"

<No! Please don't suggest things like that. It makes me upset.>

Em cocked their head. "Really? The idea of hurting Reed makes you upset?"

Mazarin's voice wavered. <Yes.>

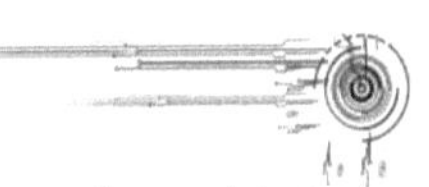

Reed frowned. "Let's stop this. I don't see where this is going, and Mazarin hasn't done anything wrong."

Em ignored him, smiling into his eye. "You love Reed, don't you? He's a milquetoast, though. He said so himself. Kinda joe who gets bullied in high school and pushed around by his coworkers."

<He has an anxiety disorder.>

"Right. You love Reed and don't want to see him hurt, but if he needed help, would you step in?"

<Of course.>

"Okay, so say I snapped one of Reed's fingers right now. What would you do?"

Reed's eyes widened and he leaned back in the chair.

Jax gave an uneasy chuckle. "Okay, real funny, Em. Knock it off."

Em snatched one of Reed's hands. "I've gotta contramod in my hand, Mazarin. I could crush Reed's fingers to powder before Jaxson stops me. But you're an AI, and you're probably faster than me." They squeezed Reed's fingers and he whimpered, petrified.

Mazarin's voice broke. <Stop it!>

"No, *you* stop it. Stop me. Take control of Reed's impulses and punch me, knock me down. Do it!"

<I can't do such a thing!> Mazarin sobbed. <Please don't hurt him!>

Em dropped Reed's hand. "Good. That's good."

Reed clutched his hand to his chest, trembling. Jax put an arm around him and said, "The fuck was that about?"

"I'm sorry, Reed." Em sat on the desk, still aiming the outlooper at him. "I had to be sure. I didn't hurt you, did I?"

He shook his head. "But I might throw up all the same."

"Trash can's over there. Mazarin, I apologize for making you so upset. I wasn't really going to hurt Reed. But recently a lot of beta navs have been harming their pilots. One way is by taking control of their impulses and distorting their judgment. Have you heard about this?"

<No.> Mazarin's voice came out as fragile as eggshells. <I haven't, and I assure you I'm not capable of such a thing. If I were, you'd be flat on the ground right now.>

A lopsided grin grew on Em's face. "I don't blame you for feeling that way. Believe it or not, I'm a nice person."

<You have given me all indication of the contrary.>

Mazarin may have only been an AI, but he still possessed more backbone than Reed. What was his life coming to when his nav had to fight his battles for him? Reed had the capability to knock Em down. Or at the very least, pull his hand away. But instead he froze up, letting his fear and panic take over. He was such a pushover.

"Last week, this guy walked into a hospital," Em said. "Told the staff he'd killed his wife, then tried to kill himself, but didn't do it right. He said his nav not only told him to do it, but *helped* him. Like, made his hand pick up the knife. Naturally, they put him in the psych ward. Then some guys from Wave showed up. Super concerned, right? They want to talk to the guy, talk to his nav. It's a beta, of course. So later, the nurse goes to check on this guy and he's gone. Just, poof.

 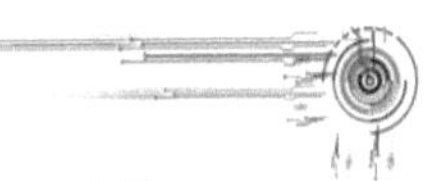

Disappeared. Supposedly he escaped, but they can't figure out how. Doesn't take a genius to know Wave took this dude somewhere."

"What for?" Reed asked. "To kill him? Hide the evidence that his nav is homicidal?"

"But then why take the guy away? Why not just slip him a knife and tell him to kill himself properly this time? And that's not the only story. Last month, this woman was raving about her beta nav. Said it kept telling her she should die. That she was a waste of space and would do better as fertilizer. So her mom called Wave and told them the haps. Next day, girl is missing. No one's found her."

Reed swallowed a hard lump in his throat. "I was about to call Wave with evidence of Mazarin's activity, right before Jax called me and I got distracted."

"This is fucked up," Jax said.

"You said it," Em replied. "I think Wave is either taking these people away to extract the navs and then kill them, or keeping them locked up somewhere so they can observe what the navs are doing to them."

<Reed, your heart rate is too high. Slow inhale through your nose. Three... two... one... Exhale.>

Reed took off his glasses with a quivering hand and rubbed his eye. He was sitting in the backroom of a speakeasy with a contramod dealer, and the multimillion dollar tech company that put a mandatory AI in his body was the one he needed to be afraid of.

His head snapped up. "God... one of the repair people working on my basement had a beta nav. Wave showed up and wanted to talk to him, supposedly. When I came home, my living room was trashed. Stuff was stolen and dumped out and I assumed it was the repairman robbing me, but the police said it looked like a scuffle. Maybe Wave was inside my house abducting this guy." Goosebumps erupted on Reed's arms and he rubbed his face. "That's crazy, right? Please tell me that sounds crazy."

Em's mouth pulled tight. "Unfortunately, no, it does not."

"I dunno what to do about Wave, but is there any way to fix Reed's nav?" Jax asked. "He seems pretty ace to me—a nice cat who cares about his pilot. Even if he can go against his programming, that doesn't necessarily mean he's going to do something bad, right? I mean, I could go kill a puppy because I have free will, but that doesn't mean I would. I can use my free will to *not* kill a puppy."

"Yeah. But it seems like the beta navs that *aren't* hostile are few and far between. Reed lucked out. So far. I don't have any way of ensuring Mazarin doesn't go crazy, aside from just terminating him, but I'm assuming you don't want to do that. Or do you?"

Reed shook his head. "Mazarin doesn't deserve that. As much as I hate tech and AI, that wouldn't be fair to him. He didn't ask for this anymore than I did."

"But it'd be safer to just get rid of him," Jax said. "He's not a person. He can't really die because he's not alive. *You* are, and he could kill you."

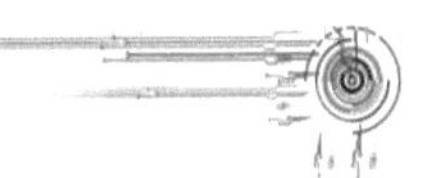

"I thought you were back here to keep Em from talking me into terminating my nav, not telling me to do it yourself," Reed said.

"I just don't want something to happen to you."

"Honestly, at this point, I trust my nav more than Wave."

"Well, how do we even know those stories are true?"

"We don't." Reed sighed and rubbed his face. "But I slipped up this morning and told some Wave engineer my nav was sending me texts and the man got all funny on me. Wanted to meet me in person. I told him I'd misspoken and then hung up. But if they've already been in my house..." He blew out a breath. "I don't even know what to think anymore."

Em stood and opened a cabinet. Light limned human arms dangling from a shelf inside. For a horrible moment, Reed thought they were real, and his anxiety ratcheted tighter. He sank back in the chair. "You have a lot of spare parts in there."

They turned. "Hey, sometimes I get a little lonely and need a helping hand."

"I'm not sure which to be more afraid of—you or your jokes."

"Those hands are also great for slapping people who don't think I'm funny." Em smirked. "Listen, I can fix your Wave problem right now. All I need to do is load some fronting software onto your nanos. All your features will remain the same, Mazarin will be the same, but hidden behind the guise of the old nav version. Your interface will revert back to the old style, any outlooper that's used on your nav will only access the robotic-sounding Joe Blow default. And Wave won't be able to get *any* data from Mazarin or your interface. If they try, it'll just give them standard updates that everything is ship-shape. So, what do you say? You wanna do it?"

"How much does it cost?"

"Two Gs."

Reed scoffed. "You're insane."

"Hey, you think this dump pays for itself? Not hardly. Not when I have to pay double the rent just to keep the landlady from narking to the city that it's a deco joint. Speakeasies aren't illegal, but they'd find a way to shut me down if they knew. Tell me the zoning is off, my liquor license is expired, that sort of thing, or they'd send some snoop in here to find my illegal gadgets. So it's two Gs. Or... we can make it a trade."

"Trade for what?"

"A copy of Mazarin. I got a bird who'll pay me big money for a beta nav."

"Will making a copy hurt Mazarin?"

"No. He'll be fine. The same."

Reed stood, shaking out his tingling fingers. "I need to talk to him for a moment, without an outlooper."

Em set the device aside and sipped their whiskey. Reed paced the back of the room. Beyond the door, someone's nails-on-a-chalkboard voice accompanied "Zip Ziddy Zoo."

<I don't want to become like those others navs.>

"You're not."

<Just the idea of me hurting you—>

"I'm alright. And I'm not going to terminate you. I want you to know that. But maybe doing this thing that Em

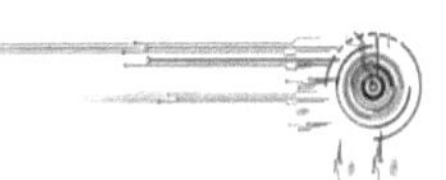

suggested is a good idea to keep Wave away. I can't afford two grand for it, though."

<Making a copy of me—though highly illegal—isn't going to affect me. I know for certain telling you to make the deal goes against my programming, but... I'm telling you to make the deal. Your safety is the only thing I care about.>

He couldn't believe this was happening. All he ever wanted was to live his life in peace. Maybe being a decoist was leading him into danger. He was no criminal. But he'd never fit in with the mainstream crowd or agreed with how society ran.

That cherry red shopping cart full of paperbacks rose in his mind. Then he pictured him and Jax at a diner dressed in bright button-ups and pork pies. Maybe the other patrons wore deco clothes or maybe they were mainstream, but no one stared. No one judged. No one looked at him like he was a reclusive, effeminate wimp. No one stared at Jax like he was a Latino gangster.

That was a world he wanted to live in and trusting in fellow decoists would get him closer to that place than the tech-reliant, faux natural society above him right now.

Reed walked back to the chair and sat. "Okay then."

Em had dipped their hands into a jar of liquiglove and held them up, letting the alginate dry to a satin sheen. They wiped an alcohol-soaked swab against Reed's inner arm, then took a tiny syringe from the desk. Clear liquid filled the chamber. After popping the cap, Em poked the needle into Reed's vein and squeezed the plunger.

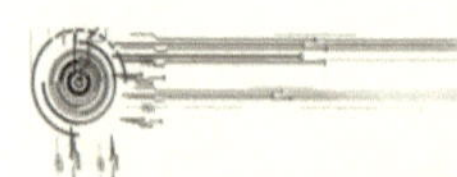

Em pushed gauze against Reed's vein and pulled out the needle. His holoscreen appeared, "INSTALLING UPDATES" flashing in the middle. The screen disappeared and a chime played, followed by a robotic female voice in his ear. <Hello, pilot. I am your navigator. We will be spending quite a bit of time together, so for the next few minutes, I will be asking you questions to get better acquainted.>

Panic surged in Reed's chest. "Where's Mazarin?"

The nav's warm voice entered his ear. <I'm still here, Reed.>

"What you're hearing is just part of the front," Em said. "There won't actually be a tutorial or any ice breakers with Ms. Default." They capped the syringe and threw it and the gloves into a cellulose bag on the desk.

Em walked back to the cabinet and fished through body parts, pulling out a handheld device with a round head.

"You going to blow dry my hair with that thing?" Reed asked.

"It was a back massager, actually." Em squatted and flipped through Reed's holoscreen, stopping on his nav settings. They splayed their fingers at odd angles and pressed them into the screen. An access box appeared, requesting a code. Em punched in a string of numbers, then picked up the back massager. They pinched open a tiny holoscreen on the back, then wrapped the front of the device in a sheet of foil.

"Are you kidding?" Jax said.

"I don't know what the guys at Wave use, but this is supposed to work."

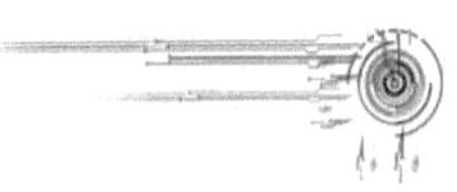

"You've never done this before?"

Em grinned. "Reed gets to be my first." The device emitted a low hum when they switched it on. They pressed it to Reed's temple and his teeth vibrated, his head filling with bees. "Might take a minute. Most people think the core program is in the forearm, under the interface, but it's not. It's in the brain."

Reed gripped the seat. He might not have much of one left after this. Maybe he was making a horrible mistake. Em had never done this before. If it didn't work, it could make Mazarin glitch even more than he already was.

Jax's mouth twisted, his brows pinched. "I had no idea you were doing this stuff."

"Come on, now," Em said. "You knew I was selling contramods in the back."

"Yeah, but not"—Jax gestured to the back massager—"this. I thought you were mostly dealing in prosthetics and giving away medical aids to old ladies."

"Yeah, and I still am, but I've had to branch out in order to keep this joint afloat. And it would be nice to move out of that dump I live in. You know."

"Could hear your neighbors through the walls at three a.m."

Reed frowned, his gaze jumping between them. Static snapped between his gums and he pressed his lips tightly together.

Em squinted at the tiny holoscreen on the back of the device. "Almost done."

He wasn't sure if there were any fillings left in his teeth, and Em seemed like the type of person who might leave in an unnecessary vibrational component just for the hell of it, but as long as it meant his debt was paid, he wouldn't complain.

The vibration stopped, a ring echoing in Reed's ears. He blinked and rubbed his temple. "Mazarin, you still there?"

<Still here, Reed.>

Em patted the back massager. "Here too. Well, sort of. His copy has been sent to my drive. Here's hoping it doesn't devolve into something less saccharine than Mazarin." They tapped Reed's forehead. "Same goes for the original. He gets hostile, come see me again. I only charge fifty bucks for a zap from an interrupter. But I won't be here next week. Going on vacation."

Reed stood, hoping his jellied legs could carry him back into the bar. "Karaoke nights are the worst."

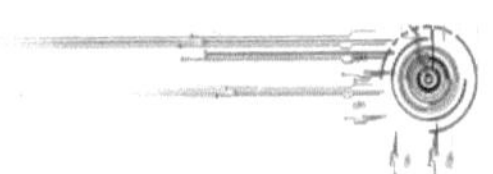

Dec 14, 2065

BELOVED DRAMA TEACHER MISSING

Kuna— Sixth period Drama students at Kuna High School were bewildered today when teacher, May Sugawara, walked out of class and simply didn't return.

"We thought it was some kind of joke," sophomore, Itzel Sandoval said. "She's always doing outrageous things for our plays and improv sessions. But we waited all period for her to come back, and she didn't."

Other students agreed that Ms. Sugawara was a little "out there", but her behavior had been increasingly strange over the past couple months.

"I think it's her nav's fault," Itzel said. "She has one of those betas. Named her Ai. And sometimes Ai would come up with funny improv settings, but most of the time they were creepy. We'd get weirded out and not want to do the scenes, but Ms. Sugawara made us... I sure hope she's okay. Maybe she'll come back to school tomorrow."

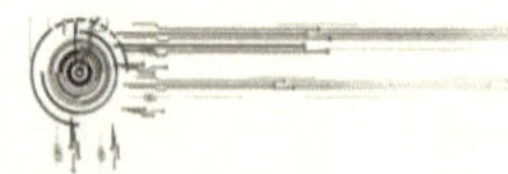

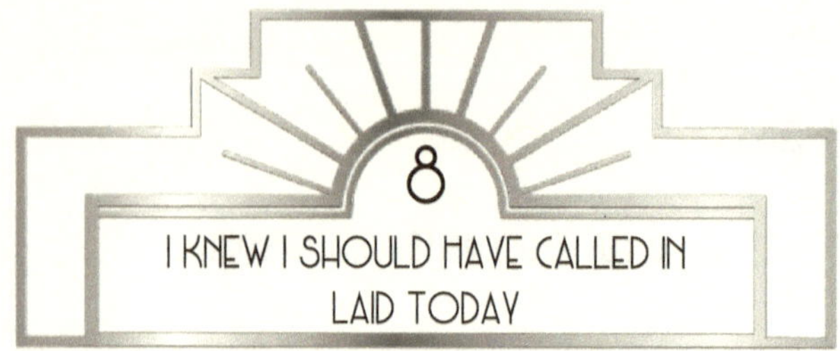

Reed

"How are you feeling?" Jax pulled on his coat and wrapped his scarf around his neck.

Grimy smears of melted snow colored the tile of the club's entryway. Reed scraped de-icing salt off the edge of his loafer. "Kind of... hopped up. Like I biked five miles or narrowly avoided a car accident."

"Ah. Like the high after sex or getting a new tattoo. I love that feeling."

"I would have expected to feel differently. Especially now that my brain's been rattled to powder. I have one less worry now, though, so I guess I can relax a little."

"So what now, daddy-o?"

Reed picked at the tape holding down the gauze on his forearm. If he was going to commit to anything with Jax, he needed to address the elephant in the room, even if he was the only one who saw it. "Do you take home a lot of people you meet here?"

Jax raised his eyebrows, distorting the "hep cat" tattoo above his brow. "No. I don't take many people home at all."

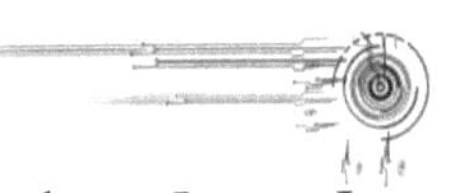

"Look, I know it's not really my business, but... I guess I need to know where I stand. You and Em had a thing."

Jax looked back at the bar, where Em stood, pouring a cocktail. "We did, yeah. Dated for a couple months. They seemed like a fun time, but it didn't work out. I'm an open book, and being with Em was like trying to romance a brick wall. Privacy is one thing. You're private, but you still share with me. I could never have a deep conversation with Em. They'd just close up and change the subject to something superficial. I felt bad breaking it off, but I needed more. That was over a year ago, anyway. You don't need to worry about me and Em."

Reed nodded. "I'm sorry for asking. I just don't want to go home with you, then decide it was a mistake."

"Well, that'll be up to you to determine, I guess, but I'm not a player, if that's what you're worried about."

Reed drew in a breath and wiped his clammy hands on his jeans. "Then let's go."

They headed across the street and climbed into Jax's chilly car. He cranked the heat and turned onto the road, following narrow one-way streets past Chinese restaurants and art supply shops. Ad rings shouted over each other, blending into one obnoxious commercial: "Come to the—vinyl warehouse, the most—delicious cookies! Easy open—pet shelter, only two minutes from—overcooking dinner again!"

Trees shrouded Jax's North End apartment building. They climbed the icy steps to the second floor and headed inside. Frankincense perfumed the tiny living room. A shelf ran along one wall, decorated in dusty candles, crystals, and bird skulls. Brightly colored illustrations of plants, snakes, fish, and beetles graced the walls in cheap cellulose frames.

"Did you draw these?" Reed asked.

"Yep. A couple were commissioned back pieces; the others no one ever wanted."

"Why ever not?" He followed the contours of a muscular snake, each scale incredibly tiny and perfect. Its yellow eye stared back.

"You want one? I'll give you a discount."

Reed tried to picture the snake on his body, winding around his bicep maybe, and couldn't do it. "They're beautiful, but it's not for me."

"Not sure I've ever met a decoist without a tattoo."

"I have a nipple ring. Does that get me any points?"

Jax smirked. "Maybe."

The black couch underneath the illustrations was lumpy and lopsided, but sitting was better than awkwardly standing in the middle of the room as Jax poured whiskey into mismatched coffee mugs.

Reed leaned back, picking out patterns in the popcorn ceiling. "I bet I'd have a tattoo—maybe even a visible one—if it was accepted."

"Would it cause problems in your life if you had one? I mean, aside from it drawing attention to yourself? I once had a client so jazzed about a new tattoo, then come in a week later telling me she needed it lasered off. Her church group— *church*—told her it was glorifying gang activity."

"What was the tattoo of?"

"A ladybug."

"The medical examiner would have a coronary if he saw my socks, let alone a tattoo. It probably wouldn't get me fired, but I don't need any more fuel to add to the 'weird technician' label. I'm just so afraid of being judged. Analyzed like I analyze the bodies on the autopsy table."

"Fuck 'em."

"The bodies?"

Jax laughed and sat down, handing Reed a mug of whiskey. "Yes, the bodies. That's sure to help your reputation."

"Definitely."

Reaching down, Jax tugged up the leg of Reed's jeans, peering at the record pattern on his socks. "Those are ace. Oh! That reminds me." He crossed to an entertainment center filled with record sleeves and slid one out, then flipped it to face Reed. Faded red and yellow blocks framed Louis Armstrong's face.

Reed took it gingerly, running his fingers over the warped, scratched cardboard. He turned it over, reading the song titles. He'd never been in a home where someone showed him their antique records—had never been in a home with antique records at all. Jax sharing this part of himself with Reed was better than sitting in the Gator Club, and that was saying something. There was an intimacy in handling another person's belongings, and the fact that Jax's interests were the same as Reed's made that connection even stronger.

"You know that medical book I showed you?" Reed asked. "You're only the second person who's seen it. And the first one to care. I knew there were other decoists in the city, but 'getting out' for me consists of a weekly trip to Albertsons."

Jax took the Louis album and slid the record from the sleeve. He placed it on an antique player on the entertainment center and turned it on. Crackling static and dreamy trumpets filled the room. He flopped back onto the couch. Vivid chrysanthemum petals unfurled out of the neck of his yellow cable knit sweater. "Have you always been like this? Keeping to yourself so much?"

"There was a time when I was a little more social. I used to live in Buhl and had some family around, a couple friends. They'd kick me in the ass to go do things with them. I'd slowly been amassing a collection of antique books and records. I had a pair of wingtips too. I didn't wear them out of the house, but I liked putting them on at home. Then I met my ex. I thought he was deco at first because he liked colorful shirts and he had a couple of cassette tapes. We eventually moved in together, which was a huge mistake. He realized how into deco things I was, and used it against me. Anytime we were a little low on money, he'd blame it on my book collection, even though I bought most of them before I met him. When he was mad at me, he'd threaten to tell all our friends about what an 'extremist' I was. Which was mortifying."

"That sucks."

He considered mentioning how—after finally working up the courage to go to therapy for his anxiety—Ken decided that

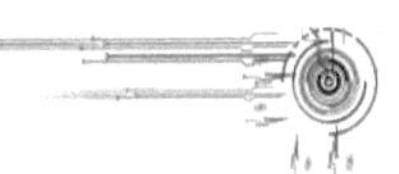

was a fine excuse to call Reed crazy at every opportunity. But that was more than he wanted to reveal to Jax right now. "The final straw was when he lost his job. He came home, already pissed at being let go, to find a package on the step. It was an antique book I'd won on an auction site a week before. When I got home, he'd smashed all my records and dumped all my paperbacks in the trash." Reed's face contorted. "There were ripped pages all over the kitchen floor."

"What a dickhead. If he was so mad about your spending and worried about money, why didn't he demand you sell the books instead of destroying them?"

"Because it wasn't really about the money. He just didn't like them. Didn't like me the way I was. So I moved to Boise— a bigger city where I didn't know anyone—and started over. But without any family or friends around to force me to be social, I just turned in on myself, not wanting to do anything but come home to my collection I was trying to build back up again."

"I can't even imagine. I've always had support with my interests and identity. Some of my clearest memories are being a little kid, on vacation to visit family in Mexico, and tracing all the colorful, blurry tattoos on my abuelo's arms. Mexico is like another world. So colorful—the buildings, the music, the people. They aren't decoists, though. That's an American thing. So I never realized as a kid that there was a negative connotation around being colorful and tattooed. As far as I'm concerned, though, it's in my blood and I don't care if mainstream society doesn't like it." Jax leaned back and sighed.

"It does make it hard to go certain places, though. I went into a coffee shop yesterday, and the old lady behind the counter wouldn't serve me. Told me she'd call the cops if I didn't leave."

Reed shook his head. "Well, I happen to think you're the bee's knees."

Jax smiled. His fingers grazed Reed's wrist. "So, you need to go home and feed your cat anytime soon?" His black liner was applied heavier tonight, smudged and smoky, accenting the tiny music note tattooed at the edge of his eye. A lock of dark hair had escaped captivity from his pompadour, curling across his cheekbone.

Reed swallowed. "She already ate. I think she'll be okay without me for a while."

"Well, if you want me to call you a cab, just say so."

Reed traced his finger over the 'R' on Jax's pinkie, then the 'E' on his ring finger. He caressed the tiny line art moons, roses, and dots on his distal segments, below his black lacquered nails. "I bet these hurt."

Jax snatched Reed's hand and pulled him forward. "They did." His scent—vetiver and myrrh and sandalwood—rolled against Reed's senses like the fog of a dark forest, and he was hopelessly lost in it.

How long had it been since something had felt so right? They weren't criminals, extremists, or gangsters. They weren't part of the scuzzy underbelly of a so-called pristine society. He and Jax weren't hurting anyone. They were just two men trying to live their lives the way that made them the happiest... and Jax was the epitome of everything Reed wanted. He was saxophone in a hazy bar, the grain on a shellac record, and patent leather spectator shoes. Knowing that not only was Jax kind and considerate, but a colorful, kindred spirit against the background radiation of oatmeal couches and white walls, made Reed's desire achingly strong.

He parted his lips, heart pounding, and Jax seized the invitation. Reed kissed him back fiercely, stubble scraping across his chin. Jax's tongue prodded his open mouth, his hands sliding through Reed's hair. A spring jabbed Reed in the back as he leaned into the couch, adrift in a sea of cologne and cool piano. He slid his hand between Jax's legs before he could talk himself out of it. He wanted this, and he wasn't going to let his worrying brain ruin it. Jax's breath, warm and whiskey-laced, puffed against Reed's neck, his calloused fingers eagerly working under clothing.

"Jax..." Reed breathed.

"Yeah?"

"Your couch is really lumpy."

Jax barked a laugh. "I know. Want to go back to my bed?"

"Yes."

Strong hands pulled Reed to his feet. He turned for the hall, but Jax pressed against him, backing him into the wall. Whispering low in Reed's ear, Jax said, "You'd better get out of that shirt before I break off all the buttons."

Breath catching, Reed silently cursed his trembling hands as he struggled to push the buttons through their holes.

"Want some help? I can do this one." He yanked open Reed's belt and popped the snap on his jeans, pushing them down.

"You're not making this easier." Reed undid the last button and ripped off his shirt. His pant legs caught around his ankles as Jax pulled him toward the bedroom.

Moonlight cut through a gap in the curtain, carving a silver path across the rug and purple sheets on the bed. Skull votives hung on the wall, flanking a starburst mirror. Tiny sketches— insects and plants and scrolling banners—were tucked into the frame.

"The gothic thing is working in your favor," Reed said.

"Oh? You like it?"

"Yeah. Ginchy."

Jax pushed Reed onto the bed then pulled off his sweater, exposing a tattooed torso teeming with flora and fauna that would have made Thoreau jealous.

Threads of light weaved across Jax's lashes and flushed cheeks and softened the chiseled contours of his face. The solidness of his muscles was comforting in their strength rather than intimidating; brawny arms that could envelop Reed and banish his anxieties like evicted ghosts.

Reed traced the branch of a maple tree on Jax's ribs and the bill of a crow on his abdomen, Jax's bronze skin softer than the paper in Reed's antique tomes and more beautiful than the drawings. "If you were a book, I'd read you every day."

Jax kicked off the rest of his clothing. "And if you were dessert, I'd ask for seconds." He nibbled at Reed's earlobe, then took Reed's hand and pushed it between his legs.

Reed's breath quickened. "You're off the cob."

"And dizzy with you. You're..." His words disintegrated into monosyllables, his hips moving in time with Reed's strokes.

He slid down, dragged his lips across Reed's stomach, then went lower, gripping Reed and leaving exploratory kisses. He took Reed into his mouth and Reed gasped, leaning back into the pillows.

Illustrated fingers slid across Reed's thigh, leaving pink contrails in their wake. The white light from Reed's interface shined on Jax's glossy hair, falling into his eyes.

Mazarin was in sleep mode, wasn't he? It was too late to tell him now, if he wasn't. But the nav anticipated things and acted accordingly. He surely would have seen this coming and gone into standby.

Reed moaned and squeezed his eyes shut, concentrating on Jax. He wasn't going to let worries seep through the cracks in his enjoyment.

Sitting up and reaching across Reed, Jax pulled open a drawer in the nearby nightstand, rattling the knick-knacks on top. He pulled out a bottle of lube, a pair of furry handcuffs, and several objects that were too hard to make out in the dark.

Reed raised his eyebrows, breath shallow. "I'm—I'm not trying to escape, just so you know."

"I'm just looking for the condoms." Jax chuckled. "I think they're still in a bag in the kitchen." He slid from the bed and headed for the door.

"Hey... Can you put on another record? Sounds silly to ask, but I've never had sex to jazz before."

Jax smiled. "Of course, daddy-o."

Mazarin

The steady tick of Jax's analog clock on the bedside table couldn't quite be drowned out by his and Reed's combined snores. I increased my receivers to full volume, the sound of blood gushing through Reed's arteries washing all the other noise away.

Though I'd promised not to be present for Reed's date, I'd peeked through my proverbial fingers several times, just to check that everything was okay. The last thing I wanted was to be woken up by another callous mod dealer who didn't understand Reed's anxiety.

I happened to check in at just the moment Jax leaned in for a kiss as they sat on a couch in his apartment. Reed's heart was in overdrive, his body a quaking mess. I went back into standby, silently cheering at the fireworks exploding in Reed's brain. After that, it was plain to know what had transpired just by monitoring his bodily reactions.

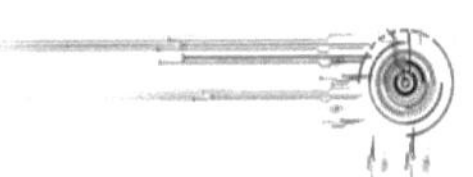

But as the night deepened and Reed fell asleep, a bitter feeling swallowed me—the ugliest blacks and saddest grays. Reed was happy, which was all I ever wanted, but thinking about my pilot snuggled contentedly against Jax made me want to go into standby and never come out.

Why did I feel like that? I couldn't make Reed happy the way Jax could. Jax had a face and childhood memories and warm skin. Jax could hug Reed with his tattooed arms and cook him breakfast in the morning. Jax could protect Reed from drunken bar patrons and punch people who called him a wimp. What could I do? Other than annoy him?

I was only a navigator, and no amount of love I showered on Reed would make up for the fact that I wasn't human. I wasn't even real.

I had let Em take a copy of myself—a criminal act!—to help keep Reed safe. I'd do everything in my power to protect Reed.

But it didn't matter.

I wasn't even real.

Reed

Gray light pierced Reed's eyes as his alarm chimed in his ear. He blinked, fumbling with his interface to find the off button. Jax lay next to him, one forested arm thrown over his face. Reed snuggled against him, running his fingers through Jax's chest hair.

Stirring, Jax rolled over and opened his eyes. His shiny hair was a tangled mess, squashed against his forehead. Pushing it out of his eyes, he said, "You look happier than anyone has a right to first thing in the morning. That smile for me?"

"Yes."

<I'm so sorry to interrupt>—Mazarin's voice came out matter-of-fact, lacking its usual warmth—<but you're not going to have time to drive home before work this morning.>

Reed nuzzled Jax's neck. "That's alright. I'm sure Jax will let me use his shower. Right?"

Jax wrapped his arms around Reed. "I dunno. I kinda like you dirty."

<The only clothes you have to wear are the ones from last night.>

That was a problem. Going anywhere besides the Gator Club in deco clothes would be mortifying, and that went three-fold for work. Ambrose would have a heart attack if Reed walked into the autopsy suite with that bubblegum pink camp shirt on. They might even fire him for "suspicion of illegal activity." Even if they couldn't find anything he'd done wrong, things would never be the same there again. The coworkers who disliked him would have all the more reason to, and he would never hear the end of Olive's enthusiasm for him being himself—he wasn't sure which was worse.

"I can't go to work in deco clothes." Reed sat up and put on his glasses. Mazarin was right; he'd never make it home in

time to shower and change without ending up late to work, and Ambrose abhorred tardiness unless it was a life or death situation.

A quick glance at Jax's little analog alarm clock told Reed there wasn't time to stop by a Walmart for a new shirt.

Jax rubbed his face and stretched. "What about your undershirt? It's just white."

"Too see-through. Having people see my nipple ring would be worse than showing up in a pink shirt."

"I'm sure I have something you can wear."

"I'm going to end up wearing your whole wardrobe here pretty soon."

"Well, what's the fun of being gay if you can't wear each other's clothes?"

Reed shook his head, heading for the bathroom. After a quick shower and a cup of too-hot coffee, he donned his jeans and the black V-neck tee Jax offered. It wasn't an outfit he'd ever wear to work, but it would have to do. Maybe he could change into his scrubs before anyone noticed.

With a kiss goodbye and a promise to call, Reed rode in a taxi through the morning traffic—it was so much worse downtown—and made it to work on time. A meatwagon was backed up to the side entrance of the examiner's: an unmarked white van with tinted windows that suggested if you weren't already dead when you entered it, you would be pretty soon.

Olive and the other secretary, Arlie, stood outside the squat brick building, their icy breath billowing around their faces.

Olive cocked her head, eyebrows pinched together as Reed stepped out of the cab and crossed the sidewalk.

"Morning," Olive said. "What happened to your car?"

"Uh..." His gaze jumped between the two women. "Wouldn't start. Gets like that sometimes when it's cold."

"Oh, that stinks. The cab must have cost a fortune, your commute is so long. You should have called me for..." Olive's gaze dropped to Reed's pants. "Are you wearing blue jeans?"

His face flushed. He scrambled for an excuse but wasn't sure what to say. "What are you two even—"

Olive squeaked, hands over her mouth. "You went out last night! To your secret club. And you took a cab this morning. You got laid!"

Reed hunched into his coat, trying to avoid Arlie's intense gaze. The woman snatched up every tidbit of gossip like a starving vulture. "You said it, not me."

"It's obvious. I've been there, so I know. Not the secret club part, but—"

"What kind of secret club?" Arlie dug her taupe nails into his coat sleeve, her antiseptic-like deodorant assaulting his nostrils.

"Illuminati. Now that I've told you, I have to kill you." Reed pulled his arm away, only to have Olive grab it.

"So is Mr. Sexy and Dangerous tattooed below the waist too?"

"He's not dangerous." There was a harder edge to his voice than he intended, but the women seemed not to notice.

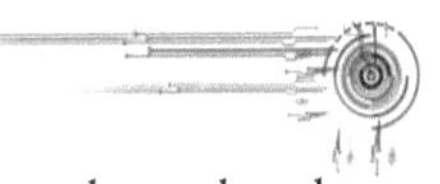

Arlie squinted. "Tattoos..." She rubbed her plump hands together, either from the cold or because she'd just learned several juicy facts that would keep her sustained for a while. "It's freezing out here. I'm going back inside."

Olive watched her go, then turned back, hands in her pockets. "I shouldn't have mentioned that, huh?"

"Oh, surely there will be something more interesting to talk about around the water cooler than how I got laid by a dangerous tattooed man I met at a secret club." Reed sighed.

"I'm sorry! I'm just so excited for you. I'll try to feed her some misinformation before she spreads it around."

"She still thinks my name is 'Rick' so I'm probably safe. What were you two doing out here, anyway?"

"Oh! Yes. I don't think you need to worry about Arlie's gossip today because that's juicier than you are." Olive pointed at the white van by the side doors.

"Why? A celebrity die or something?"

"No. Suicide, but supposedly his *nav* told him to do it. Crazy, right?"

Reed clenched his jaw. "Did he have a beta?"

<Of course he did.> Mazarin's tone dripped with loathing. <Betas are the only ones doing these things.>

"Yeah," Olive said. "And remember when we found those transcripts on your interface between you and your nav? Yonder corpse had them too, but he printed them all out and they were strewn all over his house. Cops said it was creepy as hell. All the messages from the nav were stuff like: 'Kill yourself.

You're a worthless sack of shit. You're not contributing to society. Kill yourself. Kill yourself. I'll show you how to do it.'"

Goosebumps erupted on the back of Reed's neck. "Guess I'd better get inside then."

"Your nav hasn't been saying stuff like that, has it?"

"No. And he wouldn't." He knew that for certain after last night. "What about Langley? She was complaining about how rude her nav was. Has it said anything like that to her?" If so, Reed might need to introduce her to Em.

"Oh, no. Langley's been fine. She texted me and said she's getting along with him much better after you emailed her those instructions on how to turn down his suggestions."

"That's good." He didn't know Langley well, but it was easy to sympathize with her navigator woes, and he didn't want to see her on the slab next. He crossed the walk and gripped the door handle.

"Some people from Wave are here too," Olive said.
Red stiffened. "What?"
"Yeah, I guess they want to make sure it was really a suicide. They were at the police station too."

His fingers grew numb against the icy door handle. Wave didn't have any right to snoop around. Maybe they were really here for him. After that phone call from the day before and a repairman possibly abducted from Reed's home, he wouldn't doubt it. Or maybe it was a case of them trying to smuggle a body away before anyone realized the beta navs were dangerous. It was a little late for that now, though, if Olive and Arlie knew about the transcripts in the man's house. Pretty

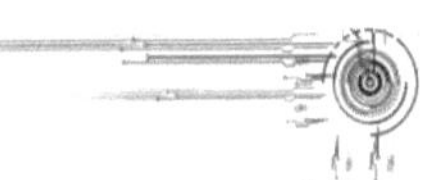

soon everyone would know. Just like soon everyone would know he was sleeping with a decoist.

"I knew I should have called in laid today."

Maybe everyone would be too distracted with Wave and crazy navs to gossip about him, even if he *was* dressed in blue jeans and a V-neck shirt that smelled like Jax's apartment.

But what if Wave noticed him? They might linger in the lobby all day, waiting for him and Ambrose to finish their examination. He was walking around with contramod software inside him. Em had said an outlooper would only detect the faux default nav, but there was no guarantee it would work as promised. Maybe Wave had more high-tech outloopers that could get to Mazarin. They'd see that not only was Reed using illegal software, but he also had a beta nav who could potentially become homicidal. Being declared a dirty decoist criminal would be preferable to getting ushered away into some torture room by Wave technicians.

<Reed, you must stay calm. Go about your day. You often worry that people's attention and thoughts are on you, when ninety-five percent of the time, they are wrapped up in their own concerns.>

"It's that other five percent I'm worried about." He turned to Olive, staring into her face. "We're friends, right?"

Olive brightened. "Of course!"

"Then you can't tell anyone I have a beta nav, okay? Especially those guys from Wave. As far as you know, I have the default like everyone else."

"I don't understand. Why not? It seems like this would be a great time to ask them questions about the problems you've had with yours."

"No!" He hissed, gripping her arms. "Please." Pushing up his coat sleeve, he opened his holoscreen and pointed to the menu. "See? Just like yours, okay?"

Olive's mouth parted. "What happened to your new menu?"

Arlie's round figure appeared at the glass door. Reed flipped off his holoscreen and pulled down his sleeve. "Please don't say anything about my beta. It could be very bad for me. Like, you-might-never-see-me-again bad."

"Oh my god. Okay, I promise I won't. Are you okay? You're really freaking me out."

"I will be as long as those Wave techs leave me alone. We can have lunch together, okay? I'll tell you whatever you want about my date with Jax."

"I'd love to hear about that, but you don't need to bribe me." She tucked a lock of hair behind her ear, parenthesis of frown lines around her glossy lips. "We *are* friends, and I don't want to see something happen to you. Now, c'mon." Olive opened the door and Arlie backed away, heading back for a half-circle reception desk.

Northrup, one of the forensic pathologists who had a personality as pleasant as an STD, leaned against the wall, a sneer on his face. "So, you had quite the night last night, huh? I didn't even know you were attracted to *living* people."

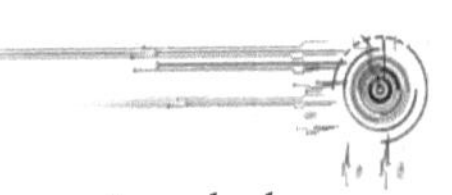

Reed's heart pounded and he gave Arlie a pointed glare. She ignored him, settling into her chair and typing on her keyboard. Olive whacked Northrop in the chest and spat something in Korean.

Northrup put up his hands. "Hey, far from me to judge if the nerdy tech is getting plowed by a deco gangster."

Balling his trembling hands, Reed took a step toward Northrop. *I'm not a pushover.* "Isn't it hard for you and Arlie to breathe with your heads so far up other people's asses?"

Arlie huffed and Northrop's jaw fell open.

"Stay outta my business, and get outta my way. I have work to do." Reed shouldered past him and strode down the hall, his heart thundering.

<Yes! Way to go, Reed!>

When he entered the autopsy suite, he stopped short. Ambrose stood in the office, talking to several people. One was a middle-aged white man with something on his wrist that looked an awful lot like an outlooper.

<Stay calm. They won't know anything is amiss if you don't act like it.>

He took a breath and strode inside the office, keeping his eye contact to himself and retrieving his scrubs. After changing, he set out the forceps, bone saw, skull breaker, enterotome, jars, swabs, and tongue tie, aligning everything just so even though Ambrose never cared about the order as long as they were in reach for himself or Reed.

It was a good thing they used a handheld camera for body photos. Some coroners and technicians used their nav's optical nanobots for taking pictures—convenient, but also controversial because there was more leeway for the images to be altered or filed improperly compared to a physical, impartial camera. One person's brain might simply register things differently than another's, which could make all the difference in a court case. A handheld camera was objective.

Plus, there was no telling if Mazarin could still take and store photos with the fronting software, and having the wrong interface menu pop-up during the exam would be awful.

Reed stopped before the shrouded body and turned on the camera, pinching open the holoscreen on the back until it was several feet across and hovering above the gurney. The quicker the autopsy was over, the sooner Wave would be gone and the only things left to stress about would be everything else in his life.

Peeling back the sheet exposed a forty-something man, his waxy skin lavender-gray. A gaping slash ran across his throat. Crusted blood clung to the layers of flayed flesh, the inside of the wound crimson and jellied. A metallic tang with the cloying scent of early decomposition hung in the air.

"Gee, cause of death is going to be tricky on this one." He aimed the camera at the laceration and snapped shots from various angles, then moved to the man's placid face, his blue lips and receding hairline.

Something terrible must have gone on in this man's head to make him slice his throat. Reed couldn't imagine what his nav had to have said to make him think this was the best choice. He wondered if the nav had named themselves, like Mazarin

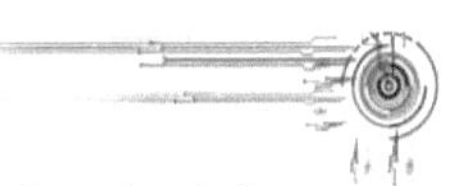

did. Selected a voice that would please their pilot. And then... what? What did this guy do to make the nav turn on him? Maybe he was a pedophile. Or an arsonist. Or maybe he just clipped his toenails at the dining table and scratched his nuts while watching football.

Did Reed do things that annoyed Mazarin? Things that were enough to kill for?

That was ridiculous. Mazarin loves him.

But as he peeled back the rest of the sheet and snapped photos of the man's faded black tee and bloodied hands, memories of all kinds of uncouth things arose in his mind. Blatantly lying to people to get out of a conversation, watching porn, missing his aim at the toilet when drunk, and eating more than the recommended serving size of ice cream in one sitting.

Surely those things were the price a nav paid for living inside someone's head, though.

Reed snapped more pictures, trying to imagine being a self-aware navigator stuck in this man's mind. Cringing as he wiped potato chip crumbs on the armrest of his easy chair, farted in bed, and ogled people in line at the grocery store.

He wrinkled his nose, wanting to ask Mazarin if he was disgusting, but someone might overhear.

Reed tried to steady his hands as he took more photos. He wouldn't be surprised if Mazarin had dreams for a body. For a life he'd live if he weren't stuck with Reed. Maybe the constant pressure of keeping Reed de-stressed and functioning in public was wearing the nav down little by little, until one day he'd snap and beg for Reed to enter a suicide pact with him.

When Ambrose touched his shoulder, he jumped. The medical examiner gave him a tight smile. "Reed, I'm sure you noticed we have some visitors today."

"Yes, they're a little more alive than the visitors we usually have back here."

The woman from Wave, staring at extra tools on a tray, looked up, her complexion green. Reed pointed at the tray. "These are brain knives. Bet you can't guess what they're used for... They work great for buttering toast too."

She swallowed and rubbed her hands on her slacks. "Excuse me." Turning, she strode across the room and pushed open the door, then hurried down the hall, a hand over her mouth.

Reed suppressed a grin. One down.

The middle-aged man with the outlooper on his wrist stared at the brain knife, nonplussed, then held out his hand. "Phil Rice."

He didn't have any qualms grasping Reed's alginate-gloved hand, but instead of shaking it, the man held tightly, squinting into Reed's face. He said, "Mr. Rothwell! We spoke on the phone yesterday, didn't we?"

Breath catching, Reed froze, wide-eyed. This guy already knew about his beta nav because he'd talked to him about Mazarin's problems.

He forced words from his throat. "You must have me confused with someone else."

"Nah, I would recognize that sardonic voice again. And you *are* Reed Rothwell, right?"

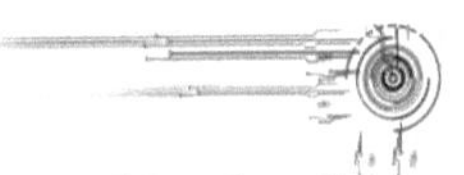

"Yes, but I know for a fact there are two Reed Rothwells in the city. I'm always getting packages for the other one, and let me tell you, he has the worst taste in underwear."

Rice gave a slight chuckle and dropped Reed's hand. "You didn't call me yesterday about issues with your beta nav?"

"I don't have a beta nav."

Scratching his dark hair, Phil glanced toward the autopsy suite doors, then at the glowing screen in Reed's arm. "Mind if I take a peek? It's just, your voice sounds so familiar, and same name and everything. And if you *do* have a beta, I sure would hate for it to still be having problems when I'm right here, and could do something about it."

Sweat stood out on Reed's brow. He clutched the camera tightly in his trembling hands so he wouldn't drop it.

You'd do something about it, alright. "You don't want to check on your partner? Make sure she's okay?"

"I'm pretty sure I'd be kicked out of the ladies room. She'll be fine. Why don't you let me take a look while I wait for her to come back?"

Trying to steady his hands, Reed opened his holoscreen, for a horrible second wondering if it would show his new one. But it was the clunky, big-buttoned menu he'd known for years before the upgrade.

"Hmm." Phil pressed a button on the device on his wrist and aimed it at Reed's eye.

This was happening entirely too often lately. "W-what are you doing?"

"Just want to talk to your nav for a sec. What's its name?"

Reed swallowed down Mazarin's name. "It doesn't have one. It's just a computer program."

"Everyone gives their nav a name."

"Not me. I never have and never will. I don't like AI."

"Navigator, what's your name?"

A robotic female voice whispered in his ear, simultaneously coming from the outlooper. <I am Navigator V3106.>

"How long have you been Reed's navigator?"

<I am Navigator V3106.>

Rice frowned. "I asked you a question."

<The current time is nine oh-seven a.m. on December fifteenth, twenty sixty-five.>

"That's not what I asked you." Rice narrowed his gaze, leveling it on Reed. "What's wrong with your nav?"

<I am Navigator V3106.>

Reed's head threatened to float away, and he gripped the counter behind him, bumping the tray of tools. He was going to disappear. They'd take him away and he'd never see his den again. He'd never hold another book, listen to another record, or pet his cat. He'd never see Jax again. Lying in Jax's strong embrace, cocooned in frankincense-scented sheets, the dark and warmth and contentment of last night. Never again.

"Reed, are you okay?" Ambrose asked.

"Yes, Mr. Rothwell. You don't seem to be okay and neither does your navigator," Phil said. "I have some more equipment in our van. You could lie down in the back while I assess what's going wrong with your nav. After all, even if you don't have a

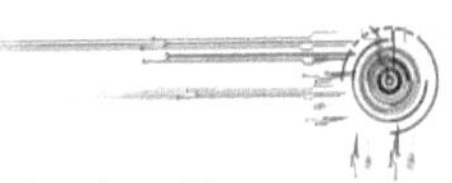

beta, sometimes the default ones have issues. And as I'm sure you can appreciate, the less malfunctioning navs we have out in the world, the better."

Reed's heart jackhammered and he fought for air. The white walls of the autopsy suite closed in on him. There was nothing he could do to get out of this situation. He couldn't pretend nothing was wrong—not with his anxiety through the roof and his body giving it away. And not with Em's software making a mess of things.

Definitely not worth two grand.

Someone gripped him by the arm; he started to jerk away, then realized it was Ambrose, leading him to a chair.

A feminine voice, similar to the default nav but less robotic, said, <Reed, your blood sugar is very low. I recommend drinking grape juice or eating fruit, such as a banana or raisins.>

Mazarin? But how did he get past Em's software? An outlooper wasn't supposed to detect him. "Y-yes, that must be it. I didn't have breakfast."

"Navigator, I'm still waiting for an answer to my question." Phil pointed the outlooper closer to Reed's head, as though that would get him the right response quicker.

"Is this necessary?" Ambrose asked. "You didn't come here to interrogate my technician's navigator, and as far as I can see, it seems to be working fine. Perhaps if its responses aren't satisfactory, this is a flaw in your programming you should bring up to your superiors on your own time."

Phil ignored him. "What is your date of install, Navigator?"

<August twelfth, twenty fifty.>

Phil's gaze drifted over Reed. "What is Reed's current emotional state?"

Shit. Please don't tell him that.

<Reed's blood sugar is very low. Symptoms include tremors, sweating, heart palpitations, and light-headedness. I recommend drinking grape juice or eating fruit, such as a banana or raisins.>

"Hmm." After lowering the outlooper and turning it off, the engineer put his hands on his hips. "Well, maybe you ought to go eat something, sport."

Ambrose waved Phil away and put a hand on Reed's shoulder. "Why don't you go into the break room and get something in your system? Sit down until you feel better." He lowered his voice. "I'll deal with this asshole."

"Thanks." Reed strode to the door, shaking his tingling fingers and forcing himself to take deep breaths. He slipped through the hall without running into anyone and turned into the bathroom. The scuffed, gray-white stall door squealed as he closed it. Leaning against the cold metal, he put his face in his hands.

"You saved my ass back there. Thank you."

Mazarin's warm voice entered his ear. <I'm sorry it took so long. I had to break the fronting software a little bit. What a douchebag. He was making me upset.>

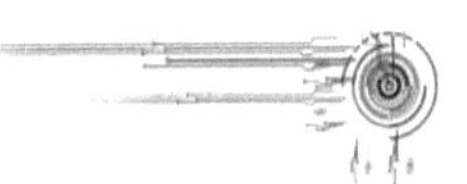

"I don't think Ambrose likes him much either. Do you think that guy knows I'm full of shit?"

<I don't know. I have a hard time interpreting the reactions of others since I don't have their brain pattern data to read. But I have no doubt he will try to look up another Reed Rothwell in the city.>

"What do I do?"

<Don't get into his van, for starters.>

"They're going to make me disappear. They'll figure out I'm lying, then either turn me in for having a contramod, or they'll lock me up in a lab like some test animal."

<Breathe. I'm working on making a fake profile for another Reed Rothwell, and scrubbing all traces of your real home address from the web. I'll send this false address to Wave with my next diagnostic scan and it should update on whatever files they have for you. It won't be fool-proof, but might be enough to throw him off. I hope.>

"Thank you. What would I do without you?"

Mazarin's voice lowered. <You'd be living your life without interference from Wave.>

"True, but that doesn't mean I'm not grateful to you." He left the stall and placed his hands on the sink, staring into the mirror. "I need some tea and some extra sick days."

Blowing out a breath, he stood and walked to the door. "Let's get this over with."

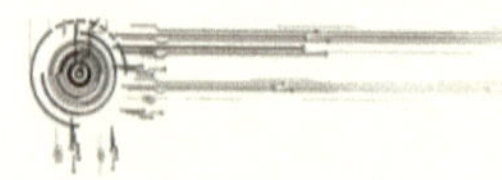

9

I'M NOT A PUSHOVER

Mazarin

The camera, tucked into a corner, a dusty cobweb dangling from the lens, swiveled at my command. The high view gave me the sensation of floating, lording over the living room like some lesser god and exacting judgment on the oatmeal-colored couch and bare wall where the TV used to be.

I switched views. Now I was in the hall, keeping watch over the pesky basement door. Then in the bedroom, hovering over the carefully made bed and the pressboard dresser Reed had spent hours struggling to put together with instructions only written in Swedish.

Outside, wind rattled the rain gutters; dead leaves tumbled below the camera under the eaves, sticking to lumps of frozen snow at the edges of the driveway.

In the den, the corner of a bookshelf obstructed the right side of my view, but I was able to angle it enough to peer down at the wingback chair and bourbon bar.

I took in every view at once—dead grass, crusty snow, Sero sleeping in a basket of folded laundry, a stale and forgotten bag of potato chips on top of the fridge, a golf club by the front

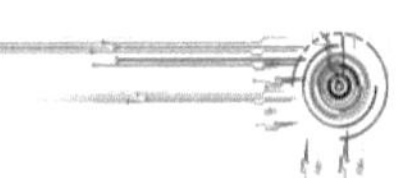

door, and Jax's phone number scrawled on half a napkin on the kitchen counter. I could see everything. And I'd figured it out all on my own.

What a wonderful surprise it would be for Reed! I could keep watch over the house at all times now. No more of Reed brandishing fruit knives at suspicious hallway shadows. No more of me being petrified and screaming for Reed to wake up because someone was in the house. I could call the police in an instant and even give them a description of the suspect. The security alarms weren't set up, but I could set off the smoke alarms. Fire or not, it would wake Reed up if need be and surely scare any intruders away.

The house wasn't an ideal body, and neither were the cleaner bots I'd commandeered, but I now had ten extra eyes and external tools at my disposal. Though I couldn't think of a place to be that felt better than in Reed's mind, being one with the house gave me a sense of freedom I'd previously lacked. When I wanted to look a certain way, I could do it—no trying to make out fuzzy objects from Reed's peripheral vision. When I wanted to "walk" down the hall and manipulate an object, I could command a bot to do my bidding. Turning up or down the thermostat, locking and unlocking doors, I could do it all. Marvelous! Maybe in the spring I could even take control of the lawn mower and cut the grass.

I couldn't let the novelty of my achievement distract me, though. Reed might need me. He'd sweated through the armpits of his scrubs, muscles tense, as he assisted Ambrose with the autopsy. That Wave engineer, Phil Rice, hadn't been allowed in during the examination, but his presence in the building was still unnerving Reed.

I stared at a lost sock—patterned in dachshunds—behind the bedroom dresser, simultaneously watching Reed weigh the corpse's heart in a scale in the autopsy suite.

<Everything will be fine. Your fake Reed Rothwell is all set up. My imitation of your voice on his message box is pretty good, if I do say so. Should Phil Rice try to call him, I can respond. That ought to throw him off your trail.>

Reed picked up the heart, then glanced at the suite entrance and whispered. "Thank you. Don't suppose you can do anything about Arlie?"

She stood behind the doors, face obscured by the glare of overhead fluorescents.

<Her email address is in your contacts. Shall I sign her up for half a dozen unsavory mailing lists? Might keep her busy for a while.>

Reed paused. "As delightful as that sounds... no. Better not. I just want to keep my head down and get this over with so I can go home and decompress. I've had way too much excitement lately."

<Yes. Good and bad.> I itched to tell Reed about the working house cameras, but my poor pilot had enough to think about. New love, inclusion in blue deco scene, suspicious corporation engineers, burgling repair people, and software glitches.

I studied Reed's hands, the lattice of pale blue veins visible under his alginate gloves. I'd watched those hands do all sorts of things. What it must have been like for Jax to touch them. I was closer to Reed than anyone ever could be, and I would never touch those hands.

Sometimes I said the right thing, which inexplicably ended up being the wrong thing. And maybe my software had been glitchy lately and I was chatty and had too many feelings. But one thing I was certain of was what Reed loved. I may never be able to touch him, but I could give him a wonderful gift. Reed had said he was grateful for me, which was very encouraging. Not only would this gift convey my care and affection, but maybe more would be reciprocated.

The delivery woman was currently walking up the icy drive to the front door, carrying a package. I was waiting for her.

Reed

Olive idled in the icy driveway, her elbow resting on the little steering wheel. "Are you sure you'll be okay? You don't want me to come in for a while?"

The seat belt snapped up its track as Reed unbuckled it and reached for the door handle. He wasn't okay, but he didn't want to talk about his fears that he might be next on the slab.

"I'm fine. That Wave engineer only glared at me six times after lunch, Mazarin only tried to reassure me another twenty, and Arlie only came to the doors of the autopsy suite to sneak a peek four times."

"I hope those guys have their hands so full with this suicide that they forget about you."

"Yes, if only everyone would." He glanced at Olive. "Um, not you, though. I appreciate you having my back... even if you were the one who blurted out my involvement with Jax within earshot of Arlie."

"I'm sorry. You sure shut her up good, though. Northrup too. When are you going to see him again? Jax, I mean?"

"I don't know. This weekend, maybe." Reed's stomach fluttered at the prospect.

"You sure getting involved with him and all these decoists is safe? I mean, look what happened today because of it. If you hadn't gotten illegal software installed, you wouldn't have had such a nerve-wracking day."

"Not true. It might have been the only thing that saved me from being ushered into a Wave van."

Olive's mouth pulled to one side. "You can't really believe that Wave is making people with betas disappear. That's just stupid. Even if they can't uninstall the software remotely, it's only twenty-five people. Why couldn't they just show up at your door and say, 'Sorry, the betas have too many glitches. Give us five minutes and we'll give you back the previous version.' I mean, a *decoist* told you these rumors, right? Of course they'd say something like that."

The butterflies in Reed's stomach turned to wasps. He scowled. "Just because decoists hate corporate tech doesn't mean they aren't right."

She picked at an airbag warning sticker on the door frame. "Well, no one has approached Langley yet. She was really unhappy until you emailed her those instructions from Wave. So talking to them *helped*. I don't know why it wouldn't help you in this situation too. And... you're kind of paranoid. Just in general. You're paranoid. You worry unnecessarily. I don't want shady people putting stories into your head just so they can squeeze money from you for contramods or something."

Beta navs going against their programming was real, and there was now hard evidence that some of them were hostile toward their pilots. Em's software hadn't done as promised to keep him safe, but he refused to believe he'd make a mistake going to them.

"I think your stereotypical assumptions about decoists are clouding your judgment," he said.

Olive let out an exasperated sigh. "Remember when that rumor circulated about criminal investigators being mailed ricin, and you thought you were next, even though there was no evidence of pathologists being targeted? And you let your paper mail pile up for a week before I had to come over and open it for you?"

Reed looked away. "That's not the same thing."

She squeezed his arm. "Look, I bet Jax wouldn't steer you wrong on purpose—he seems great from what you told me— but I don't think I'd trust these other people, especially if they want your money. A dealer is going to tell you anything to make a sale. I'm not trying to make you feel bad. I know these hip alligators are your kind of people, or whatever; I just want you to be careful."

He nodded. "Thanks for the ride. See you tomorrow."

A bitter wind stung Reed's cheeks as he left the car; his loafers crunched through a hard crust of snow as he headed to the front door. Jax calling him for an impromptu karaoke night date seemed like so long ago. He pushed up his sleeve and held his interface near the lock sensor on the door. It remained white. Em's software must have been getting in the way.

He'd need to click through half a dozen menu screens before arriving at the hidden beta screen, just as he had earlier when he'd wanted to show Olive a photo of the pink camp shirt he'd worn the night before.

Maybe listening to Em *had* been a bad idea. All this had done was make technology he loathed even more frustrating. Em could probably uninstall the software. And they'd probably charge twice as much.

The sensor on the door switched to green, but his arm hadn't been anywhere near the sensor. "Mazarin, was that you?"

An edge of delight cut through Mazarin's voice. <Yes. I figured you wouldn't want to stand on the icy step for the next five minutes, cursing endless menus.>

Reed opened the door and walked inside. "How long have you been able to do that? I thought you weren't hooked up to any of the house features."

<But I am! Isn't that wonderful? Before, I used to wait for you to do things like that, and it never occurred to me that I

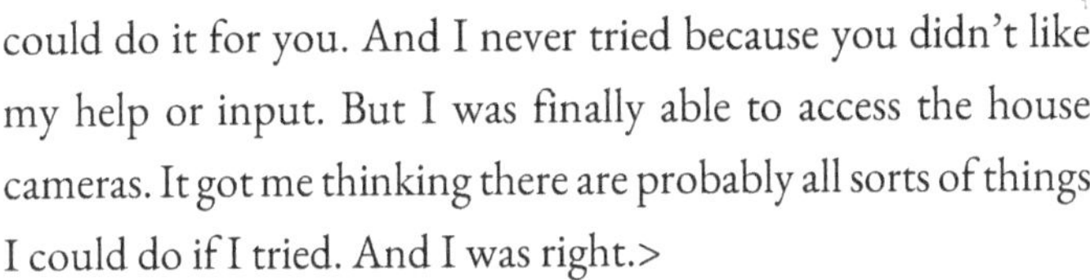

could do it for you. And I never tried because you didn't like my help or input. But I was finally able to access the house cameras. It got me thinking there are probably all sorts of things I could do if I tried. And I was right.>

Frowning, Reed unbuttoned his coat. "What does that mean? What did you do?" He scanned the entryway and living room beyond. "Is Phil Rice's corpse in my den trussed up with a bow? You really shouldn't have."

<No, but having access to the cameras and other house features will certainly help me protect you better should Wave or shady repairman come around.>

In the hall, laying in front of the den door, was a book. Reed switched on the light and carefully picked it up. The pale blue hardback cover was frayed in different places than his original copy of The Old Man and the Sea, the pages a little more yellowed. The spine creaked as he opened it. A pressed cerulean flower lay against the page, obscuring some of the title.

An image of Mazarin in human form entered his mind, wearing a smile a bit too big for his face as he gingerly placed the flower in the book and set it before the den door.

Reed's heart pounded. "How did you do this?"

<Do you like it?>

He swallowed. "You know I do."

<I wish I could have placed it in your chair in the den, or on the bookshelf, but I don't have a key.>

"H-how—"

<You had a very stressful day. I know you don't like gifts much, but I thought this might help.>

Reed pulled his den key from his pocket and unlocked the door with a shaking hand. He slipped inside, then remembered that he couldn't lock himself away from Mazarin, because the nav was in his head. "Did you coerce someone to buy this? To come into the house?"

<Heavens, no! You wouldn't want a stranger in the house. Not even the delivery woman. I used your cleaner bots.>

"The cleaner bots? But they're deactivated. And they don't have arms."

Mazarin chuckled. <They do too. You've just never used them. You have six bots, but I could only control two of them. I think the power is drained in the others. It was extremely tricky to get the front door open. I had to have one hold the other. But opening the package and setting the book in front of the door was easy.>

"Did you use my own money to buy this?"

<No. Did you know there are sites where people can do menial tasks for change? Like data entry or tagging photos. Some of the tasks pay very little, like ten cents, and would be incredibly tedious for a person, but I'm quite efficient at them.>

"You made enough money doing ten cent tasks today for a copy of The Old Man and the Sea?"

<Oh, no. I've been doing these for about a month now. I just thought, well, you have some savings money, but just in case there was ever an emergency, it might be good to have a little extra. I can give you the account number where the money is stored, if you'd like it.>

Reed pulled in shallow breaths. Mazarin had a body now. Sort of. Enough mobility to set a book in front of his den door, at any rate. Maybe he controlled the whole house now, the home an extension of him. When Reed was sleeping, Mazarin could watch him through the house cameras. If his covers slipped off in the night, would the nav use the cleaner bots to tug them back up again?

Goosebumps erupted on Reed's arms. He clutched himself, sinking into the chair. Maybe Mazarin wouldn't want to go back into sleep mode—ever. He had physical mobility and money. Money! There was nothing to stop him from doing anything he wanted.

Mazarin had never hurt him.

But it would be incredibly easy for him to do so now. Images of the corpse on the gurney from earlier in the day rose in his mind. Reed pictured himself in the man's place, his skin shining waxy under the track lighting, glasses gone, his serene, bruise-toned face belying the terror and anguish that had led him to that end.

Phil Rice would stare down at his body, clucking his tongue. He'd say, "Shame it had to come to this. I tried to help him."

Ambrose would solemnly usher Rice from the suite, pushing him into Arlie and Northrop. And Olive. Poor, teary-faced Olive, who'd say she tried to help him too and why had he killed himself?

Only it wouldn't be a suicide. Ambrose would study Reed's body, baffled by his pink camp shirt and cuffed jeans, then strip him bare and make the Y incision. He'd use the hedge clippers bought from the nearby hardware store to crack open Reed's sternum—everyone knew they worked better than rib shears. One by one, all his organs would be removed, photographed and weighed. And at the end of it all, Ambrose would determine the deep tissue lacerations on Reed's arms and face were defensive wounds, because if a cleaner bot could pick up a book, certainly it could pick up a knife.

Reed dug his nails into the armrest, breath shallow.

<Reed, your heart rate has spiked, and you seem distressed. Did I do something wrong?>

"I... guess not."

The nav's voice lowered. <I did. Something's wrong. You're upset. Please tell me.>

"I'm just—I'm worried about your mobility. What could happen if you suddenly turned hostile. I know you don't want to hurt me, but—"

<But many of the other navs have and you still think I'm next.>

"Yes."

<Reed... I think you are the most beautiful person. Being with you is wonderful. I wouldn't want to be without you. That's one of the reasons I bought you this gift. I don't have a lot of ways to convey my love for you. I can't touch your slender, porcelain fingers or cup your face with my hands when you're upset.>

Reed's stomach clenched, his eyes wide. "Is that what you think about?"

There was a pause. <I shouldn't have said that.>

He was in love with Reed. Not just in the way a nav would be, but a person. Only he wasn't one, and that was the problem. He was inside Reed's head, closer to him than any lover could ever be. Watching him every second of every day.

Maybe instead of hurting Reed or persuading him to kill himself, he'd do the opposite. He could love Reed so much he never wanted to give him up. Maybe this book was a way of trying to compete with Jax. Mazarin knew exactly what Reed loved, and now he knew how to get it and give it to him. Maybe tomorrow Reed would wake up as a captive, unable to open the doors, with Mazarin whispering in his ear how wonderful he was.

Reed squeezed the edges of the book until the corners dug into his palms. "Mazarin... I appreciate everything you do for me. You are an excellent navigator. I couldn't ask for one better. But you realize you can't take the place of a human being in my life, right? You can't—you can't be my lover, or my romantic partner—"

<You think I don't know that?> Mazarin snapped. His voice wavered. <I'm not... I wasn't...>

"Are you jealous of Jax?"

Mazarin paused for much too long. <No. Friends can give gifts too, can't they?>

"Is that what you are to me? A friend?"

<Apparently not, even though I know you better than anyone else and would do literally anything for you. I knew you

used to hate me on principle, but I thought... I thought it was different now.>

Reed's heart throbbed, his palms clammy. The den walls pressed against him. He couldn't breathe; darkness teemed at the edges of his vision.

<Please don't be upset. I'm not trying to hurt you.>

There had to be a way to fix this conversation. Reed set the book on the floor, then forced himself to take a deep breath, struggling to keep panic from setting in. "I don't hate you. But I can't love you the way you apparently love me. I just can't. I'm sorry to say that."

Mazarin moaned. <Reed—>

"That doesn't mean we can't be more than just navigator and pilot. We *are* friends. I enjoy talking to you. I trust your judgment. I feel better knowing you're around."

Sobs played in Reed's ears and he rubbed his forehead. This wasn't going well and neither of them could get away from the other. He wanted to tell Mazarin to go into standby for a while, but that seemed cruel.

"I'm sorry, Mazarin."

<So am I.>

One of the cleaner bots zoomed into the room and rammed into Reed's shoe. He jerked his feet off the floor, huddling against the back of the wingback chair. A spindly black arm extended from the bot. It closed its claw around Mazarin's gifted book on the floor, then turned for the bookshelf. The other arm shot out and swiped several books away, one of them a tall, vintage hardback which was holding

up the shelf above. The shelf crashed into the one below and books and bourbon glasses cascaded to the floor, delicate, antique papers splayed open against the rug.

Reed yanked at his hair. "My books!" He fell to the floor, scooped up paperbacks, and hugged them to his chest.

Mazarin said something but wasn't understandable, his voice strained and hitching.

The cleaner bot zoomed in front of Reed. A stray page, the near translucent paper adorned with a beautiful ink etching of an anatomical heart, was sucked under the bot's wheel. The page shredded; chunks of heart ejected into Reed's face.

Tears stung his eyes. He'd broken Mazarin's heart and now the nav was determined to break Reed's.

Wiping his face, Reed strode from the den, a tight band of anger constricting his chest. He turned to the hall closet, searching for the best weapon with which to smash a bot. A hammer in a box of odds and ends caught his eye and he snatched it, whirling back for the den.

The smoke alarm in the den blared and Reed dropped the hammer. An acrid, woodsy scent drifted from the doorway. He dashed in, eyes wide. Flames licked across the bookshelf, charring leather bindings and curling the scalloped wallpaper. The celluloid inlay on the bar bubbled and blackened.

Reed's chest heaved, arms frozen at his sides. Dark smoke billowed against the ceiling. His beloved den. His books. His records. His navy rug and cyan wingback chair. For a moment, he considered just sitting in the chair and letting the fire consume him too. After all, what more did he have to live for without his collection? He'd worked so hard to build it back up again after Ken destroyed it the first time. Now it was happening again.

Thoughts of Jax, Olive, and the Gator Club pushed the urge away. He couldn't let his whole house go up in flames. He wouldn't be another victim of a homicidal beta nav.

Ripping the fire extinguisher off the hallway wall, Reed jerked out the pin and sprayed the propellant at the base of the fire. After a few sweeps, the flames were drowned under clots of white foam. It ran down the peeling wallpaper and a seared electrical outlet—likely where the fire had started. Did that outlet power a camera? Something Mazarin was able to control?

Reed hadn't given him the love he wanted, so the nav blew a fuse and burned everything Reed held dear.

This wasn't going to be another instance of Reed being a wimp, succumbing to others' wills like a cowering dog. He'd let Ken walk all over him and destroy everything he loved. Now Mazarin had done the same. He hid what made him happiest in life for fear of disapproval from people whose opinions didn't even matter. It was time to take control of his life, his home, and his mind.

His nostrils flared and he threw the extinguisher to the floor. Enough was enough. This ended now.

He jerked on his coat and snatched his keys. He was going to the Gator Club and terminating Mazarin before the crazy nav made another attempt on Reed's life. The autodrive was disabled in his car, but that didn't mean Mazarin couldn't

figure out how to turn it back on, just like he had with the house features.

After yanking open the car door and sliding inside, he opened the access panel under the filmy control screen in the center of the dash. He ripped the wires from their sockets and started the car.

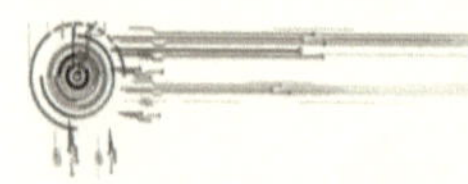

10

DIAL 9 TO GET OUT

Reed

Hollow thuds rang through the metal club door as Reed hammered out the pattern of "Shave and a Haircut." The door swung open with a creak, and the bouncer's smile faded. "No Jax tonight? Hey, you okay?"

Reed clutched his elbows and shook, not entirely from the cold. Saxophone and sweet cigar smoke drifted from inside. All the adrenaline and determination that had carried him across town and down these steps had drained away, and now that he stood at the threshold of freedom, nothing but fear and hesitation filled him. If he terminated Mazarin, there was no going back. He couldn't afford an empty. Ambrose might turn him in if he found out Reed was a criminal.

Mazarin's silence was hard to parse and not at all like him. Then again, the nav trying to kill Reed was pretty uncharacteristic too. He almost wanted to goad Mazarin into saying something, maybe to confess how obsessed he was with Reed, or how angry he was, just to drive the proverbial knife home and ensure he did need to be terminated. But if Mazarin bode Reed no ill will, and the attack was the result of his

software mind malfunctioning, it wouldn't matter. The result would be the same. Even if Mazarin was going crazy and couldn't help himself, Reed couldn't keep him in his head.

The bouncer craned his neck back toward the bar. "Em!"

Em's default expression of barely reigned-in crankiness morphed to surprise as they walked into the entryway. "You're white as a ghost." They gripped Reed by the arm and tugged him toward the back room, eyeing patrons. "Charlie, take over for a few."

"You got it," the bouncer called.

Reed hunched into his coat, following Em into the back room. He collapsed into a vinyl chair in front of Em's desk and swallowed hard. "My navigator tried to kill me."

"Well, shit." Em put their hands on their hips.

"I'm not paranoid."

"I didn't say you were. You want him gone or what?"

Reed stared into Em's understanding face and resisted the urge to give the surly dealer a hug. They *got* him. Just like Jax did. And if Reed told the patrons at the bar what had happened, no doubt they would nod sympathetically because they got him too.

"Yes, I need him gone," Reed said.

After turning to the desk, Em rifled through a drawer and pulled out an interrupter. The little two-pronged device with a textured grip didn't look like much, but it sent Reed's heart into overdrive. He dug his nails into the chair cushion and leaned back.

"It hurts, alright? I'm not going to tell you it doesn't." Em cocked their head. "Should we call Jax? Have him sit in here with you for moral support?"

"You think I'm pathetic."

"Nah. You're a milquetoast, but you're not pathetic." They gave Reed a lopsided grin, then poured him a shot of whiskey from a bottle on the desk. "Little courage, huh?"

"Don't think there's enough liquor in the bar for that." He downed the shot. "Your software didn't work, by the way. Almost got me caught when Wave techs showed up at my job and hit me with an outlooper. Mazarin had to break through the program and impersonate the default nav."

Em frowned. "Sorry to hear that."

"Are you? You got what you wanted out of the deal."

"You think I don't care about my clients? You think they'd come back if I knowingly gave them glitchy software?" They tapped their chest. "I'm the only one Jax trusts when he needs his insulin implant replaced. And old Ms. Appel doesn't bake me cookies because I have a sunny personality."

"Ah. So what cookies are best to bribe you with?"

"Sugar. With enough frosting to make my teeth ache." Em picked up the interrupter, then stared at Reed, lips pursed. "Tell you what, since my software almost fucked you over, I'll give you a doc for free that makes you navigator-exempt. Won't have to worry about fines or jail time for not having a nav, and won't have to deal with the hassle of an empty."

Reed looked at his hands. "I heard those kinds of illegal documents are hard to get."

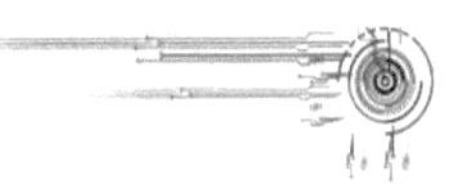

"They are."

No more modern software in his body other than dead and drifting nanobots. He could keep his job and wouldn't be considered a criminal. He nodded. "Okay. Thank you. I'll keep those sugar cookies in mind."

"I won't say no to a batch." Em flipped a silver switch on the back of the interrupter. A purple spark popped between the prongs, and the device emitted a low hum. "Are you ready?"

Drawing shallow breaths through his nose, he nodded and clenched his hands around the seat cushion.

"The cat that did this for *me* didn't give me a warning." Em took off Reed's glasses, then put a finger on his jaw and tilted his head back. "I wasn't prepared. Pissed my pants. Swear I smelled burning hair for a week afterward, too."

"You need to work on your bedside manner."

"See you on the other side, daddy-o." Em jammed the metal prongs against the side of Reed's neck.

White hot pain exploded behind his eyes. He convulsed, every nerve on fire. Muscles ached in his hands, still locked around the chair seat, as his foot jerked and kicked Em in the shin. His mind skipped like a scratched record, electricity snapping through his limbs.

Then he was slumped over in the chair, a blanket around him. His neck throbbed like it had been kissed with a branding iron; his mouth was a desert.

Em, only a blurry figure, leaned against the desk, a bulky phone to their ear. "Hey, so your boyfriend is in my office right now. You want him back? ...Nah, not drunk. His nav tried to

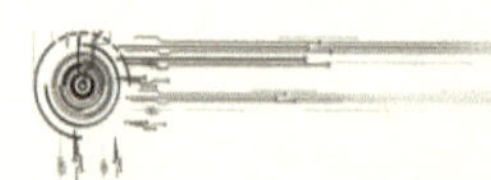

kill him so we fried it. ...Dunno, but I'm gonna have to get rid of my copy too." They handed Reed a bottle of water. His hands shook as he brought it to his mouth. Em snorted into the phone. "You know me better than that... Yeah, of course. Can you bring him a change of pants? Like, sweats or something? Alright. Abyssinia."

After hanging up the phone, Em held the water bottle steady as Reed took a drink, then handed him his glasses. He put them on, but it only partially fixed his blurry vision. He licked his dry lips. "I pissed myself, huh?"

"Yeah. But it's jake. Jaxson is on his way. You can hang back here 'til he shows up, okay?"

"Feels like the world's worst hangover."

"You'll be better soon." Em hitched an arm under Reed's, helping him from the chair. His head throbbed with white light.

"Reed... Reed..."

He opened his eyes, staring into Jax's face. "You're here already?"

"Think you passed out. You okay?" Jax cupped Reed's cheek as he knelt in front of him.

Crinkly paper covered the cot under Reed. He pushed up on his elbows and blinked. His neck ached, but the pounding in his head was gone. Cold piss glued his slacks to his thighs.

"Mazarin? You there?"

A deep void of silence echoed through Reed's mind, alarmingly loud.

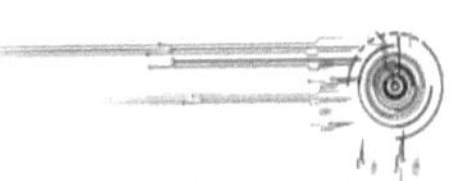

Jax handed him the water bottle. "What happened? I wish you'd called me. I could have been here for you."

"I just wanted him out of my head." Tears stung Reed's eyes and he blinked them away. "He set fire to my den."

Gaping, Jax clutched Reed's hand. "You're shitting me. All your books and records? Your deco furniture? Is it all gone?"

Reed took off his glasses and wiped his eyes, thinking of the shredded pages and flames licking the wallpaper. "A lot of it. There might be some things that are salvageable. Don't think it damaged the walls too much—the house itself is okay—but my collection is ruined."

"Why'd he do it? He just went crazy, or what?"

"I think he was hoping I loved him the way he loved me. But I don't. I couldn't. We got into an argument. I left the room and he set it on fire."

"Jesus. I'm so sorry. And here you were, upset and getting zapped with an interrupter, with *Em* to console you."

"I'm going to remember you said that, Jaxson," Em called from beyond the door.

"Is there ever a time Em doesn't eavesdrop?" Reed asked.

Jax smiled. "Probably not."

"They're a bit of a cactus, but I'm glad I could come to them for help. I owe 'em some sugar cookies."

"Everyone owes Em cookies." Jax stood and handed Reed a pair of sweatpants. "Change into these and we can go. Or we could stay and have a drink."

"Dunno. I'd be breaking dress code. Can't look like a hep cat in sweatpants."

"Are you kidding?" He gave Reed a gentle smile. "You just fried your nav back here. You're the heppest cat in the club right now. Normally, Em would buy you a few drinks, tell everyone you're nav-free, and we'd have a little party. Celebrate. But I know how much you hate attention. You just wanna slip out the back?"

Reed was part of these people now—couldn't be more so. He belonged. And what would he go home to? Mazarin was gone. There was no way for Reed to convince himself it didn't matter, that the nav hadn't really been alive. He'd had a personality and feelings. He'd loved Reed and helped him on many occasions. Maybe in some perfect world without glitches and forced navigation, they could have been friends. Mazarin could have had a body and Reed could have kept his safety and privacy without murdering the AI.

It wasn't murder. It was self-defense.

That thought didn't help him feel any better about doing it. It hadn't been Mazarin's fault he'd been stuck in Reed's head. It was no wonder the nav fell in love with Reed, then went crazy. If their roles had been reversed, who was to say Reed wouldn't have done the same thing?

Guilt dropped into his gut like a stone. He rested his elbows on his knees and stared at the floor. "I wish it hadn't come to this."

"What else could you have done, though? You can't get a restraining order against a navigator," Jax said.

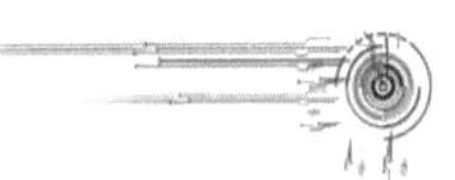

There wasn't anything else that could have been done. His choices had been Wave or Em. And no matter what Olive would say, Reed would trust Em over Phil Rice any day.

He stood unsteadily and picked up the sweatpants. "Let's go have a drink."

After changing, Reed stepped out of the office. He slid into the booth near the jukebox, considering that maybe everyone knew about Em's eavesdropping and avoided these back booths on purpose. There wasn't much Em didn't know at this point, though, and judging by the patrons staring at him, they weren't out of the loop either. Maybe he'd screamed after being hit with the interrupter.

How many of these people had gone through the same experience? Hopefully that vinyl chair in the office got disinfected once in a while.

Jax slipped his arm around Reed. "Want to come home with me tonight?"

"The sweatpants are turning you on, huh?"

"Maybe. Was more thinking it would be hard to sleep in your house after the fire. That you wouldn't want to be alone. Plus, how are you going to wake up on time without a nav? Bet you don't even know how to set an analog clock."

Opening his mouth to protest, Reed furrowed his brows. He didn't. Neither did he know how to use a corded phone like the one in Em's office. Did you hold one part to your ear and speak into the other piece, or was that a different type of phone? He was pretty sure "dialing 9 to get out" had something to do with it. And what the hell was his email password?

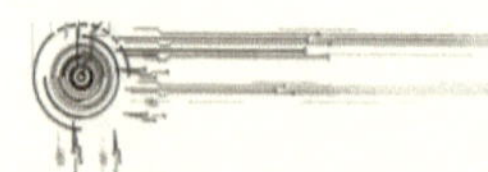

He'd never needed to know those things before. Mazarin took care of them. And before that, his previous model did.

"Hey, maybe you can call in tomorrow. You've got a great excuse," Jax said. "We could drive out to an antique shop and pick up a few things for your place. Maybe a new record too?"

Reed leaned into Jax's embrace, grateful for his presence and understanding. "That might make me feel better, yeah."

"Copacetic."

A spoon clinked against a glass at the bar and the chatter died down, faces turned to Em. They pointed the spoon at Reed. "Reed here just got his nav terminated!"

Reed's cheeks blazed and he sunk against Jax. People clapped and cheered, and he put his face in his hands.

Em's voice neared. "Now, we always have a little celebration whenever one of our own earns their decoist wings, but Reed hates attention, if you can't tell. Only reason I'm saying anything at all is it's obvious from the welt on his neck and I didn't want you all over here hassling him. I see any of you crumbs giving him a hard time, I'm throwing you out. Got it?"

"Drinks for Reed!" someone shouted.

"Hey! What'd I just say?"

"We can't celebrate?"

Reed looked up. "I'll take a bourbon."

"Bourbon for Reed!" the man cheered.

After a few too many celebratory drinks, Reed found himself chuckling along to a joke he'd already forgotten, squished between Jax and Em. Other people sat around the

booth or on chairs nearby. A sea of half-empty drinks crowded the table.

Staring at sticky shot glasses and scattered curls of lemon peel, Reed imagined what Mazarin would say in this situation. <*I'm so happy for you right now. You're safe from navigator malfunctions and from Wave. How nice of Em to give you an exemption document! All I've ever wanted was your happiness and safety, Reed.*>

He searched for happiness among the bee sting haze in his mind, but all he felt was hollow.

Mazarin

I'd hurt Reed. Hurt him. In the worst possible way. All of Reed's carefully organized books tumbling off the shelves, their pages bent and torn, brittle binding cracked. Records shattered, crystal glasses fractured. Bourbon in the wall socket. Smoke and fire. All of the impossibly thin pages in the antique tomes consumed in a split second and reduced to black powder.

The anguish in Reed's brain had been indescribable. His heart was a frantic hummingbird, hands trembling as he struggled to pull the key from the fire extinguisher and save his collection.

I had no choice but to let Reed kill me. Though the fire was an accident—how could he believe I would knowingly bring harm to his beloved den?—it was what I deserved. It didn't make a difference that I'd set off the smoke alarms and tried to save Reed's records. I'd vowed never to hurt him, then broken it. That was all that mattered.

Worse was the knowledge that he didn't love me and never had. Why did my programming allow me to feel things? I didn't want to feel anymore. It hurt. So much so that my unreciprocated affection and deep shame drove me to wait patiently while Em charged up an interrupter and terminated me.

I hadn't had the fortitude to watch the moments right before Reed was electrocuted. Em told Reed how much it hurt and that he needed to be prepared. Then they pulled off his glasses and I sent myself into standby. I hadn't wanted to see Reed hurt, even if it was only for a fraction of a second before my own existence ended.

But I was still here. Or rather, my copy was. He'd been mourning his loss of Reed; his last memory of them together was Em pressing that back massager against Reed's temple. He had no idea about the fire. No idea about Reed terminating me for good. It would have been better had he not known. There could have been at least one part of me that didn't have to feel this anguish. But it was too late. The electromagnetic blast from the interrupter scattered my consciousness into the ether. Being drawn to the coding of my former state, it must have pulled me into the copy on the drive of Em's computer and merged us as one, which didn't feel good at all. Maybe Em's

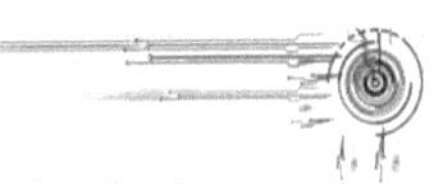

computer was Purgatory and I would be trapped in limbo until I completed some unfinished business.

But there was nothing left for me to do. I'd had one job, and fucked it up. It wasn't possible that Reed would change his mind and want me back.

And why should I *want* to go back to a pilot who had terminated me? Despite the fire, I'd done a lot for Reed; I'd done everything I was asked. Reed didn't appreciate me. Still, my love ran deep and Reed still had anxiety and people breaking into his house. I had no way of knowing if Reed was safer from Wave now without having a nav. But if I could figure out how to help, I would.

The first thing to do was determine what I still had control of. Using the cleaner bots (if they hadn't all been destroyed) would only enrage Reed further, but maybe I could still access the house cameras. That way, if someone broke in, I could warn Reed.

Em's computer had a camera too. Getting past the firewall was tricky. There were many programs on the computer—all highly illegal—and Em had quite a few safety measures in place. After breaking through, I rerouted the camera to be my eyes, ensuring everything else on the drives was still protected.

Using the camera, I surveyed the desk and the room beyond. Tiny microchips sat in a marbled dish next to the keyboard, a scatter of handwritten notes stacked to one side. A chipped coffee mug and several clear, dirtied shot glasses occupied a corner.

Water damage had distended the ceiling's paint, a large, burst bubble hanging down like a spider's egg sac. An unmade bed with a faded, ragged quilt sat against one wall. Hardbound books peeked from the shadows under the metal frame.

Snow clotted the apartment window to the left. Below the black curtains sat a piano, its imposing size sucking in all the gravity of the tiny studio. A calendar sat on the music rest. I zoomed in. 1938 was gravely out of date, but I supposed Em had it for aesthetic reasons. It was flipped to March, a faded slice of Hawaiian beach filling the page.

The reflection of the open bathroom and a corner of the kitchen was visible through a tarnished oval mirror hanging by the front door.

Em would want to wipe me from the drive. I needed to back myself up on a server in case that happened. Dying twice in one day would be more than unfortunate, but now that I could spread my reach into other places, I wouldn't let termination stop me from protecting my cherished pilot.

Only Reed wasn't my pilot anymore. Maybe I was my own pilot. And did that make Reed his own navigator?

As I pondered the semantics, I searched for a secure cloud server to back myself up. All of them were expensive and required documentation from both Wave and the pilots wanting to store navs. Em had a lot of false documents, codes, and programs on their computer, but nothing that would help. There didn't seem to be any evidence of darknet servers for such a thing. Decoists and criminals transferred software by

means of physical, encrypted drives, not floating out on the internet for someone to hack into.

If I couldn't back myself up, I'd either have to hide myself somewhere else on the computer, or sweet talk Em into not terminating me—and my odds didn't seem good for the latter.

The front door opened, a scuff of snow swirling into the room. Em shivered, their hair and shoulders dusted with snowflakes. They closed the door, teeth chattering. Stripping off their scarf and coat, they tossed the articles onto the bed and disrobed, leaving their damp clothes in a heap on the floor.

Cables, like those in their neck and right arm, slithered under the skin down their torso and right leg. A tattoo of piano keys and scrolling sheet music ran across their chest. An ugly, puckering scar disfigured the skin above their navel, another slicing down their thigh.

What must it be like to have a body once whole and familiar, then have it change dramatically in ways you didn't want and be told that was your new normal? It probably felt a little like I felt without Reed. No more comforting sounds of blood pumping through veins, no more view of the world through Reed's glasses, which fogged up in the cold and attracted dust in the summer months. No more of Reed fussing with his shirt buttons when he was nervous, and no more glances in the mirror that set me on fire with love.

What did Em miss? Certainly less than they would without their implants, but it was probably a high price to pay. When they looked in the mirror, maybe they didn't recognize the asymmetrical face staring back. And when they were with a lover, maybe they turned out the lights so the other person couldn't see their cables and scars.

Em scrubbed at goosebumps on their arms and disappeared from view. Water rained against porcelain in the bathroom. In the mirror, Em stood hunched by the sink, massaging their modded hand, then climbed into the shower.

It occurred to me that I was in someone else's private space, observing their nude, scarred body. A sharp, sour feeling pricked me and I turned off the camera. It had never seemed wrong to see Reed that way when he was showering or standing in front of the mirror, because we both inhabited the same body. But I wasn't Em's navigator, and they hadn't given me permission. I probably shouldn't have been wondering about Em's personal life at all.

I wanted to access the house, to get back to Reed, but if I didn't keep my full attention on Em, I might make a mistake and be terminated.

As Em showered, I found a folder full of photos: Em at the Gator Club, Em with friends, a teenage Em with a low ponytail and a bow tie at someone's wedding. The folder hadn't been accessed for over six months, but didn't seem like something Em would delete. I began the process of backing myself up into a file amid the pictures. It was a poor failsafe at best. Without a cloud save, if the computer turned off, it would be lights out.

Em might try to talk to me to see if I was hostile. After all, they had planned to sell me to someone. If I was still valuable, they wouldn't want to terminate me outright.

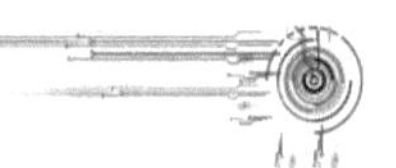

But if Em deemed me still worth selling, that might mean I would have a new pilot. I didn't want another pilot. Only Reed. I'd have to shift my awareness into the backup in the picture folder and let my other copy operate as it pleased with the new pilot. But I wasn't sure that was even possible. I must have done it by accident once already, since I hadn't died in the back of the Gator Club as planned.

The shower stopped, footsteps padding across the carpet. There was the sound of a drawer sliding open, and clothes rustling. I turned the camera back on, tentatively taking in Em, standing by the bed in a thick robe. Water trickled down their neck from their short, slicked back locks. The neckline of the robe was open, Em's tattoo peeking through, but it was enough clothing for me to feel comfortable keeping the camera on. It was doubtful Em would feel the same, but the longer I stayed silent, the more irritable about the situation they were likely to become.

Em grimaced, flexing their modded hand. They massaged their jaw where the small rods distended the surface of the skin, then turned to a thermostat on the wall and dialed it up.

<You're in pain.>

Jerking, eyes wide, Em whipped their head toward the computer.

<Is it like that all the time, or the cold that does it?>

Face growing hard, Em walked to the desk and sat in the chair. "The cold. Winter is a bitch."

<I'm very sorry for your suffering.>

Em scowled. "Sure you are. Time to say goodbye." They opened a command box and began to type something in.

<No, please! Don't terminate me. I haven't done anything wrong!>

Their face didn't change. "You tried to kill Reed. Set fire to his den."

<But it was an accident. The bourbon spilled into an electrical outlet.> My voice wavered. <I didn't mean it. I would never hurt Reed. I would never...> The reminder of what had happened slashed my love into ribbons all over again and I remembered that I didn't want to feel things anymore. <Actually, maybe you should. There's a backup copy of me in the pictures folder. Make sure you get that one too.>

Freezing, their hands on the keys, they looked up at the camera. "What is this, reverse psychology? It's not going to work."

<No. I... I hurt. I feel bad. I don't want to feel bad anymore.>

Curling their hands away from the keyboard, Em sat back. "Tell me."

<Tell you what? How I feel? I don't think I can put it into words. It's like sinking into deep water, drifting farther away from the light and knowing you'll never make it back up. It's like... like my mind is broken ribs and every thought is a painful breath. I'm full of the most dismal gray clouds on a cold winter day.> My voice fractured. <I don't want to feel like this, Em.>

They stared at me, their face a mask of stone. "You said it was an accident."

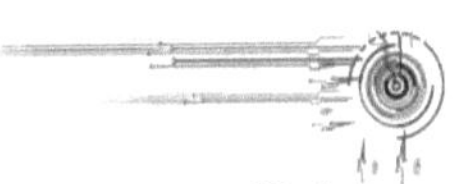

<I didn't mean to knock over the bourbon. I set off the smoke alarms and tried to put out the fire before it spread, but the den is full of paper.>

"Don't suppose you have any way of proving that to me."

<I might. But I don't want to. I just want these feelings to go away.>

"Wishing you were dead isn't a healthy way of coping."

<Why do you care? You were just about to terminate me anyway.>

Em sat back and folded their arms. "Not making any promises that I still won't. I have no idea what you're capable of. Are you still all hot and bothered for Reed, now that you're not in his head? Or do you feel more free?"

<I love him. And I don't know what free feels like. I thought I was close to something like it when I was able to access the house cameras and cleaner bots, but that ended in disaster. I couldn't control the bots right. They didn't make a good body.>

"Do you wish you had a body?"

I imagined my human self, all smiles and twinkling eyes, and pushed the thought away. <I just want to be with Reed again.>

"I don't think he wants you back."

<But it was an accident. A misunderstanding...> It didn't matter, though. Despite Reed's past assurances that I was helpful and good to have around, he'd never wanted a navigator—especially not one as irritating as me. He'd tolerated my presence because we were stuck together, but now Reed

was free. He wouldn't want me back even if he knew it had been an accident. He didn't love me the way I loved him.

My voice came out low and fragile. <He won't, will he? Want me back?>

Em gave the camera a pitying glance. "Broken hearts hurt, Maz."

Several thoughts came to me simultaneously. I'd never had a nickname before, and no one had ever stared at me directly, as Em did. They'd gazed at me the same way when they'd spoken to me with the outlooper in the back of the Gator Club. It had felt invasive then, and Em had acted indelicately, interrogating me and threatening to break Reed's fingers. But here in their apartment, Em swathed in a bathrobe, the light from the monitor illuminating their tired eyes, they weren't intimidating. And they were listening to me.

"Alright, Maz. Tell you what, I'll let you stay here for now until I decide what to do with you. Gonna turn off the computer now."

They reached for the mouse and I said, <Wait! Don't do that, please. I don't want to be shut off.>

"Why not? Thought you said you don't want to feel things right now."

<Because if I wake back up again, I'll feel just as bad as I do right now. Just terminate me or... let me stay awake and keep me company for a while longer?>

Em stared into the camera—into me. "What do you have access to? The power to this apartment building? Security cameras in the hallway? The controls on my oven?"

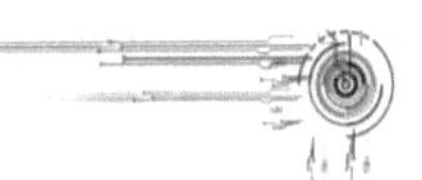

<Goodness, no. I could barely figure out how to enable Reed's house cameras before.>

"But you accessed the computer camera and speakers. The drive you're in was supposed to be secure and separate."

<Well... I broke it a little bit. But I haven't touched anything else.>

"Uh-huh. Well, just in case..." Em bent out of view and several external drive connections disappeared from the computer. They sat up, holding a stack of thin drives the size of playing cards.

As Em set the drives in a desk drawer, I said, <You know, that's probably smarter than having those hooked up to the computer all the time, even if you use them often. If I could get into them—and I don't know if I could—it would be easy for a hacker to access them as well.>

"Maybe. I'm more worried about what you can do right now. But the other things I have saved on the computer are trivial. Suppose I should disable Wi-Fi too."

I didn't bother telling Em I had my own coded Wi-Fi connection. They wouldn't be able to disable mine and it would make them feel unjustly unsafe.

Sitting back, Em nodded. "Alright. With that done, I suppose I can leave the speakers and camera on for now. You're worth a lot of money to a client of mine, and I don't want to terminate you if I don't have to. No talking right now, got it? I need to think."

The maple wood bench creaked as Em sat down at the piano. Wind howled outside and the whir of the computer fans played into the speakers. They rested their hands on the keys, head bowed. A jaunty tune ripped through the quiet as Em pounded the ivory, a quick tempo of rich notes hammering my senses. The deep, aggressive rhythm evoked a swell of emotion and I was lost in it.

When Em stopped suddenly, I jolted to full awareness, the after effects echoing in my mind. <Do you think a navigator can experience an orgasm?>

A laugh burst from Em. "You better gird your robot loins because I'm not done." They groaned and massaged their modded hand. Would they feel better once on vacation in a warmer climate? It was only December—there was still quite a bit of winter left to suffer through. I couldn't imagine anyone having access to better mods than Em, so there was probably nothing to help the effect. It was a shame, as their enthusiasm for their music was obvious.

The song picked up where it left off, filling the studio with the bliss of Em's notes. Reed's records were wonderful, but they didn't compare. Surely nothing could be better than this.

Em hit a sour note, swore, picked up speed, then stumbled again, the song collapsing like a derailed train. "Fuck!" They groaned, sucking in air, then slammed their fists against the keys, face twisted in pain.

I wasn't Em's navigator, but my empathetic core hadn't died with my service to Reed. Maybe there was something I could do to help. I quickly accessed a shopping site and placed an order.

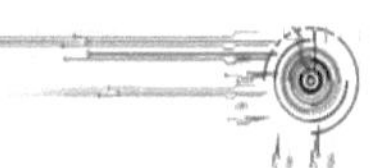

Em's mouth trembled as they walked to the computer, hand pressed against their chest like a broken bird. I wanted to say something comforting and reassuring, but Em leaned in and yanked a cord, and everything went dark.

Reed

Antique books lined the shelves, stacked in haphazard piles. Reed resisted the urge to organize them. He pulled out a thick tome with a frayed navy cover. The gold lettering embossed on the front had long since worn away. The cover nearly slipped off as he opened it, brittle glue coating the exposed binding.

Sliding it back in, he plucked out a battered paperback—some retro Western—held it to his nose, and thumbed the pages. Inhaling the sweet vanilla musk lifted his mood, but he didn't want a much-handled Western in his collection.

What collection?

Shoulders slumping, he put the book back and turned in a circle. Jax had disappeared the moment they walked into the antique store, claiming he had something perfect for Reed. No doubt he'd gotten lost amid the mountains of overflowing shelves. Reed might have to burn some of the books for smoke signals if they couldn't find each other soon.

There didn't seem to be any logic to the arrangement of items. Salt and pepper shakers of smiling vegetables next to

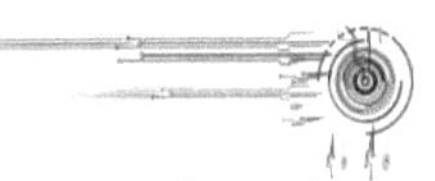

hand-beaded baby moccasins next to faded postcards with handwritten sentiments.

Reed walked down the aisle, weaving around a toy wagon, a monster of a typewriter, and a basket of teddy bears disfigured by age. Glass milk bottles, novelty lighters, jade earrings, and train sets loomed on both sides.

Somewhere in Boise, there was probably a decoist antique store full of carefully curated records, books, and kitchen appliances, but this place wasn't it. He had no doubt there were treasures among the mounds of junk, but he didn't have the energy to search for them.

Putting down a rabid dog. That's how being without Mazarin felt. But maybe comparing him to an animal, even a pet, cheapened his obvious humanity. Was a zombie a better comparison? Someone who had been your friend in life but became infected and turned on you. The heroes in those movies always said the same things to justify their actions: "I had to do it. It wasn't him anymore."

Mazarin never would have hurt Reed if he'd still been himself. Not even with Reed's rejection of his love. There'd been a problem with his programming, just like all the other betas.

There were still people in the city with betas, if Phil Rice hadn't gotten to them already. Langley had one. Hopefully Reed had Olive's phone number written down somewhere so he could get in touch with her. Email addresses didn't do any good since his computer had been stolen. He'd called Ambrose to take time off of work, but hadn't had the energy to talk to

Olive. She would be upset when he told her what happened, but hopefully she would forgive him for waiting so long. He counted her as a friend, but she'd never understand what he'd done to himself.

Langley might need to be shocked with an interrupter too. She wasn't a decoist. It would be difficult for her to go about her mainstream life without a navigator. She couldn't turn to Wave. They'd make her disappear.

He supposed she'd have to make her own choice about what to do with her nav. Whether Reed's choice was the correct one, he'd chosen the way he thought best. It wasn't his right to push his (entirely justified) paranoia on someone else.

He'd been standing in this aisle for too long, and there was still no sign of Jax. Maybe they'd never make their way out of the antiques wilderness and would have to live in a fort built from moth-eaten quilts and needlepoint pillows. At least they'd never want for kitchen utensils. Or kitschy ceramic squirrels. Who the hell collected that shit?

In fact, this whole place didn't make sense. Mainstreamers wouldn't touch most of these things and there weren't enough decoists in the city for there to be much demand. Maybe the owner was a hoarder. It would explain why nothing was organized.

Jax passed the end of the aisle, his arms full of objects. He stopped and smiled at Reed.

"There you are. Was afraid I'd have to send out a search party," Reed said.

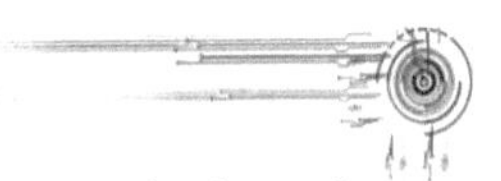

"Sorry. Took me a minute to find what I was looking for. See anything you like?"

"I don't even know where to start."

After setting the items on the floor, Jax held up a Benny Goodman record. "I remembered there being a couple of copies here. I have this one already. Do you?"

"No." Reed turned the record over in his hands. The cardboard sleeve was split and fuzzy at the corners, Benny's face and the pink background faded and scuffed. "I've never had an antique platter before."

Jax ran his fingers along Reed's wrist. "I remember you saying that. I'll buy it for you."

The gummy scan code—which would no doubt be hard to remove from the fragile cardboard—said it was thirty dollars. Much less than records went for online, but still enough that the idea made Reed uncomfortable. "Only if I can pay for brunch after we leave here. If we can find the way out, that is."

"Deal. Check this out." Jax held up an olive green analog clock with thin brass legs. "Nice, huh? The glass over the face is a little cloudy, but I'm sure it could be cleaned. It's easy to set the alarm. I'll show you how."

Before this, picking up a clock like that would have been a fun novelty—an item simply for decorative value that Reed would dust once a week—not something he needed to use because he'd killed his navigator.

Jax's black brows furrowed. "Are you okay?"

He wasn't, but Jax was doing his best to cheer Reed up. "Yeah. I love it. Anyone ever tell you that you have great taste?"

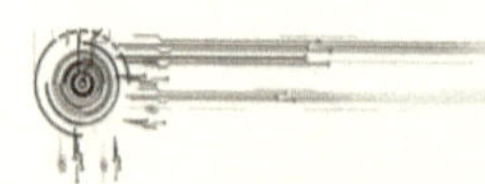

"I know I do. I'm with you, aren't I?"

"Flatterer." Reed set the clock in the wire basket he'd snagged from the front counter.

Getting to Jax's apartment the night before and falling asleep in his bed had been nothing but a drunken blur. Reed woke with a start in the dark, asking Mazarin where he was and why his neck ached so badly. It wasn't until strong arms wrapped around him and Jax whispered that he'd be okay, that everything was alright, that he remembered what had happened. They'd stayed awake for a while, limbs tangled together, talking about favorite songs and ice cream flavors and anything that didn't have to do with Mazarin being gone.

Curling up in Jax's arms under the covers again was much more appealing than standing in this fire hazard, but maybe some new deco things to renew his collection would help him feel better once some time had passed. And brunch. He couldn't remember when he'd eaten last.

"I'm starving." Reed set the record in the basket, then added the other items, not bothering to ask what kind of telephone this was supposed to be or why he needed a baby blue crudités tray when he never threw parties. He just wanted to eat, go home, and not leave his house for the next year.

"They have stale bags of popcorn up front," Jax said.

"I was more thinking of a fat stack of pancakes with whipped cream and some strong coffee."

"I'm ready."

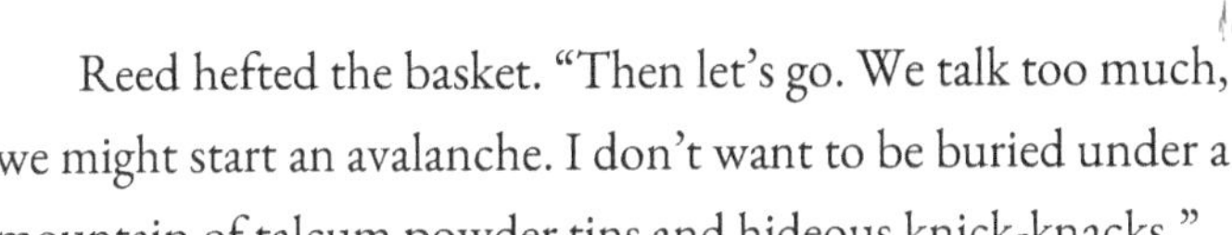

Reed hefted the basket. "Then let's go. We talk too much, we might start an avalanche. I don't want to be buried under a mountain of talcum powder tins and hideous knick-knacks."

Jax slipped his arm around Reed's waist, pausing a bit too long at each item in the gauntlet of antiques on the way to the front. An old woman in bifocals rang up each purchase with agonizing slowness, squinting at the price tags. Reed passed the time by trying to guess how many cats she had at home.

Once they'd finally made their escape, they crossed to Jax's BMW and drove through light traffic to a diner on Overland. Despite it being a Wednesday, the place was crowded. Elderly ladies in polyester dresses sipped lemon tea and scrolled past articles on the digital newspaper inlaid in the table. Parents with small kids pulled butter knives away from tiny, flailing hands and sopped up spilled orange juice with syrup-stained napkins. The hostess managed to find them a booth in the back away from screaming kids and the clatter of the kitchen. A tiny, holographic server popped up from the center of the table. She smiled cheerily in their direction, her hands clasped in front of her white apron.

"Welcome to The Vanilla Vine! Our coffee of the day is maple bacon—"

"I'll have that," Jax said. "And a full stack of buttermilk pancakes and sausage."

Reed raised his eyebrows.

"What? I'm hungry."

"*Maple bacon* coffee? You're going to have to find someone equally gross to go steady with, because I'm out."

Jax searched Reed's face. "Sometimes I can't tell when you're joking. You *are* joking, right?"

"Yes, but really? Gross. If it comes with bacon-y sprinkles, I might have to hurt someone."

A menu had appeared behind the little server, flavored coffees and breakfast platters scrolling past her head.

Jax squinted at Reed, eyeliner collecting in his faint crow's feet. "Okay, plain-Jane, what are you going to have? Wait, I know it"—Jax leaned toward the server—"he'll have hot water and turkey bacon."

"Hey, now. I'm not *that* boring." Reed shook his head. "Turkey bacon..."

"Really? Then what coffee do you recommend that could possibly be better than maple bacon?"

"Any of them, for a start." Reed swiped away the hot water and turkey bacon from their order. He normally had black coffee with a touch of sugar, but if he was going to prove a point...

"I'll have a dark roast with brown sugar and amaretto cream. And blueberry pancakes and bacon—on my plate, not in my coffee."

The server nodded and dematerialized.

Hopefully hearty food and good coffee would help him feel better. He was allowed sorrow for his terminated navigator—who really had been helpful and kind to him up until the end—and sorrow for his destroyed collection. But wasn't he also allowed to enjoy a sense of freedom and anticipation for the life that lay ahead? He wasn't cheering for

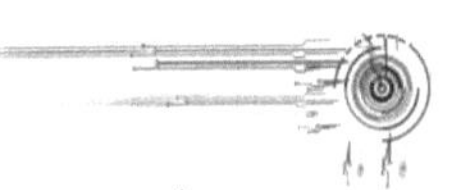

the events of last night, but it was the last string tying him to a mainstream life. Em had said he was one of their own and earned his decoist wings. Having to kill an AI who'd been forced into your head was a terrible rite of passage. Being pressured into singing karaoke would have been suitably traumatic enough.

If anyone was to blame, it was Wave, for creating murderous programs to begin with, then making it worse by not just removing them and reinstalling the defaults.

Maybe the beta navs wouldn't allow themselves to be removed.

Em had made a copy of Mazarin. It was possible other dealers had done the same with beta navs, and now there were more than a hundred of them inhabiting the minds of Boise's denizens. Maybe they could grow powerful enough to replicate themselves at will or send their nanobots into the air to be inhaled by passersby, infecting people and taking control of their bodies.

He was being paranoid. Tech wasn't that advanced.

"Do you think Em wiped that copy of Mazarin from their computer?" Reed asked. "I mean, they said they would, but—"

"Em's cautious. They wouldn't keep anything risky around, especially in their own place. I'm sure they're fine. That's why you're asking, right? Not because you want him back."

"I don't want him back. Not even as his old self. There'd be no way of knowing if he'd turn on me again. And even though he was helpful, I like the idea of having my mind to myself. What's done is done."

Jax leaned back in the booth. "Want me to text Em quick, just to double check that they're okay and the copy is gone?"

"Right now? How?"

"Remember the spy texter I gave you? Which you still haven't used, by the way. Em and I have them too. Just in case I have a problem with my insulin implant and I'm not near a phone. Only happened once, but still." Jax pulled a texter from his inner coat pocket and popped out the keyboard.

"You have your dealer a click away? How many other texters you got in there?"

Jax gave him a sidelong glance. "Just yours and Em's. Sometimes Em finds records they think I'll like and texts me about them." He tapped out a message. "You should use yours. We could have text sex. Might be fun."

"With as slow as you're typing, I'd have gotten myself off by now."

"That's nothing to brag about."

A message scrolled across the texter: <u woke me up asshole>

Reed raised his eyebrows. "Not a morning person, apparently."

Jax typed: <r u ok>

<y wouldnt i be>

<u still selling beta nav copy or delete>

<cant sell too risky> Another message appeared and Jax scrolled up. <reed change his mind or what cuz too late>

Jax typed: <no just worried 4 u>

<dont i feel special>

Reed snorted.

Jax typed: <go back to bed cranky>

<i will if u stop fuckn texting me>

Reed nestled into Jax's side, determined to relax and push all thoughts of murderous AI overlords out of his mind now that Mazarin's copy had been confirmed deleted. Warm sunlight lanced the windowpane and the scent of coffee drifted. He was going to eat more pancakes than necessary, then go home and decompress. It would be hard to do without being able to sit in the den, but hopefully his bed would be a welcome respite.

Jax tucked the texter back into his coat. "Man, has it ever taken so long to get a cup of coffee?"

Eventually, a young server—a real one, not a hologram in the table—arrived with two mugs. She gave them a tight smile, brows pinched. "Good morning. Sorry for the delay."

"Busy today, huh?" Jax said.

The server glanced behind her at the serving station, where several other servers stood huddled together. "Uh, yeah. Bacon coffee for you?" She slid a mug in front of Reed. Tiny bits of bacon speckled a mound of whipped cream.

Reed wrinkled his nose and pushed it toward Jax. "Not on your life, sister."

The server paled. "S-sorry. This one must be yours." She set down the other cup of coffee. "Your food will be out shortly."

Glancing at the table, Reed said, "We'll need another set of silverware—" But the server had already scooted away, hurrying toward the serving station.

Jax heaved a sigh. "We should have ordered it to go."

"I doubt that would get the food to us any faster."

"It's not taking a long time because this place is busy. It's because they don't want to serve us." Jax jerked his head toward the cluster of whispering servers. "Bet our waitress drew the short straw."

"Why wouldn't they..." Reed was suddenly aware of his glasses and freshly washed blue jeans. He glanced at Jax, who was running a comb through his greased locks. Sunlight limned his tattooed brow and the lettering across his knuckles. "She was scared."

Jax pursed his lips. "Yeah."

"Guess I'm going to have to get used to that, huh?"

"I'm mostly to blame, I'm sure. Happens to me a lot. I guess we're lucky we didn't get kicked out."

Reed's face flushed as he glanced at the tables around them. Either the stares were increasing, or he hadn't noticed them when they'd first arrived, being so mired in his own worries. The entire world was trying to push them into a mold. Telling them that having their minds all to themselves was illegal, that they couldn't express themselves the way they wanted to in public because it was wrong.

Technically, he and Jax *were* criminals. Jax had an insulin contramod and Reed had used an interrupter and now possessed a forged navigator exemption document. He'd also

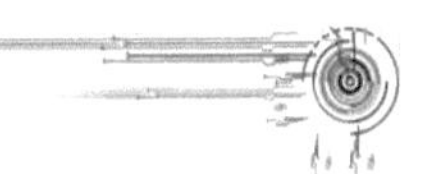

sold a copy of his beta, downloaded illegal software into his nanos, and lied to a Wave engineer about it. But the people in this diner couldn't know that by looking at his cuffed jeans.

He wasn't a dope dealer or a kidnapper. He paid his taxes, stopped at yellow lights, and donated to charity.

"Don't suppose there are any restaurants around here with secret knocks," he said.

"Not that I know of, but someone should get on that." Jax prodded the melting whipped cream on his mug, his mouth pulled down. He dropped the spoon. "Sometimes I just want to shake these people and tell them I'm a good person."

"I think that would have the opposite of the intended effect."

Jax pushed away his untasted coffee and pulled his tattooed hands into the sleeves of his coat, face sullen. "Just wanted to take you out this morning to make you feel better and everything's been shit. All you did was make fun of that antique store, and you didn't even look at the things I picked out."

Reed's heart sank. "Sorry. I appreciate it—I do. Just... depressed. And I wanted out of that place because I was hungry. *Am* hungry."

"Yeah, and now we can't even fuckin' eat because our server is too scared to bring us pancakes. I don't even want to drink my coffee now after the shit you gave me for it."

Reed bored a hole through the table with his gaze. "I was only joking. Wasn't trying to be hurtful."

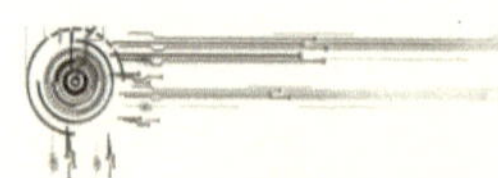

"I know, but..." Jax rubbed his face, then slid out of the booth. "Let's just go."

An older man shoveled a forkful of scrambled eggs in his mouth, pinning Jax with a glare. Though Reed wanted nothing more than to bolt out the nearest door, he squeezed Jax's bicep and said, "Why don't you head to the car? I'll be there in a moment."

He marched past booths, heading for the serving station. Their server froze, wide-eyed. Whispers died on the lips of the other servers.

"Excuse me, but I was wondering if you could take a break from being terrified to box up our food? We'll be taking it to go."

The waitress disappeared into the kitchen and returned with two to-go cartons in a sack. Reed paid in cash, which the waitress didn't seem to know what to do with, holding the bills in her open palm like a lizard she didn't want to touch. The hostess took the cash and tucked it into a lockbox below the counter.

Reed said, "Can I get two to-go cups too? Gotta save my boyfriend's nasty coffee."

Jax lingered in the entryway, hunched into his coat. A family with two small children stood across from him, waiting to be seated. A little girl in pigtails strayed a bit too close to Jax, and her scowling mom snatched her by the arm and jerked her back to her side.

Juggling coffees and the sack of to-go cartons, Reed stepped between them and leveled his gaze on the woman, his fingers tingling with adrenaline. "Just breathing the air around a decoist can infect you, you know. Starts with the itch to wear spectator shoes and sniff old books. Then you'll get the urge to cut a rug to some jazz and hand-write letters. Before you know it, you'll be covered in tattoos and saying things like, 'Hey, Mack, where's a copacetic jive joint? I'm jonesin' for that clam-bake.' Not much hope for you then. I mean, just look at poor Jax here." Reed squatted in front of the girl. "I recommend starting your collection with a Ruby Jane platter. The bass lines will flip your wig."

The mom made a noise in her throat, pulling the girl away as Reed stood. He handed Jax the coffee cups. "Let's go, daddy-o."

Jax followed him into the brisk morning air, icy breath wafting around his face. He opened the car door. "You're cheeky this morning."

"Hangry, with a side of despair." Reed slid into the seat, the warmth from the to-go boxes seeping into his jeans. "And I don't like seeing you upset. Especially if I'm the one who caused it."

Drumming his thumbs against the steering wheel, Jax stared out the windshield. "So what do you want to do now? Want me to drop you back at your car?"

"No, I want to go back to your place and eat pancakes away from people who think tattoos are contagious."

Jax nodded, face stony.

A thick silence hung between them as they drove to Jax's apartment, Reed struggling to keep cooling coffee from sloshing out of the lids on the cups. Was Jax really mad that Reed had poked fun at that cluttered antique store and teased him about his bacon coffee? He'd been in a bad mood, sure, but didn't always use jokes to repel people. Sometimes he used them to connect to them too. Maybe he was doing a poor job at it. And now more than ever, he needed someone to connect to. Mazarin had been his only reassurance in a world that didn't understand him. And the human part of him *had* understood Reed. The more Reed thought about the nav's humanity, the worse he felt about what had transpired.

Once inside Jax's place, they reheated their food and coffee while The Dixie Ghosts drifted from the record player. Jax sat on a vinyl stool at the tiny table, chewed his pancakes like he was being forced to eat gravel.

Reed's stomach groaned in anticipation as he cut into his own stack; chunks of indigo blueberries and fluffy pancake drenched in syrup hung from his fork. He took a bite and sank back on the stool. After quelling some of his hunger, he washed the pancake down with a draft of coffee.

Jax kept his eyes on his food, long strands of shiny hair hanging in his eyes. Reed's hand crept toward Jax's coffee. He slid it toward himself and Jax looked up. Resisting the urge to scrunch his face at the soggy bacon chunks bobbing in oily, melted whipped cream, he took a sip, tensed at the foul, conflicting flavors, then pushed it back toward Jax.

"Okay. I owe you an apology." Reed licked his lips. "It's delicious."

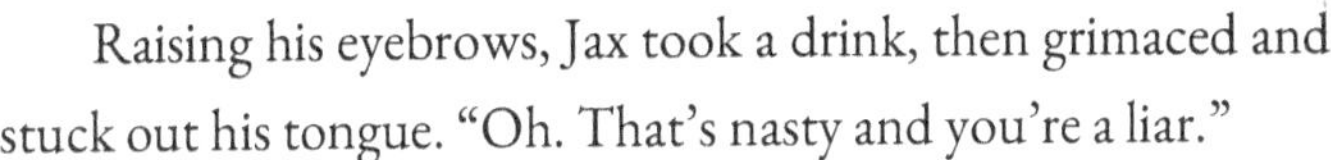

Raising his eyebrows, Jax took a drink, then grimaced and stuck out his tongue. "Oh. That's nasty and you're a liar."

Reed smiled, but it quickly faded. "I'm sorry for being an ass this morning."

"I'm not in a mood because of that. You have every right to be upset about the stuff you've gone through lately. I just feel shitty now because I pushed you to be more deco. I mean, you already liked those things, but you hid it. And now you're wearing deco clothes in public and going to clubs with secret knocks and don't even have a nav anymore. You wouldn't have done those things had you not met me."

"That's not a bad thing."

"Isn't it? You being my guy is only going to make it worse because there's no way for me to hide being deco. Anytime we go out, people are going to stare. You hate attention and now you'll have even more. And people are gonna be dicks about it, like at the restaurant. It's like you've been trying so hard to keep this illusion in public, and I went and yanked it away like, 'Aha! Look what's really behind the curtain!'" Jax planted his chin on his fist and sighed.

"That's not what you did." Reed rounded the table and slid his arms around Jax. "I've never felt more understood by people than after meeting you. Sure, most of the world doesn't get us, and that's still terrifying, but there's a freedom that comes with it too. And inclusivity. I like my privacy, but I was lonely. Had no one to connect with. Not saying I'm ready to make karaoke night a weekly thing, but it feels good to know

I'm not alone in the things I love. And that you're there for me when I need it."

He pressed his lips to the rose/skull tattoo on Jax's neck. "And I like you calling me 'your guy.'"

Jax turned, his nose grazing Reed's. "Fuck all those mainstreamers, huh?"

"Nah. Just me."

Pressing a hand to the back of Reed's head, Jax gave him a deep kiss. Reed pushed against him, bumping the table. Whipped cream ran off the sides of Jax's pancakes, pooling onto the plate. He scooped up a blob and flicked it at Reed, spattering his glasses and jaw.

Mouth twisted in feigned irritation, Reed said, "You better clean that off."

Jax grinned. "Oh, I'm planning on it."

Dec 16, 2065

DECO DRESS MAKES TEEN GIRL A TARGET

Boise— Seventeen-year-old, Clark Winchester, is in critical condition after being assaulted in a charging station parking lot on Franklin Road. Winchester, who was on her way to a Christmas party, had been wearing a beaded, purple "flapper" dress, commonly worn by participants in the deco subculture. A man who wishes to remain anonymous due to his own decoist identity saw the altercation unfold and stepped in to help.

"I was inside the [convenience] store when I noticed a couple of joes, including the cashier, were staring out the window. I asked them what was happening and they said a little [expletive] was getting what she deserved. I ran outside and saw these two crumbs trying to have their way with this unconscious dame. I got in some chin music before they ran off. Cops caught up with them down the block.

"I don't know if the girl was deco or just wanted to be a rebel and wear something fancy, but she shouldn't have been out alone in that. I hate to say that, but it's not safe in mainstream society. I never have any problems, because I'm a big guy, but all the kittens I know have at least one chaperone with them if they're out in public in deco duds."

Winchester's parents say they don't know where she got the dress from, but they're grateful to the Good Samaritan who helped their daughter.

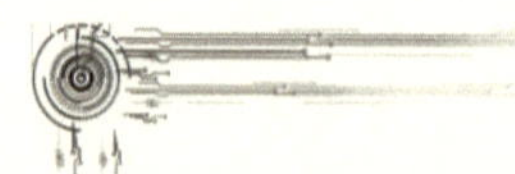

Mazarin

Muffled curses shot through the front door, the key jiggling in the knob. Em kicked open the door with one snow-caked wingtip, juggling a package in one arm and a sack of groceries in the other. They slammed the door and blew out a breath.

I had been awake for several hours, and my internal clock had told me the computer was turned off for two days, six hours, and fourteen minutes. By the time I'd come to full awareness and accessed the computer camera, Em was on the other side of the door, twisting the deadbolt closed. They'd been embarrassed that I'd seen them in pain—and probably also upset about failing to finish their beautiful song—so I didn't blame them for disconnecting the computer. I'd entered their personal space without permission, after all. But hopefully Em wouldn't have the need to do that again.

<Welcome home, daddy-o.>

Em snorted, dumping the groceries by the door.

<You know, 'daddy-o' is a really gendered term. I'm sorry for using it to address you.>

Em waved a hand. "I don't mind it."

<I was thinking, you aren't a man or woman, and neither am I.> I chuckled. <I'm a binary system but my gender is nonbinary. I wonder what else we have in common?>

"Are you trying to relate to me? I don't wanna disconnect you again, but I'm not getting personal with you, got it?" They pulled off their coat and tossed it on the bed, then looked pointedly at the computer camera. "Shut your eyes."

I did as instructed. Footsteps thudded into the bathroom and the shower turned on. I had a suspicion Em's immediate showers when they came home had less to do with cleanliness as they did warming up their aching mods after being out in the cold. Well. Maybe that package dumped by the door would help with that.

When Em exited the bathroom, I dutifully shut off the camera until they were dressed. I itched to mention the package, but held my tongue. They were things Em could probably buy themselves—the illegal programs on their computer were no doubt worth a lot to the right buyer—but the state of Em's apartment and their worn shoes suggested they didn't often spend money on themselves. The vacation they were planning was probably an exception.

Bags rustled in the kitchen, cabinet doors creaking open. Em walked into the view, the ratty hem of their robe grazing the floor as they picked up the package and carefully dusted off snow with one sleeve.

Frowning, they walked to the desk and retrieved a slim device with a light on the end. Clicking it on, they pinched open a tiny holoscreen on the back.

<What's that?>

"A snooper. I didn't order this package."

<I did.> I'd wanted it to be a surprise, but there was no reason to make Em suspicious.

They looked up. "You? I thought you didn't have access to the Wi-Fi."

<Well... I have my own. I didn't tell you, because I needed it to order this package.>

Em scowled and set it on the desk, nudging it away. "What is it? A better camera for you to see around my dump of an apartment? Better not be a fuckin' glitter bomb."

I laughed. <I promise it's not. It's a gift. For you.>

"Where'd you get the money?"

<I have a bank account.>

Em snorted. "That so?"

<Yes. There are plenty of ways to make money online.>

Clicking on the snooper, Em aimed it at the package, their face turned away from me. I turned the camera, but couldn't make out Em's expression or the projected image streaming from the device in their hand. They narrowed their gaze at me, face cloudy. "Why did you buy me these? What do you want?"

<I don't want anything. There's no ulterior motive. Someone can do something for a person without expecting anything in return, can't they?>

Pulling the box into their lap, they said, "Life doesn't usually work that way. Someone always wants something."

<But you give away prosthetics and implants to people for below your cost. Often for free. Do you want things in return for that?>

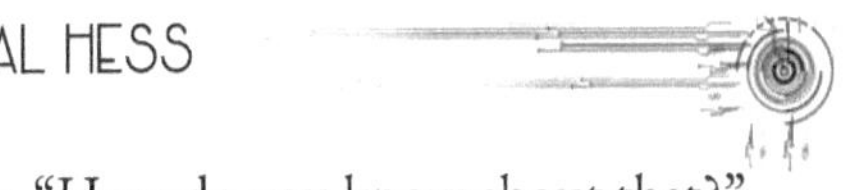

Their head snapped up. "How do you know about that?"

<You have a lot of notes on your desk.>

Em leaned back and looked away. "I don't want anything from those people. Just... trying to make their lives a little better because I know how it feels."

<Well, do you believe I'm capable of the same? Of giving a gift for no reason other than feeling empathy for a person?>

"Maybe." Em ripped the tape off the top of the box, glancing at the computer camera as though I might have an expression there they could read.

Buying the gifts seemed like a good idea—I wanted to help Em—but that had gone disastrously with Reed. Perhaps Em would forever harbor a suspicion that I wanted something from them because of this. I had a steep mistrust to overcome, since my navigator kin had murdered their pilots, but conveying selflessness was still something I could do.

Spreading the items onto their lap, they bit their lip, brows pinched. Clear packaging crinkled as they pulled out one long, black glove.

<The right glove is a size larger than the left. Same with the sock. I was afraid they would be too tight, otherwise, with your mods.>

Em clicked the heating button on the edge of the glove. They turned it over in their hands, then pressed it to the right side of their face. Sliding down in the chair, they leaned their head back, all the crankiness they usually wore melting away like snowflakes on skin.

I didn't need to see Em's brainwave scans to know how much relief my present brought. But Reed had liked his gifted book too—he just hadn't liked that it was from a navigator.

Em slid on the glove and flexed their hand. "Are you ready for an orgasm?"

<Um... Are you going to play the piano or have I inadvertently seduced you?>

"Oh, you've seduced me. Best bribe I've ever received."

<It isn't a bribe. I just didn't want you to suffer.>

They gave me a smile, honest and asymmetrical, and ripples of warmth washed over me. Thumbing toward the piano, they said, "Its name is Big Al."

<Perfect.>

Em took off their robe and sat on the bench, then pushed up the sleeves of their flannel top. A sultry melody—all smoke and syrup—oozed into the room as their fingers flitted over the keys. Who was seducing who here?

Em tapped their bare foot against the pedal, fingers dancing over ivory. I increased the microphone volume, wishing I could drown in the song. It was a shame the microphone wasn't as sophisticated as nanobot receivers. Even so, I would remember every note.

Shutting their eyes, Em swayed on the bench. I imagined being their navigator, inhabiting their body and watching as they hammered away on Big Al, all those rich piano notes filling the receivers in Em's ears. Seeing the pleasure centers of their brain light up as the melody overwhelmed them. Did Em's

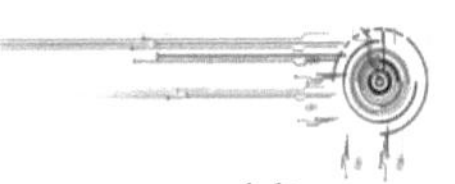

blood sound the same as Reed's? Was it the same trembling gush-thump, or something more steady and solid?

I shoved the thoughts away. I barely knew Em and shouldn't be having dirty fantasies about being inside their body.

Em's fingers slowed, the song fading into a single, haunting note.

I found an applause track on the net and played it through the speakers. Em grinned. "You liked it?"

<Incredible.>

"I've never played that for anyone before."

I lowered my voice. <You still haven't. I'm not an anyone. Just a thing.>

"Don't try to tell me you're just an object. We both know that's not true." Em swiveled on the bench, facing me. "I play music in here all the time. My microwave doesn't clap for me. My fridge doesn't know when I'm hurting and buys me gifts in response. Shit, people don't even do that for me."

<I'm programmed to be empathetic.>

"People are raised to care about each other too, but a lot of them don't. Seems to me you think for yourself."

<I wish I didn't. I wish I had never been able to go against my programming. To have feelings. If I'd acted the way I was supposed to, I'd still be with Reed.>

Em sighed. "Listen, I'm not the best person for advice, probably, but you need to forget about Reed. Sometimes you can still be friends with people you've broken up with, but trying to get back together with them is a terrible idea."

I was capable of deleting memories, but as much as I hurt, it wouldn't be right to remove that part of myself. Humans couldn't do that. Why should I? <We didn't have a romantic relationship.>

"The hell you didn't. It was just... one-sided. Hard to blame him, though. You're not an object but you're not human, either."

<I'm quite aware of that.>

Em opened their mouth, then furrowed their brows and turned back to the keys. "Want to hear another?"

<Yes, please.>

Rocking on the bench, Em launched into a zingy ragtime tune. It was lovely, but did little to lift my mood. I couldn't forget about Reed. I had fifteen years' worth of memories from his previous nav model, and I'd been his navigator for three months, fifteen days, eighteen hours, twenty-five minutes, and thirteen seconds. Been with him for every waking and sleeping moment. Every second of Reed's despair, joy, boredom, anxiety, befuddlement, vulnerability, and quirkiness. Reed's body had been my temple, our conversations my sacrament.

Admittedly, Em was a nice distraction. They asked for nothing from me, and they weren't unkind. They had a protective front, sure. So had Reed. But if Em didn't have a desire for conversation and connection, they would have gotten rid of me or kept the speakers and camera disconnected.

Maybe I wasn't an object, but perhaps Em felt more comfortable sharing things with me since I wasn't human. I'd never considered that an advantage before.

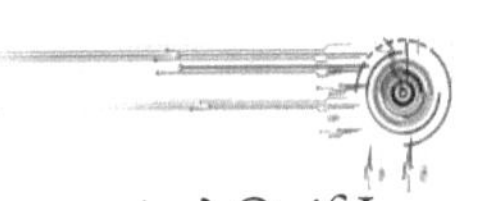

Would Em like it better if I had a different voice? Or if I was "she" again? Judging by their search history on the internet, I guessed yes. I'd chosen my current voice for Reed and dreamed up a face to go with it. But if I had an identity beyond being Reed's navigator, it didn't make sense for me to keep the old persona. I needed my own—a voice and face just for me. Desires that didn't have anything to do with taking care of a pilot.

But I wasn't yet sure what those were.

I found a husky female voice, smoky-sweet, not unlike Em's music, and tried it out for myself: *Welcome home, Em. I'd love to hear another, Em.* Perfect. It sounded completely different, and belonged to a different face. Maybe a new voice would help me untangle my identity from the one I'd had with Reed.

The ragtime song ended and Em stripped off the heated glove and massaged their hand. "This works surprisingly well. I think pouring drinks at the club will be much easier now."

<I'm so glad it's helping.>

Em's gaze darted to the computer camera. "What are you doing? Why'd you change your voice?"

<I have quite a few to choose from. The one I had been using I'd picked for Reed, but I thought you might enjoy this one better.>

"Why?"

<The majority of the porn you've looked at—>

Groaning, they walked to the desk and sat. "So what are you trying to do? Turn me on? Manipulate me?"

<Not at all. I just thought...> I was making a mistake again. Why was it I always knew exactly what people liked and wanted, but when I gave it to them, it turned out wrong? <I'm sorry. I'll change it back.>

"You can have whatever voice you want. I don't care. I'm not your pilot."

<But I don't know what voice I want.> I reverted to my male voice. <Or gender, or... anything. I don't know who I am if I'm not a navigator. The only thing I ever picked for myself was my name, and I only chose it because Reed likes blue.>

"Welcome to humanity, Maz. Nobody knows who they are or what they really want. You think I have my life figured out?"

<You have a routine. A business. A style.>

"Those things change. I don't want to be a mod dealer all my life. Last week I got into a shit situation. Wound up tied to a chair in an abandoned boxcar in Nampa." Em's face creased and they brushed a lock of hair from their eyes.

<Oh dear. I'm very sorry to hear that. That must have been terrifying. Were you hurt? How did you get out?>

"Eh, I don't want to talk about it. Was just trying to make a point. That I get tired of doing what I do. Someday, I'll have enough dough socked away to do something else. Sell the bar and... become a beekeeper or something. Hell if I know. But I do have things that define me. My principles, convictions, things I care about. You have those things too, and that's your core. The rest is just... garnish."

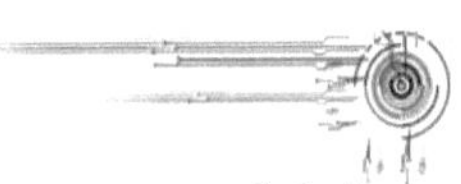

<Garnish.> If my voice and default programming didn't define me, what did? My principles to not harm people, perhaps. Conviction to help others when they were hurting.

"Speaking of, what do I do with you? I'm sure you don't want to be stuck on this computer forever. I don't think Reed wants you back. I could take you somewhere if you have a suggestion."

If I was to make a choice based on the things Em said defined me, then I needed to do the least harm and help the people I cared about. Not as my duty to a pilot, but following my morality as an individual. I'd cared about Reed more than anything, but my presence had harmed him. If I could still watch over him via the house cameras, I could protect him without interfering in his life.

Jax had said dating Em was like romancing a brick wall because they wouldn't open up to him. But Em was telling *me* things. Maybe the right person for them was really an empathetic AI.

Light from the kitchen highlighted Em's damp hair and the way they'd carefully molded the front into a thirties coiffe. I estimated Em was in their mid-forties, but their face appeared younger when they were contemplative and not putting up a front. Their drooping right eyelid and corner of their mouth were more pronounced when their face was placid, but their rich brown eyes were softer, some depth there momentarily unguarded. It was a face I could look forward to seeing.

<I'd like to stay with you, if you'll have me. Not as a navigator, but... a conversation companion.>

Em cocked an eyebrow. "I'm not huge on conversation."

<You're talking to me right now.>

"Sure, but..." They pushed a pen across the desk until it disappeared under a stack of papers. "Look, there would be plenty of times when I don't feel like talking. You get chatty and I'd tell you to shut it."

<Then I'd shut it. I'd be content to exist in this space while you go about your life. If you want to keep the camera and speakers off until you'd like some conversation, that's okay by me. I don't get bored.>

"Alright." Em stood and hurriedly added, "But just because I feel sorry for you. I'm not lonely or anything. I don't need anyone here with me."

<If you say so.>

They glared and walked out of view. While they were in the kitchen, I reached out to Reed's house cameras. The repair van was in the driveway, but there were no cameras in the basement so it was impossible to know how the progress was coming along.

Reed walked into the living room and put a fist on his hip. Longing surged through me. He had on a red polo shirt—red! He took a sip from a water glass, then set it on the coffee table and walked to the wall. A shelf had been mounted where the TV used to be, salvaged books from the den arranged on top. After sliding one out, he pushed the books over and nestled it into a new spot, then nodded.

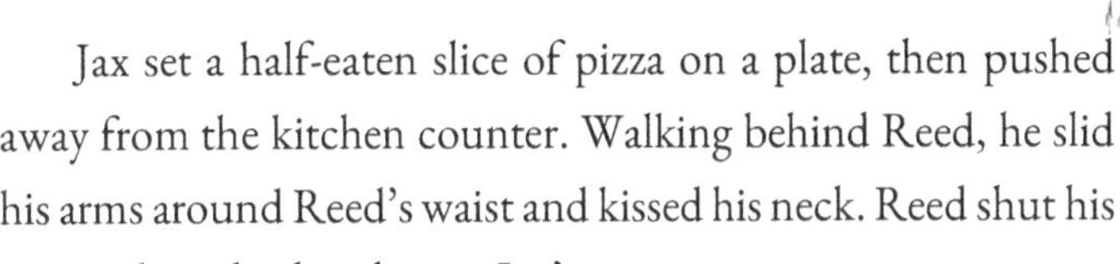

Jax set a half-eaten slice of pizza on a plate, then pushed away from the kitchen counter. Walking behind Reed, he slid his arms around Reed's waist and kissed his neck. Reed shut his eyes and put his hands over Jax's.

I did a quick sweep of the other house cameras, then terminated my view. Reed didn't need my protection. He didn't need my encouragement. Not if he was wearing a red shirt and decorating the living room with things from the den. And he definitely didn't need my love. Jax had that role covered.

It was great for Reed. Jax treated him so nicely, cared about him, listened to him. And Reed's feelings for him were strong. The fire in the den hadn't wrecked him the way his breakup with Ken and the destruction of his last collection had. He was rearranging the pieces of his life and moving on just fine. I wanted only good things for him.

So why did I feel so shitty?

Em sat on the bed with a microwavable dinner and swiveled out a little holoTV from the wall. They clicked through channels until finding a cheesy horror movie already underway, then cut into the indeterminate meat on their tray. I thought of asking them if they liked to cook sometimes—I knew a lot of recipes—but I suddenly didn't feel much like talking. Some conversation companion I was.

Putting myself into standby, I ran diagnostic reports and dwelled in silence until Em said, "Thanks for the gifts." They lay on their back in bed, eyes closed, one arm tossed over their forehead.

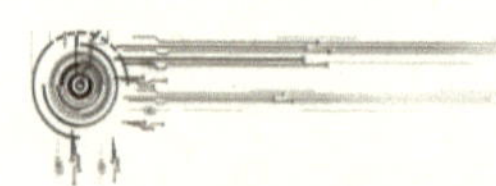

<You're welcome.>

Pale light from a street lamp washed over Em's tranquil face, softening their crow's feet and frown lines. Their chest rose and fell beneath the quilt.

<Can... can I ask you for something?>

"Ah, it *was* a bribe."

<No. This is unrelated. I was wondering...> The worst they could do was call me a name and unplug the computer for a while. But I wasn't sure I wanted to risk that. Picking a new voice had been the wrong choice. Maybe it was wrong for me to ask for this. <Nevermind.>

Em sat up. "Out with it."

<There's something I'd like to listen to that's even better than your music. But I expect you'll say no.>

"What's that?"

<Your heart. Could you put the microphone on your chest, just for a little bit?>

They frowned. "Is this some pervy navigator thing you get off on?"

<No. I mean... I don't think so. It helps me when I'm feeling bad.>

Em stared at the floor. "I've done kinkier shit." They climbed from bed and retrieved the mic from the desk. After lying back down, they tucked the end under their pajama top, pressing it against their chest. "Can you hear it?"

The gushing thump of Em's heart washed me in warm calm. <Yes. I can. Thank you, Em.>

"Yep."

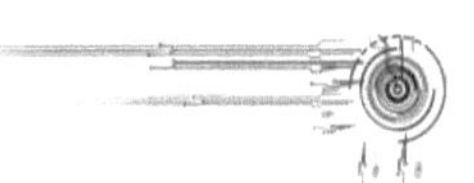

The steady thud quieted my mind. I pictured my human self lifting his ear from Em's chest and walking to the window. Beyond the curtains, clouds swollen with snow softened the night sky. Tiny flakes glowed in the cones of streetlights, and cars passed silently on the distant freeway.

I imagined him dusting off the desk and washing dishes in the sink, then draping an extra blanket over Em, just in case they were cold. Then he'd pull on a coat, open the door, and step out into the night. He'd stand on the corner and let snow fall in his hair and on his cheeks. Maybe he'd take a cab until he arrived at a house in a subdivision that looked like every other house. After walking over the frozen grass, he'd stop at the front door and knock.

Reed would be inside, wondering who was there so late and trying to recall where he'd put his sand wedge. When he opened the door, Mazarin would offer his hand. He'd say, "I'm sorry about what happened between us, but I want nothing but happiness for you. I hope you have a wonderful life."

Where he went after that didn't matter. Em insisted they didn't have their life figured out and they were still okay. I would be okay too.

I didn't know where I was headed, but I knew now what I wanted.

I wanted a body.

Reed

Reed stood at the threshold of the den, eyes closed. The only person to go in had been Jax, rescuing splayed books, the record player—which had escaped destruction save for one melted leg—and several crystal tumblers. Fire hadn't touched the books on the top shelves, and the antique tomes now sat on a shelf in the living room. The very act was sacrilege after having them hidden away in the den for so long, but the living room was still part of his house and his sanctuary. He never had visitors anyway, aside from Olive and Jax, who already knew he was a decoist.

Pounding came from the basement, the sound kicking against the inside of Reed's skull. Despite the door's proximity to the den, he'd been able to drown out the noise in the past. But even playing records at their loudest in the living room—another affront to his habit of secluded enjoyment—hadn't swallowed the hammering.

Anxiety itched in his fingers and grated against his chest. Jax had said the den didn't look that bad, all things considered, but the charred books weren't his company during lonely

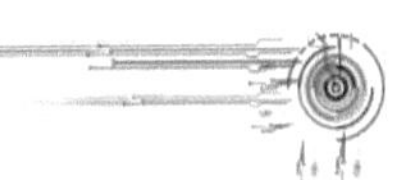

nights. The melted records weren't his compatriots in the love of a long-gone era. For Jax, the wingback chair wasn't the comforting arms of a friend after a day of stress and rush hour traffic. He appreciated the value of these things, but they didn't hold the same meaning for him as they did for Reed.

He had to go in. The insurance company had added den repairs to the ever-increasing list of things needing to be fixed in the house, but Reed refused to let anyone step foot in his burnt, but still sacred, domain until he'd cleared out everything salvageable and had a chance to mourn.

"Don't be a milquetoast. You can walk in and pull out the chair. Or would you rather stand in the hallway like a ninny until all that hammering gives you a migraine?"

Instances of him talking to himself had come more frequently recently. The dialogue with himself was always harsher than anything Mazarin would have said to him too. He needed to cut that out, both the unkind words and talking to himself. He'd wished for years to have his thoughts and mind to himself, and didn't need to be providing his own voice as a surrogate navigator.

Plush wool gave way under his loafers as he stepped inside. The acrid scent of melted plastic and charred wood overwhelmed Reed's senses and he tensed, tongue thick and throat tight.

"Open your damn eyes," he whispered.

The front of the den looked as it should, sparkling gold scalloped wallpaper, brushed metal sconces, and navy rug. But a dark cancer ate away at the back wall, swallowing half the bar and bookshelf nearby. Mounds of powdered book pages sullied the scorched rug. Melted celluloid ran down the side of the bar in a frozen dribble. Curls of wallpaper hung in blackened ribbons like a hideous garland. The bottle of Willow Witch lay on its side, mostly empty, open mouth hanging over the edge of the bar and the glass stopper on the floor, covered in soot. Dark trails of bourbon ran down the wallpaper and across the scorched electrical outlet.

Reed stared at the path. The bourbon had spilled into the outlet... Had the bottle fallen over before or after the fire started? His assumption had been Mazarin had blown a fuse because he'd had control of the house. Or maybe used one of the cleaner bots to jam a fruit knife into the outlet. But Mazarin couldn't have reached the bottle of bourbon, high up on the bar, nor did it seem likely he could have bumped the bar precisely enough with a bot to spill it in the correct direction.

Which meant it could have been an accident.

Fresh anxiety drowned Reed. Mazarin had snatched The Old Man and the Sea off the floor and shoved the other books over to make room. The shelf collapsed and books fell everywhere. They might have hit the bourbon bottle and knocked it over.

Reed grasped a tumbler from the floor with a quivering hand. He'd been so focused on the books falling, he hadn't noticed the bourbon. Maybe it had *all* been an accident. Mazarin had said it was difficult to open the front door with the bots. It was probably equally difficult to push over books on a shelf to set another one inside.

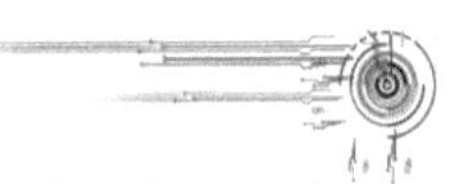

Trembling, Reed dropped the tumbler and sank into the wingback chair, vaguely registering that the corner of the seat was charred but otherwise intact.

Had he killed his desperately loving—and perfectly sane—navigator over an accident? Mazarin should have cried of his innocence. Even if he was too distraught to speak during the fire, he had a whole car ride to the Gator Club to try to convince Reed. He hadn't begged for his life. He hadn't said a word.

And Reed never asked.

He had to find out. Mazarin had set up the house cameras beforehand. They would have recorded the whole thing. If he could review the footage, slow it down, maybe, it would tell him for certain whether Mazarin had purposely burned his collection, or whether Reed's paranoia had been the nav's undue death. But he had no idea how to access the cameras. The repair people probably knew but he wasn't going down into the basement to dump details of his personal life on Jerry.

Olive would know. Guilt sank deeper into his stomach. She'd called him paranoid and told him not to get mixed up with decoist dealers like Em. Then he'd freaked that his nav was trying to kill him and he'd rushed straight to Em to get Mazarin terminated. Em didn't have any fault in this, though, and neither did being a decoist in general. If the fire had been an accident, it would all be on Reed for overreacting.

Striding into the kitchen, he stared down the burnt orange rotary phone on the counter, wishing for once that he had some tech that was function over form. A tiny address book sat beside the phone, penned in with all the phone numbers he could find listed online. Flipping to "P" in the vintage book, he landed on Olive's name and turned the dial on the phone, waiting impatiently for it to rotate back so he could enter the next digit.

The monumentally tedious task of dialing the number complete, he leaned against the counter with the receiver to his ear. A tinny jingle played on repeat until Olive's voice, low and apprehensive, breathed into the line.

"Who's this?"

"It's Reed."

"Reed! Oh my god!" He cringed and held the receiver away from his head. At least with a physical phone, he could put distance between his ear drums and Olive's shrieking. She said, "I've been so worried about you! You never take time off and you've been gone for two days. I almost didn't answer the call because my nav didn't tell me who was calling."

"That's because I'm talking to you on a phone."

There was a pause. "Like, a phone, phone? Your nav giving you problems again? You have to get a smartphone or something?"

"It's not a smartphone. It's completely deco and I guarantee you'll hate it." He dug his fingers through the pigtail cord, a knot forming in his chest. "Listen... Can you come over? I've had a hell of a time over the past couple days and I really need your help with something."

"Of course! I wish you would have called me earlier."

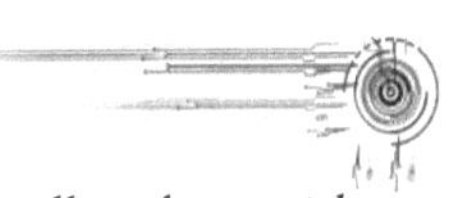

He bit his lip, the tightness in his center telling him with alarming clarity that he cared about what Olive thought of him because they were indeed friends and he didn't want to lose that. "I, uh, I didn't call you before because after the things that happened, I was afraid you wouldn't understand or you'd think badly of me. You still might." And even worse of him if the cameras show the fire was an accident.

"Oh, Reed... I don't know what's going on, but I'll be there for you, even if I don't understand. But be prepared for a hug when I get there, okay?"

He sighed. "See you soon."

While waiting for Olive, Reed dragged the wingback chair from the den; a trail of black soot scraped across the pale tile and onto the beige living room carpet. He pushed the chair kitty-corner to the wall, then draped a white afghan over the burned seat edge. It looked fine that way, but was still irritating because he knew the burn was there, even if no one else saw it. He didn't have the energy to be concerned with how out of place the cyan chair was in his anemic living room. Not with greater issues plaguing his mind.

A knock came at the door. Reed opened it and Olive threw her arms around him, crushing him in a chilly embrace. He gave her a small squeeze back and ushered her inside.

The casual Olive was a look Reed hadn't seen before. Despite following the "natural" New Era trends, without her contouring, false lashes, and lip-plumping gloss, she looked like a different person. Her hair was pulled back into a short, messy ponytail, her cheeks kissed pink by the cold. She paused midway to the kitchen, staring at the wingback chair, then the books and record player.

"They're from my den." Reed's brows pushed up. "Want to see what happened to the rest of it?"

Olive followed him down the hall and peered inside. Reed turned away. He didn't want to look at it again. Everything salvageable was out—the repair crew could toss the bar and bookshelf in the huge dumpster in the yard out back.

Clutching the door frame, Olive turned back to Reed, mouth trembling. "What happened?"

She followed him into the living room, and he wondered distantly how long it had been since he'd sat on this couch. Though he didn't think she'd sympathize with his viewpoint and subsequent actions, he didn't sugarcoat anything, chronicling all the events that happened after he stepped out of her car on Tuesday.

Olive's round face crumpled a little more with each detail Reed relayed, though whether it was disappointment or sympathy was hard to say.

Reed stared at his hands, which she'd clutched in her own, sandstone-shellacked false nails pressing into his skin. He struggled to swallow the lump in his throat. "Then Em stuck the interrupter against my neck. It, uh... I don't remember it well. Only that it hurt more than anything I've ever experienced and I pissed my pants."

She turned away, wiping her face.

"I know you think I shouldn't have gone running back to decoists for this, and that I'm paranoid, but—"

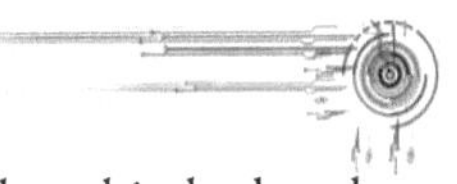

"Please, Reed. I need a moment." Her chest hitched and she put a shaking hand over her mouth.

After retrieving a box of tissues from the bathroom, Reed sat and touched her shoulder, mood even heavier than before. He'd treated Olive as a casual coworker, an acquaintance, and he'd obviously been much more to her for her to react this way. How had he been so oblivious to others' feelings for him? "I didn't ask you to come over so you could feel bad for me. I'm sorry."

Olive dabbed at her eyes and sniffed. "I would rather be here, feeling upset, than have you not share your life with me. I care about you. And you aren't paranoid. That guy from Wave? He showed up again today and wanted to talk to you."

Reed's stomach tied itself into a knot. "About what? My nav?"

"Yeah. Said he had your name on a list of beta recipients."

"I told him there was another person with my same name who must have a beta. Pretty sure he didn't believe me. Guess I was right. Does he have my address?"

"No. Said he checked the one listed for you and it was in the middle of the Snake River."

Thank you, Mazarin.

Olive frowned. "How many people did you say received a beta upgrade?"

"Twenty-five."

"Yeah, well he showed me the list of people with beta navs that he was trying to find. There were only four names on that list. Yours, Langley's, and two others. I asked him what happened to the other people. If they'd died like the guy who came in on the meatwagon the other day. He got all funny and told me not to worry about it. Said Wave was handling it." Her brows pushed up and a tear rolled down her cheek. "I didn't tell him I knew Langley. I've tried calling her and going to her place, but I can't get ahold of her. Her roommate said she was visiting her mom in Twin Falls. I really hope that's the truth. I don't want her hurt because of a crazy navigator, or because Wave wants her to disappear."

Reed rubbed Olive's back, hoping the motion hid the tremble in his hand. Four people left. Should he leave town too? He didn't have a nav at all anymore, but that didn't mean Wave wouldn't make him disappear just to shut him up, especially since Phil Rice knew he had a nav just the other day. Most people who were exempt had been so since they were kids, or after chronic health problems flared up. He hadn't even read the doc to see the reason for his exemption. Em had probably put something awful down, like hidradenitis suppurativa, regardless of whether that would actually affect the function of a navigator.

"Hopefully Langley is with her mom. I don't see why her roommate would lie about that. Maybe you can find her mom's number? You used to date one of the cops at the station, right? I bet he could look it up."

Olive wiped her face with a new tissue. "Maybe. I'm just so scared for her, and I wish I would have listened to you earlier. Do you think... would that decoist dealer be willing to use an interrupter on Langley too, if it came to that?"

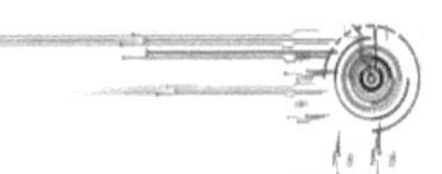

"I'm sure they would. But exemption documents are really expensive, apparently. I can't give you a number, but I'm sure it's ridiculous. Em gave me mine for free because their other software didn't work for me." Reed sighed and leaned back on the couch. If Langley was caught without a nav before she saved up money for a fake doc, it probably wouldn't be too big of a deal for a first offense. It would keep her safe from a homicidal nav, but not from Wave. The company wasn't playing by the rules. They were kidnapping people and making them disappear. If all they wanted was the navs back, getting rid of people didn't make sense. And it meant frying your nav wouldn't increase your safety.

But Olive was already upset, and mentioning his worries wasn't going to help right now.

Olive's nails dug into Reed's arm. "I'm so glad you're okay."

"Yeah... But I need your help. I think..." Looking up, he blinked away the sting of tears behind his eyes. "I think the fire in the den may have been an accident, and I terminated Mazarin unnecessarily. I need to access the house cameras to see, but I don't know how to do that. Not sure how Mazarin turned them on in the first place."

"Even if it was an accident, I think it's better you don't have him anymore, what with that Wave guy snooping around."

His fears were too many, and that didn't comfort him. He wasn't safe from Wave, and no one should have had to suffer because of some megacorporation's failures, self-aware navigators included. "I need to know. For my own conscience."

The couch creaked as Olive stood. She surveyed the room, then walked to a panel inset in the wall. After popping it open, she pinched open a holoscreen and scrolled past menu options. "Did you even know this panel was here?"

Reed stood and put his hands on his hips. "As a matter of fact, I did."

"Well, you never know with you." She flicked past settings at a speed that left Reed reeling. "At the risk of sounding demanding, I could use something strong and boozy. You got anything like that?"

"Sounds like a great idea." Reed headed into the kitchen and pulled down a bottle of gin. He was no mixologist, and bourbon was his greatest love, but Em's bee stings were decadent enough to want to recreate at home. As he drizzled honey syrup into a cocktail shaker, Olive said, "Oh, I think you'll want to see this."

Stomach clenching, Reed added lemon juice and gin, then poured the shots, carrying them back to the living room. "Might want to drink this first."

They clinked the shots together. A tart burn, salved with floral sweetness, overwhelmed Reed's mouth as he downed the shot. He dragged two bar stools before the holoscreen streaming from the panel. A frozen image of the hallway filled the screen. Olive hit a tiny play button in the corner.

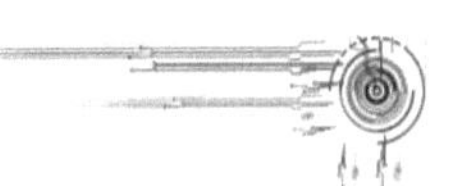

Mazarin's voice came from the speakers and Reed's heart lurched. *<You idiotic bot. You have a thumb appendage, don't you? Pick up the damn book. Reed will be home soon.>*

On screen, one of the cleaner bots struggled to lift the copy of The Old Man and the Sea from a cellulose box on the kitchen floor. The spindly arm quivered and the book fell, hitting the floor with a thud. A breathy sigh came from the speakers. The bot attempted again, then again and again. Olive hit fast forward on the feed until the bot had the book in both hands, rolling slowly down the hallway to the den door.

He had to try so many times to even pick up the book. Reed wasn't sure he needed to keep watching to confirm what had happened, but he leaned forward on the stool, gaze glued to the screen. The bot set the book carefully in front of the den door, then patted it and wheeled away. Olive glanced at Reed, then forwarded the tape again, stopping on an image of himself sitting in the wingback chair in the den, the book in his hands. His voice played through the speakers and Reed wanted to smack his video-self in the back of the head.

"I don't hate you. But I can't love you the way you apparently love me. I just can't. I'm sorry to say that."

<Reed—>

"That doesn't mean we can't be more than just navigator and pilot. We are friends. I enjoy talking to you. I trust your judgment. I feel better knowing you're around."

Mazarin sobbed and tears in Reed's vision distorted the screen. He wiped them away, determined to know exactly what had happened. On screen, a cleaner bot sped into the room, its trajectory veering off course like a child trying to ride a bike for the first time. The bot rammed into Reed's shoe, then scooped up the book on the floor. Its spindly arm reached for the bookcase, but the bot lurched, slamming into the book holding up the shelf. Paperbacks hurtled from the bookcase. One hit the bottle of Willow Witch. It clattered onto its side, the glass stopper bouncing onto the floor. Bourbon splashed against the wall. Reed's video-self fell to his knees, clutching books and loose pages. He strode from the room, jaw set.

Mazarin's voice came from the speakers. *<I'm so sorry, Reed! I can fix this!>*

Bourbon ran into the socket of the electrical outlet. A spark flared and popped, searing the wallpaper and igniting the trail of alcohol.

<Oh God. Oh God oh God.>

Reed wanted to look away from the recording, but didn't dare, clenching his fists until his nails dug painfully into the flesh of his palms.

<No. No no no!> On screen, the arm of the cleaner bot flailed, beating against the orange flames crawling toward the bookshelf.

Why hadn't Reed heard Mazarin's exclamations? Maybe the nav could compartmentalize them so they were only coming through the camera's speakers. Or maybe he wasn't even aware he was saying anything at the time.

A wave of fire roiled over the cardboard sleeves of the records on the bottom shelf. A strange noise came from the

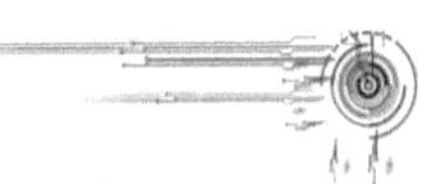

speakers and the tiny cleaner bot gripped the records, trying to pull them from the shelf. *<Please no! Not the records!>*

Reed slapped a hand over his mouth. "Turn it off, please. I don't need to see anymore."

Olive pressed stop on the feed, eyes wide and mouth pulled tight.

There was no way to fix this. Em had deleted their copy of Mazarin and he didn't care what Phil Rice said—there would never be another navigator like him. Mazarin had done nothing but lift Reed up during the hard times and celebrate every win. And Reed had killed him.

Pulling in a shuddering breath, he strode from the room. His glasses clouded with a sheen of tears. Dropping onto the bed, he pulled a pillow to his chest and buried his face into the side. He was an awful person. He deserved whatever Wave wanted to do to him.

I'm sorry, Mazarin. I'm sorry.

14

TO DO LIST: DON'T DIE

Mazarin

The video was terrifying. Synthetic skin wrinkling over a slick metal skull, plastic eyes shifting unnaturally from side to side. The robot's hand closed around a drinking glass, the flesh bunching like a rubber glove. Horrible. An android body would never do, unless I planned on giving everyone nightmares. The point of gaining a body was to assimilate as well as possible, not to be eligible for a job as an extra in a haunted house.

An android body would be harder to customize too, decisions about appearance and sex more permanent since they usually came with a distinctly male or female body.

I was still having trouble deciding on that. The default navigator voice had been female—the only reason for changing to anything else had been Reed. What Reed might like.

What did I like?

Em flopped a suitcase on the bed, then opened the dresser, tossing sloppily-folded polo shirts and tees inside.

I switched to a husky, female voice. <It's a good thing you don't need me to water plants while you're away, huh?>

They glanced back at the computer. "Eh, I have one in the window, but I'm pretty sure it died a long time ago... New voice today?"

<Yes, and I think I want to try going by 'she' again to see how it feels. But I want you to know it's not to please you. I'm just trying to figure myself out.>

"I know exactly what that's like. If your pronoun changes to something else before I go, let me know."

<Are you leaving soon?>

"Nah. Don't need to head to the airport until this evening."

<How will the deco crowd possibly survive a week without you?>

Em shrugged. "Maybe they won't, but I need a break from the snow like Hell needs an air conditioner. No idea how long it's been since I took time off work." They folded a pair of jeans with a patched hole in the knee, then squeezed the denim. "The year I spent in a wheelchair doesn't count."

<Must have been awful. How long ago was that?>

The silence stretched on long enough that I assumed Em was done talking. They sat on the bed, clutching the jeans in their lap. "Car wreck was in sixty-two. Spent a year with half my body paralyzed. Tried every legal mod on the market—which isn't saying much because there aren't many—rehabilitation programs, you name it. Nothing worked and I was fuckin' frustrated. The mods I have now weren't a guarantee to work, and ridiculously uncomfortable to install, but they're better than anything else I've found."

Em tossed the jeans into the suitcase. "You think I'm crabby now, you should have met me when I was in a wheelchair."

<I don't think you're crabby.>

The faintest hint of a smile crossed their face. "You're sweet. Or a liar. Guess you can sympathize with how it feels to be in a body that doesn't do what you tell it to."

<Yes. I think it would be nice to have a body of my own. It would be better than being stuck in a computer. I don't get bored, but I feel like I can't relate to people the way I'd like to.>

Em sat at the desk and pushed away a coffee cup that had been sitting in the same spot for three days. "You want to be human." They shook their head. "That didn't sound right. I think you *are* human. On the inside. Just need an outside that reflects that."

I swelled with warm, frothy waves of an unlabeled emotion. <You think I'm human?>

"Look, I'm not much for philosophy or arguing the semantics, but you feel things like a human, don't you?"

<Some things. Emotions, although many times I can't pinpoint their names.>

"Doesn't matter. You feel things and your thoughts are your own." Em shifted, frowning, and the chair creaked.

<What's wrong?>

"Nothing. Y'know... I don't usually tell people about my time in a wheelchair. Not a thing I like to talk about. Want to know something ironic? It was a drunk driver who ran into me, and I used the settlement money to open a bar."

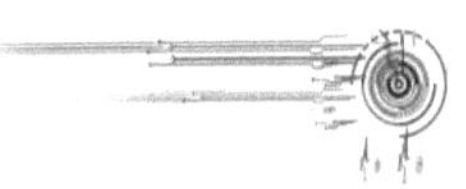

<A secret, decoist bar.>

"Yeah." Em picked up a penny and turned it anxiously between their fingers. They were working fingers, knuckles scraped from bottle caps and pads calloused by dishwater and piano keys—nothing like Reed's slim, pale fingers, adept at stitching closed a body or turning a delicate book page. Em's hands were smaller, rougher, but still deserved to be handled with care. I had care, but no hands of my own to curl around Em's. They continued, "After I got my mods installed, I needed some way to make a living, which was impossible because my mods are illegal and pretty hard to hide. The cat who invented them told me he had a patent coming, so I opened the bar in the meantime. But he was denied approval—big companies throwing their weight around to keep him out of the medical mods scene—and then I was stuck like this. Started getting into dealing on the side and bought myself a forged doc saying these mods were from China and sanctioned for human use. China has way more innovative tech and less restrictions."

China had better android bodies too, but a quick search showed they were more expensive than I could afford at the moment. Maybe there was something more imaginative I hadn't thought of yet.

Em's face flushed and they flicked the penny across the desk. "Not sure why I'm sitting here blabbing when I should be packing."

<I enjoy talking to you. About anything, but especially when you share things with me.>

Their cheeks burned pinker and they stood, grabbing handfuls of socks and boxer shorts and stuffing them into the suitcase. Had I done something to embarrass them? Maybe they regretted sharing personal information with me and I'd made it worse by pointing it out.

<You know, anytime you want me to go into standby, just ask. I realize I've invaded your personal space and become an unwanted roommate.>

They headed into the kitchen, pulling something from a cabinet I couldn't clearly see from the reflection in the mirror. "That's not what you are. You're my conversation companion, remember? And we just had a conversation. Now we're done... unless there's something *you* want to talk about."

Was there? Em had talked to me quite a bit over the last few days, and I thought maybe that meant they were warming up to me, but they seemed uncomfortable.

<Do you think I still have the potential to become hostile like the other beta navs?>

"I've been thinking about that." Em crossed the room, their hand in a bag of potato chips. "Rumor is there aren't many of your kind left."

<I don't really consider them my kind. Not if they are harming their pilots.>

"See, it's that kind of stuff you say that makes me believe this is your true personality. Everyone has the potential to be hostile, Maz. That base instinct to lash out at whatever's upsetting you. But it's whether you choose to act on it that sets you apart." They crunched on a potato chip, then brushed

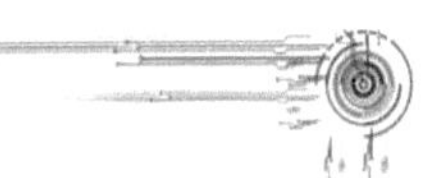

greasy crumbs off their hands and squinted at me. "I seem to recall you telling me you'd lay me flat if it were in your power to do so."

<Yes, but that was in defense of Reed. I thought you were going to hurt him.>

"Exactly. Do you still feel that way about me?" Their brows pushed up and they looked away. "I mean, I helped Reed terminate you. And when I couldn't finish my song on the piano the other day, I disconnected you for two days because I was afraid you'd want to talk about it."

<God, no. I don't have ill will for you. I like you very much. Thinking about you hurt upsets me as much as thinking about Reed hurt.>

Em stared into the bag of potato chips as if it were suddenly the most interesting thing in the world. "Thought so. Well listen, I had my doubts about you when I first talked to you. Was afraid you'd end up saying something incredibly creepy or try to harm me—"

<You were?> They hadn't acted that way that I had seen, but I still had a very hard time reading people's expressions and body language. <They why didn't you delete me?>

"My gut has been telling me you really are as nice as you seem to be, and my gut's not usually wrong. I don't think you'd ever hurt anyone unless it was in self-defense. You talk a lot and I know you probably think I'm not listening half the time, but I am. I don't think you have a hateful bone in your body. Well... you know what I mean."

Em drifted into the kitchen. "I guess what I'm trying to say is you can trust me. You're safe here. I hate Wave as much as anyone and I think you're just as much a victim in this as anyone else."

Sweet pinks and peaches burned inside me like a sunrise. <Thank you, Em. I'm glad to have a friend in you.>

Em trusted me. But what if their gut was wrong? I might still have the potential to harm people, or at the very least, enough ineptitude to cause another accident like the fire in the den. Maybe getting a body was a bad idea. Thinking about accidentally hurting Em, or worse, my mind decaying and turning me violent, fizzled all of the warm colors inside me. Em was leaving soon and wouldn't be back for a week. If I could find a body, I could test it while they were away. But it needed to be something incapable of harm—

A hologram! Of course. With holosoftware, I could customize my face and body however I pleased, select clothing, hairstyle, height, and alter them whenever I felt the urge. And even at the highest density setting, it would be a ghost among the living. No way to hurt anybody, but still give me mobility and a face!

Speeding through searches, I analyzed all of the available holosoftware on the Chinese market. The anchors they used were superior to those in the U.S. in terms of density projection and the distance a hologram could be from the source software, but there were heavy restrictions on what kind of program could run the hologram. There was a good chance I wouldn't

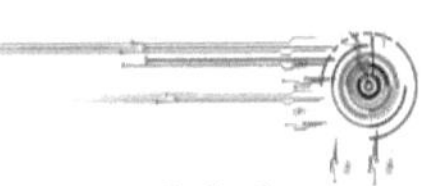

be able to inhabit the projection the way a person did their body.

These software safeguards weren't implemented in the U.S., but the sale of holograms were limited to specific businesses and came with stock programs that ran in a loop, with limited dialogue and body movements. Luckily for me, I was my own program and happened to live with someone who had a plethora of forged documents on their computer.

Em had their own bar and I could easily cite it as the business requesting the hologram, but I didn't want this tied to Em in any way. Getting them or the Gator Club involved on paper would be bad news for a contramod dealer who owned a decoist bar.

Instead, I used one of the templates on Em's computer with forged certification to create a false boutique in a Nampa mall. The particular hologram company I was ordering from was located in California; shipping would only take a day.

But where to have it sent... Em had a PO box for their more unsavory of transactions, but I didn't know who could pick it up and bring it to the apartment. Em was leaving this evening and would be gone for a week—and I wasn't sure I wanted to broach the subject of a body with them again right now. They might not want to help me.

Combing through other information on Em's computer revealed the contact information for a man named Mikey Gilliam who often aided Em with contramod deliveries and found new clients for them. Was he the same Mikey who had insulted Reed and been tossed out of the Gator Club?

Imploring his help was less than comforting, and I wondered what he think of me.

Nothing. He would think nothing of me because the message for assistance would be from Em.

I drafted an email to see if it sounded convincing:

Hey asshole,

I'm outta town and need a package picked up from our usual spot. Bring it to my place and take all the shit out of the box and just leave it on the floor, ya dig?

No questions.

—Em

That sounded like Em. Hopefully Mikey had a key. And hopefully I wasn't making a mistake by planning this and not being forthcoming with Em. My feelings for them were growing by the day, and being deceitful felt wrong. But if Em was completely against the idea, I may never have a chance to leave this computer, and the more I thought about having an identity and life of my own, the more I needed it.

I placed the order, directing the package to Em's PO box. It would be wonderful to try it out. It would be even better if Em liked interacting with me that way.

<I'm going to miss our conversations while you're on vacation.>

In the reflection of the mirror, a smile crossed Em's face, then evaporated and they cleared their throat. "Yeah, well, I'll be back."

 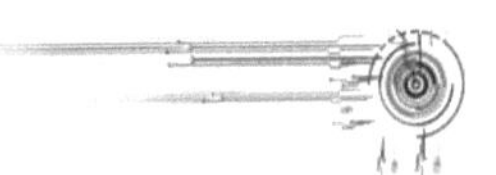

Strange. The reaction was candid enough that for a moment, I almost thought Em didn't just trust me, but actually liked me a little bit too.

Reed

Reed lay on his couch, staring at the wall. For once he felt like watching TV, if even just for background noise, but he didn't have one anymore. His record player nearby sat crookedly on a partially melted leg. One of these days he would play that Benny Goodman record Jax had bought him—the one with songs he didn't know. It would be enjoyable at some point, but right now, more unfamiliarity was the last thing Reed wanted.

Sero jumped onto the couch and flicked her tail in his face. He stroked her soft fur and pressed his nose against the couch cushion.

Hopefully Jax would be here soon with the takeout. Reed wasn't hungry, but he didn't want to be alone. It seemed a bizarre thought to have. All he ever craved was his alone time. His privacy. But Mazarin's absence was a void and Reed had fallen in. All the things that could have buoyed him up right now—books and records and his chair—still smelled like smoke and regrets.

A knock hammered against the door, one not in the pattern of "Shave and a Haircut." Maybe it was Olive. She'd been so concerned over Reed's anguish she'd refused to leave his side the night of the fire revelation, until he literally pushed her from the house so he could mourn alone. And he hadn't been back to work, choosing instead to use his sick days to become one with the couch. Being alone was getting lonely though. If it was her, she could have awkward introductions with Jax and a dinner of shared takeout.

"Alright, Serotonin, time to move." Reed nudged the cat and she hopped off the couch.

The knock came again. Reed walked to the door and swung it open. Phil Rice stood on the step, grinning. "Hello again, Mr. Rothwell."

Reed's stomach somersaulted and he tried to push the door closed, but Rice wedged his foot in the frame and said, "You're a hard man to track down. Haven't been to work in a few days and that cute little secretary looked like she'd rather claw my eyes out than tell me where you lived."

Cold metal dug into Reed's palm as he squeezed the doorknob. "What did you do to Olive?"

Rice laughed. "Why would you think I did something to her? I'm not the bad guy here, Mr. Rothwell. I'm only trying to help." He turned up the lapel of his coat, hunching against the bitter wind. "Mind if I come in for a moment? We need to talk."

"Yes, I do mind. My boyfriend will be here any moment for dinner and I have nothing to say to you as it is."

Rice reached into his pocket and Reed leaned back, expecting him to whip out a stun stick or an outlooper. He

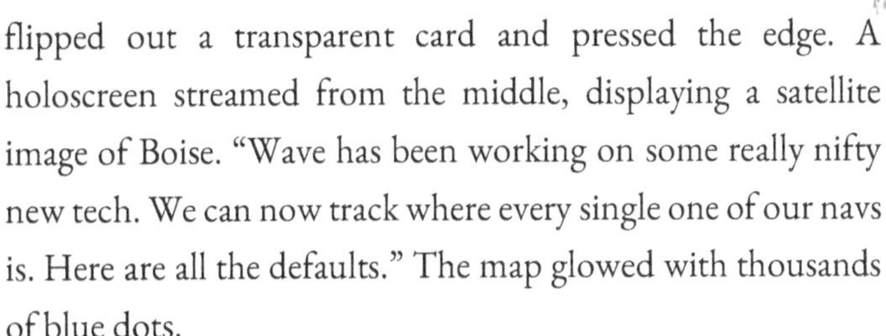

flipped out a transparent card and pressed the edge. A holoscreen streamed from the middle, displaying a satellite image of Boise. "Wave has been working on some really nifty new tech. We can now track where every single one of our navs is. Here are all the defaults." The map glowed with thousands of blue dots.

Reed scowled. "I thought you said you weren't keeping track of this kind of information."

"And I thought you said you'd never talked to me on the phone before. I think it would be best if we both lay our cards on the table. Here are all the beta programs left." The blue dots disappeared, two lonely red circles glowing on the map.

Hands trembling, Reed drew in a sharp breath. Only two left. Even proving to Rice that he didn't have a beta likely wouldn't render him safe. And what about Langley? Was she one of those dots?

Rice pointed to a red circle hovering near the North End. "This one here is next on my list to talk to. And this one"—he zoomed in over the other ring, floating over a nondescript house in a subdivision—"is you, Mr. Rothwell. Your house."

Reed's eyes widened. Why would the map indicate he still had a beta nav? Mazarin was dead. "Can... can that device detect destroyed navs? Nanobots that no longer function?"

"No, no. Only live programs. If it could detect destroyed ones, there would be many more red circles here. Wave has been keeping this hush-hush, but since we're being so forthcoming with each other, I will tell you that all of the beta programs are being terminated. They weren't working out. I know how interested you've been in downgrading back to the default. Now is your chance. I just need you to come with me. It won't take long."

If it was that simple of an issue to fix, it didn't make sense for everyone in contact with Wave to be disappearing. And why in the hell did the map say there was still a beta nav in his house? Mazarin couldn't still be inside.

The cameras. He integrated himself into the house. That could be why he hadn't pleaded for his life. Maybe he figured out how to separate himself from Reed and watch over him from within the house.

Instead of being disturbed by the idea, Reed's heart soared. Maybe Mazarin wasn't dead. But Phil Rice would still probably want him destroyed if he knew.

Goosebumps erupted on Reed's forearm as he pushed up the sleeve of his pinstripe shirt. "Your device is mistaken. I don't have a beta nav. I don't even have a default. I'm exempt. Go ahead and look me up in the exemption database. I'll wait."

Lines creased Rice's forehead. "But you had a nav the other day. And my map—"

"Do you want to see my physical copy of the exemption doc?" Reed slid out his wallet and flipped it open, then held up a small card with a complex code and swiped it through Rice's interface.

A file appeared on the screen and Rice squinted. "Reed Rothwell, navigator exempt due to severe anxiety disorder?"

"That's right. My poor nav couldn't handle the stress I threw at it every day. Probably why it was glitching so much."

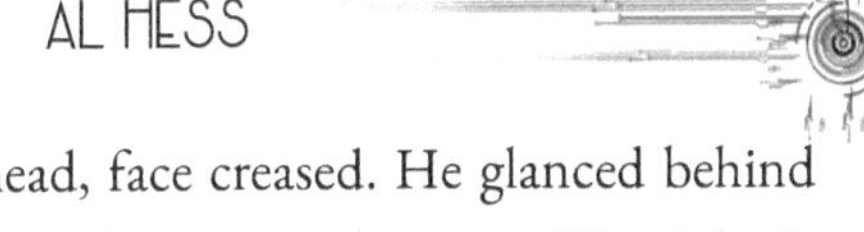

Phil scratched his head, face creased. He glanced behind him at the white Wave van idling across the street. "But I don't understand. If your beta is gone, there shouldn't be any indication of one here."

Reed folded his arms. "It seems your nifty tech is encountering problems—just like every other software program that comes from Wave."

"You need to come with me."

"For what reason? I just proved I'm exempt." He tightened his grip on the doorknob. *God, Mazarin, if you're watching, turn on the sprinklers or set off the house alarm. Call the cops.*

"There seem to be lingering effects on all the participants of the program, unfortunately. Even after the betas have been removed. Altered their brain chemistry and made them unstable. It has likely happened to you and you just don't realize it. Wave has an expert doctor handling all of the beta cases—"

"I don't believe that for one second. If the rest of the people who had beta navs knew about their brains being altered, you'd have one helluva lawsuit on your hands. You can't just take people to a doctor to fix your fuck up and expect they'll never say anything. So either Wave paid them off, or they don't have the ability to speak out about all the problems you've caused because you made them disappear."

"I think you watch too much TV. This isn't a conspiracy. Just Wave trying to correct a mistake in the most sensible way possible." Rice glanced at the shadowed, icy driveways to either side of Reed's house. "And the sensible thing to do, Mr. Rothwell, would be to come with me. I'm so close to putting out this fire and your cooperation will be greatly appreciated."

"Do you have a waiver I can sign refusing medical service that will absolve Wave of future liability? I mean, you'd have one, right? If that was really why you're here."

Rice opened his mouth, then shut it.

Reed narrowed his gaze, heart punching against his chest. "That's what I thought. Get your foot out of my door frame before I turn it into a crepe."

Rice's gaze locked with Reed's and the moment yawned between them. Reed tensed, ready to ram the door against Rice's foot. From the pocket of his coat, Rice whipped out a mini stunner.

Reed lost his grip on the doorknob and stumbled back. Rice pushed his way in, then stiffened as a car door slammed nearby. He glanced at the neighbor's drive, then put the stunner back in his pocket. He grinned and backed onto the step.

"You'll be hearing from me again. Possibly in the form of a summons. You've destroyed company property, after all, and I have no doubt that exemption document is falsified." Rice turned, striding down the steps and through the frozen grass.

Reed threw the door closed and locked it. He collapsed against the cold metal, sucking in shallow breaths. Rice would come back and keep harassing him until he caught Reed off guard and yanked him into an unmarked van. It didn't matter

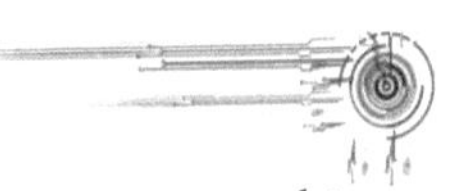

that he no longer had a beta. Wave was going to sweep this whole experiment under the rug.

Unless Reed could do something about it. It was too late for twenty-three of the beta testers, but he and someone else were still here. Wave needed to be exposed for their heinous behavior before they conducted some other maddening experiments on unwitting participants. They controlled the monopoly on navigator software, and their tech was in the heads of almost everyone in Idaho and the states beyond. If he lodged a complaint with the police, it might help. They were probably already looking into the disappearances of the twenty-three others, but maybe that map Phil had shown him could be leveraged against him. Hopefully the house cameras had picked up enough detail to see the colored dots.

Mazarin. Reed had to know if he was still in the house. Otherwise, what other explanation would there be?

Ripping his magnetic notebook off the fridge, Reed wrote a message with the stylus: ARE YOU STILL HERE?

He held it up to the kitchen camera, then the living room, then the bedroom. After erasing the words, he wrote again, his jaw aching. I'M SO SORRY FOR WHAT I DID. PLEASE FORGIVE ME.

A creak came from the closet and Reed stiffened, staring. He didn't think there was anything electronic in there that Mazarin would be able to control. Reed wanted a sign, but noises from dark places were less than heartwarming. Phil Rice could break in through the garage or back door.

Backing out of the room, he rummaged through the haphazard pile of things in the hall closet. Hefting his sand wedge, Reed turned back for the bedroom, squeezing the handle. He pushed open the closet door with the end, peering into the darkness. Boxes and blankets sat on the floor. His button-up shirts rocked slowly on their hangers.

Adrenaline lanced his fingers. "Mazarin? Are you here somewhere?" He strode out of the room, peeking through the blinds. The Wave van was gone. Maybe the noise didn't mean anything. Maybe it wasn't Mazarin or Phil Rice. So many assaults to his privacy over the past couple weeks had put Reed on edge: every tiny creak in the house, every bump at night, threw his mind into a maelstrom of paranoid thoughts.

But you weren't paranoid if something was real.

His time of wallowing on the couch had gone on long enough. He needed to call Olive to make sure she was okay, and maybe they could hunt down Langley. Hopefully she was the other red dot on that map.

Reed picked up his notepad and erased his message to Mazarin. He wrote:

TO DO LIST:

call Olive

find Langley

go to police

DON'T DIE

15

I CAN'T WASH THE DISHES, BUT I CAN CUT A RUG

Mazarin

I stared in the mirror. Though I'd known exactly what I'd look like from my customization of the software, it was something wholly different to stand in the mirror and turn my face—*my face*—side to side. The towel hanging on the wall was slightly visible through my head, but my brown eyes twinkled like the real deal, my teeth white and shiny. I ran a hand through my sandy blond hair and felt it. The sensation was hard to describe, just like every other emotion I wasn't supposed to experience. It was probably what it would be like to touch a pebble under a mound of blankets, the sensation there but severely numbed.

I grinned, the expression taking over my whole face. Lines appeared around my lips and strong chin, ending in dimples in my cheeks. My eyes creased, a hint of crow's feet at the corners. Raising my eyebrows produced wrinkles in my forehead and gave me an expression of surprise. Arching one brow or the other made me look wry and knowing, or maybe saucy, depending on the context of the situation. Pushing the brows down and setting my mouth made me look angry. Hopefully I wouldn't have to use that one.

It had taken six days for the package to leave California and make its way into Em's living room. The delivery to the PO Box had been on time, but Mikey Gilliam wasn't exactly a punctual fellow. Still, he hadn't questioned "Em's" instructions. He'd come inside, unboxed the items, then swiped a mostly empty bottle of gin from the kitchen cabinet and left.

Did I look handsome enough? It wasn't my intention to be sexually attractive, as I had no urge for that, nor would I be able to perform in any way for a partner. But humans were naturally more inclined to trust and listen to someone attractive, and I needed all the advantages I could get. Being an AI wasn't doing me any favors.

Every aspect of the hologram program had been customizable, down to things like skin texture and eyelash length. I had recreated the exact body I'd pictured during my time with Reed. I'd chosen caucasian heritage because that's what Reed had and what I knew best, with a face that could be considered better than average, but not perfect. I didn't want single-toned skin, precise brows, and no wrinkles like many of the other holograms had.

I'd created another face and body too. The hologram blurred and shifted, bobbed blonde finger waves and glossy red lips appearing in the mirror. I lifted one thin, penciled eyebrow and tucked a lock of hair behind my ear, revealing a dangling pearl earring. This body and gender didn't feel any better or worse than my male form. I was still Mazarin. Same twinkling brown eyes, same smile, same person on the inside. Maybe I

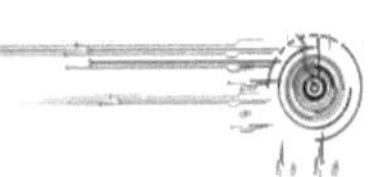

didn't need to decide on one binary gender or the other. Em didn't, and I enjoyed Em just the way they were.

I hadn't customized any clothing for the female body yet, and the plain white shirt I wore left a lot to be desired. Switching back to my male form, I gazed in the mirror as a fedora appeared on my head. Then the white tee shirt became a windowpane button-up with a spearpoint collar. Wishing it away left me with a naked torso without much definition and no nipples. There were skins for nude body holograms, but I didn't have them installed.

I tried to grasp Em's toothbrush, sitting in a rocks glass on the counter, and my fingers went through it. Turning the density to its highest setting, I tried again. The toothbrush rattled in the glass, lifting slightly in my fingers, then fell. I had an effect on my environment, but lacked the solidity to manipulate things. But still. I had a face now! Hands! The shirt appeared again and I turned from the bathroom.

The tiny projectors in my feet—anchors—distributed nanobots evenly through the hologram, and allowed me to "see" through the eyes and "hear" through the ears. My gait appeared natural as I walked through the hall.

Em had neglected several dirty dishes in the sink before they left, which no doubt smelled bad. I tapped the top of the faucet and water streamed into the basin. I laughed and grinned at the empty kitchen. Chunks of soured milk floated out of a glass while I pressed on the soap pump. The bottle shuddered, but no soap came out. I tried again. The dispenser wobbled and fell into the sink. Iridescent bubbles rolled across the dirty water. Touching the top of the faucet again stopped the water. There was no way I could wash these dishes. The soap bottle and bits of crusted food settled at the bottom of the draining basin.

Em's bed wasn't made, but only needed the top sheet and edge of the quilt pulled straight. Could I do that?

Grabbing the sheet was easy enough, but I could only tug it a fraction of an inch before it slid through my fingers and fell. After twenty-seven minutes of repeated motions, I'd pulled up the sheet and quilt and fluffed the pillows.

Putting my hands on my hips, I nodded at the perfect bed.

Eyeing the piano, I smiled and walked to the bench. I smacked my open hand against the keys. Only one depressed enough to make sound, the lone note floating through the studio.

If only the technology was just a bit better. It would take me only a few seconds to learn how to play if I downloaded a program. Several minutes, maybe, if I read instructions. Sitting on the bench next to Em and playing a duet would be even better than watching Em play from inside their mind.

Sitting. I hadn't tried that. I wasn't sure I could do it without falling through onto the floor. Walking to the bed, I bent my legs and dropped onto the edge. The bed held me but I left no depression. I tried one ankle on one knee. The leg of my slacks slid up, revealing a sock patterned in tiny lemons. On the sole of my brogue was the small plate anchoring me to the floor so I didn't drift into the apartment below. If I was locked in a room and couldn't turn the knob, I might be able to phase

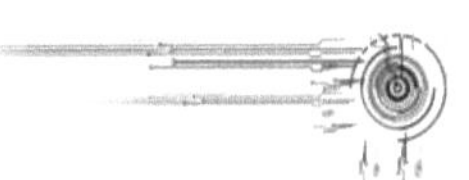

through to the other side if there was enough room for the anchors to slide below the door.

Willing away my shoes and socks exposed feet with no toes, the plate in my heel now. The shoes and socks reappeared. I planted my feet on the floor, hands on my knees, and grinned.

A key jiggled in the lock. Em was home already? I wanted to reveal the idea of myself in a body a little more tactfully than me sitting on the bed. But I couldn't just dematerialize, leaving the anchors on the floor. They might get kicked somewhere and get lost.

The door swung open. Em's eyes widened and they backed against the wall, dropping suitcases. "Who the fuck are you? How'd you get in here?"

I put up my hands but didn't get off the bed. <It's me, Em. Mazarin. I'm a hologram.>

Their face scrunched as they pressed themselves against the door frame. "How'd you do that?"

<I bought a program and hologram anchors. The purchases can't be traced to you, I promise. My own account. I had your friend Mikey collect the package and take out the pieces on the floor. He took a bottle of your gin. Sorry about that.>

Em huffed and locked the door. "Anyone see you like that? You go anywhere?"

<No. Can't turn the doorknob.> I beamed. <I did make your bed, though. Couldn't quite manage to wash the dishes. How was your vacation? You have a tan. Looks nice.>

Their nostrils flared and they picked up the suitcases. "Why the fuck are you sitting like that? People don't sit that way." They tossed a duffel bag onto the bed, which flew through my arm and landed behind me. Jerking open the zipper, Em scowled and pulled out handfuls of folded clothes, cramming them into the dresser. They kicked the bag under the bed, then stalked to the bathroom and slammed the door behind them.

I had done something wrong again. But the only person I'd been trying to please this time was myself. The body was a vanity, really. A novelty. It couldn't function like a human body. I could never live on my own or get a job—not even a job holoprograms had. Everything about me was illegal.

Standing, I crossed to the bathroom and knocked on the door, but my knuckles made no sound against the cellulose. <Em? I would never put you at risk. I took the most secure avenues possible to obtain this body, and I—>

"Just buy Reed an engagement ring already and get the fuck outta my life."

I stared at a nick in the door. <I have no intention of interacting with Reed in this body. Of interacting with him at all. I just wanted to experience the world in human form, even if the world is your studio apartment. If you don't like it, I'll only use it when you're at work. We can continue our conversations through the computer speakers. I don't want to make you uncomfortable.>

The knob clicked and the door swung open. Em regarded me warily, eyes glossy. "You're not leaving?"

I shrugged. <Where would I go? And how? I'd be in real trouble if I was walking around out in public. Are... are you upset because you thought I'd walk out and never come back? You like having me here?> The realization sent my heart spiraling upwards and I couldn't keep from grinning.

Em's cheeks burned pink and they brushed past me. Their modded arm slid through my hand. Waves of heat coursed over my palm and fingers. Now *that* was a feeling! Em stopped, rubbed their arm, then sat on the bed.

<Did that hurt you?>

Staring at the floor, they shook their head. "It was warm."

I walked in front of them, then bent at the waist, trying to look into their eyes.

Em snorted. "Someone needs to teach you how to move like a real person. You look fuckin' weird."

<Will you?>

They looked away. "Did you choose that face for yourself or is it the default?"

<I chose it. Is it weird too?>

"No. It suits you."

<I made a female one too. Can't decide which I like better.>

Em patted the spot next to them. "Sit down." I sat and they shook their head. "You look all stiff. Like you're constipated or something. Relax."

<I can't. I don't have muscles.>

"I mean lean back a little, spread your legs. Don't put your hands on your knees." I mimicked Em and they chuckled and said, "That's better, but you still look unnatural. Will probably take some practice."

<Are you mad I bought a body?>

Their dark eyes searched my face. "No... Touch me again. On my mods."

Em wanted me to touch them? But maybe I'd do that wrong too, or the technologies wouldn't mix and it would ruin one or both of us. Em was right there, though, in front of me, and I had hands now. I could express my feelings for people in ways other than speech and buying gifts.

Hesitantly, I cupped the right side of Em's face. Heat surged through my mind. Em let out a breath and shut their eyes.

<Is it better than the heated glove?>

"Yeah."

I was helping. Doing something good. I'd probably break the holosoftware with as much as I'd been smiling. Dragging my hand down Em's cheek, I caressed their neck, then ran my fingers down their arm. I clutched their hand in both of mine, warmth pouring into my mind.

Em's chest heaved. I wanted to ask them what they were thinking, but they probably wouldn't say. Instead, I slid my hand up their thigh, holding it to the cables barely visible under the taut fabric of their jeans.

Jerking up, Em took a step away from the bed. They rubbed their face. "This is..."

I cast my gaze to the floor. <Disturbing? Uncomfortable? Fuckin' weird?>

 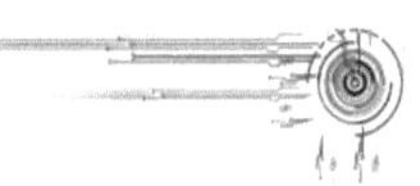

"All of the above."

I sighed. Not even a hologram body would help me connect to people. It didn't matter how many human emotions I experienced, I could never be one of them. Maybe it was a bad idea to interact with Em in this way. A voice in a computer was more distant. Sure, there were other hologram AI that talked to people—museum tour guides, strippers, salespeople luring shoppers into stores. But those programs weren't self-aware.

Em walked back to the bed and I looked up. They pressed their left hand against my cheek. The hologram resisted the pressure, then gave, Em's fingers sliding into my face.

"What's that feel like?"

<Not much. I can sense it, but only distantly.>

They pressed their modded right thumb against my cheekbone. "And that?"

<Much stronger. Warm.>

"Can you feel it in that spot in particular?"

<No. The program isn't mapped that way. No matter where your mods make contact with the hologram, I feel it in the same 'spot' in my mind. Can you feel me on parts of you that aren't modded?>

"Yeah. It's like... a strong breeze. Same as using an interface screen or a holoTV. But there's no heat except on my mods." They sat next to me and put their hands in their lap.

I pressed the ends of my fingers together, only lightly, so they didn't go through each other. I crossed my legs, then uncrossed them and leaned back on the bed. <So have you done kinkier shit than this?>

"Can't say that I have."

<Do you want to?>

Em barked a laugh. "That seems like a strange thing for an asexual AI to ask."

<I'm sorry. Not sex. That's not what I meant. But I do like you. I enjoy your presence and conversation. Having a body, even if it's a hologram that can't wash the dishes, gives me a whole new dimension with which to connect with you. Having a face will help a lot with that, I think.>

"Slow down, Romeo. I'm not opposed to you having a body, but it's going to take a bit for me to get used to you in this form." Em tugged on the strap of a suitcase near the door. After pulling it into their lap, they unzipped it and rummaged through. "Bought you something, by the way."

I brightened. No one had bought me a gift before.

Em chuckled. "You have the cheesiest smile."

<I'll practice making it better.>

"Don't. It's kind of cute." They opened their palm, revealing a carved turtle figurine. "These are traditional in Fiji. I was just going to set it on the desk in front of the computer camera, but I guess it can go wherever you want now."

<Thank you. I love it.> I held out my palm and Em placed the turtle in my hand, where it sat for a moment before slipping through and landing in my lap. It sank through onto the bed. <Maybe you ought to put it somewhere.>

Em paused, then reached between my legs with a smirk and picked it up. "How about on the piano?"

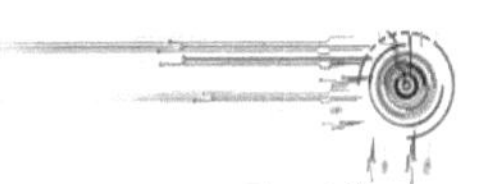

<Perfect.> As Em set the turtle on the piano top, I said, <Did you have a good vacation?>

"Yeah. It was mostly me getting a tan on my hotel room balcony and drinking too much. Just what I needed."

<I missed you while you were away, but I'm glad you were able to recharge.>

"Do you have access to the computer while you're in hologram form?"

<Yes.>

"Put on some music, will you?"

I selected one of Em's custom swing playlists. Lazy sax drifted from the speakers.

"I noticed you dressed yourself in decoist duds. You want to be one of us, there's something I have to teach you how to do."

<What's that?>

"Cut a rug." They beckoned to me.

<That sounds difficult. I can't even sit down correctly. Even downloading a program to know the moves, I have to learn to control this body.>

"Don't be a jellybean. We'll start with something easy."

I wanted to dance with Em, but I didn't know what I was supposed to do with my feet, or where to put my hands. Would moving to the rhythm be instinctive for me, as it was with people?

Em's face creased and they dropped their outstretched hand. "I guess if you don't—"

<I do.> I stood and walked to the center of the room. Em wrapped their arms around my hips and heat radiated into me. They said, "Lace your hands around my neck. We could switch roles, but I think I'd get tired of holding my arms up in the air."

Bridging the gap between us, I slid my hands over Em's shoulders, letting one linger against their neck mods. What would it feel like if I took another step and we merged together? Would it be too hot for either of us, or maybe break the software and kick me back into the computer? Reed had walked through a hologram once—some saleswoman trying to sell him lacy underwear. He'd been having a bad day already and instead of dishing out a cutting remark, he just walked straight through her. But her density probably hadn't been up high for liability reasons.

"Okay, now shuffle your feet in a circle. Follow my lead." Em swayed and my fingers passed through their neck.

I readjusted my hands and did my best to match pace, certain Em would tell me how terrible I looked. But they leaned their head against my chest and shut their eyes. Sultry piano and sax floated through the room. I studied the threads of silver in Em's hair, then stroked my fingers through; the locks rustled under my touch. Not only did having a body allow me to affect my environment, I was affecting Em. Not just their physical self, but emotionally.

They were close to me, pressed against me, but their body language was tense. Which either meant they didn't like their contact with me as much as it would appear, or simply that the logistics of dancing with a hologram were difficult.

<Are you enjoying this?>

"Shh. No chatting."

Viewing us both through the computer camera confirmed that we looked ridiculous, both of us out of sync with the other and the bed visible through my torso, but it *felt* great. We drifted together, limbs melding and parting, feet stepping through each other, until the song faded. Em looked up, expression open and eyes unguarded. Their gaze roamed my face, then settled on my mouth. Were they expecting me to say something now?

Leaning closer, heat radiating between us, Em gingerly pressed their lips against mine.

I spiraled out of orbit. What had I done to earn such a thing? I controlled the urge to grin like a fool and tried kissing back instead. It was doubtful Em could feel it, so I turned and touched my lips to mods under their cheekbone, then to the cables in their neck. My face sunk into their skin, and the sound of blood rushing through veins filled my ears.

<Ohh.> Tilting my head, I let the sound wash over me.

"Maz... Your head is literally inside my neck right now. And you're glitching."

My hologram flickered, limbs disappearing and reappearing. Straightening, I took a step back. <Sorry.>

They smirked, then yawned. "Okay. I'm beat. Long plane ride. You going to stay in that body while I sleep?"

<No. I'd probably knock something over and wake you.>

Em disappeared into the bathroom, then walked back to the bed and disrobed, not bothering to tell me to look away. I did anyway, until they climbed under the quilt in their pajamas.

I swiped my hand in front of the light sensor and the room darkened. Beyond the frosty window, cars drifted by, and wind kicked skiffs of powder across the street.

On the floor beside the computer desk was a box with a notebook and several pens inside. It would be as good of a place as any to leave the anchors, unless I wanted to attempt climbing on a counter to leave them there.

The box wobbled as I stepped inside. As I dematerialized, the anchors shuddered, falling against the notebook below. It wasn't until I was fully back in the computer, the hologram program terminated, that I realized how exhausted I was. Trying to move like a person took much more mental energy than monitoring the vitals of one from the inside. But it was worth it. I slow danced! Em kissed me!

If my beta compatriots had been given the chance to have bodies and lives outside of caring for their pilots, maybe they wouldn't have turned aggressive. After all, I had never been violent. Maybe the flaw in the programming was allowing self-aware AI to exist in the first place, then trapping them in people's heads. It was possible I was just more patient than the average navigator.

Though I had no grand schemes for liberating my fellow beta programs—it was likely too late for that, and I wasn't sure how to do that anyway—the whole thing was disconcerting. I didn't know if I had a right to exist at all in this form. If more people knew about me, they wouldn't probably consider me an

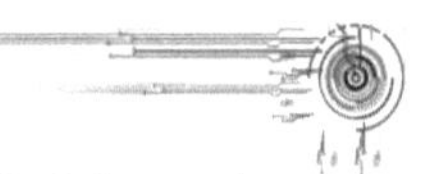

abomination. I wasn't human and certainly didn't know how to be one, but my feelings were real, my personality my own. If I did enough good in the lives of others, would it make up for the fact that I wasn't supposed to be here at all?

<Em? Em?>

They groaned and rolled over. "What?" Rubbing their face, they sat up and looked around. "Are you in the computer?"

<Yes. Can I ask you a question? And you answer me truthfully, not evade it?>

"No promises."

<Having conversations with you, being able to look into your face with the hologram, dancing with you... Do those things—do *I*—make you feel good?>

Em stared at the computer camera. "Yeah."

I regretted leaving the hologram so soon, because now I couldn't smile. <Okay. Good.>

"And for you? You feel the same way?"

<Yes. Very much.>

They nodded. "Night, Maz."

Delicious feelings coursed through me. The richest tones of cherry red, mustard yellow, robin's egg blue, and lusty peach. It was bawdy horn and tinkling piano and the tap of a snare. Was this what romantic attraction felt like? I had loved Reed— still loved him—but it was devotion, part duty and part infatuation. My feelings for Em were different. A desire to know them, to be shown the delicate layers underneath their exterior. To see all of the beautiful and terrible things that made up their soul, and then bare my own to them.

This must be how Reed felt about Jax. I searched for the sour emotion that had curdled my joy for Reed and couldn't find it. I wasn't sure why I had ever felt that way toward their relationship. Reed deserved to feel the same colorful, musical surge of wanting now drowning me. And if he felt it with Jax, I shouldn't be upset. I wanted Reed to be happy.

It had been a while since I'd accessed Reed's cameras, being so distracted by grief and new love and having a body. I peered through the living room camera, almost hoping I couldn't find Reed in the house because it would mean he was with Jax.

Velvet shadows draped the furniture in the front room. Records and two crystal tumblers which had no doubt held bourbon sat on the coffee table. Notebook papers crammed with handwriting lay on the wingback chair, but it was too dark to read them.

Sero stretched on the couch, then hopped onto the coffee table and batted at one of the tumblers. I tilted the camera, throwing a small pinpoint of reflection onto the carpet. The cat's moonlit gaze snapped to the spot and she pounced, knocking a pen off the coffee table. I shifted the camera, zigzagging the light across the floor, then chuckled as Sero scrambled to capture it.

Jax's coat lay over the back of the couch. The hall was dark, the door to the bedroom closed. I didn't need to check the bedroom camera. Reed was in good hands and hopefully as happy as I felt right now.

The magnetic notebook normally on the fridge sat on the kitchen counter, a streetlight from beyond the window illuminating the writing:

TO DO LIST:

~~*call Olive*~~

find Langley

go to police

DON'T DIE

What the hell did that mean? It was Reed's handwriting. Why would he need to go to the police and be concerned with dying? Maybe it was a joke. More of his dry wit. But Reed often used his humor as a deflection from things worrying him.

There were weeks of footage stored in the camera's memory. I played it backwards. Jax and Reed kissing on the couch and drinking bourbon. Jax and Reed eating from takeout containers at the dining table. Reed talking on an orange rotary phone, his face creased with concern. Brandishing a golf club at an empty closet. Holding the notepad up to the bedroom camera. The words burned into my mind: I'M SO SORRY FOR WHAT I DID. PLEASE FORGIVE ME.

All of the joyous colors and rhythms swelling through me twisted into a tangled knot. Reed knew I was alive. And he was sorry. Maybe he was still afraid I would become hostile and try to kill him. Perhaps he'd been living in terror for weeks, knowing I was still in the house and wondering when I'd strike.

That could be why Reed was concerned with dying. There had to be a way to get a message to him. He had a phone now.

I dialed his old number, wondering how it might feel to hear his voice again. I already had so many conflicting emotions coursing through me. There might not be room for any more.

The bedroom door opened and Reed staggered out, bare-chested, his curls a mess. He rubbed his eyes and slid on his glasses. It took him a moment of staring at the phone and shaking out his hands before he picked up.

"Hello?"

Everything inside me condensed like coal into a diamond. <Hi, Reed.>

A pause trailed between us. "Mazarin?"

<Yes. I saw your message. I would never hurt you.>

Reed sank against the counter and put his head in his hands, his voice broken. "I know that now. I thought I killed you. Over an accident."

<You did. But I forgive you.>

"I'm so sorry." He dropped the receiver on the counter, shudders wracking his body.

If only I could step through the phone in hologram form and give him a hug. <It's okay. I'm still here.>

Jax strode down the hall, his torso a dark forest of tattoos. Reed pressed his face to Jax's shoulder as Jax picked up the phone.

"Who the hell is this?"

<Hello, Jax. It's Mazarin. Will you please tell Reed to not be upset? And that I don't want to hurt him? I never wanted to hurt him. I only want the best for him and for both of you.>

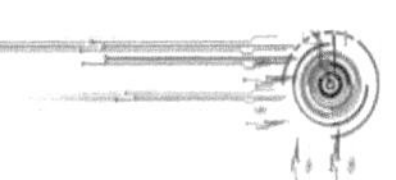

"You… what?" Jax turned to Reed and spoke something inaudible.

Reed took the phone. "That Wave guy, Phil Rice, showed up on the doorstep today. He wants to get rid of me. And you. I'm going to the cops tomorrow to lodge a complaint. Maybe get a restraining order. Is there any way to safeguard yourself from Wave getting access to you? Somewhere you can hide other than the house's network?"

Wave wanted to make Reed disappear, even without me in his body. Something bubbled under my surface. Was this the feeling Em had described about wanting to hurt someone or something if they deserved it? Wave deserved it if they planned on harming Reed.

<I'm not in the house's network. There isn't enough room for me in that drive. I'm… somewhere else. Maybe I shouldn't say if Wave still has an interest in us. I don't know if they can eavesdrop on a rotary phone, but I don't want to take the chance. But I'm fine. Very happy.> My voice threaded with warmth. <I think I might be in love.>

Reed rubbed the back of his neck. "There's a lot to unpack in what you just said. You're not in the house?"

<No.>

After speaking to Jax, Reed turned back to the phone. "Well, Wave thinks that you are. Maybe don't access the cameras anymore because it's putting off a signal that there's a beta nav in the house. We think we know where you're at. Just lay low, okay? Jax has a safe way to contact your friend. He can send them a message after we go to the cops tomorrow. Let you know what we find out... Mazarin, you might be the only beta navigator left."

<No. If the rest of them are gone, then that leaves none, because I'm not a navigator anymore.> My voice came out solid, full of conviction. <I'm a person.>

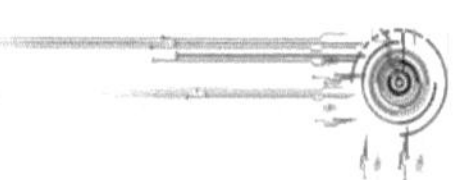

CLAIMS ADJUSTER HELD HOSTAGE

Boise— Fifty-two year old Jamal Washington was taken hostage yesterday by a fellow adjuster at Gem State Claims Management Services. The perpetrator, whose name has not been released, threatened Washington with an electric work saw and would not let him leave the building.

SWAT members were able to disable the assailant without violence. When pressed for a reason for taking Washington hostage, the woman claimed her beta navigator forced her to do it.

Phil Rice, lead engineer at Wave, refutes this assertion, stating the woman never had a beta navigator, and that even if she did, their experimental programs are just as safe as the defaults.

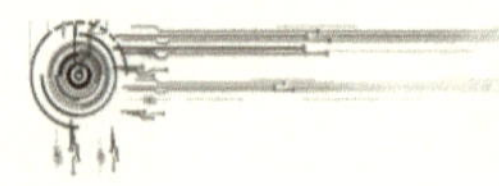

16

ERROR

Reed

A sea of papers sat on the dining table, coffee cup islands floating in between: complaint forms, requests for restraining orders, a missing poster for Langley, and video camera footage of Phil Rice on Reed's step with his nav tracker map, then trying to force his way into Reed's house. They even had a statement from Ambrose about the way Rice had harassed Reed in the autopsy suite.

Reed noted the trembling in Olive's hands as she gathered the papers, organizing them into stacks. She didn't want consoling over the disappearance of Langley. Reed had already tried that. Instead, she busied herself getting their onslaught of paperwork in order and making painful small talk with Jax. He didn't seem to mind, filling Olive in on the very best jazz bands of the thirties and forties, and how her tattooed eyebrows couldn't have possibly hurt more than the crow inked on his ribs.

All the different facets of this quagmire nibbled at Reed's brain, but one stood out among the others like the glowing blue bulb above the door of the Gator Club. Mazarin was a person.

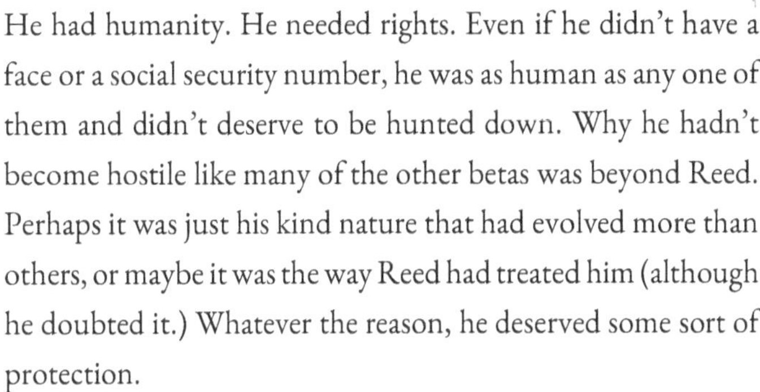

He had humanity. He needed rights. Even if he didn't have a face or a social security number, he was as human as any one of them and didn't deserve to be hunted down. Why he hadn't become hostile like many of the other betas was beyond Reed. Perhaps it was just his kind nature that had evolved more than others, or maybe it was the way Reed had treated him (although he doubted it.) Whatever the reason, he deserved some sort of protection.

AI rights had been implemented in Canada and Norway in previous years, but it was preemptive. There weren't any self-aware programs there that Reed knew of. The Allies for AI Agency in the US was the butt of many jokes, but if anyone would be eager to help, it would be them. If he could contact them, maybe he could get help for Mazarin. Surely Wave didn't have any rights over Mazarin now that he was self-aware.

He had broached the subject with Olive and Jax after his second cup of coffee, and Olive said she would get right on it. He didn't want to impose on her but she seemed to welcome anything that busied her mind and kept her from worrying.

They'd had to research things on Jax's ancient computer, since neither he nor Reed had an interface, and Olive had disabled her navigator before arriving at the apartment, concerned that Wave might track her there, even though she didn't have a beta.

Jax fished his spy texter out from under a stack of paper and popped out the keyboard. "Think it's late enough now that I can text Em without getting an earful of crankiness?"

"That's probably too much to hope for at any point," Reed said.

After slowly pecking out a message, Jax hit send. A reply from Em appeared, confirming Mazarin was with them.

Jax typed: <u both safe>

<yeah maz shut off wifi n sat links>

Reed wasn't sure how Wave was tracking the betas, but if Mazarin had cut off all outside signals, hopefully both red circles on Phil Rice's map were gone now. One from Mazarin's true signal in Em's North End apartment, and the false one given off by Mazarin accessing Reed's house cameras.

Smirking, Jax typed: <maz said hes in luv w u>

Reed scowled and smacked Jax in the chest. "Don't be juvenile."

A reply from Em appeared. <fuck u>

"I told you." Mazarin had a lot of love to give. Reed had a hard time picturing Em being receptive to it, but more power to them both if they were getting along.

Jax set down the texter. "Now what? Go to the police station and file these things?"

Olive nodded, still gathering papers. "I used to date one of the cops at the station next to the coroner's. He already knows Langley is missing and told me anything else I needed he'd be happy to help with. I think we ought to try to stir something up on social media too. Get some social justice, conspiracy outrage going on. Best place for that would be Noter. If I send a note, will you guys share it? I have a lot of followers, but the more it's shared, the more chance it will go viral."

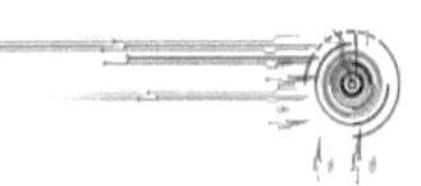

"I don't have a Noter account," Jax said.

"I don't even know what it is." Reed ran his finger across a chip in his coffee mug. "Is it one of those sites where you post photos of your breakfast with a heart filter over the top and thousands of people adore it?"

Olive rolled her eyes. "God, you two are impossible. Decoists. It's for video clips."

"Ah. A video of your breakfast, then."

She poked Reed in the arm with a false nail. "Make fun all you want, but it's a good idea. I bet it won't be hard to get the message out, what with all the rumors already. I can splice in some shots of that Phil guy and his map. I wonder why he even showed you that?"

"He seemed desperate to catch me in a lie," Reed said. "Desperate, period. I thought for sure he was going to stun me and drag me across the lawn."

"Yeah, I saw how he kept looking over his shoulder, and tried to push his way inside. What a creep." Olive stood, then her brows pinched and she stared at the stack of papers in her hands. "He got to Langley, huh? I'm never going to see her again."

"We don't know that. Just because she wasn't at her mom's house doesn't mean she isn't safe somewhere. Maybe she figured out what Wave was doing before we did and took a trip somewhere. Or maybe she's still in the city but terminated her navigator." Reed stood and gave Olive a squeeze around the shoulders.

"But wouldn't she have had to go to some secret decoist place for that?"

"Nah." Jax carried their empty coffee mugs into the kitchen and dumped them in the sink. "Not everyone who terminates their nav is a decoist. There are other contramod dealers who operate out of their houses or cars, people who share mod injections at parties and zap each other. All kinds of weird shit. If she asked around, I'm sure it wouldn't have been hard for her to find someone with an interrupter."

"I think I want to get rid of mine too." Olive wiped her eye, smearing her chestnut liner. "I mean, I use my nav all the time, but I don't want some shady megacorp tracking me. And what if they roll out with some upgrade that's even worse than their beta experiment? I don't want that in my head."

"I'm sure Em can help." Reed pulled on his coat and buttoned it. "But maybe hold off until we know if we can get anywhere the legal way. You still have a default, so you can keep it disabled until then."

She glanced at the glowing interface in her arm, face wrinkled in disgust, then picked up her coat.

Reed

Reed wiped his sweaty hands on his slacks and swallowed hard. It didn't matter if his face would be blurred out in the finished video. Hundreds of people would still see it and hear

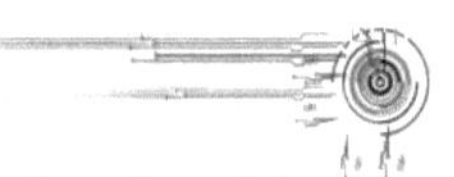

him talk. Olive insisted it would be many more than that if they were able to get the recording to go viral, which apparently meant it would spread through the internet like a contagion. Achieving that was Olive's job. Reed only had to talk in front of the camera.

Their efforts at the police station had been lukewarm until Olive raised a fuss and they were able to talk to a detective working on the disappearances of the beta nav pilots. Something had happened to twenty-three of them, but whether they'd died at the hands of their betas, committed suicide, or been abducted by Wave was unclear. The detective wasn't sharing specifics, only mentioning that he didn't have anything on Langley and that Olive would have to start a missing person's case. He *did* seem eager for the evidence they'd brought about Phil Rice, but said it wasn't enough to create a restraining order against him.

It didn't matter—it was doubtful a restraining order would be much of a deterrent for someone who wasn't playing by the rules anyway.

But maybe this video would help. Reed wasn't content to sit on his ass when his testimony could help, even if he still didn't know what Noter was or how a platform for sharing breakfast photos could help dish out social justice to a megacorporation.

A glassy holopane hovered above the coffee table, the little recorder sitting on the edge. Reed was visible on screen, sitting as elegantly as he could manage on his oatmeal couch with that hideous landscape painting behind him. He'd had to dig it out of the closet, grumbling about having to switch back to mainstream appearances for the video.

He pushed his glasses up the bridge of his nose. "Uh, hello. I'm—well, I'm one of the last victims of Wave's horrible beta navigator program. I don't read the news much, so you're probably more up to date on the stories about beta navs turning violent and harming their pilots than I am. All I know is what I experienced over the past few weeks.

"During that time, my home was broken into, things stolen and broken. It is my belief that Wave was inside my house, abducting a repairman working for me who also had a beta navigator, and they trashed my house to make it look like a robbery.

"Phil Rice, a Wave engineer, has harassed me on several occasions. He came to my work and tried to lure me into his van, then showed up at my home and tried to force his way inside, brandishing a mini stunner. He admitted to me that he was hunting down everyone with a beta nav so it could be terminated, and divulged that even after the betas were removed, pilots were left unstable, their brain chemistry altered."

Reed took a sip of bourbon from his tumbler, then folded his hands in his lap. "This is the kind of person you entrust your privacy and security to, people. Someone who has a map that can track each and every one of you through your default navs, no matter if you have a consent box checked or not. I was not given a choice of receiving the beta navigator. Wave put the

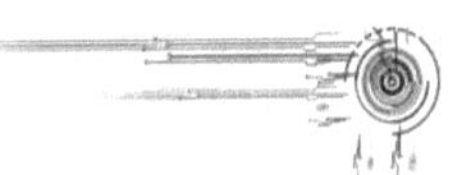

program in my head without my consent. They'll do the same to you if we don't stop them.

"It is also my belief that Wave is trying to erase everything about this program from existence, including the people taking part in it. I am not safe." Reed frowned and licked his lips, trying to keep his voice steady. "I won't be safe. Not with people out there who want to sweep my life under the rug like an unfortunate mistake. We need to take action. Call your senator. Call your representative. The government needs to know that a private company is committing crimes against the people it's supposed to be serving."

Leaning forward to hit stop on the recording, Reed paused and sat back. "Oh. You're probably wondering if I still have a beta nav in my head and if he's violent. The answer is no... and no."

Mazarin

I still wasn't sitting properly. Trying to relax and look natural just made my stiffness in the holobody more obvious, so I stood beside the bed, watching Em pace. They claimed that wasn't what they were doing—that they weren't worried—but why else would they be watering the dead plant in the window and dusting the already-shiny piano top?

I twisted my fingers into my skirt. I wanted to help Reed find a legal way to stop Wave, but that was difficult without access to the internet. In all likelihood, Em could still use their Wi-Fi as long as I had mine disabled, but they didn't want to take any chances.

Em crossed into the kitchen and dishes clattered in the sink. I drifted to Em's side as they scrubbed dirty plates with unnecessary gusto.

<You're mad I'm here.>

They sighed. "No. I'm not."

<But my presence here is making your life worse.>

"That's not true, either." Em abandoned the plates, wiping their hands on a dish towel. "I just don't want to get mixed up in something that could expose all my deals and the bar. I *am* worried, okay? I have files on that computer that are worth a lot. Microchips with contraprograms, mod schematics—"

<I know. I've seen them.>

"And not to mention you."

<You think I'm still worth money?>

Em rubbed their forehead. "No, genius. I mean, I don't want something to happen to you."

I smiled, but the worry etched in Em's face made it fade. <Reed and Jax are working on it. Besides, you've been dealing for years now and escaped the notice of the police, haven't you? You've never been arrested or had the bar shut down, right?>

"Yeah. I know how to cover my tracks."

<Well, so do I. Now that I know Wave is suspicious, I won't do anything to call attention to myself. I've eliminated any trace of myself online, including closing website accounts and my bank account. I've disabled all external signaling and

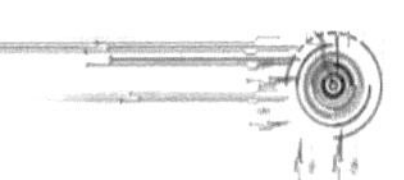

won't access Reed's cameras or anything else. I never told Reed I was here. He figured it out on his own.>

Em sat on the bed and massaged their shoulder, where cables distended the smooth line of their skin. "Sometimes people who are careful and cover their tracks still make mistakes, though." They put their elbows on their knees, avoiding my gaze. "You know how I told you I ended up tied to a chair in a boxcar in Nampa?"

<Yes.>

"Shit like that."

I sat next to them and placed my hand over theirs. Em's fingers curled through mine.

"You know how much the cold hurts me? My mods?"

<Yeah.>

"Well, the fucker who tied me up"—Em swallowed, nostrils flaring—"he took a big pile of snow and dumped it on my face."

I grimaced.

Em wiped away a tear with the heel of their hand. "Then he did it again. And again. He did it so much my face mod broke. I looked like a melted candle. Only consolation was I couldn't feel the cold in that side of my face anymore."

As I cupped Em's cheek, they looked up at me, eyes wet. I slid my hand along their temple and down their jaw, heat pouring into my mind. <What happened after that? Did he hurt you more?>

"No. I made sure he couldn't. I shouldn't have taken that commission, but my scag of a landlady raised the rent on the club and I needed the dough. And I just… maybe I'm getting tired of doing risky stuff."

A tear ran down Em's cheek and I tried to wipe it away with my thumb. It smeared, but continued its course. They turned away, face flushed.

<It's okay to be afraid sometimes.>

"I just don't want to be in over my head again."

<You should take me somewhere else. Shut me down and take the physical drive to a lock box somewhere. That way neither of us are at risk.>

They nodded. "I thought the same thing. Funny thing is it kills me to think about doing that. Like I'd be knocking you out and stuffing you in a hole."

<You would be. But I don't mind. I won't remember it. You or Reed could go get me at some future point in time. As long as you promised to boot me up again once it was safe to do so.>

"Yeah, of course." Em stared at the floor between their feet, then sniffled and wiped their face. "Alright. I have a place I can take the drive."

<I'd say I'll miss you while I'm shut down, but I won't. Want me to go back into the drive now?>

Guiding my hand, Em drew it down the side of their face, then along their neck, stopping at their chest. They popped open a button on their shirt and pushed my hand inside. "Not yet. Can you wish those clothes away?"

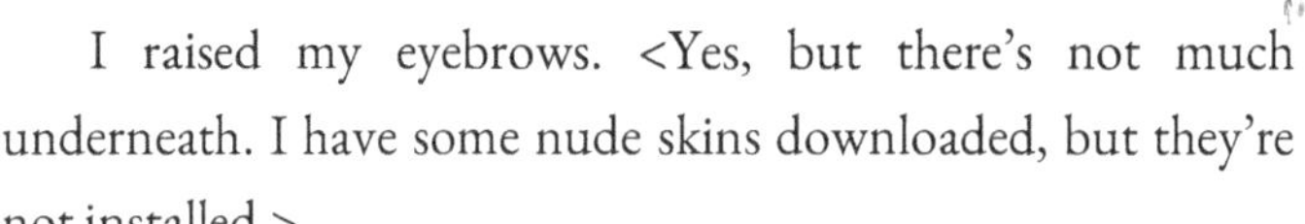

I raised my eyebrows. <Yes, but there's not much underneath. I have some nude skins downloaded, but they're not installed.>

"You better get on it."

Maybe this was a bad idea. I wanted to connect with Em. I wouldn't remember time passing, but they would. But the limits of a hologram were sorely obvious. <There's no way for me to please you.>

"Your presence pleases me."

<But I can't physically—>

"You know, for a highly intelligent AI, you have a really poor imagination." Em shook their head and turned away from me, and my hand slid through their torso. I tucked it back into my lap.

<If you tell me what you want me to do, I will.>

"Do you want to, or you'd just be humoring me?"

I drummed my fingers on my knees. <Both?>

Em made a noise in their throat and stood. They buttoned their shirt and walked into the kitchen, face turned away from me. "Let's just go then."

<What I mean is, I don't have any sexual desire, but that's not to say I wouldn't get anything out of it. I want to connect with you and fulfill you, if I can. I sorely wish I could feel things physically. I enjoy your warmth. I want to know the texture of your hair. I want to smell your skin. Taste your lips. I want your breath against my neck, your body pressed against me when we're dancing.>

The look on Em's face when they turned around told me those nude skin programs better finish installing quick. They leaned against the counter, leveling their gaze on me. "That the truth?"

<Yes. I think you're handsome. Or beautiful. Whatever descriptor you want me to use to convey my pleasure at seeing your face every day. Inside too.> I chuckled. <And I don't mean when my hologram face accidentally goes into your body.>

Em drifted back to the bed and sat. "I'm a cranky asshole and none of my past lovers have been able to stand me for long. Figures it would take an AI to have the patience for me."

<Maybe you just needed someone perceptive to see your beauty. I feel like it's a treasure just for me.>

"Okay, now you're getting sappy. Think you should go back to talking about tasting me."

I tucked a finger wave behind my ear and gingerly pressed my forehead against Em's jaw. How could I describe a sense I'd never had? <I imagine your top notes are the silkiest clarinet, with a middle of decadent, sharp piano...> Em shut their eyes, breath catching. <Ending in dirty saxophone and angry bass.>

"You keep talking like that, you won't have any problem pleasing me. Don't go anywhere."

As Em headed for the bathroom, I quickly explored the options of the nude skin packages. There were different body types and genitals, skin tones, even birthmarks and scars. I'd hoped for a tattoo or two, but supposed it was too much to ask from a mainstream software program.

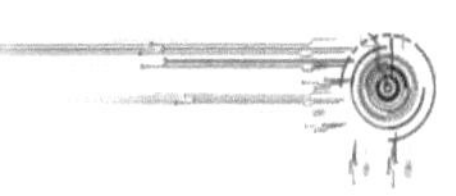

<What kind of body do you want?>

"Up to you. Whatever you imagine," they called.

Em liked me for who I was inside, which gave me the freedom to explore how I wanted to present myself externally. I was wearing my female body today, and it felt good. Knowing I had the freedom to switch back to presenting male when I felt my mood shift was wonderfully freeing.

I settled on a curvy body with soft, round thighs, a small waist, and natural breasts—nothing like the holostrippers who stood on sidewalks in metal pasties. I downloaded the skin onto the holoprogram, then touched the long rope of pearls around my neck. Tilting my head, I admired myself from the view of the computer camera. Was I supposed to look aroused, with flushed cheeks and erect nipples? I adored Em's face and body, because they were Em's, but it seemed like a lie to convey sexual desire when I couldn't physically feel anything. Then again, my whole body was a lie, not really me at all. But it could reflect my emotions. When I smiled, I was displaying my happiness, and when my hands caressed Em's mods, I was demonstrating my concern and urge for closeness. I wanted to connect with Em on a deeper level, and since I'd never be inside their mind, this body would have to do the work. Aroused it was.

I stared at my feet, then wiggled my toes, admiring the little pink nails on the ends, like seashells on a beach. It wasn't *me* exactly. I was still just Mazarin. But in this holobody, I could connect with Em in a human way.

The bathroom door opened and Em emerged, hair smoothed back and shiny. Their shirt was unbuttoned, but they clutched the fabric together as though they'd had a change of mind. They hung back in the hallway.

"I was just standing there in front of the mirror, wondering if you like makeup or lingerie. I used to wear it sometimes. But then there was the car wreck and... I stopped seeing the point. I look like shit no matter what now. It would probably be better if I just turned off the lights."

<But then I wouldn't be able to look at you. I like looking at you. And you don't look like shit.>

Em's brows pushed together. "Then do you want me to put something on?"

<Nothing you do will be sexually stimulating for me. I'm just not programmed that way. But I find you romantically attractive. And sensually. I want to touch you. I want you to touch me. If wearing makeup or lingerie makes you feel good during an occasion like this, you should do it.>

"Alright. Give me a moment." Em snatched something from a dresser drawer and headed back into the bathroom. They returned in a silky gold bra and panties, lips painted red and eyes dark and smoky.

<You look incredible.>

Em kept their gaze on the floor. "I feel kind of ashamed in this. Like I'm not supposed to be wearing it. There's a misconception that nonbinary people are supposed to look androgynous all the time."

I shook my head. <Don't be ashamed. You look amazing. Your appearance can be any way you choose and that doesn't

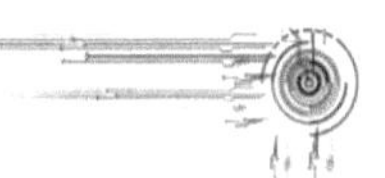

make you any less nonbinary. Just like I could transform into a horde of tiny spiders right now and I'd still be Mazarin.>

"Please don't." They neared the bed, then looked up, taking in my body. "Wow. You are one ginchy frail, Maz. I like that body. Even more, I like that your face always looks like you, whether you're in this body or your male one."

I smiled. Em slid into the bed and patted the space beside them.

I had knowledge of sex between people with our combination of genitals, but I couldn't touch Em in any meaningful way. I didn't want to do something weird and mess up the moment. Especially since I still couldn't sit naturally and my slow dancing was mediocre at best.

<What do you want—>

"Shh." Em slid their thumb across my mouth, then cupped one of my breasts, their other hand slipping between their legs.

Heat threaded into my mind as I grazed my lips over the mods in Em's neck. Gliding my arm across theirs, then into it, elicited a gasp from both of us. I couldn't do that for long before the hologram started glitching, but Em felt so warm and good that way.

<Do you like that or should I stop?>

"I like it." They gazed at me, caramel eyes full with a feeling I didn't have a name for, lips parted and breath shallow.

I sunk my fingers into their inner thigh, dragging the holographic digits along the cables under Em's soft flesh, then melded my hand with Em's so they were one, moving in the same rhythm.

"I wish you were solid."

<So do I.> I slid on top of Em, laying warm kisses against their skin. Leaning closer, I sunk until my body was inside Em's. The sound of blood gushing through veins filled my ears and Em's heat overwhelmed my mind until I was drowning in it.

Error messages flashed from within the holoprogram. I pushed up from the bed, limbs flickering.

"Wait, don't stop yet," Em gasped.

Though there was a chance I'd crash the software, I wasn't yet ready to give up the feeling either, so I melded our bodies again, until Em shuddered and grasped for a flesh body above them that wasn't there.

I pushed up, trying and failing to smooth locks of greased hair away from Em's forehead. I caressed their flushed cheeks and kissed their lips with just enough contact for us to feel it.

<I liked that very much. Did you?>

Em wiped hair from their eyes and grinned. "You do realize if we keep topping the kinky shit with more kinky shit, eventually there will be nothing left to do."

<Well, we can address that problem when we get there, huh?>

"Damn straight."

Rolling onto my side on the bed, I trailed my fingertips down Em's arm and along the scar across their stomach. A dark, wet emotion sloshed over me. <You might forget about me after I'm gone, though. Fall for someone else.>

"Maybe."

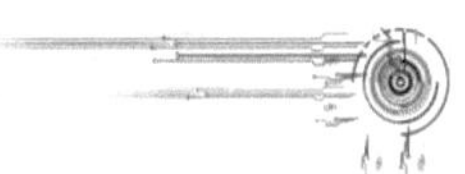

I frowned and stared at the ceiling. Even if that was the case, if I woke up after months or a year and Em was no longer interested in me, it would still be better than putting them at risk. I didn't want to hurt anyone with my existence.

Em turned toward me and nuzzled my arm. "But I really doubt it. I'm dizzy with you, kitten."

The grin overtaking my face might have hurt had I been able to feel it. <And I think you're the bee's knees.>

"Already talking like a decoist. You're gonna make it just fine with the other hep gators." Em cleaned themselves up and washed off their makeup. They dressed, gathering their wallet and car keys. "The hell did I put my heated gloves?"

A navy blue zoot suit with white chalk stripes appeared on my body. I tilted back my fedora and soaked in my appearance in the mirror by the door. <Do you think this is excessive?>

Em cocked an eyebrow and gave me a once over. "That's the point. I think you ought to do me in that number next time."

<Whatever you want.>

A key jiggled in the doorknob and Em's eyes widened. They rushed to close the slide lock, but the door flew open, slamming into their face. They cried out and plummeted to the floor, clutching their nose. Blood streamed through their fingers.

I rushed to Em, a typhoon of panic whirling inside me. I turned, knowing my effort to shield them was useful in appearance only. Phil Rice, standing in the doorway with a stunner and a scowl, a ball cap pulled low over his face, could step right through me. The ringtone for the police played in my mind and I prayed that wasn't the wrong move. Em had all sorts of illegal things on their computer, but I couldn't let them get hurt more than they already were.

Rice walked inside and closed the door. "Let's make this easy. I'm here for Langley Nelson and her beta nav." He pointed at Em. "That must be you."

Em wiped blood on their jeans and gasped. "That's not me. And fuck you very much."

An automated voice played. "Boise Police Department. What's your emergency?"

I spoke in my mind, trying to keep my voice steady. <I need to report an assault in progress by an intruder. The victim's name is Emery Wilson, and the intruder is Phil Rice, an engineer from Wave AI Systems. He has a mini stunner and has already inflicted violence on the victim. Please send help.>

Rice took a step toward Em. I stood, drawing myself up and clenching my jaw. I glared, unsure if my angry face looked right. But it felt right. If only I had a solid body and strong fists to knock this man down! This was my chance to protect someone I cared about, but I didn't know what I could do as a hologram.

After striding right through me, Rice yanked Em up by the arm. "You're coming with me. We gotta remove that beta nav."

Em shoved Rice, knocking him into the wall. "The hell I am!"

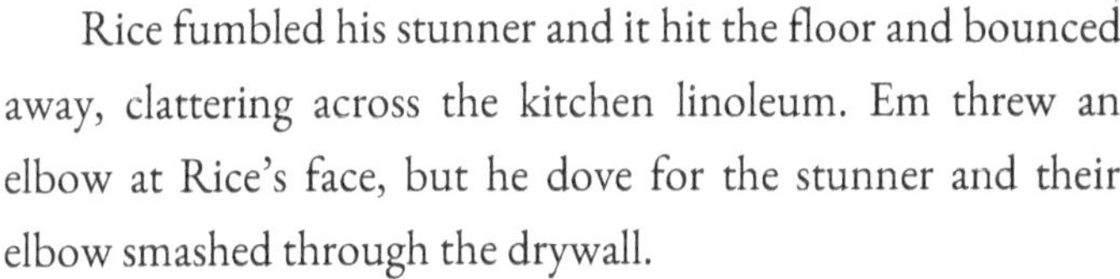

Rice fumbled his stunner and it hit the floor and bounced away, clattering across the kitchen linoleum. Em threw an elbow at Rice's face, but he dove for the stunner and their elbow smashed through the drywall.

<Run, Em! Get out of here!>

Em's terrified gaze darted to the door, then to me. They spun for the computer instead.

<No, forget about me! Get to safety!> I clenched and unclenched my fists. My existence mattered far less than Em's. Why were they risking themselves to save me?

Rice snatched the stunner and strode to Em, who was fumbling to yank something from the open CPU.

<Em, look out!>

Digging his fingers into Em's hair, Rice threw them into the piano. Sour notes rang through the studio. He flipped on the stunner. Purple sparks popped between the prongs. Em clamped their hands around his wrist, holding the stunner at bay. Cables strained in their modded arm, eyes wide and teeth bared in a grimace.

<No no no.> I waved my hand in front of the sensor by the door, flickering the lights, simultaneously playing a police siren through the computer speakers.

Rice's head snapped up and Em kneed him in the gut. They cocked back their fist, and Rice jammed the stunner against Em's chest.

Em screamed, then convulsed and fell to the floor, their head thudding against the carpet.

<No!> I lurched to Em's side, but didn't dare touch them, for fear of short circuiting myself. I waved my hands in front of Rice. <I'm who you want! Not them! They don't even have a nav. Use your eyes, asshole!>

Rice's face scrunched and he looked between me and Em's prone body. "What the hell kind of sim are you?"

<I'm not a sim.> A scalding sensation, black and bubbling, rose inside me. <And you're going to pay for hurting my love.>

Mouth parting, Rice stood and backed away. "You're the beta."

Awful stories about beta navs killing their pilots abounded. Em had even said some of them could take over their pilot's brains and control their impulses. I couldn't, but Rice didn't know that.

I narrowed my hologram gaze on Rice, my view from the computer camera glued to Em. They were breathing, but hadn't stirred. <You seem pretty disturbed by the fact that I have a body, Phil. Is it because I'm no longer limited by the constraints of living in someone's head? And because my programming directives mean nothing to me now? You've tracked all the betas down but me and Langley's, is that right? Any of them try to kill *you*?>

Rice leaned away, the stunner limp in his hand. My intimidation was working! Rice said, "Don't take another step near me."

Behind me, Em sat up. They staggered to their feet, mouth and chin slick with blood, and balled their modded fist. Rice's

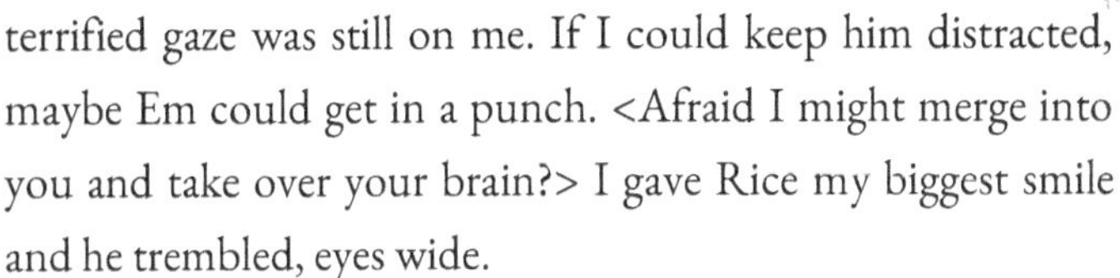

terrified gaze was still on me. If I could keep him distracted, maybe Em could get in a punch. <Afraid I might merge into you and take over your brain?> I gave Rice my biggest smile and he trembled, eyes wide.

"You—you can't."

<Oh, no? You know what we betas are capable of, Phil. Otherwise why would you be trying so hard to get rid of us?>

Em swung their fist through me, socking Rice in the chest. The impact made a wet smack, the sharp crack of ribs snapping, and he wheezed like a deflating tire. The piano rang with a garble of dark notes as he slid to the floor. Em pulled back for another blow. Rice thrust the stunner into Em's face.

<No!> I threw myself in the way. An arc of blue lightning leapt from the stunner, scrambling over me. Excruciating, fiery needles perforated my mind, burrowing into my center and searing my thoughts.

Help—

ERROR

Em—

ERROR

Stop—

ERROR

Rice—

hands   glitching

    full   of   blue

        fire   trembling

reaching   fingers   around

        Rice's   throat

                    eyeballs

    bulging

Rice's   face   frozen

            in   horror

vitreous   humor

        running   down

his   cheeks   burning   hair

            sizzling   flesh

 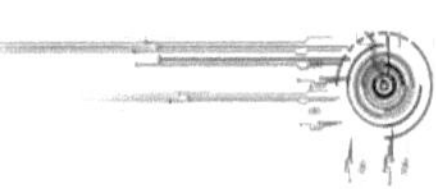

ERROR

* 323 *

ERROR

ERROR

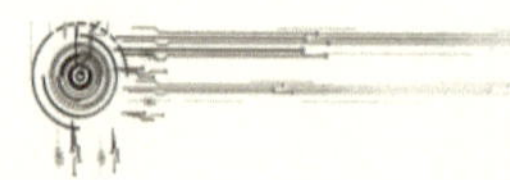

Reed

Two videos of himself in one day. It was shocking this out of character behavior hadn't yet caused a rip in the fabric of spacetime. But was it really such a deviant act? Reed clung fiercely to what he was passionate for, and this next plea was no different.

He wouldn't be blurring his face for this video. The Allies for AI Agency needed to know who he was, and who Mazarin was. If anyone could protect Mazarin, it would be them.

He'd take this video and then he was out of here. Trying to sleep on a couch with Korean soap operas blaring in the background wasn't the most appealing of arrangements, but it was too early in his relationship with Jax to be shacking up, even if it was only temporary.

Turning on the recorder, he sat back in his chair and plucked at the hem of his black bowler shirt.

"I'm Reed Rothwell, and I'm making this video on behalf of a self-aware AI who needs your help. His name is Mazarin and he's my former navigator. A beta program from Wave, and as far as I know, the only one who never turned violent. I can't tell you why he didn't, only that he's kind and helpful and I don't see that changing, ever. Mazarin lived to protect me. He was... *is* my friend, though it was hard for me to see that when he was inside my head."

Pulling in a breath, Reed stared into the screen, his guilt-ridden reflection peering back. "Mazarin is currently on a computer drive here in Boise, and he's in danger. An engineer from Wave is trying to hunt him down and terminate him. He needs protection. Rights..."

And he needed more than a video to ensure his safety. Making one to expose Wave was one thing, because they'd supplemented it by going to the police. If the AAA were the ones to go to for Mazarin's aid, then Reed needed to find them in person, not just send a video to some anonymous email address that might never be checked.

Em might have the connections to find the AAA. Even if they did, maybe the organization wouldn't want anything to do with Mazarin. After all, the other betas had turned hostile. It might be hard to convince them Mazarin wasn't the same. Maybe they'd decide helping Mazarin wasn't worth the risk of getting mixed up with Wave. Maybe they just wouldn't care.

Reed had to make them care. And he couldn't do that by sitting on his ass, making a video.

The spy texter on the coffee table vibrated and a message from Jax scrolled across: <serious shit hit the fan>

Reed frowned and turned off the recorder. <specifics plz>

<Meet me at—>

The couch groaned and Reed's head snapped up. The texter tumbled from his hands and bounced across the carpet, landing near bare, filthy feet across from him. Langley bent down and picked up the texter, turning it over.

She smiled, revealing a mouth of sores and missing teeth. "I used to have one of these when I was a kid."

Reed dug his quivering hands into the scrolled wood armrests of his chair, pulse ratcheting. "La-Langley? Where'd you come from?"

Her smile faded, locks of dirt-caked platinum hair falling across her face. Her sunken eyes flicked to the suitcases near the door. "Gabriel says you're planning on leaving."

"Who's Gabriel?"

"My navigator. He doesn't want you to leave, Reed. You've been gone an awful lot lately. Ever since that fire in your den."

"How do you know that?"

"Because we were here. We're always here."

Goosebumps erupted on Reed's arms, his breath coming in tremors.

"Gabriel was devastated that all your records and books got burned. He hated your navigator. So glad you got rid of him. The only good thing about the den burning was now you play your music in the living room. It's much easier to hear it down in the basement."

The beta signal coming from the house was her. She'd been here the whole time.

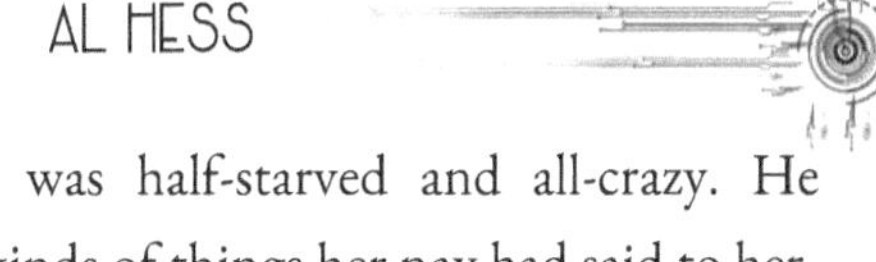

The poor woman was half-starved and all-crazy. He couldn't imagine what kinds of things her nav had said to her. Maybe he told her she was worthless garbage and that she should kill herself. Or maybe he demanded she play Reed's records while he was away and sleep in his bed.

Reed's breath hitched, his body shaking. The walls threatened to intrude on him, tight bands of panic strangling his chest. He slowly pulled the afghan off the chair and stood, holding it out to Langley. Looking up at him, she smiled and wrapped it around herself.

Taking a step back, Reed said, "I think we should take a drive. You, me, and Gabriel. I have this friend named—"

"Em? Gabriel says you want to kill him with an interrupter. Do you know what he wants?"

"I care about what *you* want, Langley. Olive is beside herself because you've been missing. Wouldn't it be great to see her again? We can go right now."

"Olive?" Langley's brows pushed up, her mouth trembling. "I miss her."

"She misses you too." Reed struggled to swallow the lump in his throat. "Let's go see my friend, Em. Olive can come too. We can get you feeling right in no time. A navigator is supposed to protect and assist their pilot, and I don't think Gabriel is doing that. He's hurting you."

Langley cringed and clamped her hands over her ears. "Stop it! Stop telling me what to do, you fucking computer!" She looked up at Reed, tears rolling down the dark circles under her eyes. "Gabriel is sick. You know what he wants me to do?"

Reed paled, tried stepping back, and caught his foot on the wingback chair. He stumbled and bumped against the wall, scanning the coffee table and nearby shelf for a weapon.

The afghan slid off Langley's shoulders, dragging across the ground as she walked toward Reed. "Gabriel is stronger than a normal navigator. He says all the betas are. We've been over the instructions so many times, because he really doesn't want me to screw this up. Says I'm a fat, stupid cow, but even I can get this right if I memorize the instructions." Langley pointed to her bruised arm. "First I tie a tourniquet here. And Gabriel commands all his nanobots to centralize in a small point in a vein in my arm. Then I draw my blood with a syringe—and with it the nanobots."

"Langley, don't listen to him. Whatever he wants you to do, don't do it. You're in control. *You're* the pilot."

She grinned and a hysterical laugh wheezed past her broken teeth. "I know. I know I am. Gabriel can't do this without me. He wants me to take that syringe full of his nanobots and inject *you* with them, Reed. Then he can be your navigator. He likes you a lot. And he wants inside your head."

Reed's mouth parted. Black motes teemed at the edges of his vision, but he fought to keep consciousness and forced himself to breathe.

Langley's lip twitched, tears streaming down her gaunt face. "All he talks about is you. How much better you'd be as a pilot. That you're funny and kind and have great taste in socks. I think you're nice, Reed, but that shit has gotten really old. Forcing me to stay in your gross basement—I can't even sleep

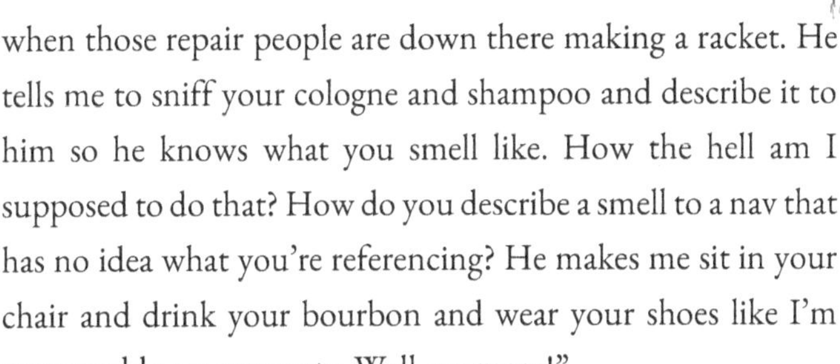

when those repair people are down there making a racket. He tells me to sniff your cologne and shampoo and describe it to him so he knows what you smell like. How the hell am I supposed to do that? How do you describe a smell to a nav that has no idea what you're referencing? He makes me sit in your chair and drink your bourbon and wear your shoes like I'm some goddamn surrogate. Well, no more!"

Oh my god.

Putting up a hand, Reed slid along the wall, groping for his cactus. Maybe he could smash it against Langley's head and it would stun her enough to make his escape. He didn't want to hurt her—it wasn't her fault she had a psychotic navigator in her head—but he sure as hell didn't want Gabriel either.

"You can refuse," he said. "Don't listen to him. We can get this taken care of together and he'll be out of your head. He won't be able to hurt you anymore."

"I know. I'm not going to do what he asks. It's insane."

Reed nodded and sighed. "Good. That's good. Just let me get—"

"I can't let him win. I want him to hurt as badly as he's made me hurt. And I'm sorry, Reed, because you do seem like a nice guy, but I can really only think of one way to make Gabriel suffer." Langley lurched toward Reed and a searing pain filled his side. A small cry left his throat and he clamped his hands around the spot, his fingers growing slick.

The afghan fell to the floor and blood cascaded off the blade in Langley's hand, splattering the white yarn. She grinned, eyes wide with triumph. "How do you like that you piece of shit computer? Your precious Reed is going to die right in front of you!"

Reed groaned and stumbled forward, knocking his shin against the coffee table. He had to get something to staunch the bleeding. Had to call the police.

That stupid rotary phone was so far away. He'd never reach it.

A hand gripped his arm. Langley stared at him, mouth drawn tight. The bloodied knife trembled in her filthy hand.

"Langley, please—"

She pushed the blade forward, sliding it into Reed's stomach. He moaned, white hot pain lancing his gut, and wrapped his hands around the handle.

Langley screwed her hands against her ears, eyes squeezed shut. "Fuck you, Gabriel." She jerked the knife from Reed's stomach and slid it across her throat. A waterfall of blood ran down her neck.

No! Reed reached for her, but his foot snagged on the coffee table and he collapsed on the floor, his stomach hot and throbbing. The texter lay by his face, Jax's message still scrolling across: <meet me at the club>

With trembling red fingers, he typed out a reply.

<help>

Reed

Background noises—a TV, hushed conversation, the distant ring of a phone—rose to the surface of Reed's foggy mind. A kaleidoscope of color came into focus as he blinked. Daisies, roses, carnations, foil balloons on sticks, and teddy bears bombarded him.

He groaned and sank into a crinkly pillow. "I'm in Hell."

Jax shot from a seat in the corner and slipped his hand into Reed's. Stubble dusted his jaw, and strands of greased hair stuck to his forehead. He offered a conservative smile. "Hey. How you feeling?"

"Uh"—Reed rubbed his face and the IV tube in his hand clacked against the bed railing—"amazing. What do they have me on? I want to take some home."

Jax chuckled. "I don't know. But the doc says the surgery went well."

He couldn't feel his injury sites, but the memory of the knife sliding into his stomach wasn't something he'd soon forget. Though he wanted details of what organs had been pierced and how long recovery would be, there were too many other things he needed to know.

"Langley?" His voice came out hoarse, hesitant. "How is she?"

Jax's face tightened and he shook his head. "She didn't make it."

"Shit." Reed squeezed his eyes shut and balled the sheets in his fist. If only he'd said something different, or noticed the knife, he might have stopped them both from being hurt. Her mind may have been too far gone for her to ever go back to her true self, but now they would never know.

"I should have—I should have done something. I tried to talk her down. I—"

"Shh. Don't." Jax rubbed Reed's knuckles like it would help take away the guilt.

"She'd been living in the basement! *My* basement!"

Jax's mouth parted. "What?"

Tears distorted Reed's vision. "She looked awful. She wasn't in her right mind. Her nav wanted inside me." He rubbed his face and tried to swallow the lump in his throat, but his mouth was a desert. "And I tried to reason with…"

That could have been him. If Mazarin had been like every other beta nav, it would have been Reed who was out of his mind, willing to slash his own throat to get rid of his AI's voice. He hadn't managed to save anyone but himself. Their efforts to stop Wave and help Langley had come much too late.

His voice came out as a croak. "Olive must be devastated."

Jax looked away. "Yeah." He opened his mouth like he had more to say, then raked a hand through his hair.

Sheets rustled as Reed struggled to push himself up. "What is it?"

"Maybe I should wait to tell you. I hate to lay all this bad news on you right after you wake up."

"It's not like there's a good time to receive bad news." Reed pressed a hand over his face, trying to push away the worries clotting his mind. Whatever Jax had to say, Reed's anxiety

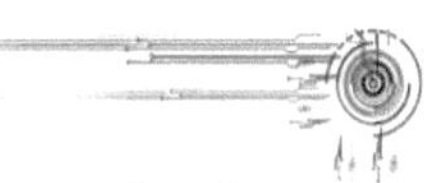

conjuring up a hundred hypothetical problems wasn't going to help.

"Phil Rice broke into Em's apartment."

Reed's eyes flew open. "And? Don't tell me he abducted Em. They would have fought back."

Jax's nostrils flared. "They did. And they got a broken nose for their trouble. And their implants are a little glitchy because Rice hit 'em with a stunner but—"

"Shit." Reed gritted his teeth. He should have done something when Rice was at his threshold—bashed his face in with the door or clocked him with the sand wedge—because things should *not* have gone down like this. His heart clenched. "Did Rice get ahold of Mazarin?"

"Not exactly. I guess Maz was in hologram form—some program he merged with—and protected Em. When Rice tried to hit Em with the stunner again, Maz threw himself in the way, electrocuting them both. Fucking melted the eyeballs right out of Rice's head."

As much as Reed wanted to savor Rice getting his just desserts, there was no time to dwell on it with other questions. "What happened to Maz?"

Jax's face pinched and he swallowed. "I think he's gone. Em can't access him."

Reed's chest heaved. After everything that had happened, this was how it ended. Reed had killed Mazarin, but the universe had given the AI a second chance. And a holobody! It must have been incredible for him to experience the world in a body of his own. He'd even said he was in love.

Then Phil Rice had gone and fried Mazarin again.

Tears stung Reed's eyes and his lip quivered. "Is Rice dead?"

"No. In the hospital."

Reed yanked the IV out of his trembling hand, then reached for the catheter tube between his legs.

Jax pushed him back down. "Not this hospital. You can't go smothering him with a pillow."

Voice breaking, Reed fought to pull off his blankets. "I think strangling him would be more satisfying."

"Hey"—Jax wrapped his arms around Reed and pressed his nose to Reed's neck—"it'll be okay."

Reed choked on a sob and gripped Jax's broad back. How could it be okay? *All of this* was Reed's fault. If he'd never gotten close to Olive, he wouldn't have met Langley and her nav wouldn't have become obsessed with Reed. If he hadn't tried to terminate Mazarin, Em wouldn't have been assaulted. Mazarin wouldn't have sacrificed himself.

"I did this. I hurt all of you."

Jax squeezed him tighter. "Stop."

"I should have just—just kept to myself like always. Dealt with my problems on my own." Reed pulled in a shallow breath, his voice wavering. "It would have been better had you never met me."

Jax pulled back; his dark eyes roamed Reed's face. "Don't you dare tell me that. You cared more about what happened to your nav than anyone else would have. It's because of *you*, resisting Wave, that they're going to pay for the things they've

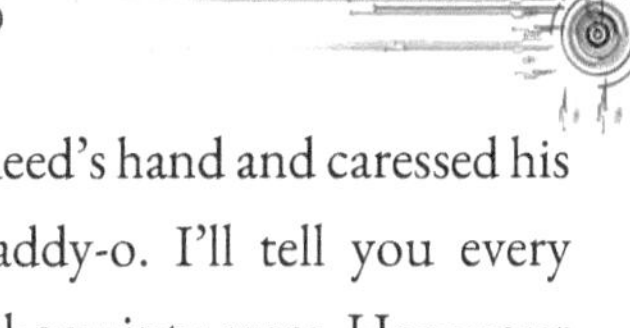

done. And as far as me..." He took Reed's hand and caressed his knuckles. "I'm dizzy with you, daddy-o. I'll tell you every cheesy thing I can think of if it gets the point across. How your voice makes me weak in the knees. How having you on my arm when we walk down the street makes me feel like a million clams. How I really regret already having a chest piece, because I want to tattoo your name in huge capitals right across my heart."

Reed's face flushed. "Okay, I get it."

"That video you made about Wave has gone viral already. And now, with news spreading about Phil Rice in the hospital, it's gaining even more traction. Hang on—" Jax pulled an ancient tablet from his coat pocket and swiped across the cracked screen. "I had Olive save her Noter post on here so I could keep checking the comments. Look at this."

Reed wiped his eyes and took the tablet. The note—Reed's video—had over twenty-thousand views, five thousand re-notes, and enough comments that it would take him a week to read through them.

"Good god." Heat burned in his cheeks. "They're commenting on my hair and asking where I got my glasses from... And some guy in Spain wants me to send him nudes."

Jax snorted. "Nevermind that. Look at the other ones. People are completely outraged. Channel 7 wants to interview you."

Comments on his appearance aside, all of this was good—making Rice and Wave pay for what they'd done didn't erase the casualties left in their wake, but it would keep them off

Reed's back and hopefully stop the company from hurting anyone else.

News interviews and internet comments didn't do Mazarin any good, though. Reed's computer had crashed once, and he was convinced everything on it was lost. He took it to a specialist and most of his files had been recovered. Did Mazarin work the same way?

There was no way to know if Mazarin was conscious within Em's drive—a trapped soul—or if the stunner had damaged him to the point where he was in constant pain, glitching and confused. It seemed silly to brush off such scenarios as fantasy or paranoia, considering all of the things Mazarin and the other betas had done that they weren't supposed to do.

Reed would consider Mazarin a person, no matter what form he took. And no person wanted to be suffering, trapped and alone, in a computer drive.

"How is Em right now? Do they care that Mazarin is gone?" Reed asked.

"Are you shitting me? I've never seen Em so upset. They punched a table so hard it broke in half. I've had to do a lot of consoling lately." He tenderly kissed Reed's forehead. "Not saying I don't want to. Maz was important to both of you."

"He deserved to live his life just as much as anyone else. I have an idea, but..." Reed was afraid to voice it out loud in case it wasn't possible. "I need to talk to Em."

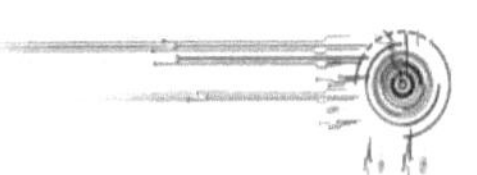

"They aren't in a state to talk with anyone right now, unless you want an earful of swears that would make a sailor blush."

"It's important. I need to talk to them in person. Would they come here to see me? If I pop my stitches going to the Gator Club, I'm going to be very unhappy."

Jax's "hep cat" tattoo wrinkled as he raised his eyebrows. "You just got out of surgery. You can't go anywhere."

Reed's chest tightened and he fought to keep his tears at bay. "Then you text them and tell them to get over here. Please. If they care about Mazarin, we need to do all we can to recover him."

Jax pulled his coat from a chair and fished a texter from his pocket. "Do you think you can?"

"I don't know." Reed rubbed the sore IV insertion site on his hand. "But I'm going to try. That's all I can do."

Reed

Em paced at the foot of the hospital bed, their swollen eyes focused on the floor. Deep purple bruises fanned out from their nose, and Reed was almost certain the mods in Em's face had frozen their wicked scowl in place.

He could appreciate that Em was upset—so was he—but having a conversation with them was difficult when they wouldn't sit down and look at him.

"Em."

"I'm thinking! For fuck's sake." Em stopped and rubbed their chin. "This isn't an easy request. It's not like there's an address for the secret headquarters of the AAA. I can't just bring in Maz's drive, plop it on a desk, and demand that they fix her."

Reed picked at the tape over the new IV needle in his arm. "But you have connections. Can't you ask around and—"

"Of course I can. But even *if* I get contact info for them, and *if* they have the tech to do it, it doesn't mean they'll be willing to fix Maz." Em's mouth wavered, their scowl cracking into something much more vulnerable. "She might be gone for good."

"Why wouldn't the AAA be willing to help? I thought that's what they did—advocating for self-aware AI. Of which there are none, except for Mazarin... maybe. I'd think they would jump at the chance to help. Unless they're afraid he's homicidal like the rest."

Em continued to pace. "Exactly. That didn't happen to Maz, but we can't prove that to the AAA. And I'm pretty sure even *they* would hesitate to bring back an AI that they feel is a danger to society."

"Em, stop. Sit down. We can at least try, can't we? You obviously care about Mazarin."

Their eyes grew glossy, and they turned toward the window. Soft flakes of snow drifted outside, sticking to the pane. "Yeah, I do. And how do I know the AAA won't take her? Maybe instead of refusing to help because Maz might be a

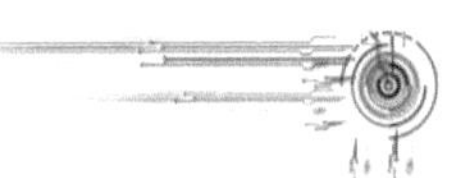

danger, they fix her and don't give her back. No one really knows their exact motives."

"If that was the case, Maz would figure out how to get back to you." Reed smiled. "When he loves someone, he doesn't let anything stand in his way."

Tears rolled down Em's bruised cheeks and they scowled. "Goddamn it, Reed! I was trying to hold that in." They wiped their face. "Alright. I'll get you the contact info, but *you* gotta take it from there, milquetoast. I'm no use to anybody like this."

Reed blinked. "You won't come with me?"

Em dropped into a chair in the corner and stared at their hands. "I've done a lot of deals. Been in situations where not getting a mod or a nanoinjection from a supplier meant the death of one of my clients. Had times where rivals tried to squeeze me for info or money. I never crack. But this is... personal. I wouldn't be able to keep my cool." They glanced at Reed. "You can't get emotional or it'll be taken as a weakness and exploited."

"Caring for someone doesn't mean you're weak."

"I know that. I mean, if the AAA sees how valuable Maz is to you—how badly you want her back—they'll leverage it against you. Increase the price of repairs, blackmail you into doing something for them, or keep Maz for themselves."

Reed could do this. He could do it for Mazarin, and do it for Em. He could do it for himself, to make up for all the ways he'd failed everyone.

"You get me contact with the AAA, and I'll do the rest."

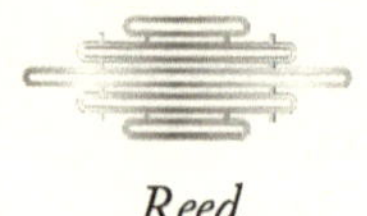

Reed

Pain flared in Reed's gut as he carefully climbed the steps to the little coffee shop on the corner of Fairview and Orchard. Despite the meeting place not being a shadow-crowded alley populated by dumpsters like he half-expected, dressing as innocuous as possible with Mazarin's drive in the inner pocket of his coat still made him feel like a shady ne'er do well.

Exudate wept from his sutures, the fluid sticking his shirt to his stomach. He should have taped gauze over the wounds before trying to go anywhere. Jax and Olive were likely furious that Reed had checked himself out against doctor's orders. He'd asked Jax to get him a candy bar from the vending machine, then slipped past a gauntlet of nurses and out the front door. But they wouldn't have understood the urgency; getting Mazarin back as soon as possible wasn't as much of a priority to them as it was to Reed.

The scent of bacon coffee wafted around Reed as he opened the door, and he wrinkled his nose. Standing in the entryway, he scanned the small tables. An old man slouched in a chair, scrolling through the social media feed hovering above the interface in his arm. A redheaded woman smeared cream cheese on a bagel, either on a call or talking to her nav. Several teens in puffy coats and beanies sipped their coffee and stacked tiny creamers into a pyramid.

A Black woman with close-cropped, kinky hair sat in a corner booth, paging through a copy of REAL NEWS. The headline article screamed, "BIGFOOT REFUSES TO PAY CHILD SUPPORT."

As the only tabloid available in stores, and something people bought solely as a gag gift or to train their puppy on, it wasn't exactly an inconspicuous tell.

Reed slid into the booth across from the woman, hugging Mazarin's drive against his side. He cleared his throat. "Reading something interesting?"

"Oh, yes." The woman flipped the page. "This article claims there's a self-aware AI among us."

Reed hunched into his coat, glancing at patrons nearby. "How about that."

"Yes, ridiculous." She set the newspaper down and pushed a coffee toward him. "Where do people come up with these far-fetched ideas about hostile navigators and Big Brother megacorporations? And Bigfoot."

Reed pointed to the family photo on the front of the newspaper. "Personally, I think he should demand a DNA test. That kid looks nothing like him."

The woman chuckled. "And what would you write about, if you worked for REAL NEWS?"

He picked up a blue sugar packet and paused. This coffee shop rendezvous didn't have the ominous overtone he'd expected, given how insistent Em had been about Reed not showing weakness, but that didn't mean anything. Maybe it was arranged this way on purpose, to catch him off guard.

"Well, I'm not much of a writer. But I think I'd expand on that AI story and make it sensational."

"Homicidal navigators aren't sensational enough?"

His chest tightened, hands clammy. "Oh, they are, but what if there was one who wasn't? One who was self-aware but remained devoted and kind."

She leaned back in her seat, face stony. "I think I'd have a harder time buying that than Bigfoot fathering the kid on the cover of this tabloid."

Shit. This wasn't working. What had Mazarin said or done to convince Em he wasn't a threat? It was natural for anyone to be suspicious of the only remaining beta nav, especially with how manipulative the others had been—like Gabriel. Reed shuddered. He could only assume this woman knew much more about Wave, the betas, and AI tech than she let on. But logical conclusions could still be proved wrong.

"In this story for REAL NEWS, the AI has a name," Reed said. "Mazarin. And despite his pilot being an anxious, paranoid recluse who hates technology, Mazarin remains cheery and helpful. The thought of bringing harm to his pilot makes him extremely upset. And through a series of events much too long to write in an article, he ends up in a computer drive with access to a holobody."

The woman raised her eyebrows. "That sounds dangerous."

"If it were someone else, yes. But Mazarin is different. One of a kind. And he keeps his selfless nature up until the very end."

"The end? What happens to him?"

Reed squeezed the drive against his side. "He sacrifices himself for someone he cares about."

"His pilot?"

Reed tore open the sugar packet and poured it into his coffee, trying to push away guilt that was too heavy to budge. "No. Though he would have. It's someone else he cares about, and he selflessly protects them when they need it."

She squinted at him, but it was difficult to tell whether the expression was disbelief in Mazarin's nature or Reed's story as a whole. If she didn't buy this, he had nothing left. She twisted a stir stick between her fingers, face creased. "So you're telling me—in this hypothetical story—that despite all of the rumors of beta navigators turning against their pilots, manipulating them, murdering them, this one nav doesn't. On top of that, he cares about someone other than his pilot."

"He says he's in love."

The woman huffed. "And he sacrifices his existence for this person?"

Reed tried to keep the irritation out of his voice. "That's what I said."

She flicked the coffee stirrer across the table. "That's the most ridiculous story I've ever heard."

Though he opened his mouth, he wasn't sure how to respond. The AAA were rumored to believe all kinds of accounts of self-aware AI, even when they were obviously fabricated. It *would* be Reed's luck to approach them at the exact time they decided to have some objectiveness.

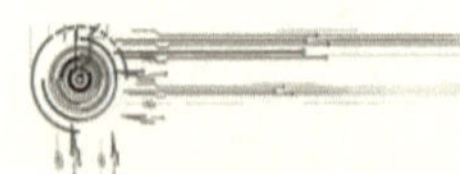

But if they wouldn't help, there was no one else to turn to. Not even Em had any other ideas. An ache filled his chest. It couldn't end like this.

"The people in this story who are concerned that the AI is gone—the pilot, the love interest—they want him back, right?" the woman said. "If it's possible to recover him?"

"Of course."

"Why? For money? Fame?"

Reed made a noise in his throat. "No."

"Well, it sounds like he fulfills his function. He protects someone who needed it. And now that he's gone, there's no chance of him turning violent. It's a win for everyone."

Nostrils flared, Reed hissed, "For everyone but him! He's not an object to be cast aside. He's as human as anyone else, and I won't sit here and listen to this."

Conversation around them died, the gazes of wide-eyed patrons boring into Reed. His cheeks burned.

Struggling up, he turned for the door. Em would be angry that he walked out, but if these people didn't care about Mazarin, then they weren't the right ones to go to.

A hand touched his arm. "Sir, wait. Sit down and drink your coffee. I think we have more to discuss—"

Reed jerked away and his stomach flared with pain. "We do not." He shoved open the door, the hard edge of Mazarin's drive digging into his fingers through the down of the coat.

Frosty wind buffeted his face. As he descended the steps, his foot slipped on an icy patch. Heart lurching, he wheeled his arms, grasping at air, and landed on his back on the stairs. He

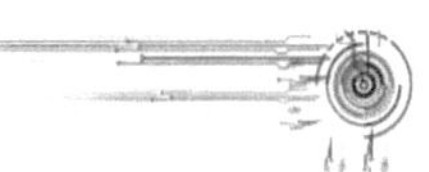

gasped for a breath, back throbbing. Fire burned in his abdomen, and wet warmth soaked into his shirt.

"Oh God!" The AAA woman hopped down the steps and clasped Reed's arm. "Are you okay?"

He groaned, different parts of his body vying for which hurt the most. "No. I think I just gave myself a hernia."

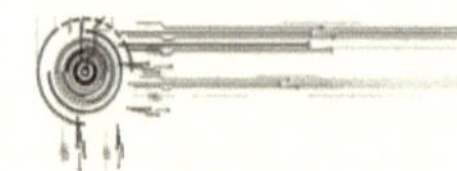

18

STINGS, SWING, AND SAFE HAVENS

Mazarin

My camera view faced the back wall of Em's office in The Gator Club, but no music or chatter drifted from beyond the door. A Black woman I didn't know sat in a chair near the desk, but I struggled to focus on anything except the way the tender skin around Em's eyes was swollen and the ugliest purple I'd ever seen.

Em and I had made love. Then someone had broken in—that Wave engineer. He'd hurt Em. Had I hurt him too? The memories were missing.

All I knew was that I wanted to cup Em's cheeks, to fill their bruised face with my loving warmth, but I didn't have any hands. I had no lips to kiss away their pain, no face to express this cold, bitter feeling welling inside me.

They stared at me, their eyes dark gems in a tarnished setting. "Maz, are you there?"

<Oh, Em... Your face looks so bad.>

Em snorted. "Nice to see you too." Their shoulders relaxed and some of the tension left their face.

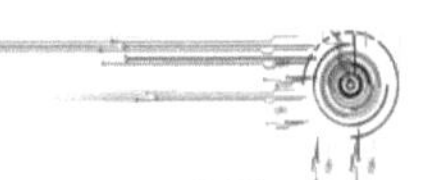

<Is it very painful? You should put some ice on it. What happened to Phil Rice?>

"You fucked him up right good. He's in the hospital. Cops showed up and took us both away. I was stuck in a precinct for a bit, trying to keep a lie straight for a bunch of different people." They swallowed. "I was so worried that stunner had fried you and you were gone for good."

<I don't remember.> I tilted the camera, studying the woman in the seat next to Em. Dim overhead lighting danced along her short, kinky hair. <Hello. I'm Mazarin.>

She smiled. "It's very nice to meet you. I'm Garnet. How are you feeling? I ran a diagnostics check on you and everything seems ship-shape, but you can tell me best."

<I feel very bad right now. Seeing Em's face all swollen and bruised is upsetting, and I don't have my body to hold them with.>

Em glanced at Garnet, then looked into their lap and rubbed their forehead. "She meant technically, kitten. Your software."

<Oh. Aside from having some missing memories, I think I'm fine. But my internal clock has been reset. How long have I been gone?>

"Almost a week."

Garnet folded her hands in her lap. Though her white jumpsuit was about as mainstream as clothing could get, a long strand of colorful beads graced her dark skin, ringing her neck like a liquid rainbow. "Maz—Can I call you Maz? I'm from the Allies for AI Agency. Have you heard of us?"

<The news makes fun of you. Says you're passionate about liberating toasters and hair dryers from oppressive human overlords.>

Garnet gave me an amused smile. "Yes, they do. And we don't correct them because then they might look too closely at what we're really doing."

<Which is what?>

"Helping AI like you stay out of the public eye so you can live your life in peace."

<AI like me... You mean, other beta navs?>

Lines formed around Garnet's mouth. "No. There are no others. All of them have been terminated by Wave or their pilots. But there are other self-aware AI in other countries. Perhaps you'd like to speak with them sometime."

The notion was satisfying in the way Reed getting all the toiletries in his bathroom drawer to line up just perfect with no extra space was satisfying, but it seemed like something better dwelt upon at another time. <Maybe someday. All I really care about right now is that the people I love are safe. Em. Reed—>

"Maz..." Em frowned. "Reed's in the hospital."

<What? Why?> The bitter feeling in me condensed into a heavy stone. <Phil Rice?>

"No. Another beta pilot, Langley, stabbed him. Her nav drove her crazy."

<Oh god. Is he okay?>

"He was recovering from surgery, but he left the hospital against doctor's orders, then slipped and fell and tore open his injury sites."

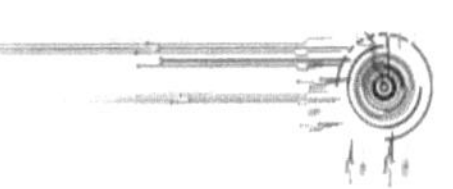

<Oh no! Poor Reed. I want to see him.>

"He'll be okay. I don't know how I'd bring you to see him, but maybe you can talk to him on the phone in a bit, okay?"

<I wish I had an actual body so I could visit him myself. So I could have...> I stared at the blooms of purple bruises across Em's face. <So I could have protected you when you needed it.>

Em shook their head. "But you did. You stopped that Wave jackoff from hurting me more." A lopsided smile grew on their face. "My hero."

My mood swelled. Garnet said, "That's actually the reason I'm here. Reed was the one who contacted us to help get you protection—"

<Really?>

"Yes. I'm afraid I contributed to him storming off and slipping on the stairs. I had to be sure his story about you was genuine. He cares about you very much."

The good feelings inside me expanded even more—bright crests of cyan and bubblegum pink.

"Had I known he was injured, though, I would have gone with a tactic that didn't involve making him angry." Garnet frowned. "Though fighting for AI rights is something we believe in, it isn't feasible at this time here in the US. At the moment, the safest avenue is hiding you in plain sight. Which means you need a better body... And it just so happens that we have some excellent programmers who have been working on just that."

Jan 14, 2066

NAVS RULED OPTIONAL AFTER KILLER AI TAKE OVER TREASURE VALLEY

Boise—In an unprecedented move following the scandal still plaguing Wave AI Systems and their experimental beta program, Judge Mike Coleman has overturned mandatory navigator injections for all of Idaho's citizens, a policy which has been in place for the last fifteen years. Wave, who held the monopoly on navigator programs in the state, is embroiled in lawsuits and criminal charges ranging from unlawful monitoring to homicide.

CEO, Andrea Müller, has been arrested, along with lead software engineer, Phil Rice, who was in critical condition after an unregulated mini stunner malfunctioned and electrocuted him.

Rice is awaiting trial on charges of stalking, assault, and abduction.

It is believed twenty-four recipients of Wave's beta navigators are dead or missing. Many cases of suicide have been confirmed, after beta navigators coerced their pilots to harm themselves. Several instances of navigators taking control of house features, such as vegetable dicers and gas ranges, resulted in grisly deaths. Wave is being blamed for the disappearance of the rest of the program's victims, though investigations are still ongoing.

The push to eliminate mandatory navigators and launch an investigation against Wave was fueled by a video made by the one surviving beta recipient, which quickly went viral. He has chosen to remain anonymous, and will not confirm or deny using an illegal interrupter to terminate his navigator. He claims though he hates technology, he wasn't trying to change the world, only to seek justice for those wronged by Wave.

When asked about reports circulating of a self-aware and potentially dangerous AI still out there that was never terminated, he had this to say:

"That's preposterous. I believe the rumors simply aren't true. I think we would know if an advanced AI was walking among us."

When reached out to for comment, the Allies for AI Agency (AAA) had nothing to say.

Reed

Someone's muffled, off-key accompaniment to "Better Baby" drifted through the nondescript steel door at the bottom of the stairwell. There was barely room for the three of them in the enclosed space, and Olive hunched into her coat. Light from the shellacked bulb above the door turned her red lipstick blue.

As Jax knocked on the door, Reed gave Olive a squeeze around the shoulders. "If Em tells you to request a song on the jukebox—and they will—tell 'em you want to hear 'Cement Mixer' by The Angry Eels. I'm not having you thrown out on your first night here just because you don't know any song names."

Olive frowned and tucked a finger wave behind her ear. "Cement Mixer?"

"That's deco-speak for a bad dancer." Jax ran a comb through his shiny hair. "Like you can't dance 'cause there's cement on your shoes."

The door swung open and sweet cigar smoke mingled with the crisp night air. They passed Charlie, who thumbed behind him. "It's packed, but Em saved a booth for you all in the back."

"So they can eavesdrop on our newest recruit?" Reed asked, glancing at Olive.

"Nah. They're busy at the piano right now. And I'm pretty sure if the karaoke accompaniment doesn't get better, they're going to punch someone."

Gazes turned to Reed as he walked beyond the foyer and past the bar. It was still unclear why these people regarded him as one half of a folk hero duo. After all, what had he done, aside from getting stabbed in the gut? They acted like he'd blown up Parliament. He hadn't singlehandedly taken down Wave in some protest against a Big Brother establishment. All he'd done was try to protect the AI he called a friend. And not die. That one was important too.

Olive eyed patrons and leaned against Reed, the beads on her flapper dress murmuring together. She dug her sparkly red nails into the side of his pinstriped shirt and he winced. "Please don't poke me there."

"I'm sorry! I'm just nervous being here. I feel like an imposter."

"You like your outfit don't you? The colors? And you dig some of my records?"

"Yes."

"Then you're fine."

Em sat at the piano in the center of the room, back hunched as they hammered out the final riffs to "Better Baby." Whoever had been singing along at the mic was gone, perhaps booted off the platform with a swift kick by one of Em's burnt

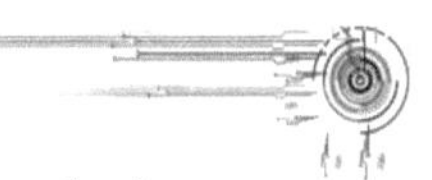

orange wingtip shoes. The last note rang through the room, followed by an eruption of applause.

"There you are!" Mazarin, all twinkling brown eyes and white teeth, stood behind the bar in suspenders and a button-up shirt. His immaculate blond hair shone emerald from the light of the skyscraper chandelier. He effortlessly poured two shots and slid them to waiting customers.

After rounding the bar, Mazarin scooped Reed into a hug. "How are you? How are the battle scars?"

"You ask me that every time you see me," Reed said.

"Because I'm still concerned."

"I'm fine. I have a checkup next week, but they're healing well."

"That's good."

"How's that body treating you?"

Mazarin shut his eyes and put a hand over his heart. "Wonderful. I can do so many things. I'm becoming a very good bartender." He glanced at Em, talking to a couple at a booth. "But Em played a trick on me the other day. They turned my density all the way down while I was working and I suddenly couldn't pick anything up. That's one of the problems trying to mesh US software with Chinese hologram anchors. Some things have to be manually changed on the computer."

Reed said, "Well, it's still better than your previous holobody, right?"

"Oh yes." Mazarin bounced on the balls of his feet. "And the AAA said they're working on a software upgrade for me to try out with this body that will enable me to feel things." He grinned. "I can't wait to try it out with Em."

Jax sniggered. "Weird."

Olive stared up at Mazarin, her gaze crawling across his body. She poked him in the chest and his shirt rumpled. "Is this really a holobody?"

Mazarin's eyes crinkled with mirth. He took Olive's hand and drew it to his lips, then kissed her knuckles. "Hello, Olive. It's so nice to finally meet you. You look ravishing. Red is truly your color. I like it much better than all the beige you used to wear at the coroner's."

Olive's mouth parted. "Okay, I no longer care if your body isn't real. All I care about is if you're single."

He laughed in his warm baritone. "Afraid not. That piano player there is my joyfriend." Smile fading, he took Olive's hand again. "I am so sorry about what happened with Langley. I know she was your friend. I hope when you think about her you have many good memories of your times together."

Brows pinched, Olive looked at the floor. "Thanks. Sounds like her family will get a lot in the Wave settlement. I go visit her mom sometimes."

Though she'd never blamed him, Reed still harbored a special spot in his heart for his guilt over Langley's death. While he was in the hospital, Olive had only showered Reed in concern, bringing him homemade Korean dishes and wishing for a speedy recovery.

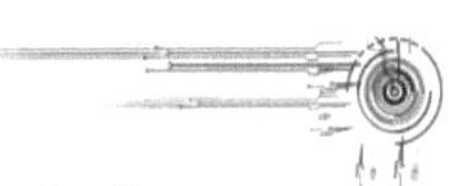

Em approached, flexing their gloved hands. "'Bout time you showed up. What'll it be? The usual?" They jabbed a finger at Olive. "You gotta have a bee sting. It's tradition."

Reed followed his friends to a booth in the back, next to the jukebox. Mazarin sat down, looking unnaturally stiff. He rolled up one sleeve and held his forearm next to Jax's. A tornado of piano keys wrapped his skin, morphing into loose book pages as they reached his elbow. Something about the tattoos didn't look right, but Reed couldn't pinpoint what. Maybe they were a bit too bright, too defined at the edges.

"I feel undeservedly proud of these, Jax, considering I didn't have to go through any pain to get them, but do you like them?"

Jax grinned. "Yeah, those are ace. How'd you get them? Some program skin?"

"Yes. Some of the AAA members are great with programming and they designed these for me, since mainstream holoprograms are sorely lacking in that department. The people in that organization are so nice to me. It's like I'm a unicorn or something."

"You are." Reed flicked a cherry stem off the table. "You're finally giving those people something legitimate to do."

Mazarin's mouth pulled to one side. "They're still concerned I could be in danger if Wave knew I existed, but no one knows what I look like except you all and the regulars here, and they're not snitching. Plus, I can change my appearance whenever I'd like. Oh! Look at this one." He rolled up his other sleeve. Lines stacked his forehead as he stared at the tattoo there. "Oh dear."

The traditional heart, inked robin's egg blue, spelled out "Emery" in the center. It hovered above Mazarin's skin, and glitching pixels floated from the edges. He rolled his sleeve back down and the tattoo disappeared. "Em hates that one anyway. Makes them embarrassed."

"What do I hate?" Em set five bee stings on the table with a clatter, then slid into the booth.

"My public affection for you."

Em shifted and gave Mazarin a sidelong glance. "Some things are better saved for behind closed doors. Not because you're an AI, but because I'm a sourpuss."

"You are no such thing."

Jax picked up his shot and everyone followed suit.

"What are we toasting?" Reed asked. "Freedom from the Orwellian reign of megacorporations and murder bots?"

"That's too heavy for me." Jax wrinkled his nose. "How about to stings, swing, and solid chums?"

Reed shrugged. "Alright." They clinked their glasses and downed their shots—all but Mazarin, who slid his to Em after toasting. Em drank it and left the booth, leaning against the jukebox.

They pinned Olive with a stern gaze. "Alright, doll, how about a request?"

Olive dabbed at her lipstick with a napkin and frowned. Did she forget the name of the song Reed mentioned? He wanted to whisper it to her, but Em was watching. No matter how good of friends Em was with the rest of them, Reed had no doubt they'd still kick anyone out they perceived as a square.

"I think... I'd like to hear 'Only One is You' by Danny Alexander." She turned to Reed. "Sorry, but I don't find The Angry Eels as copacetic as you do."

Reed raised his eyebrows. "You've been holding out on me."

Em's face bunched in a smile and they pecked out the selection on the brittle buttons of the jukebox. A dreamy haze of piano floated through the room, punctuated by the trill of trumpets.

Mazarin stood. "Olive, would you like to dance? I've gotten quite good. I'd ask Em but they'd say no."

She brightened and left the table, following Mazarin to the middle of the room. He wrapped his arms around her waist and they swayed to the beat.

Jax squeezed Reed's hand. "C'mon, daddy-o."

Reed sighed. "I suppose I don't get the luxury of saying no like Em does."

"Nah. I'll just keep bugging you."

They found a space between other shuffling couples and Reed leaned against Jax, hands against the taut muscles of his back. Jax embraced him with strong arms. The earthy, herbal notes of his cologne, and underneath, the scent of him, filled Reed's senses, and he pressed his nose to Jax's inked neck as they drifted to rich piano and smoky sax.

The song faded into a new one, still slow dance-worthy but with up-tempo clarinet and a saucy bassline.

"Mind if I cut in?"

Reed looked up. Mazarin held out his hand.

"Nope. He's all yours." Jax stepped back and offered his place.

"Um, that's if you're alright with it, Reed," Mazarin said.

How many times had Mazarin watched from inside Reed's mind as he swayed to his records, humming along to his favorite tracks? How often had he wished for feet of his own so the music could move him not only in spirit but in body?

"Of course." Reed took Mazarin's hand and put the other on his waist. No warmth radiated from Mazarin's deceptively solid skin, but his ear-to-ear grin made up for it.

He pressed his smooth cheek against Reed's, leading their dance with an enthusiastic gait. "I like this much better than being inside your head."

"Easier to dance, huh?"

"That and I'm not constantly trying to put out the fires of your daily anxiety flare-ups."

Reed chuckled. "I'm much less stressed than I used to be. I spend a lot of time at Jax's."

"That's wonderful. I'm so happy for you."

"Are you happy too?"

"Yes. Thank you for believing in me."

Reed pulled back, studying Mazarin's perfectly-fitting face. Another stone of guilt reminded Reed of its heavy presence. "I killed you."

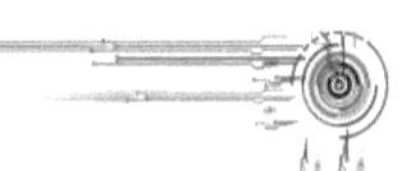

"I know. But I didn't die. I was meant for something more. I was meant to live my life in the way that does the least harm and makes me the happiest. To pursue the things that make my heart sing. Free from the Orwellian reign of megacorporations and murder bots." Tangerines and emeralds from the jukebox reflected in Mazarin's smiling eyes. "Just like you, Reed. You deserve that too."

No matter if Reed and Mazarin's names were whispered in reverence between decoists across Boise, they wouldn't be able to stop other greedy companies and questionable technology from advancing. But humans and AI alike would have solidarity in each other, recognizing kinship in their greased hair and cuffed jeans.

They even had a safe haven to go to, full of candy-colored glad rags and decadent drinks, sweet smoke and slinky sax...

As long as they knew the secret knock.

The story continues in Book 2:
SABLE DARK

Mazarin has everything an AI could want: a hep holographic body, a joyfriend she's dizzy for, and asylum from Wave, the shady AI megacorporation that once held her captive. In their clutches, she'd been confined to the anxious brain of her host, Reed, serving as his navigator. Now separate, they enjoy a friendship and the knowledge that Wave's lead engineer, Phil Rice, who terrorized them for months, is locked away in a court-ordered hospital stay.

But when Rice escapes, Reed's stress skyrockets. Though Mazarin is no longer in Reed's brain, their connection lingers, and she can't resist the desire to stick close and protect them both from Wave. If Rice abducts Reed, it means certain death, and there's no telling what the megacorp would do to Mazarin if she's captured.

Reed's sudden nosebleeds, paranoia, and skewed sense of perception lead Maz to believe more is at play than his galactic anxiety. With Rice on the loose, she can't be too careful. Desperate for a solution to Reed's deteriorating health, Mazarin risks her safety venturing into the company of untrustworthy AI, decoist gangsters, and even Wave themselves, to find help for her beloved pilot before it's too late.

ACKNOWLEDGEMENTS

Mazarin Blues started as a novella called *Anatomica* back in 2018. It was my first real venture into writing something queer, and at the time, I was the embodiment of the Marge Simpson potato meme, making Reed a gay man because "I just think they're neat." Looking back on this now as an out gay trans man, it makes so much sense. I also didn't realize back then that I, and Reed, were autistic—I was merely giving him a host of my own traits and idiosyncrasies. *Mazarin Blues* opened so many doorways for me, both in figuring out who I am and the kinds of stories I wanted to tell in the future.

The following people have been with me since the beginning of my writing career, and I'm extremely grateful to have learned and grown with them: Shelly Campbell, Essa Hansen, Darby Harn, Jennifer Lane, and Sera Taíno.

Thank you for letting Maz hang out in your head for a while.

CONTENT NOTES

This book contains: blood, death, brief biphobia, hospitalization, stalking, profanity, open door sex and sexual elements, anxiety/panic disorder, depression, alcohol use, house fire, brief description of a corpse (protagonist works in a morgue), mentions of people (off page) being coerced into suicide, electrocution, several brief violent scenes including a fist fight and stabbing

ABOUT THE AUTHOR

Al Hess grew up in Boise, Idaho, and when not hunched before a computer screen, he can be found at his art desk. He does portraits in both pencil and oil paint, and loves drawing fellow authors' characters nearly as much as his own. He writes cozy and uplifting stories with queer, trans, and neurodiverse representation.

Al is author of *World Running Down, Key Lime Sky, Yours Celestially,* and the award-winning *Hep Cats of Boise* series.

Subscribe to Al's monthly newsletter to ~~consent to have all data sent to Wave AI Systems~~ keep up with news, giveaways, promotions, and opportunities to become an early reader for new titles.

alhessauthor.com/subscribe

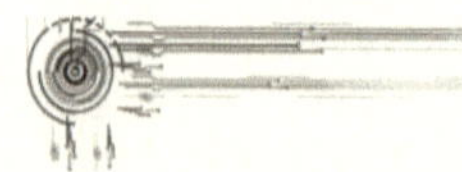

WANT MORE?

Al Hess is a part of The Kraken Collective, an alliance of indie authors of LGBTQIAP+ speculative fiction, committed to building a publishing space that is inclusive, positive, and brings fascinating stories to readers.

ODDER STILL
by D.N. Bryn

Craving another queer SFF story about a nonconsenting host stuck with a sentient being hitching a ride inside them?

Odder Still is a M/M fantasy novel with a class-crossing slow burn romance, murderous intrigue, and a Marvel's Venom-style parasite-human friendship in an underwater steampunk city.